CRUCIAN
FUSION

essays, tales, Conversations

APPLE GIDLEY

Crucian Fusion

Cover design: Richell Balansag
Line drawings: Kat Villa

Other Titles

Expat Life Slice by Slice
Fireburn
Transfer

For

Isabel and Emy
Barry, Mingo and Easy

etc

Tales

Conversations

FOREWORD

Crucian Fusion is a book of essays, tales and conversations, all of which embrace the rich history of this fascinating and beautiful island. But how did I get to St Croix?

Well, one rainy Sunday afternoon in Houston a superb view caught my eye. Framed by swaying palm fronds, yachts rode at anchor on a sea so blue I could almost taste the salt, like a rimmed cocktail glass. I shoved the laptop in front of my husband and asked, "What do you think of this place?"

"Good view. But there's a reason there are no pictures of bathrooms."

"Cosmetic," I assured him, believing the images I showed him constituted our retirement dream.

"Go and have a look." John returned to the golf on the television.

Three days later I was on St Croix.

The Agricultural Fair was in full swing, which meant limited lodging options and no rental cars. My plane was delayed in Puerto Rico so I didn't arrive until well past dusk but no matter, the smell of the tropics greeted me as I walked across the apron to the terminal. I felt at home. The taxi driver dropped me off at the top of a darkened hill above Christiansted and pointed in the vague direction of my accommodation. There were no lights and no discernible entrance. He drove off.

I chased the disappearing tail lights, shouting, "Wait! Where?"

The driver stopped, backed up and pointed to a narrow metal gate through which a few steps could be seen under an overhanging bougainvillea that swirled macabre shadows. A lamp flared as I pushed the gate and a voice called, "Apple?"

"Yes. Sorry I'm so late."

The owner of the B&B, The Breakfast Club, was kindness personified.

The renovations needed to the property I'd flown in to see were more than cosmetic but it felt right and, two days later, I made an offer. My husband is a trusting man. It was not, however, a rash decision. Italy, Spain, and Grenada, amongst others, had all been scoped. None fit the bill.

Nearly nine years later the house on the hill overlooking Protestant Cay still has a superb view but also new bathrooms, and wiring, and plumbing, and the list goes on. The jungle of tan-tan and Coralita, what my mother called 'Bride's Tears' and what I call 'that bloody pink vine', is now a truly beautiful Caribbean garden created by my husband.

Above all *Crucian Fusion* is a testament to the love I have for St Croix, the place I now call home, and a thank you.

Apple Gidley
St Croix, 2021

PARADISE OPENS EARLY

At 04:57 to be precise the cockerel beneath my open windows announces the predawn and, just to ensure the world does not fall back into slumber, he and his friends continue to cock-a-doodle-doooo until the first seaplane takes off at 7am. I can see white spray flashing from the pontoons as it bounces across the bay before rising above Protestant Cay, taking its first passengers across to St Thomas, another of the Virgins. Commuting Caribbean style.

The breeze is wafting the sheer curtains in my room and there is no need for even the fan. The sun, just starting to frill the edges of the world, promises intensity but for now is a gentle reminder of what is to come as the island wakes: bright colors and warmth that are not just climatic.

I was tired when I arrived late last night and so barely registered the room to which I had been shown, although sliding between the sheets - new I was told - was an electrifying experience. Nylon is not the coolest of fabrics for the tropics. As I look around now the decor reminds me of the 1970's. The bathroom is tiled in pale blue and the fittings show signs of sea air and age but it is spotlessly clean. The shower throws just enough water under which to bathe but I am used to living in places where water is precious.

A woman is walking her dog along the street below; its little black legs struggling to keep up with the tightening leash and her stride. Far different to the strut of the camel-colored, unfettered hound of indeterminate parentage who last night, just as I dozed off, made his rounds down the middle of the inky road, stopping only to raise Cain among those animals restrained by fences.

An occasional car coughs into life but on the whole the sounds are natural as the island gently approaches a new day. Driving is on the left as in the UK but most vehicles are also left-hand drives, which makes for interesting road skills. Middle of the road takes on a whole different meaning and is a little alarming at night when oncoming headlamps pierce one's night vision with bull's eye accuracy. A sharp swerve to the curb jars the nerves as gravel and dirt splutter before the reassuring blacktop is once again reached.

I notice rebar reaching for the skies atop what look to be lived-in homes and wonder if the same law applies here as in parts of Africa: that which allows no tax to be collected on unfinished property thus ensuring a horizon of metal rods amidst the ceibas.

Fallen remnants of the brief storm last night are being swept off the pavement outside the gate by the lady of the house. A cluster of magenta bracts from the bougainvillea climbing the outside wall forms a pile under the rhythmic swish of her broom, reminding me that being the chatelaine, mistress of all one surveys, is strenuous work. Emani will, at the agreed upon hour of nine, be presenting me with a breakfast of 'the best scrambled eggs in town'. I was asked last night as she entrusted the key to me whether I'd like them with pancakes or muffins. I opted for the more reserved latter.

And so starts my first day on St Croix, well the first day since a brief visit thirty years ago. A day of exploration and idle ambling that I predict will remind me the rhythm of life is essentially unchanged, despite the arrival of cruise ships disgorging Tommy Bahama-dressed men and scantily clad women and girls at the other end of the island. So too, I was told last night, a planeload of Danes arrive on this old, Danish colonial island, regularly each Wednesday of the season.

I pull up the images of the house I have flown in to view, just a few blocks from where I am staying. I cannot wait to see it, to learn its story. But I am reminded in this first flush of exploration the importance of looking beyond the obvious, of talking to Emani and others, and to bear in mind what is, at first glance, paradise to me need not necessarily be so for those from here. To tread carefully as I wander.

SLEEPY SUNDAYS

There is something about walking the streets, so to speak, on Sundays in certain parts the world. The air vibrates with joyous voices raised in praise to whichever form of Christianity followed, or maybe with the strident tones of the pastor haranguing his flock. Unless of course you happen upon a Seventh Day Adventist church which will not be open for business, those worshippers having celebrated the previous day. Cars, if there are any, are abandoned in no discernible order on crumbling curbs, not from a night of drunken revelry but in a rush to give thanks.

Walking down the hill on this Caribbean island earlier today, I was transported back to another island, that one in the Gulf of Guinea off West Africa's coast, and specifically to the cathedral in Malabo, Equatorial Guinea. Mass was conducted in Spanish with the singing in Bubi, the Bantu language of the island. The cathedral with its cloisters opening onto the square, catty corner to the president's place of business and a recognized palace of intrigue, was a haven of exuberant calm, if indeed those two words can be used in the same breath; the front pews taken by pious worthies intent on being seen by both the local populace and the man above.

All around me, on both sides of the aisle, rows and rows of white and grey frocked nuns of all ages made their devotions, bowing their heads like a flock of pecking pigeons eager for crumbs. As the congregation was called to take bread and wine

I was able to sit back on my pew and watch the long line shuffle to the altar. Until then I had been lulled by the sameness of their attire but as I studied the devout, many holding crosses, some gold, some wooden, on chains or strings around their necks, my eyes were drawn down to the array of footwear inching towards redemption. In place of the expected sensible lace-ups, or at least enclosed shoes, were open-toed sandals, some with low, some with high heels. Whether encased in neutral leather or gaudy plastic, the nuns' toenails made freewheeling statements of individuality; a rainbow of color to match their exultant voices as testament to their love of Christ.

A few years later and here I am sitting at a bar on the Boardwalk on St Croix, listening to *Spirit in the Sky* and four strangers ardently discussing sport. They have cycled through football, baseball and basketball with a quick skim over to hockey, the ice variety. It seems not to matter which discipline they favor because they share the opinion that "money is consistently spent on the wrong shit!" Matt, the barman agreed.

I should point out I am at the bar only because it is the one place on this sleepy Sunday island that offers Wifi, and even this is patchy. I felt beholden to try their locally brewed honey wheat ale, not my normal tipple, and have been pleasantly impressed though anticipate minimal productivity later in the day.

In the last week I have managed to slow my pace from mainland city speed to a long-dormant African amble, or maybe the *mai pen lai* attitude of Thailand. I was close to throwing out a decision to get some work done on this traditional day of rest but writing deadlines are looming and, having extended my St Croix stay, I really must pretend to accomplish something.

Funny how the mind wanders from one lived-in country to another, hence my Sunday musings. Does an essay, I wonder, count as something?

VIOLET

Smells emanating from the wood stove woke Violet. It was still dark but she didn't need a lantern to pull on the clean smock lying across the bottom of her sleeping pallet. The bell had not been rung to awaken slaves working the fields. Neither snorts from horses nor cracks from the whip, so casually unfurled to lash across a hapless back, could yet be heard.

The world, apart from Cookie and her, slumbered on.

The door of the room creaked open and Violet stood a moment. Even at eight she noticed colors not just as red or blue or green but as bananaquit yellow, dove grey, blood red. As she turned the corner she looked towards the great house and shivered before she continued into the cook house.

"Mahnin', Cookie," she said, wrapping her arms around the overflowing hips encased in osnaburg, the coarse unbleached linen worn by slaves. The ties from Cookie's apron created a reassuring bump under her cheek.

"Mahnin', sweetie, you up early." Cookie took one hand off the big ladle, used to stir the pot bubbling on the open flame, to pat Violet's arm. "Me wake you?"

"No." Violet sighed. "Mama over deh?" She nodded to the great house partially hidden behind a hedge of sea grape.

"She not here, she deh," Cookie replied. Her tone brooked no further questions. "You hungry?"

"Uhuh."

"Uhuh? Don' you uhuh me, chile."

"Yes, Cookie," Violet said, "I hungry."

"Dat better." She pointed to a mango in a wooden tray. "Have dat but eat outside, eh. And min' de smock. Mango stain." Cookie tossed a thin towel to the child. "Here, tie dis roun' your neck."

"Thank you, Cookie. Mama come when?"

"Me not know, Violet. Soon come. Now eat. Den I make bush tea."

Leaning over the door mouth step Violet stripped back the mango skin with her teeth. One felt wobbly and she took a moment to jiggle it before slurping on the stone, juice trickling down her chin. She loved mango season and delighted in being sent to gather fallen fruit from trees on the other side of the house - as long as the master wasn't sitting on the gallery, his booted legs strung along the rails of his planter's chair, his collar undone, his belly straining the buttons of his shirt as he smoked and drank. If he saw her, he would call her over. She shivered again.

Shapes became defined as the sun crept over the world. The bell tolled and dawn quiet dissolved into the bustle of the sugar plantation. Violet spat a bit of skin onto the ground and watched how fast a trail of ants formed to pick at the sweetness. She hoped her mother would appear soon.

Later, Violet, her tongue worrying the loose tooth, bent her head over a slate on the cook house table and traced her letters. Her mother watched, sometimes putting her own hand over Violet's to guide the chalk. Eliza smiled at her daughter's concentration. Her thoughts flitted back to when she learned to read and write. Taught by Miz Ida, the master's wife. When life was innocent. Before the master noticed her.

A frown marred Eliza's smooth face. A few years more and Violet would be the same age she had been when the master first took her. She shook her head, the unvoiced fear unravelling. No, surely not. Not his own flesh and blood. She rubbed her arms.

"Mama, you are sad?"

"No, child, not sad. Just thinking. You are finished?" Eliza always spoke standard English to her daughter and would not allow her to slip into the easy chat of the slaves, whose common language had evolved from a dozen African tongues to one understood by all who had made the Middle Passage, to be passed down to their children's children. She nodded at the rows of letters and smiled. "That is good, Violet. Now, I must help Cookie, and you must help Serwa wring sheets."

"I asked her why she keeps her Akan name, her name from Africa." Violet chuckled as she scrubbed the slate clean, her violet eyes shining. "She said it's because white people think her name is Sarah. And they would not like it if they knew her name meant one of noble birth. What is noble birth, Mama?"

"Born to a royal family. A king. Or here, born free!"

"I want to be free, Mama," Violet said. "Here, I not one thing, not the other."

"I know, child, one day, eh?" Eliza hugged her daughter. "Go, now you must help Serwa." Eliza watched Violet skip off to the wash house. She straightened her shoulders and returned to the task of peeling mangos to make jam to be stored in the cool of the cellar under the great house. The resentment of the other household staff made her work twice as hard.

"Tstt!" The hiss came from the doorway and, turning, Eliza saw Jeremiah. One arm raised in greeting, the other sliced off in the sugar factory as the cane grinders tried to roll him to eternity. After the accident he had been removed from the factory and put to work in the gardens, but field slaves still considered him one of them and he moved freely between the two worlds. Jeremiah, Cookie, and Serwa, and the housekeeper were the few people who did not eye her with contempt despite knowing she had been taken against her will. The master's infatuation with the slender girl with onyx skin the reason the mistress had left the islands. Her calming influence lost.

"Mahnin', Jeremiah." Eliza smiled. "W'appen?"

"De sugar boiler man, Buddhoe, he back." Jeremiah's voice was low, like a rustle in the trees. "He talk more."

"'Bout de same t'ing?"

Jeremiah nodded. He paused. "You wid he t'night?" He jerked his head at the great house then smiled when she shook her head. "I tell you later, eh. It soon come, Eliza, soon soon."

Well past dark Violet heard her mother creep from their quarters, shared with Cookie. She opened her eyes, puzzled. Her mother never went to the master when she was bleeding. She sat up as the door closed.

"Where Mama go?" she asked Cookie, whose eyes she had seen gleam in the dark.

"Not know. Maybe talk Jeremiah. Sleep now." The cook's pallet creaked as she rolled over.

Violet lay awake but still for a long time trying to put her thoughts in order of importance. The first was to keep out of the master's way. As a little girl she had not minded being dandled on his lap, and he had taken pleasure in her delight as her fingers probed the pockets always filled with some treat. But lately it had not felt comfortable. Next in importance was how to get into the library without him knowing. The books that lined the tall shelves filled her with wonder and she longed to look at the pictures of paintings. July, the housekeeper, would not give her away but Violet was not sure about the maids, especially the youngest, who never missed an opportunity to pinch her on the soft flesh under her arm. And thirdly... Violet's eyes felt heavy and she rubbed them. Thirdly, how to be noble? Free? She and her mother. And Cookie. All of them. As her eyes closed she considered moving that to her top priority.

Anticipation filtered around the cook house, the wash room, the gardens, and even the factory where Violet had run the day before to deliver a message from the master to the rough English bomba, Mr Stephens - a man loathed by the field slaves for his readiness with the whip, and avoided by everyone else.

Violet rarely left the confines of the gardens around the great house and the house slaves' quarters, made separate by the mistress years earlier. The sniggers from some of the children in the slave village frightened her. It wasn't fair. She wasn't the only one with lighter skin. There was that boy with orange hair and pale skin. No one made fun of him. She wondered if they shared a father. Or if he even knew his daddy. At least she knew. Not that that was good. Though her mother never said, Violet sensed she hated being at the master's disposal, but she had no choice if she wished to stay out of the fields and keep Violet out of them too. That was why she went, scented and clothed in silks from the chest in the corner, to his bedchamber. Why she insisted Violet practice her letters. Not that insistence was necessary. Violet loved to learn. And the Governor man, Peter von Scholten, had opened schools, so the master had to allow some learning even if he didn't let children leave the estate.

Even Cookie seemed coiled in readiness. Violet wished she knew what for. No one was saying anything. It was early in the season but perhaps a hurricane was coming, sensed by one of the old folk. No. No one was rushing around. This was different. Her fears receded until the day lost its heat and egrets headed to their rookery near the seashore. The village bell rang. A tolling like an alarm that indicated fire in the fields. Or a death. Then she heard the tutu, a conch calling from the road outside the plantation gate. The gate leading to freedom. A gate through which she had never been.

Violet ducked between the sea grape hedge and great house to a gap she squirmed into any time she wanted to disappear. Only the cats and Jeremiah knew about her hiding place and they never told. She nearly slipped out when she saw him, but his face, grim and determined, kept her hidden. Violet frowned. Why was he carrying a cane bill? He only used a machete in the garden. Then she saw other shapes, indistinguishable in the gloom, follow him, keeping to the shadows of the short mahogany-lined drive. She risked lifting her head to listen, wondering why the master and Mr Stephens did not appear. Surely they had heard the bell. The trickle of men stopped and Violet heard her name called. She eased out of the gap, straightened her smock and ran to the cook house.

"Where you been?" Cookie demanded, her tone rough. "Come," she didn't wait for an answer but hustled Violet into their room and told her to push the pallets against the door and not move them for anyone except her or her mother.

"Nuttin', no one, you hear me, chile?"

Violet nodded, tears in her eyes. "I frightened, Cookie. W'appen?"

"Maybe nuttin', maybe sometin'. Me not know." Cookie hugged her. "But you be safe here."

"Where you go?"

"I come soon, eh."

Violet nodded. Sweat dripped along her nose and seeped down her neck as she heaved and tugged pallets to block the door. Then she collapsed on one. Dim light trickled around the door frame and through cracks in the shutters, enough for her to track the passage of time until her eyes closed in worried exhaustion.

Through her dreams she heard tapping at the door, then Cookie's voice.

"Sweetie, it me. Open de door."

Violet stubbed her toe, no longer sure of her footing with the pallets out of position. Loose-limbed from sleep, she strained to move them but edged enough space for Cookie to ease through.

"Where Mama?"

Cookie ignored the question and helped Violet move the pallets back to block the door.

"I scared, Cookie. W'appen?"

"Tsst, chile. Sleep. I here. All ah good."

Tired with emotion, Violet went back to sleep and woke only when dawn broke. They moved the pallets away from the door and went to the cook house, where Cookie lit the fires for breakfast, then pounded dough. Violet watched from her perch at the table. Something was different. Cookie, her movements usually lethargic in the morning until she'd had her bush tea, was almost bouncing.

"Cookie, tell me. W'appen? Where Mama?"

"All ah good, sweetie. All ah good. Now eat, eh?" Cookie pushed a hard biscuit across the table. "Your mama, she soon come."

The day lightened but still suspense hovered in the air. Violet heard Mr Stephens roar from the village and heard Cookie's quiet chuckle.

"Not so many dere today, bukra man!"

"Where dey be?" Violet asked, her head swiveling as the thud of hoofs sounded when Mr Stephens rode up to the great house. She stood and peeped out the door and saw him fling himself from the saddle and run up the steps to burst through the front door. His voice sounded loud and worried as he shouted for the master.

"Cookie, where dey be?"

"Jeremiah, he lead dem Frederiksted. He, de boiler man, an' odders, dey take up cutlass for freedom. Soon come, chile, me hope soon come."

Violet, her eyes wide, asked, "And Mama?"

"She keep de massa busy. She good. Now bomba in de 'ouse she soon come."

Cookie was right. Her mother appeared, her smile tired but bright. The day dawdled under a hot sun. The fields went untended and even the maids' chatter was subdued as they came and went from the kitchen. Violet spent a lot of time in her hidey-hole, keeping out of the way and with an eye on the gate, not sure what she was expecting. She watched the master and Mr Stephens, their horses hurriedly saddled, canter to the gate then turn left to head east, away from the direction Jeremiah had taken. The soporific heat smothered a nervous energy until, as the long day came to an end, the village bell again rang, a long pealing that evoked promise.

Raised voices came from the village, from men at the gate. She heard Cookie shouting, then saw her standing on the door mouth of the cook house, rivulets of tears cascading down her plump cheeks. Violet hesitated. Then her mother emerged behind her and hugged the cook, tears on her face too. And laughter. Laughter, loud and joyous that rifled through the trees, through the rustling sugar cane, until it seemed as if the whole plantation was engulfed in jubilation.

She dislodged the cat on her lap and emerged from her cubby hole and ran to her mother and the cook. They drew her into their arms and danced a jig, Cookie's low breasts pushing into Violet's face as she held woman and child tight.

Violet tipped her head up and looked at the two women. "W'appen?"

"We free, chile, all ah we free!"

Footnote

General Buddhoe, aka Moses Gottlieb, worked at Estate La Grange and, due to his ability to read and write as well as his skill as a sugar boiler he was much sought out by other estates owners. As such he had greater freedom of movement than most black men, and so was able to move from plantation to plantation rallying the call for freedom.

Emancipation in the US Virgin Islands was declared by Governor von Scholten on July 3rd, 1848.

ANCHORED

I saw two container vessels come chugging in and, from the other side of Gallows Bay, I can hear the busyness of wharf laborers as they unload cargo. Along with the sound of forklifts and clatters of containers being moved comes laughter, caught on the wind and rippled across the water, usually aquamarine but at the moment reflecting the overcast sky.

One ship, the smaller one I think, is a ferry moving people rather than goods between the islands, and as I watch the activity I am reminded that once again I have a foot in two camps. Unlike the passengers from the ferry who for a brief interval were in limbo, neither in one place nor the other, I am a person of multiple places at once.

It is a position in which I am comfortable, having spent my life never entirely belonging to any one tribe. Never wholly British, or Australian, or indeed now American. Two of my cousins are known as 'belongers' due to having been born and bred in the British Virgin Islands. They both have travelled the world but their road always leads back to Tortola, where they do indeed belong, switching with ease between the local patois and the language of their birth. For me though, having had a nomadic childhood with educational stability offered through an Australian boarding school, it is the ability to slip in and out of many different circles, if not languages, that feeds my soul.

My melancholia today is coming from the scraps of paper I'm finding around this house on the hill. The scrawled notes, one a hardware store shopping list, another a reminder to phone someone, another a list of names – an invitation list perhaps. In cupboards and drawers there are ragged-edged photographs of grandchildren and the previous chatelaine of this crumbling house; this I know because of the penciled names just visible on the back, one being 'grandma'. Lodged beside a chest I found a framed pastel of an aging couple; it is a naïve drawing and, about to toss it on the skip quickly filling outside, I spotted the artist's name. It matched one on the back of a photograph and I have kept it, in the hopes the drawing can be returned to the artist.

The people from whom we purchased this home overlooking a now crystalline bay, the clouds having been scudded further west by the near constant trade winds, are the children of the original owners, both now dead. And yet there is no sense of unease as I sit here alone, just a sadness. Sadness that those same children, no longer children but my own age, did not attend their father's funeral, and when the sale of their parents' home was imminent did not take these intimate reminders. Who knows what issues a family faces, but snippets of a past life, a scrap of jaundiced newspaper dated not long after the war announcing the engagement of Janet to Eugene found in the bottom of a tool drawer, attest to a long love.

And isn't that what allows us as expatriates, or travelers, to wander the world regardless of where our immediate family happens to be? The knowledge that someone, somewhere, cares and, more importantly, cares enough to allow us the space to roam.

My husband and children are my bedrock but I do not need to be on the same bit of land as they to feel their love or support. We are currently spread around the world and yet their nearness is almost palpable, deep in the essence of me.

The ferry is leaving now and I hope those traveling, as they cross the seas and for a short while are in a liminal space, feel a sense of gratitude for the freedom given to venture beyond the limits of their tribe.

THE SOUNDS OF MUSIC

I'm alone. My spouse is in West Africa, and our grown children are on the other side of the Atlantic leading their own lives. But I am not lonely. Throughout my married life I've spent a lot of time either on my own or somewhere in the world with infants and, later, teens. I wonder sometimes whether being brought up an only child has eased both the many relocations we have experienced and the separations.

I've had a busy day, and as the sun and trade winds drop I pour a glass of wine and settle onto our gallery watching the last of the yachts drift in to harbor. I am happy to sit, sip, watch the bats start their twilight forays, and listen to the dulcet tones of Madeleine Peroux.

And as I listen I think back forty or so years to my final year at NEGS, my boarding school in Armidale, Australia, and the looming Higher School Certificate exams. Then I listened to Neil Diamond and, despite entreaties from the housemother, felt quite capable of both singing along to *Hot August Night* and revising the histories of China, Japan, Malaysia and the spread of Islam throughout the Far East. T S Elliot featured too, as did Shakespeare, Anouille and Austen. French and Indonesian were given more than a cursory nod, and social studies involved having an awareness of and interest in global affairs, a given for a Third Culture Kid although I didn't know that's what I was in those days. One science was a requirement and I had grudgingly chosen biology as something of moderate interest.

It was, however, unfortunate the school magazine offices were directly above the biology lab and therefore an easy bypass was routinely made. Needless to say I failed the sciences but managed to pass the others.

This foray into the memory archive has been brought about by guilt because I am meant to be finishing rewrites for a novel, writing a travel piece, and of course coming up with ideas for future blogs. But as mooring lights shimmer in a refracted glow on the now black bay, I realize I am now incapable of listening to music, even classical and instrumental, when working. If I attempt to recreate my teens and play music, of any genre, I find myself singing or humming along, and wholly unable to focus on the words that are meant to be flowing through my fingers.

Is this a by-product of age? I am dismayed so many people, not just young, have music playing in the workplace. Is it to make the tedium of the day flow faster? I watch as people, earphones dangling, exercise or walk to work, crossing busy city streets oblivious to the traffic yet quick to castigate, and gesticulate, to the hapless driver slamming on the brakes to avoid a pedestrian accident. Maybe though the driver is also tuned in. Or is noise, not just music, such a part of our lives now that we are unable to function without it? I wonder if it is age or if we are so over stimulated by the constant barrage of surround sound that we have become inured, or maybe even scared, of silence.

I wish I could be like Pico Iyer, the travel writer and philosopher, refusing to countenance a cell phone, but my maternal instincts will not allow me to be unavailable for my children, no matter there is little I can help them with these days, which is as it should be. However a sympathetic ear, or a gossip, is always joy across the miles.

Buying new landline phones a year or so ago the feature most important to me was the 'do not disturb' button. It is mostly in use, and should I happen to see the light flickering to indicate a caller I will wait to see who is calling before answering. Friends know to use my cell phone though there is still no guarantee I will answer. Family though are always answered. I never have an issue ignoring an incoming call when driving and one of the irritants of having a new car is the inability to switch off the insistent stridency of the 'paired' phone without reconfiguring everything every time I get in the car.

I watch my granddaughter move from one noise-making toy to another and if she were not happy to flip through her favorite books in her cot in the mornings when she wakes, I would worry she has little quiet time to absorb the world around her.

And so forty years on I find I revel in, to steal Simon and Garfunkel's term, the sounds of silence, and yet as I type and sip my wine, glancing every now and then at the harbor below, I realize there is no silence.

I am being serenaded by crickets, the chichaks are chirping as they contemplate an evening feast of mosquitoes, and the resident frog is croaking his sundown song, and there is the occasional lilt of music from the dance school down the street. Maybe after all my favorite childhood film, The Sound of Music, is really where my heart lies. Alone or with my family, but I still might not answer the phone.

OUT ON THE BOARDWALK

S oft splodges landing on my face, rain blown in and diffused through the mosquito screen, was my wake up call this morning rather than the cockerel strutting down the hill, cockscomb juddering in righteous earnestness as he crows the dawn. Sometimes he gets it wrong and starts well before the allotted time.

There is no vehicular movement yet, and yachts moored in both bays visible from the gallery are swinging on their buoys, masts swaying, in the easterly breeze. They are in recovery mode after the evening's festivities, and it's too early for church doors to open to the faithful.

Yesterday was a busy day. The territory's governor, John P de Jongh, threw a Christmas party for the island's children at Fort Christiansvaern. Tree decorating and present wrapping competitions, face painting and dancing, temptation came in the form of raffles offering I-pads and other must-have items for the kids and two nights at a luxury hotel for their parents – respite after the season's revelry. And of course Santa delighted most.

Then as dusk switched to night in the magical moment in the tropics that leaves you wondering how it happened in the blink of an eye, the Boardwalk came alive as Crucians, residents and tourists jostled for pole position to watch the Boat Parade.

Two months ago the stretch of wooden walkway lining the lapping Caribbean was a hazard to all: splintering uneven planks a lawsuit waiting to happen should an unwary tourist trip and be pitched amongst idling tarpon. The Eyeores, referring to the 'keep out' construction signs along parts of the Boardwalk, assured all who would listen, "hey man, dey'll neva finish afore de season." Awaiting the siren call for the boats to light up I admired the new Boardwalk - Hardi-plank, deep and crisp and even, providing safe passage between bars and shops and I had a moment of delight to see the naysayers had been wrong.

The crowd, a melange of colors and creeds, some sitting with legs dangling over the new Boardwalk, turned right as a police vessel with blue lights flashing heralded the start of the parade. It was then I learnt the man-in-red's mode of transport in the Caribbean is different. Down here dolphins pull his boat-sleigh. Silly of me not to have realized reindeer might struggle on the short inter-island flights. The lead dolphin, I'm not sure of his name but think it might be Bounder, also has a red nose and guides his pod gracefully through the warm waves, occasionally checking his passenger is holding tight.

The Christmas-merry crowd cheered and waved as the boat-sleigh glided along in front of the Boardwalk followed by yachts, dinghies and motor launches bedecked in thousands of colored fairy lights, quite possibly confusing to boats out at sea attempting to understand the signals. Some were decorated as Christmas trees; one a shimmering floating snow-scene above the inky dark sea; another represented the local seaplane company with glittering wings gulled out from the deck; all had music blaring across the water drowning out the cheers from land.

As the parade circled around behind Protestant Cay I left the Boardwalk and made my way back to our gallery to watch the promised fireworks. Comets with trailing tails exploded into falling stars, booms and flashes spiraled up to form giant globes of colored light, green, blue and red flickering into oblivion, ever-increasing circles of silver pinpricks led to the heavens, and aaahs from the crowd on the Boardwalk filtered through the trees and up the hill. A display to rival many seen in other parts of the world.

A squall has passed over and as the soft rain moves along the coast I see sails being raised, but still the town slumbers – a Sunday morning in the Caribbean. A time of relaxed goodwill and peace and, I think, in the distance I can see dolphins.

A RENAISSANCE COWBOY

I spend the fifteen-minute drive from Christiansted thinking of the conversation ahead. Have I got the right questions to open up the man, to learn who he is and not just the facts? What is the fundamental thing that has driven him through an extraordinary life?

He is tall and un-stooped - even at 84 - and rather than a hug, our customary greeting, we bump fists and smile behind our masks. His office is lined with photographs which seem at odds with each other. Men on horseback. Men in uniform blazers. And cattle. Box files fill the shelves and on the floor behind the desk is a backpack. It is a working man's office.

We discuss the current COVID situation. He removes his mask and tells me he is happy for me to do the same. I assure him I've been living a most circumspect life and we both breathe easier. A smile is so much more meaningful when it is seen.

My conversation is with an organized man who has sent me articles and a chapter of the book he is writing. It makes for a factual and interesting read but did not divulge the elusive key to the heart of the man. I decide to jump in.

"May I ask, Hans, are you a man of faith?"

He looks surprised. "I should think so! Do you have time for a long story?"

"As it happens, I do." I lean forward to turn on the recorder.

Born in 1936 to Frits and Bodil Lawaetz, Hans' formal education started in 1942 at the parochial St Patrick's School in Frederiksted, on the western end of St Croix. Weekdays, Belgian nuns drummed the Catholic liturgy into his not always receptive mind.

"I complained to my father." A wry smile crinkles his eyes. "He told me, 'just settle down, will you, kiddo?'."

To balance Catholicism, Sundays were spent as an altar boy at the Lutheran Church. To compound his early eclectic religious education further, he attended the Quaker Westtown School in Pennsylvania from the age of fifteen until he graduated.

But I'm getting ahead of myself.

Growing up in 1930s and 1940s St Croix - then a population of give or take 18,000 people - was very different to the bustle and traffic of 2021. Young Hans rode his horse to catch the school bus each day in the company of Normy Francis, a cowboy who worked on the farm his father managed. And Normy was there to meet him at the end of the day. Hans grew up learning and playing sports as 'a native country boy'.

In 1946, with the war over and his Danish mother anxious to see her family in Denmark after the German occupation, Hans and his brother, Bent, accompanied her on a ship from Puerto Rico to New York, where they waited nearly two months for permission to cross the Atlantic.

"We shared a two-bedroom apartment in a sixth-floor walk-up with a family friend and her two daughters," Hans recalls, leaning back in his chair with a smile. "No surprise, I spent most of the time playing baseball in the street."

I wonder what it was like for an island child of ten playing with tough city kids, but having watched children of many nationalities play ball in many countries I am reminded that, for children, a ball is a ball and it doesn't matter who's hitting or catching it.

Instead I ask, "What do you remember of the passage to Denmark?"

"It wasn't like cruising today," Hans says. "It was a cargo ship with a few passenger cabins. The waters were rough. My aunts travelled over from England and it was fun to meet our cousins. We all spent a wonderful summer in the family home in Hellebaek, about forty miles north of Copenhagen."

"Did you speak Danish?"

"No. Bent and I learnt there."

"But your parents both spoke Danish," I confirm.

"Yes, but remember, my father was born on St Croix and my mother spent her childhood here so they spoke our local Crucian dialect. So that's what Bent and I spoke."

"Do you still speak Danish?"

Hans plays with his long fingers, "No. I never spoke it fluently, but I can understand some."

The phone rings. It is his eldest daughter, Amy, home for the holidays, with a logistical issue. Hans breaks the call short and we continue.

Returning to St Croix after ten months away and missing a year of school, Hans settled back into island life and the addition of two new members of the family. One, a little boy called Ken Abel, joined the family after his mother died. Ken Abel had learning issues that his step-mother found too difficult to handle so Frits and Bodil took him in. They also welcomed Fritsie, a third son of their own in 1949.

There was no high school on St Croix in those days and not many students were able to attend schools on the mainland, or down island, so Hans expected to end his official schooling after 8th grade.

"But I was lucky. My dad's employer, Ward Canaday, set up an educational trust for me, Bent and Fritsie to attend high school and universities on the mainland. He sent brochures, and after learning Kenneth Lindquist, a young man from St Thomas, had enjoyed his time at Westtown School, I thought if it was good enough for him, it would be good enough for me."

Perhaps the decision was made easier by the fact it was a co-educational school, somewhat of a rarity in those days, located in Pennsylvania, and not as cold as New England.

"I'd never seen so many white girls," Hans says with a broad grin.

It was an unexpectedly large intake of freshmen, and dormitory space was sparse. The six tallest boys, chosen because they looked the oldest from their entry applications, were housed two to a room in the sophomore building. Hans' roommate, a Colombian, never showed up and so to mitigate the loneliness of being confined to his room from 7:30 each evening, he walked into town to purchase a small radio.

Used to the structure of both the Catholic and Lutheran faiths, Hans initially found the lack of leadership at a Quaker meeting unnerving.

"Kids were popping up and talking all around me, and I wondered what on earth was going on. Who's in charge of this?" Over the following four years, however, Hans learned to appreciate the Quaker tenet that to believe in God is to know He is all around so a building is not needed to prove one's faith.

However, before he got to that state and very early on in his time at Westtown, Hans with some trepidation answered a summons to the headmaster's study where he was told, "Young man, we're having a problem understanding you."

"I had to have tutoring, in a cold basement, on how to speak American English." Hans laughs. "The headmaster taught public speaking and juniors took turns to stand behind the podium and talk to the class," Hans recalls. "Even then, I still spoke too fast."

His eyes gleam with amusement.

"Master Test told me to stop and said, 'I shall raise my left arm every time you speed up.'" Hans grins again and raises his arm. "By the end of my speech the headmaster and all the students in the class had both their arms in the air."

I laugh with the man across the desk, whose own arms are raised in memory. I wonder what someone would think if they walked into his office.

"It was a great school," Hans continues, "four hundred students ate in the dining hall at once. Tables made up of two freshmen, two sophomores, two juniors and two seniors - four boys and four girls - and these eight would change every six weeks or so, allowing all the students to get to know each other. We learned to socialize."

We spend a lot of time laughing and I lose track of my questions, but it doesn't matter because Hans continues.

"We used KOBs."

I am completely lost.

"Kindness of Bearer," he takes pity on my confusion. "If you wanted to ask a girl for a date or write a love note to your steady girlfriend, you'd write on an 8 x 11 inch sheet of paper, fold it into a 1 1/4 inch square with the girl's name and KOB."

"Sounds very complicated."

"It wasn't. At 9:30, half an hour before lights out, all the boy's messages were put in a basket and taken by... (Hans indicates air quotes) ... a lucky boy to the girls' end of the building. He returned with KOBs from the girls. The system worked well."

Hans prospered at the school, not just academically and socially but on the sports fields, where he played soccer and baseball, and in the water becoming Captain of the swimming team as well as the baseball team. From his sophomore year at Westtown he served on the Boy's Student Council responsible, sometimes, for disciplinary issues, and went on to become chairman. In his senior year he was elected Student Body President, perhaps helped by the efforts of the Headmaster who continued to keep Hans after class to work on his speaking. Again he was called to Master Test's study but, this time, it was not his speech causing problems but rather the closeness of the boys and girls at the weekly dances. Hans was told to fix the problem.

Hans' eyes crinkle. "Having been removed from the dance floor myself as a freshman for dancing too closely with a beautiful blonde from Mexico, it was an easy fix."

"Really?" I struggle to speak through the laughter.

"In my defense, I only knew how to waltz. Bent and I had been taught in Denmark."

"So how did you fix the problem?"

"We sped up the music!"

Four years went by fast and although Hans only went home in the summers, he recalls with fondness other vacations spent with his roommate at his home in Scarsdale, New York. When he was back on St Croix he reverted to his role of cowboy and earned 40 cents an hour, along with the other hands. He did, though, get to sleep in his own bed and not in the cowboy barracks.

"From time to time, Mr Canaday would send down a vehicle for the farm. An old Jeep arrived when I was home once and I would drive it to The Morning Star Nightclub. My dad took me aside one morning and told me he didn't care what time I got home after partying but I'd better be at work in the corral by six."

"And were you?" I ask.

"You bet, he was the boss. It was tough work for all the cowboys. Most of them were from Vieques. There were no squeeze shoots then. Just catching and throwing calves." Hans pauses, "You know one of those cowboys is still with us. Guison Correa. He comes in and gets his pay check each week. He's got three daughters, all in the medical field in Houston. And a granddaughter. She did up a house at the bottom of The Beast* and rents it out to state-siders."

"I hope his daughters are safe. Houston isn't a good place to be at the moment," I comment, thinking of reports from friends living in my other favorite place in America.

"They're all fine," Hans assures me.

"You mentioned most of the cowboys came from Vieques. Do you speak Spanish?"

"Bullpen Spanish," he responds. "Guison, who now speaks good English, still only speaks to me in our own language. And I answer the same way."

The phone rings again and Hans immediately answers. He looks serious. I catch his eye and indicate I'll leave him to his call. He shakes his head and so I wait. I'm glad I do. It gives another insight to the man behind the desk. His voice is gentle, subdued. We live on a small island and I guess the nature of the conversation.

The call ends and Hans is quiet a moment. He tells me it was the daughter of a friend of a family he grew up with, who has come home after deciding to discontinue medical care for her illness. I nod and tell him of an end-of-life doula I know on St Croix who might be of comfort to the woman. I promise to connect them.

I wait for his thoughts to return to his own remarkable life.

"I was lucky," Hans shrugs his lean shoulders, "my scholarship included college and I went to Cornell to study animal science."

"Did you always want to be a cattleman?" I ask.

"What else would I study? I didn't know anything different."

Neither did he know of three surprises awaiting his arrival at Ithaca.

"My scholarship did not include meals; I was required to sign up for the ROTC for at least the first two years; and I had to pass a 'simple test' to see if I qualified as an 'apprentice farmer'."

"And did you?" I ask, not imagining this man of the land could possibly fail.

"No," Hans rocks his chair back. "I was a cowboy, not a dairy farmer. It meant I had to work each summer on dairy farms, and make written reports of my experiences." He pauses in reflection. "Cornell offered to find me placements around New York. I thanked them but said I'd find my own jobs on ranches 'out West'!"

I could see the lanky young man, in his signature Stetson, hitchhiking across America.

"In the summer of my freshman year, I hitched to a 6,000 acre ranch in the Flint Hills of Kansas. They had a large herd of Herefords they were crossing with Charolais."

"Pretty," I comment.

"Yeah. How do you know about cattle?"

"I spent some of my boarding school vacations on properties, what you call ranches, in Australia. My uncle imported a Charolais bull for his herd. I remember the excitement of it arriving."

We smile at shared recollections, from different sides of the world.

"Did you enjoy your time in Kansas?"

"It was a strange vacation. I lived with the cowboy, he was a quarter Indian, and his wife. We spent hours riding herd but didn't speak much. I was only there about six weeks when the owner of the ranch, who was Vice President of Phillips 66, asked if I'd like to work on his ranch up in the northwest corner of Colorado, in the mountains."

"Did you hitch there from Kansas?"

"No, I got a ride with his daughter and her friend. Two lovely young ladies. They dropped me off at the bunkhouse and I never saw them again! My bunk mate there was Mexican and we earned $50 a week riding herd, bailing hay and fixing fences."

I bring the conversation back to the first two provisos to his scholarship.

"What did you do about meals?"

"I worked in the kitchen canteen, first scrubbing pots and pans, but I graduated to flipping burgers."

"Do you cook now?"

"I can still flip a burger!"

We laugh again. I've seen him manage a barbecue at a Friends of Denmark event.

"And the ROTC?" I ask.

"I had to decide in my junior year whether to stay with the Air Force program and become, at graduation, an officer, or whether to drop out. I couldn't see a future in the cattle business. I didn't own any cattle or land, so I opted to stay with the ROTC. I left Cornell as the highest-ranking cadet officer."

"Always a leader," I suggest.

"Well, I'd been working with men a long time." He is modest in his response. "I guess I had a bit more maturity than some of my fellow students."

"So you had decided on an air force career, yet you still farmed each summer."

"Had to get enough credits to graduate. But in the summer of my sophomore year I took my new '49 Oldsmobile Coupe and headed for the Muck Lands of Central Florida. Worked with a Zebu cross herd of 1,500 steers weighing 400 to 1,200 pounds - most with a nervous temperament."

"Did you live with the cowboys there?"

"No. I was offered housing with migrant citrus workers, but I found a room in the attic of a private home in Tavares. I ended up playing shortstop for the town baseball team."

"Sport has featured throughout your life," I comment. "Where did you go in your junior year?"

"I had enough credits by then and needed to earn some cash. I heard a lumber company in Eugene, Oregon was hiring, and paying well." Hans chuckled. "That was a good summer."

"What happened?"

"I had a '51 Chevy Coupe and two classmates who lived in California had a '52 and '53, and we decided to drive across the States. We each found another classmate to share the driving, except mine didn't like driving at night." His eyes gleamed with laughter. "Lincoln, Nebraska." Laughter burst through.

"What on earth happened in Lincoln, Nebraska?"

"We got arrested!"

I snort inelegantly. "Okay, I wasn't expecting that." Hans' laughter was contagious.

"Yeah, 4 a.m. we got pulled over for speeding. 80 mph through town. But...." and now Hans is in full laugh, "the judge wasn't expected until 7 a.m. We got talking to the cop and after a while he just told us, 'get outta here!' So we did!"

"Speeding all the way, huh! Did you ever make it to Oregon?"

"No. Stayed in Carmel, California with my roommate and his family and worked construction. We were good with a shovel and ended up laying 17 miles of sidewalks at Fort Ord."

He ignores the ringing phone.

"So you finish at Cornell and head to the Air Force, then your father asks if you'd be interested in returning to St Croix to help with Annaly Farms."

"He injured his leg on the ranch in the '40s and it flared up again and had to be amputated. That was in '59. He'd been elected to the first Virgin Islands Legislature in '55 and was finding it hard to manage both roles. But I had a Regular Commission in the Air Force. I was based at Ramey Air Force by then and I'd rent the "Club" Cessna 172 and fly home weekends to help out."

"What changed?"

"Romance. I met a beautiful woman from Chicago. She was a teacher at the Base. You asked about faith. Well she was a devout Christian Scientist."

"Good grief. You didn't make life easy for yourself," I say, a smile tempering my words.

Hans shook his head. "We upset both pairs of parents by getting married without telling them - three months after we met. It took a while but we finally got married housing on the Base. Judy read the Bible every morning and I decided, if I was to be a good husband, I should learn more. Do you know anything about Christian Scientists?"

It was his turn to question me.

"Not much," I admit.

"They read the Bible in conjunction with their book, Health and Science. Judy was always the first reader and I became the second reader, sometimes. I credit Judy with her belief in me, in keeping us healthy. I stopped smoking and drinking for twenty years." Hans pauses, lost in memories. "We had our first daughter and it became obvious I was a family man."

"Why was it obvious?"

"I was a good manager," Hans continues. "A captain in the Air Force and had a 20-year commission, but I didn't want to be posted somewhere without them. It was 1964 and St Croix was on the cusp of a boom. The Hess Oil Refinery was opening, and the Harvey Aluminum Company was starting a refinery to make alumina with bauxite, mainly from Jamaica. Maybe it was time to go back to St Croix. Rockefeller was going to build a resort on the ranch. I figured I could get a job with them."

"But the resort didn't happen. Well, not for twenty years," I say.

"That's right. The golf course, designed by Robert Trent Jones, opened in 1965 but Carambola Hotel didn't open until 1986." Hans stopped. "Judy was instrumental in helping me settle back. And she was influential in founding Good Hope School, where she taught for fourteen years. Our daughters went there, and our grandsons." Hans slips back to the past. "Dad was tied up in politics and so I took over managing Annaly Farms after we formed the Annaly Farms Partnership with Mr Canaday, who owned the property and cattle."

"Was it hard for your father to give up control, hard not to advise, interfere?"

"No. He never tried. I guess he knew his son. He was more controlling of Fritsie when he came to work for the Farm in 1974."

"You came full circle," I suggest. "Cowboy, studied animal science, airman and back to cattleman. With a whole bunch of things in between. A real Renaissance cowboy." I smile at his laugh. "Your father, and before him Bromley Nelthropp, were committed to cattle breeding and selection. Crossing the N'Dama from Senegal, West Africa with the Red Poll, originally from England but via Trinidad, became your life's work - or part of it."

"Yeah, we developed the Senepol into fine cattle - drought and tick resistant, high milk yield, good beef quality and an excellent temperament. I never liked dealing with testy cattle. We formed the Senepol Association in 1977 with four St Croix Senepol breeders which grew to encompass the 'WC' Senepol genetics in twenty tropical countries from Vietnam to Australia, South Africa to Brazil. First we exported live cattle via plane, and then later in 50-foot trailers on ships. Some semen and embryos were collected for shipment to the United States, but there was not a federally approved facility on St Croix for collecting either for export to foreign countries. So many stories."

"Tough keeping records pre-computer days."

My comment prompts Hans to spin around and take a file from the shelf next to his desk. He shows the meticulous data recorded - the sire, the dam, the calf weight and so on.

"2018 was the centenary of Bromley starting the whole process. You know we kept the WC (Annaly Farms) brand on our herd. In recognition of all Ward Canaday did."

"A mark of the man you are, Hans, no arrogance." I glance down at my notes as he opens the backpack and pulls out a brochure he has written about the cattle reared on his ranch.

"I remember you showing me this before. When you were kind enough to speak to our Australian farming friends." I riffle the pages. "Your involvement with the Senepol is so well documented, if you don't mind I'd like to get back to your family, and Hans Lawaetz, the man." I smile but don't give him time to respond. "Your daughter Jodie was born after your return to St Croix and now runs the wholesale and retail side of Annaly Farms Meat Market, which you started in the '70s. Were you able to let her find her own way, the way your father did you?"

"I hope so. She's great. Very efficient. You know she was an Olympian? Swam for the VI in the '84 Olympics and was a flag bearer for the Opening Ceremonies in Los Angeles. That takes a lot of discipline. Something I learned at Westtown and which I hope I have instilled in my daughters, and grandsons."

"And you have very neatly brought us to my next question, thanks, Hans! Sport has played, forgive the pun, a large part in your life. Baseball, soccer, swimming. You organized the St Croix Swimming Association and were involved in the building of an Olympic length pool at the Country Day School. Until we moved here, I had no idea the VI participated in not just summer Olympics, but winter too. A thought that naturally brings Jamaica and *Cool Runnings* to mind."

"We had a bobsleigh team, too. And skiing, luge and skeleton."

Hans stood, I always forget how tall the man is, and walked to a wall of photos. "See that one," he points to a group of worthy-looking men in blazers with the Olympic medallion on the breast pocket, and identifies each and the country they represented. "It was us, in 1982, who defined the technical rules for swimming. I was involved with the Olympics for forty years. Nine summer games and five winter. I retired after the 2012 London Olympics but was elected Honorary Life President of the Virgin Islands Olympic Committee."

Conservation has also been a large part of this man's life and he was recognized by the National Association of Conservation Districts (NACD) in their Hall of Fame.

"What do you think is the main problem with farming, conservation-wise. Livestock or agriculture?" I ask.

"Erosion and overgrazing." His response is immediate. "I was told, many years ago, 'it takes grass to make grass' and it's something I've never forgotten. We have to manage our land maintenance. We're getting better but we need to do more."

Hans has stories upon stories upon stories which he tells with a self-deprecating humor, his inherent kindness showing through. His love of sports evident in his involvement with many sports in the Virgin Islands. He also played fast-pitch softball for many years. His faith in human nature and belief in giving second chances obvious by the open door to his office, to which he still goes every day. I felt guilty at closing it but, apart from the telephone, did not want to lose him to someone else.

"Judy," I say, taking him back to a painful time in his life, "she travelled with you?"

"Often, yes." Hans pauses, again. "One of the beliefs of Christian Scientists is that disease is a mental error rather than a physical disorder. Judy's mother got cancer and decided to have treatment but it didn't work." Quiet cocoons the office. "Then Judy got cancer and she refused any treatment. We had 39 wonderful, loving and harmonious years. I was beside her when she died."

Muted sounds come from the bustle of the butchery. I am loathe to break Hans' silence.

"You know I've been married three times?" His voice is strong.

"I didn't." I say. "I thought Barbara was your second wife."

"No, I married in haste. Teresa was a good rider. We'd ride in the hills. She stayed up at the house and I didn't like that my grandchildren saw us there. So we got married. It was a mistake. She wanted to take over the business. Keep me from my grandchildren. It was crazy."

I wait to hear the craziness.

"I had to get a restraining order against her. And she got one to keep me out of my house. It took 45 days for the divorce to go through!"

I am angry at someone taking this generous man for granted. I can only imagine how his family felt. I look at the photo on his desk of Barbara. A carefree photo of a smiling woman, prepared to step in and help, whether driving the tractor or helping herd twenty Senepol cattle that roam the home field, their russet coats gleaming in the Caribbean sun. A gentlewoman.

"Hans," I ask, "what happened to Ken Abel?"

"Oh," he is pulled back, "he had a difficult life. He could never really speak. After some time in South America he came home. I looked after him. Ken died in his seventies."

He is right, I think, this man is a family man. I glance up at a photo on the wall and almost tip myself out of the chair.

"Do you still ride?"

"No, I stopped about ten years ago. Had a couple of concussions from falls." He is laconic. "Decided I should look after myself."

"Good call," I say. "Did you ever play polo?"

"Not really. I came close in my freshman year at Cornell. But when I realized we had to walk the ponies around between chukkas for the varsity team I thought, 'nah'. But as a team in the fraternity league, and after a few drinks, we played a mean bareback game with broomsticks and a volleyball."

It is a morning tinged with both laughter and sadness.

I look at the man across the desk, still rubbing his fingers. A man exposed to many faiths but whose major driver is decency, fairness and a firm belief it is our responsibility to share experience and knowledge.

"I'm curious," I say. "It's over a hundred years since Denmark owned these islands. Why do you think it important to have societies like The St Croix Friends of Denmark - of which you were president for a number of years?"

"For history, in some ways a shared culture, and friendship."

The answer speaks to the man. I ask one final question.

"What do you think makes a Virgin Islander, Hans?"

He is quiet.

"Understanding, patience, faith and a love of our islands."

I thank Hans for his generous time and on the drive back to Christiansted I reflect on his answer. Hans Lawaetz, I would venture to say, is a true Virgin Islander. A Crucian.

*The Beast is a brutal road that climbs from the north coast of St Croix up into the hills and is famous as part of the Ironman and Triathlon routes.

SEAPLANE TIME

The sun creeps over Seven Hills to shimmer like a tangerine glaze across Gallows Bay and filters through palm fronds to crisscross the gallery where I sit with my coffee. It is just before seven. This I know not from the softness of the rays but because every morning on island I watch the seaplane leave on its first flight to St Thomas, the blousy and boisterous sister Virgin to St Croix.

That first flight is a far better indicator of time than the clocks on the four sides of the Steeple Building at the bottom of Church Street. It's been a number of years since the clock has told the time with any accuracy. The Park's supervisor has assured the worthy residents of this Caribbean enclave that fixing it is high on his priority list. "It's a personal thing - I want it to be accurate," he told a recent meeting of the Christiansted Community Alliance. He has not been on island long, and his enthusiasm for rigorous time keeping is at odds with the majority of islanders.

Instead it is the little seaplane, floats skimming the marina like a skipping stone, lifting with a surge of power to rise over Protestant Cay to begin its busy day connecting the islands, which provide a reference point for Crucians.

Charlie Blair is credited with spearheading inter-island air transportation, opening up opportunities for islanders to do business with the other Virgins, both American and British. A retired US Air Force brigadier general, Naval aviator, Pan-Am and test pilot, breaker of flight records and a consultant to NASA, Blair found time in 1963 to start Antilles Air Boats. His initial idea had been to provide a flying boat service from New York to various points in the Caribbean and, with that in mind, he purchased two Sandringham flying boats and later a Sikorsky VS-44. That plan morphed into a less ambitious one and he left the long-haul flights up to more established airlines. Upon his death in 1978, ironically in a seaplane accident, his wife, the Irish American actress Maureen O'Hara, ran the business until selling it a year later.

Time can be an approximation in the Caribbean and I am reminded of when living in West Africa, I bemoaned the fact many meetings I attended could run late, anywhere from quarter of an hour to two hours and longer. After showing my impatience one day I was put in my place by an elderly and erudite African who told me, "Señora, the person you are with is more important than the person you are going to see." Translated into snappy modern-day speech his words are similar to the adage, "Be Here Now!" I haven't quite been able to embrace either edict to the full extent of the letter but I do try, mostly. I don't advocate serial lateness, but really, do a few minutes matter?

The one exception is when, each time I leave this haven where I luxuriate in watching cheeky yellow bananaquits busily flit from blossom to blossom and seaplanes take off, I wander to the end of the street and request a taxi to take me to the airport. The drivers know me as 'de English lady, she on de hill' which I suppose is better than 'over the hill', but with great merriment they assure me my cab will be there, "England time, not island time!"

Seaplanes continue to provide inter-island transport and their schedule continues to be my timekeeper, but I'm not sure what I'll do when all four clock faces on the Steeple Building are back up and ticking, I mean who am I to believe?

A NECESSARY ORGAN

For a small island, only 84 square miles, St Croix offers a surprising array of cultural multiplicity from quelbe to calypso, from scuba to racing, from fine dining to roadside roti, from comedy to the classics.

Every now and then the spirit soars to unexpected heights and not always in a place of faith. Perhaps the sight of a frigate bird catching a current high over moored yachts; or the pure unfettered joy of a baby's laugh or, as on Saturday, when sound and space created harmony in the soul of those present.

I sat on mahogany pews in St John's Episcopal Church, designed and built by master craftsman Andrew Ferris after a fire in 1866 destroyed the building, itself a rebuild of the original wooden structure blown down in the hurricane of 1772. Ferris, in modern day parlance, was the main contractor. The magnificence of the rafters draws the eye ever upwards and to the balcony - a place of beauty but also stained with an ignominious past - it was where those enslaved sat during services. Ferris's elegantly proportioned stairs, pulpit and altar, also made from island mahogany, underscore the simplicity of the church, open to the Caribbean elements and the occasional pigeon.

It is those elements that have wrought so much damage to the two organs at St John's. The first, a Hutchings-Plaisted 'Tracker' Organ, was installed in 1881. Positioned on the north balcony, it is made of wood with thistles stenciled on the pipe casings. According to www.stams.org, "a tracker organ is a mechanical organ, where each key is mechanically connected to a valve for a pipe by a series of wooden 'stickers' and 'trackers'. The effect is like an old fashioned typewriter." And, for those of us in the audience interested in trivia, we were told it is also the origin of the phrase 'pull out all the stops'!

The second is modern by comparison, a 1960 Austin Organ custom built for the church, with more pipes added over the years. Hurricane Hugo rudely ripped half the roof off St John's effectively dousing both organs. The pipe organ was disassembled and shipped back to Austin Organs in Upper Montclair, New Jersey for restoration, and under the hands, and feet, of a master, the tonal quality is inspiring.

And so it was on Saturday when Peter Richard Conte, on island regularly for 25 years, played a benefit concert for the restoration, and upkeep, of both organs. Mr Conte is an organist of international repute and only the fourth Wanamaker Grand Court Organist (situated in Macy's Center City in Philadelphia), a title originating when the Wanamaker Organ with a mind-blowing 30,000 pipes was first played in 1911. Mr Conte has a string of credits and recordings to his name, has been featured several times on National Public Radio and television, and has performed with numerous orchestras.

Before each piece Conte spoke, his face tanned and animated, his well-modulated voice perhaps a precursor to what awaited the audience gazing up at the west balcony. We were not disappointed as the music sometimes thundered, sometimes whispered, and sometimes lilted, reverberating around the gracious old church.

Watching Mr Conte's hands, long and strong fingered, coax and cajole the organ into magnificence was a treat not expected. His feet danced in soft-soled shoes across the pedals. He played music I didn't know, like Alexandre Guilmant's

Grand Chorus in the style of Handel. He played favorites, the *Finale from Bach's St Matthew Passion*, then switching moods his fingers skipped lightly through Arthur Sullivan's *Overture to HMS Pinafore.* His playing of Bizet's *Carmen Suite* had most of us either tapping or humming.

The "Tracker" needs full restoration, and the "Austin" requires annual servicing - both are necessary organs if Peter Richard Conte, who plays at St John's whenever on island, or any other organist is to make our spirits soar.

And, looking around at the upturned faces, I was again impressed by the faith of ordinary people, not just here but everywhere, whose unshakeable belief that funding would and could be raised to save the crumbling buildings in which they prayed.

Perhaps I'm also a little envious!

A TASTE OF ST CROIX

Too much choice is not always a good thing, sending the most efficient of us into a panic of, well, epic proportions. The reason I'm not a shopping mall kind of gal!

Food shopping, actually any shopping or dining, was a limited and limiting experience when we lived in Malabo, our island home in Equatorial Guinea. The essentials were found after completing the circuit of the blue shop, the red shop, the freezer shop with its disconcerting strips of paper suspended from the ceiling and speckled with dead or dying flies, and the local market. The latter was good for avocados and aubergines and, if one's taste ran to bush meat, skinned monkey or pangolin hanging from hooks on rickety frames.

Returning to the megastores of Houston and where there is limitless fine dining, for any palate or purse, was overwhelming. When faced with a choice of an aisle full of cereal; or tinned tomato sliced, diced, with added onion, basil, chili and more; or loo paper of different ply, or roll size; or biscuits or breads various, I was known to freeze then wander aimlessly around until I walked out with half my list, exhausted from decision making.

Now back on an island, on and off, throughout the year, I find I have the perfect balance in food shopping: a number of supermarkets, depending on my mood and requirements, but none so big as to send me into a flat spin. And the same for dining experiences - except for one week a year!

The St Croix Foundation has, for the past fourteen years, held St Croix's Food and Wine Experience, their annual fundraiser in support of 'community and economic development, public education reform and public safety.' The 2014 theme, *Culinary Futures,* has emphasized the island's gastronomic offerings and the nurturing of youth in the food industry. Chefs, food and wine writers, and those who enjoy a good nosh descend on St Croix, filling hotels and holiday rentals and spending an inordinate amount of time discussing the latest 'new' ingredient, or vintage.

Spread through the week, there are eleven events from which to choose. Some of the choice is, as always, dictated by the size of one's wad, with a couple of wining and dining experiences running to $1000 per person. But that ticket price covers an unforgettable affair - cuisine prepared by world-famous chefs in exquisite surroundings. Richard Jenrette's home, part of the Classical American Homes and Preservation Trust, was taken over by Chef Leah Cohen of the *Pig and Khao* in New York City, famous for her blend of Filipino/Asian fusion cuisine. Or maybe you'd prefer a glimpse of Estate Belvedere, an Architectural Digest Home rarely open to the public, and a meal prepared by celebrity chefs Todd and Ellen Gray and Chef Gary Klinefelter. What better way to spend an evening than dining on the terrace of a restored sugar mill overlooking the ever-changing colors of the Caribbean.

For those with shallower wallets, A Taste of St Croix, held at the poolside of the Divi Carina Bay Resort where 2,000 people, give or take a couple, enjoy dinner and wine from the island's best restaurants, chefs, farms and food provisioners. Not only is there a Caribbean-cool party scene, but also a competition judged by guest chefs.

Eleven choices over seven days, from wine tastings to sessions for children, ranging in age from 6 - 12, about the importance of local produce and family dining, culminating in the final event of the week, Wine in the Warehouse. Music and munchies washed down with fine wines at the melee in a chilly warehouse stacked to the rafters with bottles. Documenting the evening with his acrylic-laden palette knife was Los Angeles-based artist Greg Kalamar: standing on a wine box for a bird's eye view of those milling and sipping, his painting to be sold to the highest bidder.

Whatever your taste in food, wine or fun - it's worth visiting St Croix for a taste of the island, even ForbesTravel. com says so! And for one week a year, even I can handle the pressure of choice.

THE BEAT MUST GO ON

Trade winds are the norm on this island in the Caribbean - they cool us most months of the year and when they cease to blow we all complain, bitterly. But this morning I sent a quiet plea to the man in charge of breezes and asked for a slight easing. I am nervous before each of these conversations, which means I can invariably find something to worry about. Today it was wind distorting the recording.

Stanley Jacobs went to school at the bottom of our road so I had no qualms about him finding the place. I had not taken into account two homes with similar paint jobs and so his walk was longer than it needed to be, and steeper.

"Let me catch my breath." He stands on the gallery and gazes out at the harbor, his jeans crisp and his check shirt loose.

I pour a glass of water then wait for him to sit, to get comfortable.

"You hear the shootings?" he nods across to Gallows Bay.

"Sadly, we do. Two in six days."

"These killings are retaliatory." He shakes his head, his hair close-cropped. "They are not going to stop."

"What a dreadful thought. Families destroyed," I say, only able to imagine the horror of a murdered child.

Stanley's eyes cloud behind his glasses. "And often these young men leave a small child, maybe two or three. It's very sad."

It is a chilling thought. A new generation growing up searching for somewhere to belong, even if it's a gang. This is not how I thought our conversation would start.

I dive in. "Stanley, how does it feel to be considered a cultural icon?"

"Old," he says. His laugh is deep, more a chuckle, a kind of heh, heh, heh. "That's what they tell me. But I'm a modest guy."

"I've discovered that." I think of the blanks I have drawn in my research. "The band, *The Ten Sleepless Knights*, is well documented and recorded, which is why I'd like to talk about you, the man."

There's that chuckle again. "Yeah, well."

"You were born in Vieques, how old were you when you came to St Croix?"

"About two months." He laughs. "My father was a photographer and was employed by the military. They document everything. You remember the Navy built a base on Vieques?" He continues as I nod. "Up till now they have mines, in the waters."

"So you come to St Croix, and live at Gallows Bay?"

He stands and looks down the hill for his childhood home but trees obscure the view.

"Tell me about your neighbor, the one who taught you to play *anguinaldo*, the Puerto Rican Christmas music. He taught you to make guitars too, didn't he?"

"He was old." There's that laugh again. "Maybe my age now! Guitars from sardine cans."

I think of 4-inch cans lining supermarket shelves. "They can't have been very big."

He swivels toward the table, and demonstrates how to make a guitar, then spreads his hands about a foot.

"The size of a ukulele," I suggest.

He nods. "Exactly. A ukulele, a banjo. My brothers used to make them. I was very small then but they went over to the Cay." He points across to Protestant Cay. "The tourists liked it and threw pennies, nickels and dimes."

"Well, it is music to dance to," I say.

"The entire repertoire of our music is dance, you know. You cannot sit and listen. You have to move, to tramp. That's why the truck drove so fast this Christmas. For COVID, you know. If we go slow people follow."

I know how quickly they passed through Christiansted. By the time we got to the bottom of the hill they were on their way to Canegata Ball Park after the traditional Christmas drive-by when they sing carols and crowds follow on foot.

"Were your parents musical?" I am fascinated with the thought of talent being passed down the generations. My mind flits to the murder at Gallows Bay. Maybe if music had played a part in these young men's lives, lives would not have been lost.

"My mother sang. She was from Vieques. My father, he was Crucian, he played mandolin, and my grandfather, violin."

"Do you have siblings, Stanley? Do they play music?"

"Had," he corrects me. "Yeah. I played with them, in New York."

I know gold is struck. "New York? I had no idea."

"I went to college at Lincoln, in a town called Oxford, about forty-five miles southwest of Philadelphia. I spent time in New York with my brothers. Their mother was different to my mother," he explains. "They were older. One was married to a Trini, the other to a Jamaican. And a sister. All the Caribbean people stayed together. We used to take boat rides to….." He taps his head in frustration then waves his hand. "…upstate New York, someplace."

"It'll come," I say. "Someone told me not long ago the reason we forget things is that the filing cabinet in our mind is so full it takes a time to flip through all those files." We share a rueful laugh.

"Anyway plenty, plenty people. We party. You know New York?" He asks.

"Not well," I admit.

Stanley hits his head. "Bear Mountain on the Hudson," he remembers, then asks, "You know the Beatnik? The Village?"

I nod, not able to imagine this delightful man with greying hair as a free-love-and-peace kind of dude, or following the trails of Jack Kerouac or Alan Ginsburg.

"We played at Café Wha? Off West 4th Street. You know it?"

I shake my head. Stanley is in full chuckle.

"We didn't start performing until one… in the morning." He laughs at the memory. "Down steps to the basement. Smokey. The marijuana made my throat scratchy. Heh, heh, now I am in bed by nine."

"What time did you finish?"

"5 a.m. or 6 a.m. Depend on the crowd."

"What kind of music?"

"Calypso. My brother played guitar. He was good. I was lead pan. We had conga and maracas. I played steel pan at Lincoln."

We jump back to college. "What made you choose Lincoln?"

"I didn't want to go. My teacher coerced me. He went to Lincoln. I wanted to be an artist. Paint. Me and three others from St Croix went."

"I didn't know you paint." I jump onto another snippet. "Do you still?"

"Not so much, now. Not for a good while. What I liked is abstract painting."

I mention how I feel it terribly unfair that some people are multi-talented in the arts.

"Well, art is something that doesn't stay in one place." Stanley says. "I have always liked music. You know, then," he takes us back to New York, "there was music everywhere. It was a fad. Everybody had a conga drum, or bongos, and a cowbell. People played on the streets, the steps leading up to the houses. We played in the subway on the way to Café Wha? Walking along." He gazes out to sea. "Long, long time since I go to New York." He pauses. "My grandson, he's in New York. He works in a lab. Cancer research. At Sloane Kettering."

"A medical man, like his grandfather," I suggest, referring to Stanley's time as a medical corpsman. "Does your grandson play music too?"

There's that laugh again. "Heh, heh, I give him a flute, a banjo, a saxophone. But he tell me, 'Grandpa, when I have time.'"

I take my guest back to college. "I looked up Lincoln. Some hefty alumni. Lots of musicians, and Thurgood Marshall." I tell Stanley about my connection to Texas Southern University, another Historically Black College and University (HBCU), through the University Museum and that the law school is named for the famous jurist.

"Langston Hughes, too," he reminds me.

I think of the Harlem Renaissance but ask, "Why steel pan?"

I'm getting used to indirect answers. "Maybe eleven or twelve of us from the Caribbean. Music from Trinidad. We made our own pans."

I tell him my daughter's mother-in-law plays pan in Port of Spain, and that my granddaughter has started to learn. He smiles.

"I never been there. I wish I had."

"You graduate from Lincoln then, in 1963, you're drafted. Did you go to Vietnam?'

"No. I was lucky. I got sent to Edgewood Arsenal and Fort Detrick. Two Army research facilities for military stuff."

"Because you were a psych major? Research into things like PTSD?" It is an innocent question.

"No, the other side. Into things that give you PTSD. I worked in the labs. Regular hours." Stanley is not laughing now and moves on. "Also on the neuropsychiatric ward. That was shift work."

"Were you playing music there?"

"Yeah. I played guitar and banjo with two boys from California. White boys. Folk music, Bob Dylan and Joan Baez. I liked it. But it was difficult off the base. Where I was stationed in the Deep South, we could only go certain places."

"What do you mean?"

"Segregation. The black and white thing. In Louisiana, you go to town - signs saying 'white only', 'no blacks'. I never experience that before. Coming from here, in those days there was no such thing. And in New York the West Indian people gather together. In the south it was not so good."

"What about in the Army?"

"No, no. That was desegregated by President Truman. But, of course, there were some white people who didn't like black people. You could tell."

"Jackasses," I say. My mouth is dry from the image Stanley paints. I sip water.

"Promotions, things like that, things that ran under the current."

I wonder if much has changed but bring the conversation back to St Croix.

"Did you find it difficult to come home, after the Army. To settle back on island."

Stanley looks at me in amazement. "It was home. Of course it was good to be back with my friends, and family."

I explain that I have lived in many countries and so have an attitude a little different. That wherever I happen to be, at any given time, is where I feel at home. I do not convince him.

"You start working at the Herbert Griggs Home for the Aged and start a band with some of the residents." Before I can form a question, Stanley is off and running. It is wonderful to watch his face glow with memories.

"The Simmond Brothers. The old folks," he breaks off in laughter, "my age now! They taught me quelbe and quadrille. Some of them were musical icons of their time. Then my friends and I formed a band."

"Stanley, I've got to ask, why did you call yourselves *The Vikings?*" I'm struggling with a group of men, not a blond amongst them, calling themselves after Norse warriors.

"Heh, heh, heh. Our belief of the Vikings was they were heroes. Macho-men. He-men. We had no money for instruments so we made them. Flutes. Triangles from steel rods in car brakes. Car mufflers became pipes. You know, you get a tuba sound from that. Then the *guiro*."

I look blank.

"A dried gourd, that you score with a file or blade to make ridges." His hands demonstrate again. "You play it with ten to fifteen bicycle spokes nailed into some wood. Like an afro pick. And the fife. A flute made from bamboo. It is the instrumentation that makes quelbe. Steel, squash and banjo together is what makes quelbe quelbe. We added drums. There was no drum in original quelbe."

"It's called fungi in the British Virgin Islands. Why the difference?"

"Every island has a name for scratch bands. In Jamaica they call it mento, in the Bahamas, rake. You know skin music?"

I shake my head and wonder how that didn't show up in my research.

"Skin is fife, base and kettledrum. And voice."

My head is spinning with the different instruments, and I bring our conversation back to the eponymous band and music all Crucians and imports love to hear.

"Do they play quelbe on St Thomas?"

"Yeah, yeah, but their quelbe got," Stanley pauses, "overwhelmed with other music from outside. St Thomas is commercial. We are country."

"So, *The Vikings* became *Stanley and the Ten Sleepless Knights* and you had ten band members. I know many people here know how that name came about, but tell me anyway."

"Heh, heh." I cannot help but smile at his chuckle. "One of the fathers said, 'it took ten sleepless nights to produce my ten children!'" The laugh is in full flow. "It seemed like a good name. But our numbers vary. Anything from eight to fifteen depending on who can play. That is part of quelbe culture. It is casual."

"And you all seem to have nicknames."

"And you." Stanley turns the tables. "I have not met someone called Apple before!" He asks me, "You notice how Calypsonians all have an adjective before their name?"

I nod and mention The Mighty Sparrow and Lord Kitchener. "What about your nickname?" I pause, trying to pronounce it. "Esk, Eska…."

"Eskaskolay?" Stanley helps me.

"Eskakaolay," I repeat. "Where on earth does that come from?"

The smile is broad, "Me not know. They call me that from long time ago. Some kind of drink?" The question makes me laugh. "Maybe a Danish drink, heh, heh, heh."

It is difficult to stay focused with that wonderful laugh flying around with the breeze. "Tell me where you've played?"

"All over. New York, Miami, New Orleans, Washington DC, Atlanta."

"And Denmark?"

"Four times. You know, Denmark has many jazz clubs and festivals, more than New Orleans. They like quelbe."

"How did you organize it?"

"There was a musician, Hans Pedersen and his wife, who contacted us. They lived north of Copenhagen. His band was Danish Pol Calypso. He organized many gigs for us. We played at schools, in festivals and clubs. Many places." Stanley gazes across the bay. "They like quelbe," he repeats, "and quadrille."

"Do you dance, Stanley?"

"No, no. Me no dance. But ah, me wife, Georgia," his hands move to a beat in his memory, "she could move!"

Georgia Jacobs died in 2014 after forty-five years of marriage. One of Stanley's daughters lives with him, the other nearby. They are not musical and even though he has hopes his grandsons will one day have time for music, at the moment his hopes lie with his great grandson.

"Start early with him," I suggest.

Stanley nods. "You know we try and take quelbe to the schools. After quelbe was made the national music of the Virgin Islands. We had a student band. The Quelbe Ambassadors."

"Are they still going?"

"No." Stanley looks down. "They were good. But you know, the students, they graduated and then they get busy. Some join the Army. One girl she plays flute well."

"Was that Sasha Alexander?" I remember hearing her talk on a podcast about the importance of keeping quelbe alive.

"Yes. She good, you know?" He changes tack. "You hear the plane yesterday mahnin'? A big plane. Military. Our National Guard going to Washington."

"It's dreadful!" My words are inadequate and do not convey my disgust at the storming of the Capitol on January 6th. I want to swear but that would be disrespectful to the gentleman on the other side of the table.

Stanley is distressed, silent for a moment. "It seems like it is not American. To attack the seat of government. You know what I mean?"

"It doesn't sit right, does it," I agree.

"It's out of whack."

We are quiet with our own thoughts until Stanley says, "We never practice, you know. Until Tino joined."

"Tino Francis," I confirm.

"Yeah, he pass away in 2014. He play keyboard. You know his name, DeVinci Valentino Francis? We know them by their nickname all their lives. Only know the real one when they die. Heh, heh, heh. We call him 'Folksie', also. He could read music, you know. He make us practice. Before then we practice when we perform."

Before I can ask a question, Stanley continues, "When we go to the Complex or Central High, we play quelbe and a computer program transcribed the music so students can learn. They all read music. Me, I just listen and play."

I am envious.

"What do you think of rap? The language, the beat?"

"Not much," he says. "Most times it's violence - bad message. It doesn't have much harmony - playing one chord. It sounds like quarreling, you know?"

I can only agree.

"But," Stanley continues in a reflective voice, "sometimes it is nice, and poetic."

I watch a squall cross the bay and know it is about to hit the gallery. We go indoors and I put on a mask but indicate to Stanley that he is fine as I slam windows shut. I sit on the other side of the room.

"Can I ask how old the youngest member of *The Ten Sleepless Knights* is?"

"KC - Kendell Henry. About thirty. He play with us since high school. KC plays drums, congas, steel squash and sings. And he's preparing to take over the business side of TSK, Inc." Stanley smiles at the idea of the beat going on. "And Kevin. His father is Edgie - Eldred Christian. Edgie and me, we started together. He plays banjo and sings. Kevin," Stanley reverts to the son, "plays banjo, steel and squash and is our sound engineer."

"It's great you've got a couple of younger players." I look at the elderly man with twinkling eyes and a crooked tooth. "You said, in an interview a few years ago, that you and the band hoped to record every song in your repertoire. Have you?"

"Almost. You asked me about songs about society?" Stanley mentions. "Tino, he wrote one about guys killing each other, maybe ten years ago. I have it on thumb drive. We should record it. You hear of Mighty Pat?"

I am glad I can say yes.

"Mighty Pat a Kittitian but live here long time. St Croix is his base. You ask me, before, about music telling a story. Mighty Pat, he recorded 'I Can't Breathe' after George Floyd. He incorporates rap into his music."

I nod again and say I have heard the recording. Stanley asks if I know quelbe was considered derogatory.

"Why?"

"Me not know. Country music. Scratch band. Now the music of the Virgin Islands," he repeats with pride. "We played at The Plantation, out West, long time ago."

"That was at Estate Prosperity?"

He nods. "Arthur Christiansen owned it. His daughter asked if I knew folk. I told her yes. We sang Dylan, Baez, others. I liked it."

"Do you still play that kind of music."

"Sometimes. Just for me." Stanley stands and looks out at a rainbow reaching for Protestant Cay. "I go to school, elementary, in the Steeple Building. We walk home along Church Street. You know a werewolf lived in that house?" He points across the street to a genip tree reaching over the walled garden.

I laugh, again.

"We believe it, you know? Heh, heh, heh. He one smart man. He set up a speaker in the garage - the house have a garage even back then - and he speak into the mic when he hear us coming. 'Whooo, whooo, whooo.' Oh man, we run fast. And never walk this street after dark." His laugh rumbles around the room. "Then I go to school on King Street, in the Library. Then one year down there." He points down East Street to the ruins at the bottom of the hill which, before they were the high school, was where the Danish garrison was housed back in the day.

"They keep talking about restoring them," I comment, thinking of plans yet to reach fruition.

"They should have done it long ago."

I can only agree.

"The infrastructure here, it's broken. The old bridges, the roads." He is standing above a prime example of bad roads. "You know what PhD stands for?"

I shake my head, pretty sure it's not the obvious.

"Pot Hole Dodgers!" His smile is wide at my snort of delight. We laugh together at a bumper sticker seen around town, 'Not Drunk, Dodging Potholes!'.

His stories are coming fast now as the street where we live jogs his memory.

"There was an old lady, very petite, who sold stewed gooseberries. You know gooseberries?" Stanley doesn't wait for my nod. "Cook Liza. She had a stand under the tree. She thread gooseberries on a slim stick from coconut tree leaves. One penny for one stick."

Stanley licks his lips. I wish he were preparing to play his flute, just for me. Sadly our morning is over and I walk with him to his truck. "When are you playing again?" I ask him as we puff past Victor Borge's former home.

"I don't know. This COVID is a bad thing. For everybody. We play virtually. But it's not the same. Musicians need the energy of the people."

We bump fists and I think, as I wait for him to drive away, I know exactly what he means.

I am grateful for the energy this lovely man has given me and know the quelbe beat will go on.

A NEST EGG

Every now and then we are fortunate to witness something that touches a chord - a kind act, beautiful music or dance maybe, or nature at her very best.

I have never been a lolling-on-the-beach kind of person. I prefer being in the water, and if I'm very lucky, seeing a manta ray or a seahorse or, one of my favorite sights, a cleaning station where larger-finned fish have their dental and bodywork polished by smaller varieties.

So you will be surprised to know that last Wednesday, as the sun slipped below the western horizon in a surprisingly subdued display, I joined thirty or so others on a walk through the scrub and down to the water's edge. Then I lolled, for three hours.

All for the leatherback sea turtle!

It is nesting season, and the beach at Sandy Point on St Croix is out of bounds to most humans from April 1st to September 1st, unless with an organized tour. Volunteers and researchers, passionate about conservation and in particular endangered turtles, spend the five months patrolling the area collecting data, monitoring and recording where these grand dames lay their eggs. They will also move a nest if the eggs, anything up to 80 fertilized and 30 unfertilized eggs, have been laid in an erosion area.

Given strict instructions, the group played follow-my-leader walking in single file along the crystalline waters kissing the shore. Overhead gulls, frigates and smaller seabirds circled, aware tasty morsels would soon be emerging from the depths of the sand. Wide circles drawn on the beach by volunteers, like cosmic rings, marked nests showing signs of activity. Carefully walking between the rings we headed back up the beach and settled, rather like birds quieting their feathers, in the warmth of the sand.

Our guide, Ariana, a passionate young American raised in Costa Rica, adorned with a variety of talismans around her neck, told us the tale of the leatherback sea turtle. A quiet gasp swept the circle each time a small bluish-black speck appeared, or a flipper flailed, having stabbed its way out of its shell with the help of the carbuncle, the egg tooth: then silence as we willed the tiny hatchlings to break free of the sand in which they had nestled for 65 days.

We learnt a leatherback could reach up six and half feet and weigh in at 2,000 pounds - incredible to believe as we watched their three-inch selves struggle to the surface. Clad in what looked like moldy inky-blue capes, rubbery to the touch, leatherbacks are unlike other sea turtles that have hard bony shells. Diving to and staying at immense depths, sometimes nearly eight miles for up to 85 minutes, the leatherback needs the ridges along the carapace for a more hydrodynamic flow.

The hatchlings continued to emerge, flippers swishing sand and turtles, each movement encouraging those still below to rise up. Ariana would occasionally trickle sand over the weaving clutch to keep them moving. Only as one moved away from the crowd did she pick it up and put it in the soft insulated bag, counting them in aloud with the group.

Over the course of three hours, against a backdrop of the gloaming turning to night accompanied by the lullaby of lapping waves and cavorting dolphins just offshore, we learnt the adult females lay their billiard-ball size eggs every two to three years, each season nesting between four to seven times with about ten days' break between each nesting. That could be over 500 eggs per turtle, which begs the question why such a prolific-laying creature could be endangered.

Despite nature's cleverness at camouflage, an inky carapace from above and a pinkish-white belly, the plastron, which makes it harder for predators from beneath, many fail to make it to maturity - only about one in a thousand. But we humans are also to blame for their endangered status. Leatherback sea turtles travel up to 4,000 miles between breeding and feeding, eating as much jellyfish as possible along the way - on a good day their body weight. Our propensity in using plastic bags, which we then toss away, is to blame for killing leatherbacks who mistake them for jellyfish. Our fishing practices and the erroneous belief that turtle eggs increase libido doesn't help either.

In the now glistening night we counted in 38 hatchlings and, as Ariana turned on a small red flashlight, we moved to another part of the beach away from the clarity of the night ocean to the murkier side, where reeds swayed and rocks gave protection from the patrols of hungry feeders above and below. We released the tiny leatherback hatchlings into the sea foaming at our feet, and watched, helpless, as some were tossed back onto the sand before catching the next wave out towards the cooler northern waters where they could eat to their heart's content.

Hopefully to survive, as long as they don't encounter the callousness, or carelessness, of man or the hunger of predators from the air or sea.

CHIKUNGUNYA

O r expat arrogance. Have you ever noticed how life plays wonderful little ironies when least expected? Having spent many years in countries where malaria and dengue are prevalent, where chloroquine (Sunday Sunday medicine is what we called it) left its acidic taste once a week, where long-term use of doxycycline left an unpleasant gastric condition and where Larium sent you loopy, Malarone became, in Equatorial Guinea, the prophylactic drug of choice. My husband has had a number of bouts of malaria and one of dengue – he did spend many weeks in the jungles of Papua New Guinea, but I have managed for the most part to avoid those most unpleasant of viruses.

When contemplating retirement and where best we would like to live, there were some definite 'must haves and must not haves' on our list; cheese, wine, tropical fruit and fresh milk and bread rank high on our essentials. No more anti-malarial drugs was equally high on the must-not haves list. And so it is with some consternation and a great deal of irritation that I find, having avoided the demon mozzie for 56 years, I have been caught, and in the place we have chosen in time to retire – the Caribbean.

Chikungunya is a word with which I have recently become intimately acquainted, and one which frankly I don't wish to hear again. Coming from the Makonde language of modern-day Tanzania, chikungunya means 'that which bends up' and was first noted by those outside Africa in 1952 after an outbreak along the Makonde Plateau.

For me it started over two weeks ago with very sore hands, which I put down to over-zealous gardening. I watched my fingers swell as the day progressed and it occurred to me I should probably remove my rings, but I didn't. Day two saw total body ache, which again I put down to the vicious removal of tan-tan and an invidious and invasive non-native creeper covered in small pink flowers that I have come to detest. Day three I started the arduous task of closing up the many shutters that protect our little piece of paradise from the vagaries of late-season weather systems crossing the Atlantic, as I readied for the trip back to Houston, along with Marley the cat. Wholly unable to finish the job as every bone and joint began to thrum with pain, I was fortunate to be able to call Barry, a friend who graciously and kindly shut the house down.

Now I don't know if you've flown with a cat, but I find the entire process stressful. I have become a dab hand at bribing Marley with cheese whiz infused with a sedative; though each time we go through the process I contemplate just giving it to myself. If he wasn't so unhappy when not with us, bearing in mind we hand-reared him from three days old, we would not put him or ourselves through it. However we do, and once we reach our destination he jumps from his cage and is perfectly content as I reach with shaking hands for Jim Beam. The thought of being ejected from the plane with Marley was the reason I did not succumb to tears but rather swallowed fistfuls of analgesics on the final leg of my journey from Miami to Houston.

Bent over and hobbling along the concourse at George Bush Intercontinental airport at midnight, pulling a cat cage and cursing the day I decided to become a writer and therefore become beholden to a computer, I finally made it to the sanctuary of my husband's arms.

By 4 a.m. it had become obvious I needed medical attention and so began a day of phials of blood coursing from my veins for testing, and morphine trickling in. I was hospitalized. Infectious-disease specialists tutted as my body refused to produce the expected rash, though every other symptom satisfied their desire for a sure diagnosis of chikungunya. The rash did appear the day after my release from hospital, covering my arms, legs, face and chest in a mottled hive of red bumps. Intermittent fever and headache vied for supremacy over my aching body. Apart from pain relief, keeping hydrated and rest, there is no magic pill.

Arriving for the first time on the French island of St Martin late in 2013, then quickly leap-frogging around and across the Caribbean to Central and South America, chikungunya has infected more than a million people. In El Salvador, the AP reports cases are up from 2,300 at the beginning of August to over 30,000 now (October). Health officials in Colombia predict 700,000 cases by early 2015. The US Virgin Islands declared the virus at epidemic proportions last week.

The usual common-sense preventative measures for mosquito control - widespread fogging, removing standing water, avoiding the outdoors at dusk and dawn - appear relatively ineffective. The *aedes aegypti* mosquito much prefers to be indoors, snug under beds and in closets, and typically lays its eggs in clear, clean water. Liberally covering oneself with Deet, picaridin, oil of lemon eucalyptus or other products disliked by the little buggers, and generally following preventative guidelines seems the most effective deterrent. Larvaciding, killing the mosquito larvae through water treatment which lasts about three months, is being undertaken in the USVI.

Fortunately chikungunya is rarely fatal but joint pain can apparently last for a couple of years. After nearly three weeks I find typing two pages is the limit for my hands, which as a writer is distressing but hopefully manageable, and I take solace from knowing I am now likely to be protected from future infections.

I have been severely jolted from my expat arrogance in believing that after many years of exposure I was immune to the mosquito. I have been chikungunyaed, and by God it is cripplingly painful.

THE SEMPTRESS HOUSE

eborah Hatchett sat at the open window catching purple rays of the dying sun blowing in on the easterly breeze from across the bay where men were hanged. Her hair, indistinguishable from the pristine white cap from under which it escaped in curly wisps, gave the only indication of age. Her smooth skin, almond in color, showed little of the rigors of her early life and her eyes, black flecked with pale brown, were perhaps the only sign of mixed parentage. A clay pipe, clenched in her teeth, gave an aromatic scent to the early evening. A handsome woman, still trim in a simple grey dress relieved with white lace at the collar.

Upon hearing voices Deborah leant forward and saw Eliza Sodman saunter up the hill, her infant son Aksel hoiked on her hip. A basket of notions swung from her arm. A widow at twenty-two.

But then, the idle thought brought a rueful smile to Deborah's lips, was she really a widow? It was entirely possible the striking Dane who had taken Eliza as a wife on St Croix had another wife in Copenhagen, where he had been heading when his ship went down. What matter? She was still a young woman left on her own to raise a child. Like so many free-coloreds.

Deborah laughed to see Aksel's chubby legs jump up and down against his mother's hip in response to her call from the window. The little ones kept the household of women busy. Three under the age of four.

"But no more." Her voice was a mutter. The house on Kirkegarde was full to bursting. She could take no more in. Her thoughts turned to Gertrude, the cook. A hard life and age had worn away her youthful roundness to leave a husk of hanging breasts, spindly legs and short temper. Soon she would be too ill to work. Deborah hoped her death would be quick and merciful.

The door banged as Eliza entered the house, jerking the woman at the window back to here and now.

"Miz Deb, Miz Deb," Aksel's voice piped through the stone walls, interlaced with coral. "I home."

She heard a clatter and wondered what the two-year-old had knocked over in his haste to get to her, probably with a cloth book in his hands. She smiled. He was a favorite.

And Jacob, although she tried hard not to show it. She hoped her daughter, Jane, never married, but with three children would choose more wisely now that Carl Bødker had returned to Denmark. He had left them with his name but little else, and he would never know that Jane had named her last child for him. Deborah had never liked the man. His propensity to lash out at her gentle, caramel-skinned, doe-eyed daughter, to never accept her into his house for more than a few hours' pleasure at a time, a plaything to be discarded when another took his fancy until he beckoned for Jane to return, had never sat well with her. Frederik, at nine, and even Carl at two, showed signs of a mean streak at odds with their mother. Only Jacob had his mother's temperament. But would that stand him in good stead? Probably not. It was a harsh world even for those born free. Though maybe he could pass as white. Deborah tapped her head. Really? The child was only four. She wouldn't be around to see him to manhood so what point worrying. And yet she did. For all of them.

The door burst open and Aksel tottered in, followed by his mother clutching a handful of unspooled ribbons. Deborah tapped her pipe on the windowsill and laid it aside.

"He tipped the basket over," Eliza said, her smile apologetic as she nodded towards her son. "Can you rewind them, please? I want to stitch lace onto Miz Jensen's camisole while there is still light."

Deborah nodded, gave Aksel a cotton reel to roll along the floor then started separating the colorful ribbons.

"Miz Deb," Eliza said, her eyes firmly on the organdy fabric, "Gertrude is old. Her eyesight is poor. The fish prepared this morning was not cleaned sufficiently. Perhaps it is time to replace her."

"She has not poisoned us yet," Deborah said, her tone tart. "Do you wish to take over her duties?"

"No, ma'am, I just meant maybe we should get her more help. And," Eliza paused, "Gertrude is younger than you."

"She has Sara's help, who when the time comes will be well able to take over." Deborah pulled Aksel into her lap where he settled like a mouse as she took his book from him. About to read, she looked over the child's head to add, "And, Eliza, do not be so quick to judge age. My life has not been as harsh as Gertrude's, nor yours over Sara."

With the younger children settled on their cots, and nine-year old Frederick bouncing a ball on the steps leading to the cookhouse, Jane, Eliza and fifteen-year-old Virginia sewed in the lamplight whilst Deborah, her eyes no longer strong enough for the tiny stitches needed, flicked through a catalog of dress patterns recently arrived from London. Her pipe once again lit.

The companionable silence was broken when Virginia said, "What a strange household we are." She nipped a thread with her even teeth. "All women with all boys. Not a girl child amongst us."

"I want no child, boy or girl, from you, Virginia. And Sara's Peter is almost a man, though she has little sway over him it seems." Deborah said with sniff. She had been angry when Sara became pregnant, though the girl's tearful description of rape had been so similar to her own tale that compassion trumped ire. And why should she be more irritated with a slave than a free-colored for bearing a child. They were all deemed worthy playthings for the sailors, the merchants, the overseers and even the planters who populated the island. "He needs a man's influence," Deborah added, before coughing..

"Or maybe he doesn't." Jane's quiet words silenced them. "He is only twelve. We must give him time to sort his emotions. He is angry, I know. But he is at an age wherein the unfairness of his situation is becoming apparent to him. He is a chattel."

"A better looked after one than many," Eliza said, avoiding Deborah's glance.

"But still not free to choose his own path," Jane said. "He is a firebrand at home only because he has nowhere to vent his spleen without fear of the lash. He works on the docks by day and harder than Frederick at his letters each night. I believe he could handle a position of responsibility when older."

"Oh, Jane, you see only the good in people." Deborah looked across the dim room, at the petite young woman whose hair was beginning to show streaks of grey amidst the dark.

"Not always, Mother," Jane responded. "I can find very little to say in the way of kind words about that oaf to whom Peter is tied. Mr Jensen is angling for him to move into his slave quarters. It is only because I cry helplessness to his simpering wife each time I visit her for fittings, and remind her we are a houseful of women and need Peter to carry water and generally care for the property and Gertrude and his mother, that he has not insisted."

"His wife might simper but she is one of your best customers, so have a care, Jane," Deborah said. She looked at her daughter and noted a fine line between her eyebrows that she did not remember seeing before. "You seem less, I don't know, less soft, less malleable. Is all well?"

"Is that not what you wanted, Mother. Me to be more like Eliza. To toughen up?" Jane's smile took the sting from her words.

"Yes, yes, I suppose so. But do not become too hardened, my dear. You will not find another patron if your face is sour."

"Another patron?" Jane's anger bounced around the room in eddies of outrage. "One minute you are insisting we stand up for ourselves, the next you encourage us to find a man."

"Be careful, Jane." Deborah's voice hardened. "This house, this relative ease in which we live, is thanks to a patron. And not just one."

"And your astuteness, Mother," Jane countered. "It was you who invested in property."

Deborah nodded. "But it was men who gave me the money, and from whom I learned. I am not ashamed of my life. And if some man wishes for your company, any of you girls, then you would be a fool to turn him down. You, Jane, have three children who will need educating if they are to better themselves. Carl did not leave a fortune. Your husband, Eliza, might have made you honest but what else did he leave you, apart from Aksel. A seamstress does not earn enough to house and feed a brood."

"You make us sound like whores," Virginia's voice trembled. "Sold to the best bidder, like a slave."

"No, never a whore, girl." Deborah said sharply. "And do not be naive. We are free, and free to choose who we take as a patron, Virginia. And if some lonely man wishes to take a girl to his bed, treats her well and provides for her, acknowledges her in public, that is a different matter. That, Jane, is why I did not like Carl. He did none of those things."

"He gave the children a name." Jane defended her lover.

"How does that feed them? He did not even leave you property. Listen well, Virginia," Deborah said, "choose carefully when the time comes." She looked at the girl, abandoned immediately by her father before her birth, then later by her mother. Too black for one, too white for the other. It was Gertrude who brought her to Deborah to raise. Found one afternoon, bedraggled and cowering in a storm in Free Gut, the area behind the house on Kirkegarde where freed slaves, either through largesse or manumission, set up a community.

"We might be free but we are not acknowledged as equals in the eyes of the law." Jane's color deepened. "It is ten years since we, Free Coloreds, petitioned King Frederick for more rights, less limitations. I am not so trusting as to expect acceptance within white society but there should be parity within our freedom. Is that not justice?"

"What of justice for those enslaved?" Eliza asked. "For people like Sara and Peter? Are they destined to live under the fear of the whip their whole lives?"

"Never have they feared the lash from me. But nothing will change in my lifetime," Deborah said, "despite rumblings from those in Britain who say the trade in humans should stop. Who will compensate the planters for their workers? Who will even work the fields? I do not imagine anyone freed would subject themselves to the harshness of cutting cane or picking cotton. And even if they did, does a white man's temperament change from brutal to kindly with a king's signature?"

75

"Maybe not, Mother, but that should not stop you caring."

"How dare you? Have I not been trying, certainly all your lifetime, to better our conditions?"

"And yet you still encourage us," Jane nodded to Eliza and Virginia, "to find a man to care for us. Should we not be able to support ourselves with our trade?"

"Jane, Jane, you are gullible. You have three children, do you really think you can support them, and maybe more, by sewing for the wealthy. You might have suitors now, but as your body sags, your hair grays and your eyes dim, who will care for you then?"

"What of your properties, Mother?"

"So you are reckoning on my support from the grave?" Deborah gave a coarse laugh. "It is better to wait for my death than attempt to support yourself, to find your own way."

"That is not what she meant," Eliza's voice came quietly in the gloom. "But should we really have to spread our legs to survive?"

"We all have choices, you foolish girl," Deborah said, "choices we have to live with. I chose to make my patrons pay. Their payments have afforded me the ability to live in ease in my older years. So, Virginia, I do not have to whore myself out at the grog shop, where the lowest of the low frequent and care not what they are poking."

"Mother!" Jane glared.

Eliza's laugh was forced. "So, Miz Deb, there are levels of whores. Those hoping for a grope from a drunk who will pay with liquor or pennies, those like Jane who are supported for the duration but not acknowledged, girls like me who snare a man and get the benefit of a marriage - although who is to know if there is another wife in Denmark - and then women like Anna Heegaard who seduce the highest of island society. Where do you fall, Miz Deb?"

"Be careful, Eliza," Deborah said. "Open discussion has always been encouraged in this house but you are very close to overstepping your boundaries. Is it so bad that I want all of you to have enough? We all have honest employment. I was, and now you are the best sempstresses in Christiansted, we are sought after for our work, but it does not pay for property. You must have property, girls, that is what will keep you when your looks fade and your wits shrivel along with your breasts."

Deborah stood, reached for her clay pipe and lit the tobacco with a taper from the lamp. She leaned her elbows on the window sill, drew on the pipe and gazed at lights flickering from ships riding at anchor. A canoe slid soundlessly from the inlet, behind which the gallows were built when needed. Ripples glistened in the weak moonlight like a spreading path. She would send Frederick down in the morning to buy fish from the market. She glanced down at the boy. It was time he had some responsibility.

The sound of pots being stacked drifted up from the cookhouse along with the smell of the fire being quashed. The sight of Gertrude as she slipped like a wraith into the room behind the kitchen that she shared with Sara and Peter made Deborah sigh. Eliza was right, the old woman was failing. It was nothing but pride that kept her going. Pride and determination to serve the woman who had set her free. Deborah sighed again. Life, already complicated was made so much more by the white man. Perhaps Peter would soon have to move to Jensen's quarters. Despite Jane's pleas on his behalf he was becoming disruptive and they did not need to attract undue attention to themselves. There was always someone willing to wish others harm.

The women in the room behind her had lapsed into easy conversation, broken sometimes by soft laughter. It had always amused Deborah that the women for whom they sewed felt able to share confidences with their sempstress. As if standing in a camisole gave free license to their thoughts, negated the possibility of their confessions being discussed elsewhere.

As Jane, Eliza and now Virginia became evermore in demand with those in society, it was the rule of the house that whilst they might make fun of their customers in the sanctuary of the room in which they sewed, no gossip was to be shared outside the walls of the house on Church Street.

Her pipe finished, Deborah turned into the room and looked at the young women. Perhaps she had been cruel but what point in pretending their lives would be easy. It would take little to destroy their relative comfort. Her death perhaps. Or a hurricane could wipe her properties from the island. A fire could engulf them. Send the bank notes she kept stuffed in a hatbox under her cot up in flames. Deborah shuddered and pulled her shawl tighter around her shoulders. None were thoughts not to be dwelt upon.

A mournful horn sounded from a ship out at sea and Deborah wondered where it was headed. The wind whistled in through the half-closed shutters. She was weary and her back ached. Gertrude was not the only one aging. She picked up a lantern and smiled at the scene in front of her, at her girls.

"I bid you all a good night. Do not think harshly of me. There is enough intolerance outside this house. I want only what is best for you all."

Their murmured responses followed her up the stairs to the small room she had carved out for herself - away from crying babies and rustling sheets. The night noises of those she loved.

Deborah smoothed an organdy nightgown, soft with a lifetime of laundering, over her hips, untied her cap and taking pins from her hair felt it cascade down her back. She picked up her brush and stood in front of the mirror where, unbidden, images formed of the men, those she had cared for and who had reveled in her touch. Had loved her, in their own ways. She smiled at them and deftly plaited her hair then, in an unusual act of vanity, she pushed the skin around her jawline back behind her ears. "What would you all think of me now?" she asked her flickering reflection with a soft, tired laugh.

She sank down onto the cot with a sigh, blew out the candle and closed her eyes.

At peace.

ERIKA CAME FOR THE NIGHT

Arriving behind Tropical Storm Danny and in front of Erika, I wasn't sure what to expect. I should have known better. Virgin Islanders are a hardy breed and every weather occurrence is measured against the behemoth that was Hugo, which dashed and thrashed the islands in 1989, leaving them battered and severely bruised for many, many months. In the coves of the Salt River basin there are still remnants of semi-submerged yachts deemed too expensive to salvage. Older homes, if they survived Hugo, are here to stay. Fortunately ours did.

Wednesday was spent gathering necessities. Water, batteries, paraffin, gas lighters, essential foods and Sauvignon Blanc. Oh yes, and a clever gizmo to boost cell phone power which, once home, I realized did not in fact fit my phone despite assurances on the packet to the contrary.

I have lived in countries where regular power outages were common and, with a bucket of water by each loo and strategically placed flashlights, I felt well able to handle a blackout. The evening was spent in the company of a friend at a local bar, *1884*, in case you happen to be thirsty in Christiansted. I wandered back up the hill, made a cup of tea and sat on the gallery, then boom. Sparks flew from the transformer I had just walked under and the town and Protestant Cay went black. The wind was minimal, no more than the usual easterlies that cool the island, and my confidence slipped just a little.

The insistent thrum of generators kicked in from across the bay, the lighthouse on the headland blinked green, and mooring lights from a few yachts offered pinpricks of light. It is always surprising how one's eyes adjust to the dark and what, moments before had seemed a bleary blank canvas, quickly takes on definition. After the initial surprise at the bang which sends bats and birds aflutter, sounds become more acute as animals and insects settle.

My faith in power companies has never been strong, so I was pleasantly surprised to see within half an hour the flashing lights of a WAPA truck, then a couple of hours later light blinked on around the town.

Thursday went from sunny to overcast. The day, and hours, before an expected storm are always surreal. People scurry to finish jobs, there is a run on the shops for a few just-in-case extras, hurricane shutters are trundled out or slammed shut, outdoor furniture brought in, trash cans tethered, and the air is filled with nervous expectation.

My planning, not having taken into account a lack of coffee beans in the house, sent me down the hill in search of a cup of joe. A few desultory souls ambled the Boardwalk, waiting for something, anything. Yachts and dive boats usually tied to jetties were out on moorings, gusts of wind turning them north. *Twin City*, my usual on-island coffee shop, was open. The only place that was.

A closed-up house, despite fans, is a hot house, so I spent the afternoon on our gallery, but couldn't settle. Words did not flow, and my eyes kept drifting eastwards, watching, waiting. Checking the storm's track, reading of deaths and flash floods in Dominica, did little to comfort. Words about wind shear from those safe in mainland studios merely irritated. I watched the reef necklacing the north shore, usually a gentle ripple of white capped wavelets, become a spuming crash of roiling waters.

Then, as darkness dropped like a theatre curtain, the winds picked up. Gusts that had whispered through the palms became a consistent agitated rustling, and fronds twelve feet long cracked and crashed to the ground. Crimson bracts from the bougainvillea rained across the gallery and the green lizards normally scuttling along the railings scurried for cover. And rain, much needed on the island, sparkled through the lamplight like spilled diamonds.

No boom accompanied the power outage this time. Just a sudden and angry blackness.

My daughter phoned from Trinidad. My husband phoned from Houston. Quick words of reassurance to and from them both before I disconnected, wanting to conserve battery life.

An amphora of no great value but aesthetically pleasing, and which I had considered sturdy, smashed over. A shutter from a building nearby snapped. Banana trees bent almost horizontal. Tan-tan seeds clackered. Rain hurtled across the gallery, ricocheting in through the open and, I thought, protected windows.

There was nothing to do but light the hurricane lantern, pour a glass of wine, pull a chair to the open doorway to the gallery and, in the flickering light, watch the magnificence of the storm. No thunder, no lightning. Just wind and rain. The swaying palms, like *moko jumbies*, the good spirits of the islands, danced protection around the house and I marveled at nature's rage.

Erika came for the night. It was exhilarating, but I'm glad she was only a tropical storm.

IT'S THAT TIME OF YEAR

F acing the mirror this morning as I brushed my teeth I saw a tattoo, two small letters, HQ, inked in black on the underside of my forearm and the magic came flooding back. No, no it was not a night of Bacchic-inspired revelry, but it was mystical.

The longer I spend on St Croix the more I am drawn into her spell, woven through history and wafted along on the trade winds. Like all islands in the Caribbean there are tales of mischief, of the black arts, of *obeah*. It draws its roots from Africa and, like much on that huge and beautiful continent, is often inexplicable. So it was last night.

Let me take you there.

The Garden Gala is an annual fund-raiser for the St George Village Botanical Gardens - the stated aim of the organization being 'conservation, preservation, education'. The Gardens grow exuberantly around and, in some cases over, an old sugar factory built by the enslaved. The crumbling walls which used to surround the bubbling coppers of cane juice now trail with creepers and vines. Cannonball, kapok, and tamarind trees have forced their way through courtyards laid with bricks, formerly used as ship ballast, as well as commanding space on the lawns. Bursts of magenta bougainvillea and ixora, the color of cayenne, dazzle the senses. Magic of a different kind.

The pyramid-shaped event space, open to the night scents and sounds, was decorated in purple, silver and white, with chiffon and streams of fairy lights cascading from the roof and encircling the columns. Around the perimeter were Christmas trees, temptingly dressed by different organizations and individuals, ready to be auctioned off. Centre-pieces of baubles and glittering flowers sparkled in tall glass vases on the tables. Rum and wine flowed as voices mingled and goodwill swirled.

And amidst all this was a young illusionist, Johnny Daemon, dressed all in black with lively eyes and a flashing smile. Was I swayed by his good looks? His charm? His patter? Obviously. I now have a tattoo.

"Think of the name of someone dear to you," he commanded. "Just the initials."

My youngest granddaughter came to mind.

Johnny handed me a small card on which he had just drawn a line and circle. "Write them down on this line and in the circle write your initials," he said and turned away. "Tell me," he told my companion, "when she's done. I don't want to see the letters." To me he said, "Hold the card face down in your left hand." Turning back, he asked three questions. "Where are you from? What is your passion? What is your favorite color?" He scribbled the answers on a slip of paper - England, writing, green. Or I assume that's what he wrote. I couldn't see.

Next I spread my arms out wide then pointed at him with my right index finger. We stood fingertip to fingertip for a few moments. The sound of the band filtered through the tinkle of a nearby fountain, iridescent with reflected light, and distracted me until I was brought back to the present by his voice demanding I think only of the initials.

Moving my fingertip with his, he began writing in air. An H. Then he said, "I think the next one is cursive. C perhaps? No," he corrected himself, moving my finger again. "Q. The initials are 'HQ'. Now, look at the card."

The line on which I had written my granddaughter's initials was blank, though mine remained in the circle. "But I wrote them," I gasped. "Didn't I, Laurie? You saw," I turned to my companion in confusion.

"What's that on your arm?" Johnny interrupted my protestations. And there they were, 'HQ'!

Harley Rose Quan is inked by magic on my arm for a short time, a wonderful illusion which I have no desire to understand. She will be in my heart forever - that's the enchantment.

THE ART OF A MAN

We agree to meet at Sion Farm Distillery, home to Mutiny Vodka, which might seem a strange venue for a conversation that is to be recorded. The reason though is simple. Lucien Downes is responsible for the two murals adorning the walls - one telling the building's original function as a dairy, the other highlighting its current use. Breadfruit vodka.

I am early. I settle at a high-top table next to the long, glossy mahogany counter with a bird's eye view of both the distillery and the parking lot.

Sean, the bartender, asks if I'd like a drink. I demur, explain I am working then say, "Oh, what the hell, sure." I see a grin stretch behind his mask.

Lucien saunters in and we bump fists. I hate fist bumps. They are so impersonal and I have known this man eight years. His brow raises at my drink. I shrug and suggest he order one.

"What are you having?" He looks over my shoulder at the chalkboard on the wall.

"The Queen Bee."

"Figures!" A laugh trickles around his mask.

"Hah!" I defend myself. "It was the most innocuous-sounding cocktail."

We settle with our drinks. In pre-COVID days I would have been tempted to ask if I might taste the concoction in front of him and would have freely offered mine. But life has changed. The casual freedoms of 2019 have been supplanted by anxious double-guessing of every motion, and emotion.

"You know, Lucien, I'm having a hard time finding people actually from here."

"I was born here."

"Yeah, but your parents are Trinis. Have you been there?"

"Sure. Many times. My dad is from Kelly, near San Fernando and my mother from Port of Spain. But since my grandmother passed I haven't been back. Too many memories."

"You know my daughter lives in Port of Spain? She's married to a Trini."

We talk briefly about the country that has closed its borders to its own citizens, leaving many stranded in Canada, England and the US.

"It's tough," I say, "Kate can't leave because she wouldn't be allowed back in. There are so many backstories to this pandemic."

Lucien launches into a concept I hadn't thought about.

"That's the thing," he says, "because of COVID, people have to look into things they can do, not things they can't do. Too many are complaining, waiting for a handout. We have to look outside the box, maybe turn a hobby into a business. If you can crochet. Crochet. If you can cook. Cook. You know what I'm saying?"

I nod, aware that as a writer my life has barely changed.

"You have to learn how to survive right now. Survival of the fittest."

"That's a bit harsh," I reply. "Do you think people are doing that here?"

"I think, if their main income has been compromised, some are going outside their norm. And of course a lot of people are working from home. They get jobs stateside but work from here. Really and truly, it's forcing us to upgrade our infrastructure. Both a curse and a blessing."

"Thinking about the shootings in Gallows Bay, Lucien, do you think COVID is exacerbating social issues, frustrations, the need to belong to something even if it is a gang, or is there a deeper systemic malaise?" It is not a question on the pages in front of me and I'm not sure from where it came, but I know the man in front of me will give a thoughtful answer.

He sends a rueful smile across the table. "Okay," he says, "let's give you my theory. I think there is a man-made thing, a control mechanism, that makes many more dependent on government. You're waiting six or seven months to get six hundred dollars, which is crazy, especially for a country that gives millions to other nations to help them with their people but is not dealing with their own." He sips his cocktail, his eyes serious. "Congress are still getting their salaries, their health care, but if private citizens get COVID they have to foot the bill. I'm hoping people start to realize you have to take it upon yourself to make yourself as self-reliant as possible." Lucien pauses. "As far as gangs and now. I don't think it has made much difference. It's just a different time and you have to learn to adjust."

"You're an educated man, but if people are not taught, encouraged, to think in a broader context, it's hard for them to get where you're coming from."

"You see that's the thing, man, it's an awareness. People believe they should get married, have children, have a house, but life doesn't always work out like that."

"So managing life's expectations has to be part of the equation?"

Lucien nods, "That's when you have a breakdown. People are doing what they are supposed to be doing but not making it. The people who do make it in this world are those who think outside that box. If you can peek outside, you can see the light. You wonder, 'what's out there?'"

Lucien voices another conundrum. "People have a clannish mentality and believe that if you don't participate then you're not going to be successful. But the reality is that the majority of people who are successful don't participate." He breaks into laughter.

He tells me a story of a young woman with whom he'd recently spoken. Her life plan ended with making a lot of money. Lucien's take on college surprised me.

"By the time you get out of school, the stuff you learn in school is outdated. All that money and time spent in school for obsolete learning. Now you've got YouTube!" He does have a caveat. "If you're not going into a specialty field, why go to college? You get a piece of paper and debt you spend years getting out from under. Think of the millionaires who never went to college. It's a mindset."

We are so far off script, it's time to get back to art.

"For all that, you went to Morris Brown College in Atlanta and graduated with a degree in business and information technology. Then you went to work at Pearl Paint in Atlanta, managing a number of their art supply stores. Your degree must have helped?"

"Sure, it did. We had supplies from all over the world. Being exposed to this stuff at Pearl made me realize I wanted to return to painting."

"Let's talk about that. Your 8th grade teacher, Mrs Zuhara Bilal spotted your talent and encouraged you. Did your parents?"

"Not really. My dad didn't become proud, impressed, until I had pieces in an art exhibition at Country Day School. In 2009, I think. It was an adjudicated show, and people kept going up to him and asking if I was his son." Lucien laughs. "He liked that."

"What about your mum?"

"She has dementia."

It is a bald statement in which a whole lot of sorrow is wrapped. I say how sorry I am and that I understand, having had a beloved aunt go through the same agony.

"Tell me about Pearl Paint."

"Oh man, there was some talent there. I only employed artists, kids who really wanted to make it in the art world. And some have. I had fifteen employees and nine are doing great things."

"So you mentored young artists?"

He nods. "Have you heard of Kevin Chambers?"

I shake my head.

"His sculptures are incredible. I had 28,000 square feet of stores in Atlanta and New Jersey. 60% for art supplies, 40% for craft. A sixteen-foot aisle was filled with different media. I made space for employees to show their work. To market their work." Lucien gathers his thoughts. "Break-out artists do things differently. You know Britto? The Brazilian artist?"

"I don't think so." I search my mind for South American artists and come up with an embarrassingly few number.

"He has a store in Miami airport." Lucien throws me a line.

Bright colours, pop art and graffiti float in. "Oh, yes," I say.

"His stuff is simplistic. He's a master of marketing, but his art also stands out. It's distinctive. It makes you want to buy. It's an investment."

"Do you think people should buy art for investment or pleasure?"

"Both. The first should be pleasure. Then you're getting two for one. I don't want you to buy my art because it looks pretty with your furnishings. I want your furnishings to look pretty with my art. So when you change your furnishings my art stays there. I feel very honored when people do that."

"Every piece of art I've ever bought has spoken to me." My comments makes me think of the eclectic pieces from around the world that adorn our walls, from African masks to Malaysian street scenes to Scottish lochs and everything in between. "Tell me about the first piece you sold?"

"Oh man!" A smile breaks out. "He was a guy who came in to give me an estimate for cleaning the store. He saw a piece and asked who painted it. I told him and he bought it. That felt good."

"What was it?"

Lucien reaches across for a business card I'd put out for Todd Manning, the owner of the distillery. He takes my pen and draws swirls on the back, like a lotus. "It had a maroonish background. With resin. I'll never forget the delight selling that painting gave me."

Moments later, Todd appears and we exchange cards.

"Check out the Downes original on the back," I tell him. People are coming into the bar area from the distillery after a tour. It feels good to be on the periphery of a group. COVID has affected us all in some way. The three of us chat then bump fists and Lucien and I are alone.

"How much time did you get to spend on St Croix?"

"Quite a lot. I flew down from Atlanta to stay with my dad about once a month for four-day weekends. Hey, I was the manager, I could juggle shifts. Then when Pearl went out of business, I spent longer on island but was still based in Atlanta."

"Tell me about your first show?"

"Oh man, it was funny. Me and my date for the evening, we were late because I was just so nervous. We finally arrive and a bunch of people were standing at the entrance pointing and talking. I couldn't see what they were looking at. Then I saw they were looking at my work saying, 'I'm going to buy that.' Man, it was amazing. It blew my mind. That was when I realized it was something I was supposed to do."

"Sometimes it takes a while to get to where we're meant to be." I think of my writing.

"Yeah, man, to come full circle. When I started I couldn't even draw a straight line."

I laugh at the image of this prolific artist unable to draw.

Sean goes off shift and after a couple of pleasantries with the new barman, Lucien asks,him, "Hey, man, do you know how to slab wood?" The conversation gets technical and I skim through my notes. "Sorry," Lucien says to me after the unsatisfactory finish to his chat.

"Gary McCracken slabbed our wood. He's good," I tell him, knowing it isn't helpful.

"Yeah, but he's left island."

We discuss the beauty of mahogany and I tell him about our library shelves. Planed, sanded and oiled with raw edges and spaced by painted metal piping.

"Nice," he says. "I want to use it in my kitchen. I never understand why we want to close everything away."

"Dust." I am a prosaic housekeeper. We edge back to art of a different kind. "I read that Pearl Paints went into liquidation. Shady dealings. Is that why you decided to move home permanently?"

Before he can answer, my phone rings. I grab it and excuse myself, having mentioned at the outset that I was waiting for a call from my daughter about a serious concussion. I pace up and down outside the distillery wishing I could be in Trinidad. It is serious but not long-term. I demand, if a mother can demand anything of a child, she listen to her neurologist and rest, rest, rest. I wipe my eyes and gather myself before I return to Lucien.

"You okay?" His compassion is almost my undoing. I nod and sip my drink. I don't feel like a queen bee, more like a drone running in circles.

"Thanks, sorry about that."

"No problem. That's why I don't have kids. I couldn't take all the dramas."

I'm surprised. The man in front of me is kind. "Sure there are, even when they're adults, but I wouldn't have missed it for the world. Well…" I temper my statement, "…mostly!"

I smile at the thought of teenage years. We laugh. "So, why'd you come home?"

All humor leaves his face. "It got difficult." He pauses. "My artistic career was going well in Atlanta. Same in Miami. A couple of years before Pearl closed. Man, it was cool." Lucien pauses, "As long as they didn't know who the artist was…"

I realize where the conversation is headed. "Because you're Black?"

"Yeah,"

"Oh shit," I say, my mind flies back to a conversation with Stanley Jacobs about the same issue. "Tell me?"

"You sure you want to know?"

"Of course."

"Okay, I'll give a couple of examples, from many." He pauses again. "I'm in a show, right, I'm selling well. The gallery is owned by a white dude. He tells me there's a woman who wants to meet me and I think 'cool'. I'm introduced to her, she's white, she looks at me, startled, and says, 'You're Lucien? I can't see you doing things like this, but' and she pointed to a picture of a black woman, and said, 'but I can see you doing things like that.' I mean what does that even mean?"

I have no answer. There is none.

"I told her," Lucien continues the story, "thank God I don't have your money." A sad smile flicks across his face before he relates another incident. "One time I was gallery sitting for the owner. A white woman walked in, saw me behind the desk and walked out."

I look down, ashamed for the ignorance of so many and because I cannot even imagine how that must feel.

He goes on. "Another time a guy came in, a Caucasian, and said how much he liked the art and asked who the artist was. I told him me, and he said, 'Oh, I thought you were the security guard.'"

I apologize for my race. "What do you even say to people like that?"

"You know, coming from the Caribbean, we have a different mindset. American Blacks might be aggressive to something like that. But I figured it wasn't my gallery. I just had to keep it moving. But it's hurtful. I had to keep telling myself 'you know where it's at'."

"Well, it's the measure of the man you are that you can be so gracious." I hide my face in my glass.

"Anyway, that's when I decided it was time to go home."

"Was it hard? After so many years away?"

"No. I lived with my dad until I got situated. He thought I was crazy, throwing away the chance of another steady job. But I threw myself into my art, trying to make a difference."

I think of an artist friend who used to live on St Croix but, in a stroke of irony, has moved to Atlanta. "You took over The Artist Guild Show from Laurie Ingersoll. Did you enjoy the experience?"

"Not really. I tried to make it more professional, to bring my business background to the show. It was a successful show and we made a lot of money but it rocked too many boats. People like to do things the way they've always been done. That's just how a lot of people are. The same thing with the New Blood Show at CMCA. We made money the first year and in the second we almost doubled the amount. Then things changed."

"The new director arrived?"

"Yeah." Lucien nods.

"He was a disaster, by all accounts." I remember the African American with a New York attitude. "Tell me about the Pan-Am Games," I suggest, moving the conversation away from controversy.

"Man, that was fun. I get an email that I think is spam. Then I get another one. So I call a girl I used to date from Canada and asked her if she knew anything about some fabric museum. She told me, 'they're huge.' I'm like, 'oh, okay!'"

"Then what? Which museum?"

"The Textile Museum of Canada."

"Wow! How did they find you?"

"They went online looking for Virgin Island artists and found me"

"Huh." I don't sound in the least bit intelligent but as someone ever-hoping for an agent to just 'find' me, that's all I can come up with.

"Anyway, they sent another email and told me the event was approaching and was I interested. I apologized and said 'can we start again?'"

"What was the piece?"

"It was an abstract, The Phoenix. I'll send you a picture. Anyway they were making small boats on which art from all the countries participating in the Pan-Am Games would be exhibited as sails. It was very cool."

"Sure was."

"Yeah. It was about six years after I started painting, and there I was rubbing shoulders with all these famous artists from Central and South America. So once again, it was as if something was pushing me in a direction. Something spiritual."

We are quiet in the bustle of the building. I glance at my notes.

"Art St Croix was a project you started, to raise funds for art supplies in the schools. What happened to that?

Lucien looks resigned. "It was a good idea. We ran it for two years but politics got in the way."

"Politics?" I find it hard to imagine teachers not wanting assistance with supplies. "Do you mean people?"

"Yeah, saying they'll do something then not. It got disheartening. That's why I've taken a step back from committees. Asinine behavior makes it hard to do good things."

I agree, having been on the receiving end of a disgruntled and recalcitrant board member. An incident that brought many sleepless nights and a lot of soul searching. I vowed no more boards.

"Let's get back to art. Do you paint to music?" I thought it was a straightforward question but there is a long pause before Lucien answers.

"I paint to music on my mind. I'll be listening to upbeat music, and play it again and again. Before I paint."

"Give me an example."

"This is a little ghetto. I was thinking about a song by this guy. They call him TI or TIP - he's the king of hip hop. When I was painting this week for the show at Café Christine, I had him in my head. Why is it that you play music when you're planning but not when you're painting?" It is a rhetorical question. Lucien continues, "Maybe it's because it's distracting. You're forced to absorb the music differently. If you're playing it in your mind, you're only playing what you like about it, not getting any subliminal message. When I first started painting I'd listen to music. I remember listening to Jay-Z and my work got so dark."

"I kind of get that. When I'm writing I don't listen to anything, but the other day the COVID van was going around Christiansted and that was all I could hear for hours. Way after it had left. A good message but it was driving me nuts!"

We laugh. Another group comes into the building, all masked. It is a popular venue and the noise level increases.

I recall the photo of the painting on Facebook of the porkpie-hatted young man playing pan against a bluey-orange background. The figure, his eyes shut, moves to a beat in the viewer's head. "Your latest exhibition, at Café Christine, is that where the pan boy is going? It's Kevin, isn't it? I love it."

Lucien nods. "Thanks."

"Do you paint one piece at a time?"

"No way. Four or five. Often in different media. You know, one piece can be drying so I go to another, then another. I use resins, watercolor, acrylic, fibers, raw pigments, plexiglass. You know I'm self-taught?"

It is my turn to nod. "From where do you draw your inspiration?"

"The sea, the clouds. Photos, sometimes on Facebook. I'll ask someone if I can use their image. Now I also have a muse. She's beautiful."

"Who?"

He shows me a photo of a vaguely familiar, regal-looking young woman. "Her name is Vanya Neptune."

I'm good with faces, dreadful with names. "What does she do?"

"She works at the Casino, as the main bank person."

"Well, I wouldn't have seen her there," I say, with a laugh.

"She also makes soaps and essences. I love her spirit."

The penny drops. "I know. Starving Artists, or somewhere like that."

Lucien nods.

"What are you working on at the moment?"

"A piece on Queen Mary, Fireburn. Vanya is my model. I love this empress look she has going on." He shows me another photo of his girlfriend holding a would-be torch and cane bill in each hand. "I'm going to post that next week."

"She's lovely."

"Yeah, my God, she is so dimensional, it's crazy."

"Do you enjoy commission work? If I said I want you to paint my grandmother holding her poodle on a green couch, would you do that?" I'm finding it hard to imagine the man across the table working to order.

"Here's what I do. I always want to see where the painting is meant to go. You know, for size and so on. And I want to see what kind of house they have. What style. Then I say pick three colors. So I can tie in my painting."

"And with the light?"

"Not so much. A lot of my paintings shift with the light because I use metallic pigments. So any time of day they look different. Mood lighting works best with my work. I paint at night. I procrastinate until about eleven, then I'll work until three or four in the morning."

"Good grief, I couldn't do that. I'm in bed by nine most nights!"

He laughs. "Maybe it's because that's when I painted when I was still working at Pearl. I always had the middle shift."

"What about public art? You have the murals here," I admire the wall in front of me, "and in Christiansted and Frederiksted. Do you enjoy that?"

"The one in Frederiksted was fun, it was with young apprentice artists, and Elizabeth Keith. You know her?"

"Sure." I change the tone. "I see the Art Bill has just been vetoed. What do you have to say about that?"

He grimaces and sighs. "I want to talk to the governor. And senators I know to try and get it back up. I'm going to put this out there and people can take it how they want. But the St Croix art scene did not move until I moved back. People were complacent. But everyone has stepped their game up. Why?"

I throw the question back at him. "Why do you think?"

He smiles and traces the outline of his glass. "I think I've shaken things up. Not everyone likes it. But now people are under a little pressure. It forces everyone to up their game. Competition is healthy. You know Elwin Joseph?" He sees my nod. "Have you seen his work lately?" Lucien doesn't wait for my reply. "His work is fantastic. He's jumped so far in three years. More than in the ten before."

"Are people grateful?"

"Hell, no, man. I put a show together at Top Hat, which because of the negative Danish connotations was picked up by a Danish magazine. Hey, I respect everyone's hustle. But be true. Don't talk about colonialism with Denmark. A hundred years ago. Talk about America. We can't get our mail on time. Talk about how our tax dollars are being used. Food costs here are triple the mainland. We're taxed but can't vote for president."

It is the perfect opening. "So, here's a question. Will you ever go into politics?"

"You know, at first, I really thought I'd like to. To make a difference."

I glance at the man looking into his glass and say, "You're passionate enough, but I imagine it would eat into your creative work."

He laughs, "Politicians don't work!"

I'm not going to be drawn on that particular comment. He tells me he is a strong proponent of the private sector. That by encouraging big corporations to make the VI their Caribbean and South American base, it could only benefit the islands. Lucien is also of the opinion there should be serious consideration given to adding a 2% sales tax. The monies garnered from that tax to be used to only fund free healthcare - entitled to people after five years of living, and paying taxes, on the islands.

"We have to stop waiting for a handout. Other Caribbean islands manage. Why can't we?" he asks. "We're frightened of losing our safety net. And we have to stop the brain drain. Kids go to college on the mainland but don't come back, because there's nothing for them to come back for."

Lucien is firm in his belief that the Virgin Islands are taxed without proper representation.

"Didn't America go to war with Britain about that?" I ask, a smile tempers my words.

"Right!" He laughs, but his face is serious.

"Stacey Plaskett on the Ways and Means Committee must surely help the VI get a higher profile," I suggest.

He shrugs. "I don't see how. It'll help the Democratic party. But not us. Now if she were commissioner in the Department of Interior. That would be something." He finishes his cocktail then says, "I don't understand why people don't get more riled up. We wait for a handout. We're complacent. Get a false sense of representation, security, but really we are being kept in our box."

And with that comment, Lucien has neatly tied up our conversation.

"Lucien, you're a star. Thank you so much!"

We take a couple of selfies in front of his mural. My head swirls as I drive home. Not from my Queen Bee, but from the many facets of our afternoon chat. I am once again struck, and honored, by the frankness people have with sharing their thoughts with me.

Lucien Downes - artist, entrepreneur, activist. No wonder he has time to paint only at night.

THE GREAT AMERICAN SONG BOOK

Arthur Woodley was not a name I knew. But then, I am not an opera buff. Had I been, I would have known Mr Woodley is a nationally acclaimed bass soloist most frequently associated with the Seattle Opera. His roles are many - one for which he is particularly renowned being Porgy in *Porgy and Bess*. He has also performed with Sir Neville Marriner and The Academy of St Martin in the Fields in Mexico, as well as in other countries.

Why my interest? Because on Friday evening I heard Mr Woodley sing at Whim Plantation, now a Landmark Society museum on St Croix. The setting was splendid. The windows of the rotunda-shaped room open to easterly breezes, the petrichor from recently fallen rain mingling with the smell of wax from candles sparkling high above us in a candelabra tarnished by sea air and time, the cricket chorale - all increased the audience's anticipation.

The accompanist entered first. Dr Adele Allen is an esteemed pianist and, forgive the pun, instrumental to the music scene of the island. She settled at the piano, then Mr Woodley lumbered in. He is not a tall man, neither is he big, but rather he is deep. Deep in voice, in thought, in emotion. He was clean shaven, though known to happily grow any kind of beard, saying in one interview at Seattle Opera, "Joyce Degenfelder, the Hair and Makeup Designer, was talking about a goatee. I figured, might as well grow the whole thing out, so she has more to play with!"

Born in New York but brought up by grandparents here on the island at Estate La Vallee, I can't help marveling at his path to opera. But it was not to be opera that night. Rather, the concert was a nod to American music. We travelled *Ten Thousand Miles* to Siam to hear the Rodgers and Hammerstein classic, *I Have Dreamed*, to Irving Berlin's *Change Partners* to the spiritual, *Climbing High Mountains*, and many more in between. His pitch-perfect performance made even better by the wonderful acoustics in such an intimate setting.

I spent much of the evening in tears. Something I had not warned my friends might happen. I had expected opera after all, and the only opera I know well enough to bring me to tears is *La Traviata*. But Mr Woodley's rich, mellifluous voice singing many of my father's favorite songs was my undoing.

My father was an untrained but pleasant tenor, and what he lacked in style and technique he made up for in gusto. I might have been on the other side of the world on Friday evening, but I was transported to my parents dancing on the verandah of our house in Singapore one Sunday afternoon to Ella Fitzgerald's version of *Isn't It Romantic?* with Dad singing along.

That's the wonder of music. It moves us.

And I am a woman who can be be easily distracted from the rewrites due to my wonderful editor, Jane Dean, and so it was the night following Mr Woodley's performance.

This time I found myself at the annual fundraiser for the Caribbean Community Theatre. A cabaret complete with desserts and coffee. Wine for some. The setting was not quite so magical as Whim Plantation, though the white tablecloths, decorated with bougainvillea clustered around candles and champagne glasses filled with tumbling cherry tomatoes, drew the eye from the utilitarian walls of the building shared sometimes with a congregation.

The emcee asked us to close our eyes and imagine Billie Holiday's sultry tones. But we didn't have to. Becky Bass, a twenty-five-year-old from St Croix, recent alum of Brown University and now a singer setting her sights on Broadway, took us to a dark, smoky night club with her evocative voice. Etta James, Nina Simone, Sara Vaughn were all summoned before the tempo changed with a raunchy rendition of *When You're Good to Mama* from *Chicago*, and other Broadway productions. A duet with Daniel Deane, an artist relatively new to the music scene but pleasing to listen to, and then her prowess with steel pan showcased her many talents.

I thanked both Mr Woodley and Miss Bass, for making me cry, and laugh. Both were gracious, one at the top of his career, one embarking on an exciting road to Broadway and beyond, yet such is their affinity with St Croix they happily return.

As I sit here on my gallery, gazing between sentences to the turquoise, aquamarine and navy striations of the glittering Caribbean, I am again overawed by the talent this US Virgin Island nurtures.

What can I say? Except I'm thankful to the serendipity which brought me here.

THE ODDEST PARADE
DOWN ISLAND

The Caribbean Columbus found was populated by the Taíno, a peaceable people, and the Carib, who were not. The lure of riches from sugar was great for many, and those from Europe with an adventurous or avaricious bent were keen to exploit the potential offered by fertile soil ready for the taking. Racketeers, privateers and buccaneers came too. The first waves of indentured labour came from Europe but most were not able to withstand the rigors of the climate and perished. And then came the enslaved, for which every nation involved, including those doing the initial selling or stealing in Africa, can hang their heads in shame.

Wearing the lens of the day, I would like to think there were a few relatively honorable men in the mix. Men who at least tried to treat those whose lives they owned with an element of care and dignity. That being said, I don't believe reparation can ever be fully made but neither do I believe future generations should be made to carry the burden of past wrongs.

Caribbean plantations were formed and managed by French, Danes, Dutch, Spanish and British, but worked by the enslaved. Some of the islands are still French, Spanish, Dutch or English-speaking, and so one can understand certain cultural traditions clinging on or being absorbed into modern-day Caribbean customs.

Within the British Isles there are English, Scots, Welsh and Irish. From my cursory study of the breakdown of plantation ownership on a few of the British-owned islands of the day, the Irish do not seem to have been any more predominant than the other three.

So why, I wondered, was St Patrick's Day such a major deal on St Croix, an island which has been under seven flags - Spanish, British, French, Dutch, Knights of Malta, Danish and American.

March 17th happened to be Art Thursday, a regular feature of the Christiansted calendar, wherein the many art galleries and jewelry stores open in the evening. It is a convivial event. People wander from gallery to gallery topping up their rum or wine, generously poured in each venue, chatting to artists and fellow strollers alike. I had not, though, expected green to be the foremost color of the evening. I had not received the memo. "Wait until the parade on Saturday," I was told, when I commented to one green-clad woman, who on inquiry had no affiliation with the Emerald Isle.

And so on Saturday, forewarned, we ambled down the hill to see what all the fuss was about. Crucians, those who share their island, and those just passing through staked their claim on any and every available curb, step or balcony along King and Company streets. Green of every hue imaginable was on display. Orange hair and beards also proved popular. Beads of green and gold glittered around necks regardless of sex, reminiscent of Mardi Gras. Tutus and tees teased the throng, some proclaiming with pride 'The 47th Annual St Croix St Patrick's Day Parade', others with the year's theme emblazoned across their bosoms, 'The Luck of the Irie'. Each year monies raised are donated to charity.

Why, I kept wondering? Why here? To any question asked often enough, an answer is usually forthcoming. I learned St

Patrick's Day on St Croix was celebrated first in 1969 when, and this may surprise you, a group of men who might have had a Guinness or two were sitting at Harry's Bar. I imagine the conversation went along the lines of, "Let's put a piano on a truck and drive around singing!" Shopkeepers curious about the ruckus outside their establishments came out, shoppers already wearing green followed the truck and became revelers and so a tradition was born.

Now we live on island time here and so an eleven o'clock start is not a given. Imagine my surprise when only fifteen minutes after the stated hour the wheels started rolling with the St Croix motorcycle club leading off with US and Virgin Island flags proudly fluttering.

And then they came. Marching bands and majorettes. A leprechaun, aka Gregory Worrell, followed a jeep filled with green-collared pups and collected donations for the animal sanctuary. Another, this time a leprechaun-in-training, was pulled around the parade route atop a trailer rife with rainbows and pots of gold. Shamrocks and sparkles covered every form strutting the streets. The University of the Virgin Islands homecoming queen, Angelique Flemming, waved regally from her perch on an open-top coupe, followed not long after by a banner-bedecked man in glittering trunks flexing his muscles whilst balancing on a similar vehicle. And not to be left out, a politician. Senator Nereida Rivera-O'Reilly, who was also the grand marshal, sat atop a green and white Austin Healey.

Beads were flung from floats, candies and green visors were tossed, the visors with built-in fans to cool sweating, cheering, laughing crowds intent on celebrating the patron saint of a green island across the Atlantic. To cover all bases and to ensure good fortune held, Moko Jumbies also paraded.

But the oddest thing was the music. A chorus of that perennial, The Wild Rover, played once. A lone bagpipe wailed a Scottish air, briefly, and that before the parade even started. The rest was reggae and rap with not a hint of a green jig.

There was no rain on this parade, just the Luck of the Irie!

THE DANISH CONNECTION

I am early and so drive to the end of Miss Bea Road to get a similar vantage point of the ocean to that of my next interviewee. She is an effervescent and robust 83 years, her name synonymous with Denmark's long association with St Croix. She is Nina York.

"Good morning!" A voice welcomes me as I amble up her drive so as not to disturb a hummingbird. "I think we should sit out here." Nina indicates her open gallery.

I pet the ginger tom stretched languorously on one of the chairs.

"What's his name?"

"Charlie, he's seventeen."

"He looks good on it." This is a cat whose life has been made easy. He gives me a disdainful glance and I leave him to his ablutions.

Nina disappears inside to return moments later with a bowl of green grapes, luscious in their plumpness, and puts them on the table between us. We are at least eight feet apart and I wonder if my recorder will work with the trade winds whispering through the trees.

"I've had both my shots," she states.

I know immediately to what she is referring. It is the comment, or question, on many people's lips these days. I tell her I've had one COVID vaccination with the next due in two days.

"What do you want to ask me?" Nina, as ever, is forthright.

"Let's just chat and see where the conversation takes us. Tell me about growing up in Denmark?"

She smiles and we are off.

"We lived in Copenhagen but I don't remember much about my early childhood as when I was four we moved, because of the German occupation, to Sweden. My father wrote an uncomplimentary pamphlet about the Nazis which provoked anger within the German government. And Sweden was neutral."

"Do you remember much about that time?"

"It was a Bohemian kind of life though, of course, I didn't know that word then. We moved from one place to another but ended up in Stockholm. We lived in a hotel before moving to a small apartment." Nina popped a grape. "My parents sacrificed a lot for me. I'm so grateful. I was enrolled in a Montessori kindergarten, the best school - where the royals went. I didn't speak a word of Swedish and didn't open my mouth for about two months, then suddenly I was speaking it fluently."

"It's wonderful how absorbent children's brains are," I said. Maria Montessori's book *The Absorbent Mind* floats into my consciousness.

"One thing I remember very well, once we moved back to Copenhagen after the War in 1945, was when I enrolled in a public school. Some of the students' clothing was so modest - their dresses made of paper. I felt ashamed of my winter coat." Nina gestures her neckline. "It had a fur collar. Can you imagine?"

I can't.

"You were ten when you first stepped foot in America. What brought you here?"

"That was in 1948. My father was the Danish press attaché to the United Nations."

"Is that when you learnt English?"

Nina nods, a beam lifts her expressive face. "It was a wonderful time. We were in New York three months. I had a guide who took me to Radio City Music Hall, all the sights. I still have the scrapbook I made. Even though I only turned eleven while there, the visit oriented my whole future!"

"Did your brother feel the same way?"

"I suppose so, because he stayed. He was eighteen years older than me. He ended up marrying a Swede who was in the US on a short-term visa. They eventually moved back to Sweden, so I have a niece and nephew on whom to practice my Swedish."

I am about to move the conversation along when Nina launches into the differences between her homeland and her adopted country.

"The thing about Denmark is that it is a very practical place. Everyone is well taken care of but," she pauses, "it lacks passion."

I look at the woman framed by palm trees and silhouetted against the azure bay in the distance and cannot imagine her in a life that did not fizz.

"So how did you get back to the US?" I can't believe much stood in her way.

"I finished school and applied for a Fulbright/American Scandinavian Association scholarship which, when awarded, saw me enrolled at the University of Montana in Missoula. When I arrived, at seventeen, the college considered my education so advanced I entered as a junior to study English and American history. And I took some journalism classes."

"Was writing always your goal?" The numerous articles Nina has written and translated would seem to say it was. One was a translation for Arnold Highfield of Hans West's account of St Croix in the West Indies. Another project was an educational video underwritten by the VI Council of the Arts and distributed throughout local schools about Hugo Larsen, the artist sent to document the Danish West Indies in the 1890s.

"I suppose it was going to happen. Both my parents were writers. My mother wrote fiction for Young Adults. Her books were translated into several languages. I even have a Hungarian edition!" Nina's laugh blends with the breeze. "My father was a journalist. He had a lot of contacts in the US and gave lectures here on Danish-Americans. They lived in Canada for a year after I left home. That was nice because I got to see them."

"You graduate, then what?"

Nina's animated face becomes still. I wait, not wanting to intrude as she sifts her thoughts. The cat stretches, gives his whiskers a quick swipe and saunters indoors. He presumably finds our conversation tedious. I do not.

Her voice is quiet. "My early years here were not easy. I had a bad marriage. The only good thing to come out of it was my son, Michael. It ended and I moved on."

"You must have been very young when you married."

"Yes, I was 20."

This is not a topic Nina wishes to speak about so I ask, "How did you meet Ed?"

"I was 24, and his office manager."

"That's not very original, Nina," I say with a laugh. Her smile returns and I'm sure her vivid blue eyes are crinkled behind her sunglasses.

"No. But we were together forty-six years. It was a good marriage. He was older than me. In 1963 he decided to move his electronics service center for commercial vessels, including cruise ships and yachts, to San Juan in Puerto Rico, and we stayed there thirteen years."

"Did you stay on as his office manager?"

She nods. "And I went to the University of Puerto Rico to study Spanish."

"You really are a polyglot." To be able to switch between Danish, Swedish, German, Spanish and, of course, fluent English is a gift, a talent, that makes me deeply envious.

Nina corrects me.

"No, no, my German is rusty, as is my French but that improves after a glass of wine!"

"So does mine." I laugh. "What made you decide to relocate to St Croix?"

"You know it was dumb luck that brought me here. It wasn't even my decision to leave Puerto Rico - it was my husband's. He was an electrical engineer and the Hess refinery was one of his customers and he was flying over three times a week and, while it was a business expense, it was still ridiculous. That was in 1976."

I'm about to ask about arriving on St Croix when Nina takes me back to her teen years.

"You know, it was pure luck that brought me here," she repeats. Her smile is alive with the memory. "But I had some experiences about this place from my youth. Both my father and uncle were writers, and history oriented, very interested in Danish colonial times."

I nod and think of seeing an article in which her father mentions voting for the first time. The vote was whether the Danish West Indies should be retained by Denmark or sold to the US. He voted against the sale.

Nina continues, "I have pictures of myself sitting at my uncle's dining table with his family, and my father, and on the wall are the Bärentzen prints of Christiansted and Frederiksted. My uncle also had collections of coins and stamps from the Danish West Indies. And…" Nina chuckles like a schoolgirl, "… a collection of Christmas seals."

The penny drops, and a question on my list is answered without being asked.

"Ahh, so that's where your idea for selling Christmas seals as a fundraiser came from." I jot down a note to remind myself to ask Nina more about this.

"Yes, yes. Though, in a way, it came from two sources in the same family. His daughter, my cousin, was very involved with Greenland, another Danish colony. She married the Minister for Greenland Affairs and lived there for a number of years." Nina laughs. "She started a charity publishing Christmas seals from Greenland and even managed to get the Queen to paint some. You know the Danish Queen is a very talented artist."

I had no idea.

"All these things I saw at my uncle's made an impression on me," she continues. "In a way I see my early life, say until the age of 50, not nearly as interesting as things that have happened since then."

I'm flabbergasted. Her whole life is a series of fascinating vignettes.

"Once, when I was back in Copenhagen, I went to the Danish West Indies archives because I wondered if my dad had any manuscripts deposited there." Nina grins in glee. "I had a friend who was an archivist and he helped me find the last thing my father wrote - volume one of a book about Alexander Hamilton's childhood on St Croix."

"Good grief, what are the chances?"

"I know." Nina is in full flow and we jump back to February, 1965.

"My parents visited us in PR. My dad had gotten a contract with a leading Danish newspaper to write a series of articles about various Caribbean islands, including of course the Virgin Islands. I accompanied him on some of his interviews in San Juan. One was to meet Pablo Casals. He was an old man by then but it was a remarkable moment." Nina's eyes gleam at the memory.

I wonder briefly whether the cellist had played for them but didn't have a chance to ask.

"My father had never been to St Croix but two days before he was due to fly over my mother became very ill. The doctors found a mass and she had a blood transfusion before she could fly home. The difference that made was incredible. She seemed so much better but, of course, it was very worrying and my father went back with her."

In the silence Nina's face is still.

"Well, the happy news was she recovered as soon as she got back to Denmark. The doctors could find nothing wrong. It was remarkable. I had seen the X-rays that showed a mass in her stomach."

"Gosh," I say, amazed at the human body. I begin to speak but Nina carries on.

"We were delighted but it made my dad wonder what in the world to do. Should he return to the islands, but before he could decide he fell ill."

"God, I'm sorry, Nina, to bring this all back." This is the bit I don't enjoy. Digging up sadnesses. I wait.

"He died three months later." Tears behind in her glasses glimmer but do not fall.

"Oh, Nina." I reach across the table.

"It was a tragedy." Nina's voice rasps. "It seemed so unfair. I went back for the funeral and all that." She reaches for a grape, time to gather herself. "My mother lived another eleven years and returned to Puerto Rico. I took her to St Croix one year not knowing we were going to move here."

"It is strange how life turns out." I watch the waves at Chenay Bay and leave Nina to her thoughts.

She looks down at her hands. "It was a long time ago but, you know, I felt it was a signal for me to complete what my dad didn't have time to do." Nina lapses into a silence that is filled by a couple of bananaquits, then adds, "Mother was a wonderful woman, the quiet one. My father was more outgoing, more exciting. The dominant one. But, I think my mother was the more admirable person."

It is obvious Nina cared deeply for both.

"I think I have something of both my parents in me. I went back to Denmark in August '76 to say goodbye to my mother. She had been living in a home the last few years. I had no choice, but it was a very nice one." Nina still struggles with the concept. "She died soon after and, in September, Ed and I moved here. I was glad she knew we were relocating."

"That, Nina, is the guilt we suffer when a global life is chosen. It sounds wonderful to those left behind in our passport country but it is not always easy."

"You're right, and I can truly say I never regretted leaving Denmark even though I enjoy myself tremendously each time I go back. I celebrated my 80th birthday there. Forty people, all of whom I have met in connection to St Croix."

We need a change of pace and I ask her about arriving on St Croix.

"I'd been working as Ed's office manager, mainly because I spoke Spanish. It was okay but there was something really that I felt, a pull, the more I learned about the Danish background on this island which, of course, was not the case in Puerto Rico.

"The islands are full of compelling histories, all of them different." I think of my own research.

Nina continues. "It fascinated me to discover how much this place had to offer and, back in '76, there was hardly any tourism from Denmark. That started shortly thereafter."

"What prompted the interest?"

"After the 50th anniversary of Transfer in 1967, younger people's curiosity was piqued through The Danish West Indian Society and Friends of Denmark, and they wanted to research their families. It grew from that, then in 1978 the USVI did a big promotion drive and opened a Danish West Indies office in Aarhus. That led to them asking me to become a tour guide."

I marvel at how much of our lives fall firmly into the serendipitous file.

"Since arriving, I had immersed myself in various projects - all volunteer. The first place was at Whim Great House." Nina's chuckle is contagious. "I offered to sort their books. I found they were all on little index cards and the entire collection consisted of one bookcase."

"That was an easy one." I imagine a younger Nina expecting to tackle months of cataloguing.

"I can't help but think about how things change. I served on the Board at Whim for six or seven years. We had a thousand members. It makes me extremely sad to think of that organization now."

"Such a waste," I say. The stories I have heard since my arrival in 2013 of the fundraisers and other events put on regularly at Whim, back in the day, speak to a vibrant organization. The only Candlelight Concert I attended, whilst memorable for the singing, was marred by the glint of stars through the compromised roof.

We get sidetracked by the cat who strolls out and provides light relief.

"This is a wonderful neighborhood for him, and me. Safe. You know the house sold," Nina gestures behind her, "but the new owner is pleased for me to stay? What a relief!"

I nod. "It must have been weighing heavily on you, this whole ghastly year."

Nina nods and gives a self-deprecating laugh. "Believe me, I don't envy whoever is left with the burden, probably my poor son, to sort all my stuff out."

We talk about mutual friends who recently left St Croix due to age-related ill health. I tell Nina that whilst it was a sad time, it was also a privilege to hear their wonderful stories evoked by newly-found photographs and old forgotten letters. Perhaps I am hoping to nudge her into tackling some of the boxes she tells me are stored under the bed in her spare room.

"When, or if, to leave is a horribly difficult decision to make," I say, knowing it is a less demanding one to make when of one's own volition and not through circumstance. Easy words to deliver, not so easy to live by.

"My son lives in Florida and has an apartment in his garden, maybe I can move in one day." Nina gazes at the Ginger Thomas in her garden.

I bring her back to the here and now. "Where else did you volunteer?"

"The Animal Shelter Flea Market. I'd sort donations. And I managed it for a while and made a lot of friends. It helped that I spoke Spanish. Some of the...." she pauses, searching for the right word, the first time she has done this, ".... er, ladies of the evening, shall we say, from the Dominican Republic still greet me!" Her laughter is full throated. "It is easy to make friends on this island. People are so outgoing and welcoming, and that means a lot to me."

"It also depends on your attitude, Nina."

"Well, that's true." She nods. "Another place I volunteered was at the National Parks. I was working at the entrance to Fort Christiansvaern and a Swedish woman came in and I surprised her by answering her in Swedish. Anyway, she asked me where her prints were. She had an arrangement with the parks to display historic prints and maps." Nina laughs at the memory. "I suddenly remembered and told her I knew all about them." She is almost dancing in her seat. She leans forward for a grape before continuing, "I told her I had been asked by a visiting New York couple, who owned a gallery on Madison Avenue, to translate the Danish text that went with the images. The Swedish woman was delighted and suggested I publish them."

The woman in front of me is modest.

"I said the translations were very sketchy. But she kept saying I should brush them up and publish, so I thought, why not?"

"And that is how your first book, *Islands of Beauty and Bounty*, enters the story?"

"Yes, it energized me."

I want to get the topic back to Nina's charity fundraising with the Christmas seals but she takes me there unasked.

"When I celebrated my 50th birthday at my cousin's place in Denmark, she and I discussed her work in Greenland and how Christmas seals had helped fund a housing project for the elderly. Then we talked about her father, my uncle's, collection of Christmas seals from the Danish West Indies and I said it would be fun to revive that with the aim of supporting education and training programs for VI youth."

"And off it went!" I say. Nina's birthday is in June, and I have an image of these two women sitting on a long Nordic summer evening hatching a plan.

"Yes, it was so peculiar. One of the guests was a Dane, born in St Thomas, who was a stamp artist and he offered to create the first issue. Our honorary chair was the US Ambassador to Denmark, Terrence Todman, who was from the Virgin Islands. He even attended our premiere at a World Philatelic Exhibit in Copenhagen in 1986, then we had another premiere at Government House here."

Nina's face is alight with delight.

"The whole thing got this crazy start and, of course, the Ambassador lent us huge prestige. I'd never had any marketing experience or anything like that. We raised over $200,000. It was all volunteer help. For me, it was a joy to be able to say thank you to St Croix for the many privileges it had given me."

"Why did you stop?"

"Ed got sick, and I was very busy, so the last issue was in 1999. He recovered but in 1990 I had started editing *St Croix This Week*. So many fortuitous things in my life."

I love the way my intended questions are sometimes answered without being asked.

Nina continues, "I had not been seeking a job but my friend, a journalist, Susie Jenter Tomb, was offered it. She declined because she wanted to write a book about Hurricane Hugo, so suggested I apply."

"Isn't it wonderful how life just happens sometimes?"

"What was so amazing was that in November '89, Ed and I had gone up to Stonington, Connecticut to visit his family. The woman who owned *St Croix This Week* had a house there and I had met her at a cocktail party. So many things have fallen into my lap."

"Did you enjoy the role?"

"It was demanding but I had a ball. I was told it was going to be part-time, but I had to write content, design ads, sell ads, all the bookkeeping. Trying to sell ads after a devastating hurricane was difficult - so many people who had nothing, not even power."

"What happened to the previous editor?"

"It was kind of strange. She had been away when Hugo hit and she was overcome with guilt for not being part of it and decided to call it a day."

"Did you work from home?"

"They'd had an office before the storm. But I converted an extra room in our house in Estate Bellevue into an office. It worked well because I could be at home to give Ed some TLC from time to time."

Talking about her husband makes Nina emotional but she is determined to keep going.

"We had a good marriage, it was a real love match. We shared so much - despite the twenty-four year age gap. We shared a curiosity for life. You know, he was a kind of black sheep in his family, who were a prominent family of New York architects. He was fascinated by radio from a very early age. Do you know, before I was born, he was a radio engineer in the 1936 Harvard/MIT Solar Eclipse Expedition to Siberia? He documented the whole trip, which was several months."

After hearing that, I'm not sure I agree about the black sheep comment. It's brave to face up to family expectations and follow one's own path. "When did you move here, Nina?" I nod to her apartment with the view across a field planted with palms and other natives.

"It was a bad experience. We had three home invasions at Estate Bellevue. First one, then two days later another. I got hurt in that one. He had a knife but punched me with his fist, but it still bled." Nina touches her forehead. "I screamed and he fled. Then another break in. They stole Ed's sports car but that was retrieved. It all happened in the middle of the Danish West Indies Festival."

I am shocked, and sorry I have again raked up bad recollections and say, "Did the police catch the thieves? An experience like that is enough to temper one's fondness for a place in a lot of people. It never colored your judgement?"

Nina shakes her head. "We had so much help from people - Rotary friends, neighbors, the Friends of Denmark. It was fantastic. It sounds strange but it was the best thing in a way. Ed and I had accumulated so many things over thirty years and it was time to move on. The house sold in a heartbeat, then more luck when we found this place quite by chance."

"Have you ever had pushback, Nina, from Crucians about the Danish connection?"

Nina shakes her head again.

"I've learned many good things, especially about caring. I'll never forget an event that took place when I was a tour guide for a Danish group - people mostly in their 60s or 70s. There was a Buck Island trip and on the way back one of the visitors died. It was tragic but it was handled so graciously." Nina pauses. "You know, all the employees gathered for a ceremony in the hotel lobby to pay their respects. And Pastor White, a charismatic man from the Lutheran Church, they all said something beautiful to the widow, and the Danes. I stood there and realized how much we need to learn from West Indians. I think the loyalty and caring people show for each other, and sometimes in a very difficult situation, is remarkable. The compassion was remarkable."

"And yet," I say, "we have the current situation wherein gun violence is escalating, so too domestic violence."

Nina bows her head. "It is a tragedy. Unfortunately so many young people have a lousy start. Children are brought up in the manner in which the parents were raised, the pattern of punishment and lack of self image is repeated through the generations."

We talk about those who are doing their utmost to mitigate the issues. People and organizations like Resa O'Reilly and her non-profit, Project Promise, or My Brother's Workshop who work directly with young people.

"But that's a small handful, it's not enough." Nina's sadness is palpable.

"If everyone makes a small effort it can amount to a lot."

"Yes, I suppose so," she agrees. "I've had the pleasure of helping a few students, some from very humble backgrounds, through the scholarship program from the Rotary Club and have watched them become adults contributing to their community."

I glance down at my notes, which have been pretty much redundant in our chat. I see 'buildings' underlined.

"There are many links to colonial times on St Croix. The buildings around us, built by the enslaved with bricks used as ballast from Danish ships, is probably the most obvious example. To my knowledge," I say, "our current governor is the first to not fly the Dannebrog at Government House. Why do you think that is?"

"Protocol." Nina's response is firm. "If there is an occasion I feel it would be okay to fly it. In fact, I am planning to hand the governor a copy of my book, *Our Danish Connection*, and I shall point to the picture of the Danish flag flying!"

"Preserving history so the same mistakes are not made again," I suggest, thinking of the recently published *Our Danish Connection*, a collection of articles she has written for *St Croix This Week*.

Nina nods. "Our festivals, exchanges, are now about friendships. Really we are an assemblage of exiles. In some ways that is good, but it also presents a problem as there are so many different visions of what the future should be."

"If you could wave a wand, which building would you choose to restore?"

"One church I have a special interest in is the Friedensfeld at Mon Bijou. I am told it was actually brought here as a kit."

"Wow!" A vision of Ikea floats in from the ether.

"That to me is amazing, and because the Moravian Brethren were instrumental in bringing Christianity to the population."

"That can be good and bad, Nina."

She laughs. "And I am happy to see work is being done on the Lutheran Parish house on King Street. It is a fine building, architecturally."

"You have given a lot to St Croix."

"There have been so many bounties in my life. Connections. The Christmas seals, which shops sold without any profit to themselves, helped me in turn sell ads and get to know a whole circle of business people. But that chapter of my life is over."

"Tell me, Nina, do you dream in Danish or English?"

"Both, more so in English now because I haven't been speaking much Danish lately. When *Our Danish Connection* was published, I got some interesting comments about my translations from Danish friends. They said my language was from an earlier time - it is old-fashioned - but that's okay. It seems appropriate as the book is about history." Nina laughs. "I am often told I speak like the Queen, which I think is a lovely thing to say. The Danish spoken now is coarser, not as gracious."

I look at waves dancing ashore, then at the home Nina has made her own, and think of her earlier words about fulfilling a mission her father had started - to connect two places bound by history.

Before I can speak she says, "I'm so grateful Ed and I had three years in this house together." Her voice breaks, "We brought joy to each other."

I think it fair to say she has brought joy to a great many people. This vivacious and still curious woman has lived a heartwarming and fulfilling life on an island she landed on by 'dumb luck'.

BEAUTY AND THE BEAST

I am fortunate to spend time on St Croix - the largest of America's surprisingly least known Caribbean islands. The raw beauty of her beaches and the capriciousness of the sea as it cycles from emerald to aquamarine to turquoise to steel, depending on the clouds sent scudding by the constant trade winds, never fail to delight.

History emanates off the foot-thick walls of the forts - yellow in Christiansted and rust colored in Frederiksted - telling of the seven flags under which St Croix has flown. Originally known as Ay Ay, the island has been colonized, captured, lost, recaptured and bought, by the Dutch, British, French, Spanish, the Knights of Malta, the Danish, and, finally, the US who fearful of German expansion during the First World War bought it in 1917 for 25 million dollars. With the benefits of US laws and banking regulations, strong African roots from the days of slavery, a European heritage, and a lingering Caribbean charm, St Croix has much to offer residents and visitors alike.

Green, hawksbill and occasionally leatherback turtles lumber up many of the beaches to lay their eggs, year after year. 50 to 70 days later seabirds circle the skies, watching with predatory interest as the tiny hatchlings surface through the sand and scuttle down to the ocean to start their journey north.

Cacti and scrub populate the eastern end of the island, with mahogany and genip trees towering high in the rainforest to the west. Bougainvillea, hibiscus, ixora and the island flower,

Ginger Thomas, splash color along the roadsides and hide both million-dollar mansions and less palatial homes from prying eyes. Papayas, pomegranates, pineapples and figs - delicious little bananas - grow with easy abundance. Mangos and avocados grace many local dishes, and the sea offers lobster and mahi-mahi and snapper.

Tranquility and beauty.

The islands - St Croix, St Thomas and St John - like most places have community issues, with elements of society not content to follow the rules. There is domestic abuse, too many guns in the hands of the wrong people, drug, alcohol and gambling addictions and larcenies of various kinds. All man made.

There is, though, a natural beast which lurks with vicious impunity along some of the shorelines. Known by the Spanish conquistadors as the 'little apple of death', the *hippomane mancinella*, more commonly known as the manchineel, provides a natural windbreak and fights beach erosion, ever a problem for areas facing Atlantic hurricanes. The tree, which can grow to 50 feet, can be deadly to most birds and animals, though for some unexplained reason iguana seem impervious to its toxicity.

To mere mortals its small green fruit resemble crab apples and lie temptingly on the sands. Don't be enticed. If ingested, savage abdominal pain can be expected, followed by vomiting, bleeding and damage to the digestive tract. Deaths have been reported. Don't even pick that apple up. The leaves and bark produce a milky sap which causes blindness, mostly temporary, and scorching blisters. Not only does a scratch from a branch hurt but pulsating pustules emerge over the coming few hours, adding to the misery. I have seen the pain.

If Juan Ponce de Leon, the conquistador intent on colonizing Florida in 1513 and, later, parts of the Caribbean, had survived a manchineel-tipped arrow piercing his thigh, he might have been able to attest to its ferocity. Some, though, accept the temptations. Carpenters covet the hard timber for furniture and a few risk the dangers, drying the wood naturally to neutralize the sap.

Most manchineel shrubs and trees are marked with red crosses and warnings, but signs can get overgrown. Beachgoers have been burned just by standing underneath the tree during one of the many squalls washing the islands and coasts of South America and Florida. The caustic sap can even burn the paint off cars parked under its branches. And, if burned, the air is filled with toxins causing respiratory problems.

Accepted as the most dangerous tree in the world, the manchineel is relatively rare and is considered endangered - remember, it does have some positive benefits. But really, the best thing to do, should you come upon a manchineel, is to give it a wide berth.

Beauty and the beast - part of the allure of the Caribbean.

And, should your kite get entangled in the manchineel's embracing arms, just cut the strings.

RISE UP THIS MORNING

M y father was a Gemini. As well as being a polyglot, he had an eclectic taste in music and the sounds from scratchy 45s and LPs could be anything from Schubert to jazz, Bing Crosby to gamelan, Sousa to *bierkeller* oomp pah pahs and everything in between.

It is he who introduced me to calypso. Not, as you might think, sung by the Trinidadian greats of the day, the Mighty Sparrow or Lord Kitchener or even the American calypsonian Harry Belafonte, but rather the unlikely Danish - Dutch husband and wife duo, Nina and Frederik. I never asked why a white couple sang calypso so convincingly. I learnt later calypso entered Frederik van Pallandt's life when his father was the Dutch ambassador to Trinidad. The Danish connection came, not as I had thought, through historical links to the US Virgin Islands which were the Danish West Indies until 1917, but when Dutch Frederik fell in love with Danish Nina.

It is one of life's ironies that my daughter now lives in Port of Spain, Trinidad. The country to which I swore I would not return after a year spent in the south, in San Fernando, in the mid 1980s. There is much beauty in the country but, for me, way back then it was a time of strange isolation. A difficult time politically with tensions between black and East Indian contingents. As tradition would have it, political commentary came through calypso and blared from speakers before, during and after Carnival.

When Kate extols the virtues of soca and ska, I remind her it was her parents who exposed her at an early age to the rhythms of the Caribbean. To Edwin Ayoung, aka Crazy, who won the 1985 Road March with *Suck Meh Soucouyant* and which we heard without cease when we lived there. For those unsure of the term, a *soucouyant* is a shape-changing character - by day a wrinkled old woman living in a shack surrounded by tall trees and by night, reverting to her true self and her pact with the devil, flying through the sky as a fireball searching for victims.

Trinidad and Tobago also lays claim to Calypso Rose. Born Linda McCartha Monica Sandy-Lewis in 1940, she started writing songs at 15, turned professional at 24, and at 76 and about 800 songs later claims, as the lyrics in *Calypso Queen* say, "my constitution is strong".

St Croix has just celebrated Three Kings Day. Part of the Carnival activities include competing for the Festival Calypso Monarch. Won again this year by Temisha 'Caribbean Queen' Libert. Her entry, as others, took the opportunity to highlight flaws in local politics - a time-honored calypso tradition no doubt a little uncomfortable for any politicians present. One of her songs, written by Carol Hodge, asked the question, "How could we smile? No way, no way".

Another competitor, Campbell 'King Kan Ru Plen Tae' Barnes went so far as to say politicians were worse than Satan, suggesting some get elected by invoking *obeah* - sorcery, of the bad kind - perhaps similar to the type of interference reported in the presidential election!

It would seem, having heard Meryl Streep's powerful speech at the Golden Globe Awards about the president-elect and his unvetted family and cohorts, we need entertainers of every stripe to remind the rest of us to hold our politicians' toes to the fire. To not let them ride roughshod over We the People.

Though not a polyglot, I too am a Gemini with an eclectic taste in music. My father died a number of years ago but just maybe, one day, on a giant turntable in the sky, he will listen to a tragic (or perhaps comic) opera describing the events of the Trump presidency. Until that opera or calypso is written, I take comfort, as inauguration day looms, from the music of that other great Caribbean singer, Bob Marley. Because I have to believe "every little thing gonna be alright" and that, as Calypso Rose assures us, the "constitution is strong"!

CHANEY AND OTHER COLLECTIONS

I am not a beach bunny - even stretching way, way back to my bikini days. I love the ocean - being in, under or on it. But sitting on the sand, even with a book and a beer, palls very quickly. Walking along the beach though is a different matter. There is always something to gather.

My latest collections come from the beaches of St Croix. From one, the delicate little shells of palest pink to the deepest blush. Under candlelight on my dining table they take on a translucent beauty reminiscent of a Gainsborough portrait. From another beach, I gather sea glass or, as my granddaughter Ava calls them, gems, tumbled and tossed ashore by tides and waves beginning their journey from who knows where. What start as bottles discarded by careless souls from boats, end up recycled as smooth fragments of opaque glass often used for island jewelry. Or, as in my home, placed in glass bowls to glimmer in quiet simplicity.

I still kick myself for throwing out a cache of elegant little black and white shells. Classic shells - each striation a marvel of nature's preciseness. I can't remember where I harvested them, perhaps Australia, perhaps Thailand, but I liked them enough to carry around the world for fifteen years. Then in a fit of cleaning house, probably before another relocation, I tossed them.

That is the trouble with, or perhaps the benefit of, frequent moves. Each item must be judged worthy of container space. We have a problem with books but I think have, on the whole, reached an amicable arrangement. My husband's collection of Folio Society books, and those left him by my father, always get a free ride. Reference, history and travel books too. Some novels I refuse to be parted from, *Pride and Prejudice* or *Tess of the D'Urbervilles* for example. Those which have struck enough of a chord to warrant a second, or third, reading also get a pass.

But beach novels get the heave ho - no ifs, no buts. Which, considering I am a writer and know the agonies of bringing 90,000 words to publication readiness, is very hard to do. I feel I am letting the writer-hood down but comfort myself with the thought at least the books will be available for others to enjoy, even if the author gets no royalties from the resale.

A trunk load of fabric bought from markets around the world - saris, ikat, batik and so on - has also been a constant, with pieces showing up as curtains, tablecloths, cushion covers in other parts of the world.

And there is a large box of Mexican tiles, which has been an ongoing bone of contention - with each relocation my justification getting thinner. Until St Croix. Those tiles, lovingly collected over the years, now have a permanent home and there has been a certain amount of, "see, I told you I'd use them somewhere!"

Our home on St Croix is in Christiansted. One day we will have a wonderful terrace and garden, but at the moment it is a quarry. We have enough stone to build our very own fort - never mind the one guarding the town and Gallows Bay. But it's what is between the stones that delights me.

Chaney. Lots and lots of chaney.

To people not acquainted with the islands these little bits of pottery and china might just look like, well, little bits of pottery and china. But they're not! Chaney was currency. Broken shards of table and kitchenware scavenged by children who would then file down the edges, probably on a rock, and use it as money. "I'll swap you two chaney for a stick of sugarcane" kind of transaction. Early day bitcoins! The term 'chaney' is said to be the words - china and money - conflated. Or perhaps, and I have absolutely no evidence of this, chaney came from the word 'change'. "You owe me two chaney," sort of thing.

In 2017, chaney is still valuable. Now wrapped in gold or silver and sold as jewelry to tourists and residents alike. Currency of a different kind. These little pieces of china, nearly always blue and white, have a multitude of uses - all of them artistic. They embellish lintels, become tabletops, or cover vases.

There are four distinct types of chaney: shell edge, a slightly fluted design from England around the mid 1700s; mocha-ware, off-white sturdy kitchenware with linear designs from a similar period; flow blue, from mid 1500s Germany when during the glazing process cobalt oxide blurred the design; and lastly the ubiquitous blue willow design, imported from China in the 1700s and adapted by Thomas Minton for Thomas Turner of Caughley of Shropshire. The willow design depicts the forbidden love between a Chinese Mandarin's daughter and his secretary. Upon the lovers' untimely death, the gods immortalized them as two doves, forever flying together.

And as St Croix once flew under the Dutch flag, I wouldn't be surprised if some of the blue and white fragments are Delftware.

As I wash each piece of chaney, I wonder about its story. These little shards of china and pottery - history found in our garden. History which will stay in our garden, to one day be incorporated into paving stones and risers, along with the Mexican tiles. One collection which will not be moving on.

Footnote:

I have since learnt it is illegal to take anything organic, such as a shell, from a beach in the Virgin Islands.

ACROSS THE SEA

Dust rose in a choking eddy and Taarank pulled the end of his *pagri* around to cover his nose and mouth as he moved to clamber into the back of the ox cart. Vaanee's turban, that his mother insisted he take, was stuffed into the cloth bag at his feet. His hair was slicked back with coconut oil. He turned to his sisters and brothers, framed by the village of mud and straw huts. The youngest, Shanti, lay quiet in his mother's arms. The baby was well-named. Almost as if she knew her birth coincided with her father's death.

"*Namaste, maan,*" Vaanee said, bending to touch his mother's bare feet beneath her white widow's sari. Tears glistened in her eyes as he straightened and said, "Five years is not so long. We will return rich."

The driver clicked his tongue to the ox, and Vaanee swung up beside him.

"*Alavida!*" The farewell cries followed the young men down the rutted road. Drought-stricken fields, sugarcane stalks shriveled and dry, stretched to the horizon until, in the distance, the walls of Agra rose.

Ten days, and numerous changes of ox carts later, they plodded along the wide and meandering Hooghly River to the port at Calcutta where they had been ordered to report by the recruiting agent. A uniformed guard at the gate to the bustling wharves held up a hand, his voice bored as he demanded papers.

Vaanee pulled the carefully folded copy of their contract from the pocket of his *dhoti* and gave it to the guard as Taarank hovered behind. A gob of *paan*, the bright red juice from the mixture of betel leaf and lime, landed by Vaanee's feet as the guard studied the paper. He nodded his head in the general direction of a row of warehouses, his eyes never leaving them as they picked up their luggage and walked on.

Thrusting the contract at different people they pushed towards the river until they found themselves herded into a crowded shed. Officials in khaki uniforms corralled men into one line, women and children into another.

"We go where?" The voice came from a boy, whose deep brown eyes circled the mass as he and his mother joined the twenty or so women inching forward.

"Across the sea. For many days," she answered, her reassuring smile not reaching her eyes.

Crouching down, Vaanee, said to the child, "We go to an island. A place surrounded by water. There will be much rain and we will eat bananas, and have rice and dahl, eh?"

"Tscht," Taarank glared at his brother. "Why fill his head with lies."

"How do you know that, eh? Is it not better to feel hope?" Vaanee smiled, but his heart raced.

The line of men was very much longer, Vaanee guessed over two hundred, and the brothers wondered what lay behind the doors. Quietness fell as those ahead neared the door, craning to see what lay beyond each time it opened and a man in white ushered the next man in.

Taarank clutched his brother's arm, beads of sweat erupting on his forehead.

"It is fine. Remember the agent said we would be checked. To ensure we are healthy. That is all," Vaanee reassured him. "I will go first and wait for you."

The room was stark with a gurney, a metal desk and two chairs. An Indian gestured for Vaanee to stand in front of the desk where a half-caste and an Englishman wearing white jackets scribbled on forms.

The white man glanced up. "I am a doctor. You must be examined and deemed fit to travel. Strip." The Eurasian translated the English to Hindi.

Vaanee pulled his shirt over his head and stood still.

"Everything." The Indian pointed to Vaanee's dhoti.

He unwound the length of fabric from between his legs and around his waist and stood naked. Waiting.

The doctor put strange plug things into his own ears then a cold disc to Vaanee's heart and chest and listened. Next he checked his skin, his teeth, his ears, mouth and eyes, and then, in a move that shocked Vaanee, his scrotum. With each prod, the doctor nodded and the half-caste made a note. Vaanee watched as marks filled the long sheet of paper.

"Good. You can dress through there. Next."

Vaanee clutched his shirt and dhoti to his crotch and, about to go through another door, paused.

"Please, sahib, my brother, he is next. He is anxious."

"He'll need to toughen up." The Eurasian's voice was terse.

Vaanee rewound his dhoti and waited in the cramped room. He could hear Taarank's voice rise in distress, and the Indian shouting. The Englishman spoke in Hindi, which surprised him. And the silence from his brother surprised him too. It took longer for him to appear, and when he did his face was streaked with tears. Taarank shrugged off Vaanee's arm and silently dressed. Together they moved through to the next room.

Another holding pen. As men, women and children again waited, their possessions gathered around them, children lost their inhibitions and played. Vaanee counted seventeen. He wondered what would happen if any of the men failed and their wives passed. Or the other way around. Everyone in the hall must have had to sign, or put their mark, on the same kind of paper as he and Taarank. A promise to cross the water to another place for five years. A promise of food, lodging and payment. A promise of a return ticket to India. A promise of riches.

As night fell, the doors from the medical rooms stopped opening and a rickety cart appeared, pushed in by two turbaned men. Lentil soup ladled from a vat, along with chapattis, filled the group's bellies as the clang of anchors and the shouts and grunts of Bengali *lascars* loading ship's holds drifted in. Vaanee and Taarank murmured in the dim light until Taarank fell into an uneasy sleep, his legs jerking. Vaanee watched over his brother, a worried frown creasing his brow, until he too fell asleep.

He woke to a dirty dawn trickling through metal doors on rollers from the far end of the warehouse. Yells woke those still sleeping, and the rustle of people gathering their belongings filled the subdued room. He lifted Taarank's head from his shoulder and nodded.

"Come, we go now."

The steamship, *Mars*, rode against the dock, fenders and ropes creaking. The line of men, women and children snaked up the wooden gangplank that bounced under their combined weight. They were separated before being shoved into dark and dank holds lined with wooden bunks. Vaanee, Taarank and other single men and boys found themselves at the front of the hold, married men were ordered to the middle on the port side, married women to the starboard and girls to the aft. Vaanee saw the boy he had spoken to the day before look around for his mother, or father, tears close to the surface. He took the child's hand and sat him next to Taarank.

"Why so sad? It is an auspicious day." Vaanee, smiled at his brother and the boy. "Have you forgotten today is the start of Makar Sankranti? Our next harvest festival will be far away, with new crops. But still we will sing and dance."

"And will there be kites in this place far away?" the child asked, his voice subdued.

"Of course," Vaanee replied. "And we shall eat sesame and jaggery too."

"They will have palm trees where we are going?"

"Of course. Sweet, brown palm sugar better than any jaggery you have tasted before. Tell me, boy, what is your name?"

"I am Farhad."

"Wise one. And are you wise, Farhad?"

The boy nodded, his eyes still damp.

"I am Vaanee, and this is my brother Taarank. You will be our little brother on the voyage."

The slap of ropes falling in the water heralded the start of the journey. The slap of waves along the hull heralded the long days. The slap of violence heralded dark nights when women were dragged to the deck and raped, despite the threat of punishment from the captain.

Vaanee befriended lascars working the decks. He learned the names of the seas they crossed. The Bay of Bengal. The Indian Ocean. Midway across the Atlantic they stopped at St Helena for fresh water and supplies. It was a blessed relief after the roiling waters around the Cape of Good Hope.

Lice fought for space on everybody but Vaanee worried about Taarank, who each day ate less. He watched his brother weaken as his stomach distended and he writhed in pain. Blotches like rose petals appeared on his neck and belly.

"You must eat, brother. You must stay strong. See how Farhad grows even on the thinnest gruel?"

Then came a fever so intense, Vaanee sent Farhad to beg the compounder, the ship's mediator between the indentured and captain, to come to the cramped space in which they slept, ate, defecated, and spent most of their days. Instead the boy ran back and said the surgeon-superintendent, the most powerful man aboard after the captain, was coming to see Taarank.

"You will feel better soon." Vaanee wiped sweat from Taarank's face. He watched the doctor, his face grim, examine his brother.

"How long has he been like this?" The compounder translated.

"Days. But he has not eaten for longer. It pains him."

"He has typhoid. Bring him," the doctor ordered the mediator. He looked at Vaanee. "You help."

It made no difference whether Taarank was in the hold or the medical berth. His death shook Vaanee to his core, the anguish of which was compounded by not being allowed to cremate him as was the Hindu custom. Vaanee's natural ebullience deserted him and as he watched his brother's body slide into the ocean he cried for both Taarank and himself. He felt Farhad's smooth hand reach for his.

Mars would soon be in the Caribbean but the prospect brought Vaanee no excitement. And what was the Caribbean but a strange-sounding word?

Taarank, he learned from a lascar, was one of only five to die on the voyage, a marked improvement from previous years to other parts of the Caribbean. Neither prayers to Ganesh nor the hope for a better life soothed his soul. It was Farhad who brought Vaanee back from despair. The child's quiet presence eased his pain and made the rest of the passage bearable.

After three-and-a-half months at sea, Vaanee and Farhad were penned in the hold as *Mars* negotiated, with the assistance of the harbormaster, the narrow entrance to Christiansted Harbor on St Croix, the island that would be home for five years of servitude.

The rattle and clank of anchor chains reverberated around the enclosed space as those below decks stuffed clothing into sacks. Vaanee looked at his brother's few possessions and added them to his own.

"Soon you will see your mother," Vaanee said to the child by his side. He wondered about the father whose name was never mentioned.

"I will see you again?" Farhad asked, his face downcast.

"Of course, boy, of course."

There was little wind to temper the heat rising from the wooden decks as the holds were emptied and the indentured Indians lined up. Once again they were subjected to an intrusive medical examination, this time by the Danish crown physician.

"Today is the 15th of June, 1863." The sonorous tones came from the behatted governor's representative as he eyed the bedraggled group on deck, a man whose duty it was to discharge mandates laid down by the India Government Act of the year before. "Upon, or thereabouts, this day five years hence you will be given the opportunity to repatriate to India or remain on St Croix. For the latter you will receive a bounty."

Vaanee and the others looked blankly at each other until another man stepped forward to translate the Danish into English, which the compounder translated into Hindi. Farhad fidgeted until Vaanee laid a hand on the boy's shoulder.

"Maan is where?" Farhad asked, searching for his mother.

"Tscht, we will find her when we are on land. Be still now."

Climbing down the rope ladder with Farhad above him, Vaanee wondered how the women in their saris would manage. The lighter soon filled and was rowed to shore where, after sloshing through the shallows, they were once again put in lines and told to wait. Vaanee looked around, noting the blackness of men and women, some blacker even than the blackest Tamil from Southern India. Others more light-skinned, like Indian nobility.

"She is there!" Farhad's excited voice brought Vaanee back to the present. Farhad grabbed Vaanee's hand and pointed as he made to run to his mother. "Maan, maan, I am here."

Vaanee caught him. "Wait! Let us wait a moment and see what will happen next." He kept his voice quiet but his eyes found the boy's mother and saw her head shake, an almost imperceptible movement. He looked more closely at the line of women opposite them and wondered if she was with child. "Ayee." His mutter dissolved in the general murmur around them. He kept his hand on Farhad's shoulder and squeezed.

"We must wait, little brother. You must trust me."

Another man addressed them.

"My name is Harry Rainals. I am the British Consul and am here to ensure the terms of your contracts are met." Mr Rainals waited for the translator then continued. "You will receive a daily ration of flour, rice, dhal or peas, ghee or lard, a supply of coriander seed, black pepper and turmeric. This ration, one half for a minor, will be provided at a deduction of 20 cents from the daily wages."

"Sahib?" Vaanee's voice rang out and he felt those around him edge away. "Sahib, forgive me. But what deduction for my brother. He is only ten."

The Consul glared, consulted his notes and told the compounder, who translated, "Minors, those under fifteen years of age, will be charged 10 cents."

"*Jee shukriya.*" Vaanee thanked the man. He sensed Farhad's glance, and squeezed the boy's shoulder harder.

"May I continue?" The Consul's tone was lost in translation. "You will be granted generous accommodations on the estates to which you have been assigned. I will ensure your employers comply with these terms. Work hard and well and you will return to India richly rewarded for your service."

The white man turned and climbed stone steps of a yellow building set to the side of a fort, smaller than Indian forts but still with cannons peering into the distance. Vaanee, as the swirl of strange tongues surrounded him, determined he would learn these foreign words.

Farhad wriggled under Vaanee's firm grip. "Tscht, stay still, brother. Wait."

Other white men moved towards the group as the compounder called names. Vaanee's grasp tightened as he saw Farhad's mother step forward with no glance their way. He put his hand over the child's mouth and hissed, "Be still. Wait." They watched as Indians hauled themselves up into drays, then settled on their possessions. A plume of dust following each cart as they trundled away from the harbor.

"Vaanee."

He raised his hand. "Please, sahib," he spoke through the interpreter. "This boy, Farhad, he is a hard worker. He may come with me? His mother is with child and cannot care for him. He is not wanted."

"Why should he go with you?" The words came out of the white man's mouth via the compounder.

"Because he became my brother when my own brother, Taarank, died on the ship." Vaanee felt Farhad squirm and he squeezed the child's shoulder harder. "It will be cheaper for you, sahib, he is half price. A good worker."

The white man pushed his hat higher off his brow revealing shaggy red eyebrows, and walked closer to inspect both the man and boy. He kicked the ground, shrugged and nodded. "Take the mother's name and 'is name," he ordered the compounder, "the records must indicate the boy is coming to Estate Hope and not elsewhere. I want no complaints from other planters." He turned and walked toward the same yellow building as a black man moved forward and harried twenty-one men, four women and one child to the dray.

With no time to adapt to either their surroundings, the climate or their weakened state from the voyage, the indentured coolies started work. Many, though used to field work, did not know the workings of a sugarcane plantation. Vaanee, having been recruited from the cane growing area of Uttar Pradesh, became the de facto leader, more and more relied upon to train his fellow Indians by Mr Doyle, the red-headed overseer.

Estates, unwilling to spend money on accommodations for the indentured laborers, housed them in former slave quarters. Sometimes eleven to a small, airless room. Washing, cooking and ablutions took place outdoors and bred a variety of illnesses.

It did not take long for sickness to pervade the cramped quarters. This despite the *yajna* ritual and mantras chanted with fire being burned in a pot, not a pit, before entering any of the rooms when they first arrived at the plantation by the sea. They had no priest to perform the ceremony designed to erase ghosts and negative energy but still each hut was protected by a black doll over the door, as was the Hindu custom.

Little credence had been given to the different caste, cultural and even linguistic backgrounds of the Indians. Some differences may have been lessened by the long sea journey but now, on land, they came once again to the fore. And four women amongst twenty-one men quickly roused animosity that living quarters did little to lessen. A married couple had even been billeted in a room with three single men.

To protect Farhad from harsh fieldwork, Vaanee argued he would be better employed in the village. That too caused tension amongst the women who believed a child was taking easier work from their rotation. And whilst the overseer enforced labor discipline, any domestic disturbance was deemed an issue to be resolved by the Indians themselves.

It was dysentery and death that brought the matter to the British Consul.

Befriended by an estate worker from St Kitts, Vaanee and Farhad learnt the rudiments of English from Henry. He also taught them about slavery. The more Vaanee learned, the more he believed the general attitude was that any dark-skinned person was considered inferior, of a lesser caste.

It in some ways matched the Indian caste system, ingrained from birth, wherein everyone knew exactly where they fell in the social order, an order that could not be changed even by marriage. Many Indians of higher caste, particularly Brahmans, were known to equal and better in some cases any European, a concept that to Vaanee's mind became muddled and dissolved on St Croix. That, along with squalid accommodation and the promised rations that did not appear, led to deep worker discontent.

The British Consul, learning of a young man's death at Estate Hope, visited the plantation early the next year and demanded to meet with the laborers. Mr Doyle, not happy at disrupting the workday, insisted the meeting take place at dawn.

"Sahib," Vaanee hesitated, he had never spoken English to an Englishman before. He stood taller. "Sahib," he started again, "please, not good. Many in one room. No, no ...." he searched for the word, ".... toilet." He silently thanked Henry, his Kittitian friend. "Bad for me. All."

"It is noted." Mr Rainals spoke slowly. "Who taught you English?"

It took a moment for Vaanee to sort out the strange words before he answered, "My friend."

"Good. I might need you."

"Sahib," Vaanee surprised himself with his insistence. "Daha, he, he die, like .... pig. Not good. No doctor-sahib. Man also die." Vaanee mimed a hanging.

"Yes. I know. I'm sorry."

"And eat." Vaanee could feel tension emanating off the other indentured workers standing in the quadrangle outside the sugar factory. He didn't know if it was their anger at the estate management or fear at his temerity. He glanced down at Farhad standing at his side. "No get eat. Only ...." he rubbed his fingers together in the universal sign of money.

"What?"

"'E's a trouble-maker, Rainals." Anger made Mr Doyle's voice tremble through his rough brogue. "They get food. I'll deal with 'im later."

The Consul looked at Vaanee, his hand protective on the boy's shoulder.

"He is not to be punished, Doyle."

"Work much. No food," Vaanee spoke again. The image of an older man who lived in the cell next to his swam into view. The overseer had publicly flogged him for demanding lentils and flour. "Sahib?"

The Consul nodded and Vaanee, not looking at Mr Doyle, continued, "Man he beat man. No good."

The Consul nodded again, his annoyance palpable, his face growing grimmer by the moment. Vaanee wasn't sure to whom it was directed.

"Come, Doyle."

"Get to work. Vaanee, see to it." The overseer shouted, his high boots stamping as he followed the Consul back to the Estate great house.

Vaanee and the others waited to see what, if anything, would happen. Tempers became even more volatile, particularly among the younger men, when it was discovered that not only were Indians paying 40 cents for provisions that they did not always get, but that the local work force paid only 25 cents.

Another indentured worker from Estate Hope committed suicide, one ran away and was not found. There were times, in the middle of the night as thoughts mimicked the dark, when Vaanee was tempted to flee too but Farhad, soft snuffles coming from the sleeping boy, always stopped him.

"What nonsense is this?" Rage funneled around the Indian compound like a cyclone. "We get no lentils, no flour to make chapatis, no ghee." The man, one of the oldest in the group, flung a handful of cornmeal on the ground.

"Why do you do that?" A woman screeched and darted to scrape it up from the dust.

"They do not follow their contract," said another. "Vaanee, you must talk to English sahib again."

"Me?" Vaanee felt the eyes of all upon him. "Me. It is always me who must make trouble." He stretched his neck where a whiplash wound refused to heal. "The man, Doyle, waits for me to make a mistake. And if I do not, he makes one up."

"Ayee, man. You must tell the Consul-sahib."

"Will that make it better for Vaannee?" Farhad's voice piped in, one minute high, the next the deeper tone of an adolescent.

"Tscht, quiet, child," said Manju, the oldest of the women. Her face was worn. She looked older than thirty. Raped on board *Mars*, her husband had then died, like Taarank, of typhoid and had also been tipped into the ocean. Outspoken and refusing to wear a white sari, she was treated with some caution.

"It is better you speak to the Consul-sahib again, Vaanee. You speak English. You must tell him about the beatings from Doyle," Manju said.

"What foolishness!" Vaanee laughed. "You think I can just summon the Consul-sahib? How would I do that?"

"You can write."

"In Hindi," Vaanee corrected a man, whose skin was a mess of open sores.

"Get your friend. Henry," said another.

"No. Why should he be punished for our complaints? The black men, too, have problems." Vaanee frowned.

"Not the same," said Manju.

"Why?" asked Vaanee. "They cannot leave. We have only five years to bear this burden."

"If we live five years." Aadhan spoke for the first time. He too had been subjected to the lash.

"We will," Vaanee promised. "We will return home with our riches."

"We have two more years, man. Then a sea voyage. You think we will all make it?"

"Yes, we must have faith in the gods," Vaanee answered.

"Hell is truly in the south," said Manju, her tone dolorous.

"What nonsense is that?" Aadhan said. "St Croix is similar to Calcutta. And further north than our brothers and sisters in Chennai." He chuckled. "By your reckoning, you would put every Indian south of Bengal in hell." A smattering of laughter followed his comment.

"How do you know this?" Farhad asked.

Aadhan stroked his thin mustache, his voice quiet as he shrugged and said, "I have travelled. And seen sea charts. Vaanee is right. We must have faith."

Working nine or ten hours a day, six days a week, longer at crop time when the cut cane had to be quickly transported to the factory for crushing before fermentation started, left little time for relaxation. Sometimes a group would walk to Frederiksted, the town on the western end of the island, to buy produce from the market or to flounder in the sea.

"Ayee, the sea is not like our rivers back home," Farhad said the first time they went to the beach. His delighted squeals prompted others to join him in the shallows where he chased translucent silver fish.

Now nearly fourteen, he had grown tall and sinewy after long hours in the fields, where he had moved after his twelfth birthday. Often on a Sunday he and Vaanee would go to the beach south of the town, the long stretch of white sand burning his feet as he ran into the sparkling water. Unlike many of the workers he had taught himself how to swim and dive amongst the fish and coral.

"Namaste." A man, an Indian from another plantation, called from the shore and beckoned them both. "I must speak with you."

"What is this? No more nonsense," Vaanee muttered as he wiped his eyes and squeezed water from his dhoti. His back was a lattice of scars. Doyle, despite the Consul's demand he not be punished, took pleasure in making Vaanee the scapegoat for any misdemeanor, real or imagined. He still stood tall but his face was often drawn with pain.

"Namaste," Vaanee and youth greeted the stranger.

"I am Javeed," the man said. "You are Farhad?"

"*Haan*," Farhad nodded.

"Your mother, she is from Madhepura, in Bihar province?"

Farhad nodded. "What news?" The pain of her desertion had eased, helped by Vaanee explaining she must have feared she would be unable to care for him. Of his father there had been no comment. He remembered asking why then it was easier for Vaanee to take him in. It is always easier for men, he'd replied. Farhad had wondered over the years whether Vaanee, after numerous whippings, still thought that.

Vaanee asked, "What is this about? I understand she is on the east of the island. We have not seen her since our arrival."

"She is dead."

The stark words dropped Farhad to the sand, his knees drawn up to his chin. Tears mingled with saltwater that dripped from his hair. He wondered why. Perhaps he had still hoped to see her again. Even if only on the ship back to India.

"When? Sickness?" Vaanee asked. His voice quiet.

Javeed shook his head. "Two days now. By her own hand."

"Tscht!" Vaanee sat beside Farhad, his head bowed, his feet tickled by wavelets.

"There is more." The man's voice came from behind them. "There is a child. A girl. About three years."

"Ayee." Farhad looked at the man he considered his true brother. "I do not understand. My mother would leave her why?"

"She is pale-skinned," Javeed's voice was sad. "Your mother, she had much pain. The child is a child of rape by a white man. She told me a seaman on the ship. But also the sahib here took her many times. I am sorry, Farhad. Our own people are not always kind either. Your mother was shunned by most in the village. I tried to help her."

The youth nodded. "She is where? My sister?"

"The sahib wishes to place her in an orphanage."

"No. I am her brother. I shall take her." Farhad heard Vaanee's sigh.

"Think, boy. How will we care for her? She is a baby. You are now in the fields. How?" he asked again.

"Your mother," Javeed interrupted their words, "she waited until the child was old enough to survive without her."

Vaanee shook his head, a thousand objections formed but he swallowed them all. "Doyle will be displeased. We will not get money for her food."

"I will share my rations. One more year and I will get full rations. I will fish every night."

"And who will care for her by day? Doyle will not allow you to leave the fields. He is already angry that Manju can no longer work them."

"There, Vaanee. There is the answer. I will ask Manju."

"Ayee, Farhad." His brother looked out to sea. "Perhaps the sahib is right. Perhaps it will be better for the child to go to the orphanage. She is pale-skinned. Perhaps someone will give her a home."

"*Nahin na!*" It was an explosion from Farhad. "No. My mother left me. But you took me in. I will not leave my sister to strangers. She is at your estate now?" he asked.

Javeed shook his head. "No, Farhad, I brought her with me. She is under the trees." He pointed.

Farhad stood and ran up the beach, then stopped and called back, "What is her name?"

"She is called Shanti."

Vaanee snorted, a slight smile relieved his grim face. "It seems I am to have two sisters with that name."

Doyle's anger, as expected, was frenzied when he learned of the child's presence. Perspiration, despite the lateness of the afternoon, dripped through his red eyebrows to balance on white lashes before forming a streak down his cheeks as he flogged Farhad, the first time the youth had felt the whip. After the first lash Vaanee stepped forward to try and take his place but was pushed aside. Instead he had to watch as Farhad fought tears of anger and pain as, by the fourth lash, blood flicked from his back. Two more then, grunting, Doyle coiled the whip and strode away, flinging words over his shoulder, "Any sign of trouble and I'll drown the bitch."

Vaanee helped Farhad to their room which, thanks to the Consul-sahib's insistence, now housed either a married couple or two or three men, instead of six or more. They knew not all the estates had complied with his demands and had come to believe Doyle had agreed only because he did not want the Englishman arriving unannounced for inspections.

Shanti sat in the corner watching Vaanee's every move as he bathed her brother's back with a mixture of aloe and water. In two days, she had charmed both men and Manju after the lame woman grudgingly agreed to care for her during the day in exchange for fish, and produce from the small patch they had planted.

"I hate that man," Farhad said through clenched teeth. "I hate him for what he has done to you, and now me."

"Tscht, boy," Vaanee said, squeezing the bloodied cloth, "he is not worth your hate. He is godless. We have Ganesh." He looked up startled to see Manju and the three other women at the door.

"Namaste," he said, casting a glance at the hazel-eyed child sucking her thumb. Tiny gold studs gleamed in her ears.

They returned the greeting, their eyes flicking from Shanti to Farhad. "She will be safe with us," Manju said. "We have talked. We will help care for her. She will be a child of the village."

The tears Farhad had kept at bay filled his eyes and he burrowed his head into his arms, his shoulders shaking.

"You are a good boy," Manju said. "A good brother. She will be safe," she repeated.

"Thank you, my sisters, thank you."

Both men stood and bowed to the women, with their hands together. One, Reshmi, a petite but strong girl with pert eyes, looked at Vaanee from under long lashes.

Shanti became the darling of even the most hardened of men. One whittled a doll, another fashioned a cart from a box and carved wheels. Another man returned from the Sunday market with a straw hat to protect Shanti's fair skin. The girl hoping for Vaanee's favor made clothes - a child's dhoti and shirt from his never-worn pagri and a donated threadbare cotton sari. Vaanee's concern that it would be hard to find food for her never became an issue. Like her namesake, Vaanee's sister, the child was serene, rarely crying. She slept on the mat, curled like a kitten, next to Farhad and followed both men slavishly, demanding to be picked up sometimes but more often tottering beside them as they did chores at the end of each day.

Manju, as if all the sadness of her life had lifted, cared for the little girl like she were her own when the men and other women were in the fields. A kind of calm, a sense of purpose, had enveloped the village since Shanti's arrival, as if all the pent-up emotions of servitude had found an outlet in a helpless infant.

Walking along the pebbly beach by the sea that lapped the south shore of Estate Hope one evening after Shanti was sleeping, Farhad, skimming stones, said, "It was shame, eh?" The question had been mulling since his mother's death. "Javeed said those on her estate shunned her." His voice was sad. "It was not her doing. Neither on the ship nor here." He felt Vaanee's nod. "Why then do we not feel shame? It is the same child. She is a child of rape. She is fair. Yet all here embrace Shanti. Why is this?"

Vaanee was silent as they walked. Farhad knew better than to interrupt his thoughts. He would speak when ready with his words. "I too have considered this. I believe it is because we did not know of your mother's troubles on board, nor did we know what happened at her estate. That is one thing we have to be thankful for here. Doyle has left our women alone."

"He has a black woman," Farhad said. "Henry has spoken of it."

"I know. But some white men take many women. Then discard them." Vaanee paused. "It is not just white men, Farhad. Many men are capable of brutality. In India too. Perhaps if Shanti had not been so light, it would have been easier. But your mother could not live with the shame of a bastard child to a white man, even though it was no fault of hers. She could not have gone back to your village. They would not have welcomed her, even with her money from here."

As the end of their servitude neared, conversations around the cooking pots each evening turned to repatriation or re-indenture for a further five years. The latter would ensure a bounty of $40 without forfeiting their return passage to India after ten years of service. It was a discussion that went back and forth between Vaanee and Farhad as they lay on their mats, sounds of the sea thrumming through the still night, Shanti sleeping between them.

"My village, Madhepura, is no longer my village," Farhad said in April, two months before their indenture ended. "It is backward. People with little knowledge of the world. They will not take Shanti to their hearts."

"Brother, it is many years since you were there. Perhaps it has changed," Vaanee said.

Farhad shook his head. "And you? You are happy to return to the fields around your home?" Farhad asked. "To your other sister, Shanti? Or perhaps you wish to marry Reshmi?" His voice was serious. "She makes eyes at you!"

A snort disturbed the night. "Really, Farhad! No. I do not wish to wed the silly girl. Though she is gentle with Shanti." Rain beat a light tattoo on the roof. "I promised my mother I would return with riches. But I have under $50. It is not what I had hoped."

"That is more than me," Farhad said. "But I do not want to spend a day longer in this place. Doyle is a pig." He paused. "And the voyage. *Nahin na*. I am not going back."

Vaanee, his voice reflective, said, "We, here on Estate Hope… it is unusual, I believe, with regard the child."

"I know," Farhad said.

"So, you not want to return to India at all?" Vaanee confirmed.

"No." Farhad's voice was firm.

"So, what shall we do, my brother?"

"Vaanee." The British Consul's voice rang out, "do you wish to re-sign?"

"No, sahib," he answered.

"Farhad?"

"No, sahib," Farhad replied, looking down at his sister, now just over five years old.

The same question rang along the line of indentured Indians at Estate Hope. They were watched by local laborers, many from down the Caribbean island chain. Whilst some friendships were formed, like Vaanee and Henry, there was little real interaction between former enslaved workers and indentured Indians. Due in part because the importation of Indians lessened the bargaining power for better work conditions and pay for those from the islands.

The final night at Estate Hope was one of subdued relief tinged with moments of delight. Only three men decided to sign on for another five years, and four were prepared to face the return journey to India.

"So, Vaanee," Aadhan said, his face glowing in the reflection from the fire, "we are agreed?" Reshmi sat close to him, a red bindi on her forehead and gold bangles on her arm reflecting her married status, her swollen belly showing the child growing in her womb.

Vaanee nodded, his glance taking in Farhad and Shanti. He smiled across the circle to Manju. "Yes." They were a family. Manju was not yet his legal wife but a promise had been made. Some of their combined money had gone to purchasing gold, easier to conceal from any thief or customs agent. "Yes," Vaanee repeated. "We will go with you. We will start a new life, a new community."

"Shanti?" Farhad looked down at his sister sitting in the protective enclosure of his crossed legs, her usual place. "Shanti, can you remind me where we are going to live?"

She looked up at him, her serene face broke into a grin.

"Yes, brother. We are going to Trinidad."

Footnote:

The agreement to send Indian indentured labor to St Croix was in part due to testimony in 1861 from the Bishop of Antigua. He wrote, "… in a West India Colony, perhaps, nowhere are the labourers so comfortably domiciled as in the Danish Island of St Croix; there the Labourer is invariably under annual contract, his dwelling being provided for him on the Estate. The Labourers' houses are under the inspection of the government which is equally careful to provide for them medical attendance in sickness, education for the children, and the asylums for the aged and infirm … there is no denying that a parental care is exercised by the government over the labouring class whose rights are jealously guarded at any rate; they nowhere present to the eye of the stranger such a picture of domestic comfort and healthiness as in that picturesque little island."

The treatment of Indian indentured laborers on St Croix was marginally better than elsewhere in the Caribbean. However the living conditions for both black and Indian workers were squalid rather than 'picturesque' and the death rate was high, attributed by some to there being only six medical doctors and two apothecaries on an island catering to a population of about 23,000. One reason for the lack of doctors was the need for them to have been trained in Denmark in order to set up a practice in the Danish West Indies.

Mr Rainals, the British Consul, tried through the Secretary of State for India to improve the situation. A commission of three public functionaries was set up on St Croix. Their opinion, after limited input from only two planters, stated 'the system was working well.' A statement with which the governor concurred. One reason given for the lack of care was the high cost of importing workers from as far away as India in relation to the profit gained from a declining sugar industry.

The experiment to import indentured labor from India to St Croix did not proceed after the initial five years (1863 - 1868). In 1869, James Parton of Boston wrote, "I have read the Laws relating to the laboring population of the Danish Islands, and they appear well adapted to secure rights and happiness of a people recently emancipated.... The operation of those wise and just laws prevented the Danish Islands from lapsing into the condition of Jamaica."

Mr Parton's rosy outlook on worker conditions throughout St Croix did not reflect the reality. The lack of freedom of movement of estate workers and the harshness of their conditions led directly to the worker rebellion, Fireburn, of 1878.

AMERICAN FOR 100 YEARS

I t was a good day. An easterly breeze ruffled whitecaps offshore and flowery hats onshore as women, men and a smattering of children watched marching bands and majorettes parade past the bedecked dais filled with local and international worthies.

Expectation hovered. Said dignitaries made their way to a large marquee under which islanders, long-time residents, newbies like me, and tourists, including a contingent of Danish visitors, wafted programs back and forth to move air along the humid rows.

Would Denmark apologize for past indignities? For the human tragedy of the transatlantic slave trade? Would the mainland listen to entreaties by islanders for full US citizenship allowing a vote in presidential elections?

Chatter along the lines was hopeful. Cheerful. Who doesn't like a parade, the promise of promises - even if they are later unfulfilled, the anticipation of revelry, jazz and fireworks? Meanwhile steel pans from a local elementary school and the Copenhagen Brass Ensemble took turns keeping the masses entertained.

A wreath floated in the bay. A memorial to the ancestors and, in particular, Alberta Viola Roberts, a girl taken from her family and transported to Copenhagen at the age of four to be displayed in the Tivoli Gardens - an oddity to be ogled. As fate would have it, she was buried in that cold and distant land on

31st March, 1917 - the day Denmark sold the Danish West Indies to the United States of America for 25 million dollars in gold.

The brass band struck up *Der er et Yndigtland,* and voices from the Danish contingent proudly sang their national anthem as the *Dannebrog* slid down Fort Christiansvaern's flagpole to be replaced by the fluttering Stars and Stripes. Then came the Star-Spangled Banner, followed by the Virgin Islands March, written by Alton Adams in 1920. The lyrics, 'All hail the Virgin Islands, Em'ralds of the sea', filtering around the tent in a swirl of pride, and hope.

An invocation was followed by opening remarks by Sonia Jacobs Dow, who commented that islanders were citizens of nowhere from 1917 - 1927 when the newly-acquired islands were under naval administration. We were exhorted to remember "blood, sweat and tears are inextricably mixed in this soil" and that "this celebration is more than a moment".

Each year, on Transfer Day, the proceedings are interspersed with a naturalization ceremony when new citizens swear allegiance to their new country. This year 20 men and women from eight countries became Americans to the sound of children's laughter as they rolled down the slope from the fort - their frivolity lending an air of joyful abandon to the occasion. Further proof that the US is founded on the willingness of foreigners to renounce their birth countries and apply their skills to enriching their new country.

After the temporary court was adjourned, politicians returned to the lectern. Congresswoman, The Honorable Stacey E Plaskett carried on the theme of disenfranchisement, remarking that whilst the purchase of the Danish West Indies was the most costly land purchase in US history, no provision was made for the islanders in the document - ensuring they became essentially "a marooned people".

Then came the speech of the day - spoken eloquently in a language not his own - by the Danish Prime Minister, The Honorable Lars Løkke Rasmussen. He began by saying a special bond of friendship existed between the Virgin Islands and Denmark, "a touch of common destiny that time cannot erase."

While not apologizing for bygone atrocities, Prime Minister Rasmussen did acknowledge them saying, "There is no justification for the exploitation of men, women and children under the Danish flag." He said the term 'dreamer', as founder of the first black newspaper and civil rights activist, David Hamilton Jackson, was called by a Danish governor, was in all likelihood meant as an insult, but that in today's world it would be considered an honor. He reflected on the fact that different histories, different stories were taught in both Denmark and the VI. We were reminded that "we must acknowledge what happened in the past but we can't undo the past - what we can do is look to the future."

It was a smooth transition to the announcement of a 5-year scholarship program to be given at the University of the Virgin Islands. It is students who "must take destiny into their own hands," Rasmussen said.

The Prime Minister's words were in stark contrast, both in content and delivery, to those uttered by Secretary of The Interior Ryan Zinke, who was the most the senior representative of the US government. His vacuous introduction to a letter from President Trump was a disgrace, made even worse by platitudes in the letter from the head of the free world. One got the impression the letter was a cut-and-paste job - you know the type, insert state and date, and sign here please, Mr President. No credence given to the concerns of Virgin Islanders - that of full-voting rights for citizens. An unctuous attempt to appease the USVI, America's Caribbean, without offering even a modicum of hope for improvement.

Kenneth E Mapp, Governor of The Virgin Islands, rounded out the official celebrations by commenting that, "living in the past has little value on our future. But knowing our past is important to our future."

Black limousines drove dignitaries away - the program to be repeated on St Thomas at 2pm. Meanwhile on St Croix the crowds dispersed along the Boardwalk, back to cars parked haphazardly on our street, or to local watering holes. To reconvene as the sun set in a tickle of pink and mauve over masts bobbing in Christiansted harbor to the sounds of Eddie Russell and his jazz band.

And then the boom, the hiss, the thrill of the sky dissolving in a shower of sparkling colors as fireworks saluted 100 years of being American!

MARIA HEADS FOR AMERICA'S CARIBBEAN

I t's bad news week. Actually it's been a bad news month, particularly in the two places I currently have the privilege of calling home - Houston, Texas and St Croix, US Virgin Islands.

Houston felt Hurricane Harvey's wrath as swathes of rain pounded streets, turning city and suburbs into rushing waterways. Some areas are prone to flooding and the sagacity of building homes on old rice fields and flood plains will be debated for a long time, particularly as government buyouts are sought. I imagine one word will be repeated often - greed. Of both those selling the land initially and those developing it. So too the decision of when and by how much the dams and reservoirs were opened to release pressure on old infrastructure. But it's easy to criticize after the fall, or in this case, the flood.

Then Irma barreled through another place I hold dear - Tortola - the main island of the British Virgin Islands, and a place I have been visiting since 1967. I was last there in April this year to visit my family, who thankfully are safe though not unscathed. The Dick-Reads have been an integral part of the BVI since the early 1960s; there before tourism took off and the financial institutions set up shop; before the Purple Palace took on the more sophisticated moniker of The Bougainvillea Clinic. #thatbitchIrma devastated those Virgins, reducing homes and businesses to piles of matchstick rubble. Roofs ripped off, rooms rudely exposed. Lives destroyed.

Irma also had her way with St John and St Thomas, two of the US Virgin Islands. Irma skimmed St Croix, forty nautical miles to the south, and grateful inhabitants rallied and sent supplies and succor to her sister islands.

And now St Croix is under threat.

Hurricane Maria is intent on venting her Category 5 rage on St Croix and, as I sit here safe in Houston, my heart is squeezed. For our neighbors, for our friends, for the historic richness and beauty of the lesser-known Virgin Island. And for our West Indian home which we have lovingly restored.

As I wonder what I can do to help in the aftermath of this hurricane's projected fury I am reminded St Croix has withstood nature's caprice many times. Alexander Hamilton wrote of the 1772 hurricane in a letter to his father saying, "I take up my pen just to give you an imperfect account of the most dreadful hurricane that memory or any records whatever can trace, which happened here on the 31st ultimo at night..... Good God! what horror and destruction—it's impossible for me to describe - or you to form any idea of it. It seemed as if a total dissolution of nature was taking place."

The Danish West Indies were again slammed by a vicious hurricane in 1867, with the subsequent tidal wave driving the *USS Monongahela* ashore at Frederiksted. The hurricane, unnamed in those days, was instrumental in bringing about the end of the plantation system as well as discouraging the US from purchasing the islands from Denmark.

The modern benchmark for hurricanes on St Croix is Hugo which wracked and wrapped the island in total destruction in 1989. Then came Marilyn in 1995 which killed 10, and Omar in 2008 which sank 40 boats spewing oil onto pristine beaches.

The island though is resilient, and the inhabitants resolute. Whatever terror Maria throws at St Croix, she will not win. She might dampen the spirits for a while, tamp down her exuberance and charm, but St Croix, with assistance, will rebound.

There is horror and destruction, degradation and disaster in many parts of the world but I will be doing my best to keep St Croix in the public eye. Particularly that of the US mainland, some of whose newsreaders seem unable to grasp the fact that the US Virgin Islands are the responsibility of the US. They paid 25 million dollars in gold coin for them in 1917. They should not let this centennial year be the year America's Caribbean is forgotten.

So as others gather tarpaulins and water, medical supplies and baby formula, I will be trying to keep St Croix in the public conscience. I will still launch my debut novel, *Fireburn*, based in 1870s St Croix, on October 1st, 2017. It catalogues a fictitious hurricane, as well as the historical rebellion of 'fireburn' on October 1st, 1878.

St Croix has withstood much. It can and will withstand more. It must - it is dear to me.

A CALYPSONIAN VET

"**G**ood afternoon, Doc Petersen?"

"Yes." The voice is distracted.

"My name is Apple Gidley." I launch into my spiel hoping the man will buy into it.

"What's it called?"

"*Crucian Fusion.*"

He laughs. "I like it. Sure, we can talk."

I turn in at the sign that reads 'Doc Petersen's Beach Camp' and bump along the drive. I'm not sure which house is my destination so park next to a tented area, gulp some water, square my shoulders, mask up, clamber down from Otto, our truck, and call.

"Hello, good morning, Doc?"

"In here," floats out from the nearest building.

Doc greets me, glasses perched on his nose. He is wearing a yellow, floral Hawaiian shirt and swimming shorts. His feet are bare. I glimpse, through the open door and windows, and between palm trees, a narrow beach trickling down to the Caribbean lapping the sand in brilliant sparkles.

"God, that's beautiful," I say.

"Yeah, it is. Sit, sit." Doc points to a chair six feet distant. "I have to finish this, otherwise I'll forget."

I check my notes, rootle around for my phone so I may record our chat, then watch him balance a check book.

"So," he takes his glasses off and rubs his face before reaching for a mask. "How do you want to do this?"

"I'll start with a question and then we'll see where it takes us. Is that okay?" I am learning that if I can find that magic opener the rest falls into place.

Doc nods.

"Your musical career started with a ukulele?"

He laughs, and we are off. This conversation is going to be fun.

"Lots of us had them. You could buy a ukulele for $3.50. Or make one. From sardine cans and nylon string." My mind flies to my ukulele-making lesson with Stanley Jacobs. "As pre-teens, we'd play ball then end up on the street corner, playing music and singing."

"Did you play music at St Patrick's in Frederiksted?"

He snorts, and I have the hardest time not asking, "What's up, Doc?" How clichéd that would sound. I keep quiet.

"The nuns at St Patrick's decided to form a school band and, in the 4th or 5th grade, I played the mellophone, then the mother superior asked me to play drums." Doc pauses in recollection. "I wasn't a good student."

"Of the drums?"

"No, everything. I got kicked out of Catholic school."

"Really?" I laugh. This pillar of the community was expelled. "Why?"

"Ah, let's just say I wasn't a regular attendee. I was good at skipping class, especially after lunch break. Catching crabs, or fishing or swimming. When I got older I'd pal around with older boys and the horses. Then in 6th grade, Sister Robertson taught me. She rapped me with a ruler for falling asleep in class and I tried to pull her veil off. It didn't end well."

"Were your parents mad? What happened?"

He laughs again.

"My mom never said a thing. St Pat's uniform was khaki pants and a white shirt with a green tie. So I'm dressed, go to breakfast and my mom pulls off my tie and tosses me a maroon one. I was headed to public school, Claude O Markoe. Same uniform, different tie. It was great. I had a lot of friends there already." He puts his feet on the coffee table. They are swollen. He has gout and walking is painful. "You know we all mixed together - didn't matter if someone's parent had more money than another."

"Did you still skip school, play music?"

"Not so much. I was a chunky kid so the music teacher gave me a sousaphone - you know, the instrument that wraps around the head. I still played drums and the ukulele, though I was only an average player. And I started singing."

I am longing to ask Doc to sing but instead just nod.

"When I was about thirteen we formed a calypso band - 'Sons of the Modernaires'. There were older kids in a band called 'The Modernaires'. It seemed right we'd be the sons of...." His chuckle is deep, enveloping, like his voice.

"Do you read music?" I ask.

"Not any more. I did for a while at school, but my singing was more unstructured. I listened to Lord Kitchener, the Mighty Sparrow, all those Calypsonians coming out of Trinidad. Then at fourteen or fifteen we split up and went to different schools. I went to Central High. There was a talent show and the background band were 'The Playboys'."

It is my turn to snort.

Doc grins. "I tried out, and the band - the leader was Eddie Russell - asked if I wanted to join them as singer. When Eddie left, Tarco, the bass player, took over and we became 'Tarco and the Playboys'. We played all over - at festivals, carnivals, on St Thomas and St John. And the BVI. I got a look at adult life."

"What did your parents think of all this?"

"My mother was a staunch support. She was a busy lady - a nurse, a baker, then she started a nightclub and bar. I used to sing there too."

When, I wonder, did Doc, before he was Doc and just Eugene, get time to study? To realize animals were to play a large part in his life?

"Next to the fish market was a village called Cologne, where Turtle's Deli is now. There was a bar, a gamble house rum-shop called Flatbush. Cowboys from Annaly would ride into town on Sundays. They'd tie their horses to the rail, like in a Western movie, while they went drinking. You know Guison?"

I shake my head but mention Hans Lawaetz had talked about him.

"Well, I used to pet the horses - I still remember some of the names - Tarzan and Chanka Chak. They'd be tied up till nine or ten at night so I'd take them water and some grass. I loved Sunday afternoons. You know, those cowboys would stagger out and scramble up and leave it to the horses to get them back to Annaly."

I have a vivid image of horses ambling home along rutted paths on sure hooves with their riders, in an inebriated state, swaying to their gait. St Croix of old. No fear of a lunatic racing around in the dark with no lights.

I'm brought back to the present by Doc's words.

"A guy gave me a horse to care for, when I was about thirteen. Then a year or so later I bought my first horse. That was a fine day."

Before I could ask how he could raise funds to buy a mare, he told me.

"I made good money from music gigs, and I paid $10 or $11 for her. Then I got a stallion I called Nature Boy. I had him about eight months before I learned he was stolen."

"What? What happened?"

"I knew the horse could run and back then there were races for non-thoroughbreds at Manning Race Track. I trained him on Dorsch Beach and in the hills, then entered him. He won his first race, then another time I was saddling up when a little white girl came up and started petting him. Her mom showed up and told me the horse had been taken from their home out East."

"Awkward."

"Yeah. I never bought anything from that friend again!" There's that rumble of laughter, like warm honey. "Anyway, the lady saw I was looking after the horse well and said I could keep him, as long as they could come and see him every now and then."

"Were you the jockey? Was it bareback racing?" Questions tumble as I think of bush races in Australia.

"No, no, I was too big, even then. Not all the owners could afford saddles but the jockeys had them. I raced that stallion four or five times, and won. I got a taste for racing, and winning. And training." Doc plods to the fridge. "You want a water?"

"No, thanks, I'm fine." He twists the cap, takes a swig and plomps back down. He glances up at the TV screen on the wall above his desk. It is muted but the message crawling across the CNN program offers something about the upcoming impeachment. Doc's attention swivels back to his horses. "I remember we saw a cargo plane flying over, like the one that brought the horses before from Puerto Rico. We raced to the airport to watch them unload. One was a big, beautiful grey mare and I asked how much." He laughs again. "I bought her. Spent all my money from singing on her, not just to buy her but to feed her. Here I was, a fifteen-year-old kid training and racing a champion."

"Heady stuff." I can imagine the euphoria of winning. "Is that when you decided to become a vet?"

The laugh rumbles again.

"I suppose it was. I was part of the FFA."

I know the reference to Future Farmers of America, having been a volunteer at Houston Livestock Show and Rodeo for a number of years.

Doc continues, "No one at the track used a vet, only in an emergency. We used to feed our horses on oats and molasses. And Cruzan Rum. We used that to rub their legs. And bush medicine. Witch hazel and stinging nettle, and Canadian Healing Oil. A universal panacea!" Doc pauses as if remembering the smell of camphor and creosote. "I told my teacher I wanted to be a horse doctor. He said, 'oh, an equine veterinarian?'" Doc is laughing hard. "I got muddled and thought he said 'vegetarian'. I knew there was a white guy down the road who was a vegetarian and I couldn't make the connection."

I'm laughing too at the thought of how this rather precocious teenager, rubbing shoulders with much older adults on equal terms at the race track, had confused the two.

"So, you go to Tuskegee. How was that?"

"Long. It takes seven years. First you get your animal science degree, pre-vet, then you get the medical degree. But good years. There were quite a few West Indians - thirty or forty from Guyana. But none of them were into music."

I am astounded. I don't think I've met a person from the Caribbean who doesn't sway, or play, to a beat of any kind.

"So I bought a second-hand guitar and taught myself to play."

I am given a lesson in converting a four-string uke to a six-string guitar and watch as Doc demonstrates on an air-guitar.

"A lot of calypso tunes are risqué, you know. They liked them!"

"Did you come home in the holidays?" I wonder how Doc could stay away from his beloved horses for any length of time.

"I had summer jobs at the Department of Agriculture - Ruddy Schulterbrandt worked there, the guy who used to give the horses vitamin injections. And Dr Crago, the VI State vet. I used to help out at his clinic even before I went to college. Dr Crago treated small animals in the morning then cattle and horses in the afternoons."

"After graduation did you come straight back to St Croix?"

"No, I interned at a small animal clinic in Boston, then Dr Crago invited me to join him. With Dr Hess, Paul Hess. We eventually went into partnership - in 1979."

"Where was it?" It was way before my arrival on island.

"Where the Progressive Clinic is. On Northside road."

"Oh. Kasey Canton. He saved Bonnie, my cat!" Yet another connection on this island I call home.

"Yeah, I did for him what Dr Crago did for me. Kasey worked for us in his vacations then when he graduated. Dr Hess and I had gone our separate ways by then. I didn't want any more partners so I made a deal with Kasey. Work with me for a couple of years, then we'll work something out so he would eventually get the clinic. Best decision I ever made. I retired in 2002. Ran a dog boarding kennel by the airport for a while."

I look at this man of many parts sitting on the couch and wonder how he squeezed extra hours out of each day to practice veterinary medicine, be involved at the race track and play music. It's time to get back to racing.

"Tell me about running the Randall "Doc" James Racetrack?" He is reflective.

"For a small population there is a big interest in racing. Well-off and poor want to be part of the 'Sport of Kings'."

"And queens." I think of HRH Queen Elizabeth, an avid racehorse-owner.

Doc ignores my comment, perhaps he doesn't hear.

"Back in the early 90's I got together with some people from Puerto Rico who developed a computer wagering system for small tracks, like ours. It took five years to formalize and in '98 we went to the US looking for investors. We got backing from principals at Philadelphia Park. The PR guys pulled out."

I'm getting a bit confused. "Then what happened?"

"We introduced simulcast and online betting. I developed a theory that a punter could call in from anywhere in the world but it would be logged as coming from St Croix. That way the VI Government could collect tax on winnings. As long as you kept it honest. There was one guy from Australia. Opened two accounts with $50,000 in each. One for win / place / show. One for exotic bets."

"Exotic bets?"

"Trifectas, daily doubles, that kind of thing," Doc explains. "Four years later the guy withdrew $600,000."

"Huh!" Who says betting is a mug's game?

"So the VI gets a 2% gross receipt tax and the Horse Racing Association gets 2%. It wasn't a non-profit so they paid taxes too. Eventually the partners backed out - they got a better deal from Oregon."

I can hear surf on the beach behind me. I know it's a good thing I'm not facing the ocean. Too easily distracted by the beauty and not giving my full attention to the man in the yellow shirt.

"Location, location, location," I say and look around the house where papers are spread liberally on every surface. Paintings hang, haphazardly. I'm surprised there is only one of a horse.

Doc grins. I sense another story.

"Before we had our partnership - Paul Hess and I, I was doing locum work on St Martin. I lived on the beach and decided that was what I wanted when I got home."

"I don't think I'd ever leave." The thought of sliding out of bed and straight into the sea is alluring.

"I was in the house further along." Doc points east, "Next to the Hibiscus."

I imagine the hotel in its heyday, very different to the overgrown tangle of coralita and tan-tan now growing through the floors.

"I would sit on the beach after work and play guitar and sing. Just for myself." Doc is lost in recollection. "I housesat for my sister and her husband sometimes. He was Danish. He had a reel-to-reel and I learnt all the tunes I could - blues, Brazilian, calypso. All the ones Harry Belafonte sang."

"What's your favorite?"

"I love bossanova."

"I've seen you move to that beat."

"Not so much now," he glances at his feet, once again propped up on the table. "Anyway, some guests at the hotel heard me, then the regular hotel musician, Calypso Joe, got sick and they asked me to play. I didn't have any equipment but, once I got paid, I bought some. Soon I was playing all over the island."

"How on earth did you manage your day job as well?"

"A lot of musicians like a few drinks and need all day to sleep it off. I only have the occasional rum and coke, so it was no problem. I'd play till 9 or 10, go home and sleep until 6 or 7 and start again."

"I remember a few years ago listening to you speak and play at the Synagogue. You spoke about a woman called Marie Richards. Was she a professional musician?"

"No, a nurse. I remember, as a kid in kindergarten, she'd come over and play guitar and sing. She wrote songs about food and animals. My two favorite things."

"Was she cariso or calypso?"

"Calypso. Though she could probably do both. Cariso is often extemporaneous - usually a woman, singing or chanting to a drumbeat." Doc dum de dums. "Like that. Different people come up and sing a verse."

"That's an art." It makes my careful word choice in writing seem rather feeble. I know I couldn't come up with lyrics, or even a story, on the fly.

"It is. But you know, you think of simple words that rhyme - he, she, we, tea, sea - and a basic pattern and it starts to fall into place."

"Similar to rap."

"Rap mimics the exact pattern of cariso. Cariso comes directly from slavery. *Swing Low Sweet Chariot*? You know what it means?"

I have heard the derivation but instead I tell Doc about the English rugby fans who sing it at matches. I don't go into the actions. I don't think he's impressed.

"When it was first sung it told of the need for a slave to keep her head down, stay safe because soon someone would come to take her to safety."

"The Underground Railroad?'

Doc nods.

"Even after abolition cariso, then calypso, were used to spread a political message. They still are." He chuckles and sings, "*We ain't want no percy pigtail.* You hear that?"

"Don't think so," I admit.

"Percy Gardine owned a grocery store in Frederiksted, famous for selling pigtails. He'd spoon some out of the brine barrel and wrap them in wax paper. Pigtails are used for seasoning peas and rice."

I do know that. A bit like chicken feet in Asia. Either way, I'm not a huge fan.

"Well, Percy was standing for the municipal council and one of his detractors wrote the song, *we aint want no percy pigtail.*"

Laughter echoes around the room.

"I grew up with calypso," I say. "A bit odd because I grew up in Africa and Asia. I used to cry whenever my father played *Jamaica Farewell.*" I sing, "But I'm sad to say I'm on my way, won't be back for many a day..." Doc joins me, "my heart is down, my head is turning around, I had to leave a little girl in Kingston town." We smile, and I tell him, "Dad would assure me he wasn't going to leave me." I feel sad in a happy kind of way. "Now I cry because it reminds me of him."

I pull myself together.

"Doc, you're a man of many parts - vet, musician, talk show host, writer."

Before I can go on, he lumbers to his feet and searches on a shelf. He hands me a copy of his memoir - *Tantan Tails and Tantan Tales.* It is far too thin for the countless stories this man must have.

"I think this is my last copy." He hands it to me.

I promise to return it.

"So, what have I missed? Any other talents? What about Island Center? I've heard it used to have fabulous shows. I found a photo of you and Curliss Solomon attaching foam to a new plywood floor a couple of years ago. After Hurricane Maria. I've only been once. To see the Caribbean Dance Studio perform."

Doc launches into another tale. "Penny drives, cake sales, all sorts of fundraisers to build it. The doors opened in '67. Initially it was mainly Broadway shows. I left for college in '68 so missed a lot of those early shows. But The Boston Pops came, Jose Feliciano, Nancy Wilson, and Ray Charles. Lots of great acts."

"Have you performed there?'

"Sure. And acted!"

I scrabble to keep up with the flowing stories and have a feeling this is going to be another good one.

"I'm playing at The Palms one evening and a guy at the bar asks me, 'Done any acting?'" Doc throws his head back on the sofa, his laughter circulates the room. It is hard not to laugh too.

"Oh God," I tell him, "I've been acting my whole life. He said I should audition, so me and Jackie, a girl who played piano at Frank's, both agree to try acting. I was pretty sure I could manage but hadn't realized I only had six weeks to learn the script."

"Hang on a minute," I interrupt his flow, "what was the play?"

"The Pajama Game. So we're three weeks into rehearsals and I'm still reading." Doc chuckles. "The director is getting worried. I tell him, 'relax, I can do it'. I go home, rehearse and by the next week I was off the book. He asked me, 'where did that come from?' I told him, 'I told you I could do it.'" Doc is laughing, again.

"Was that the start of your next career? Actor?" I am teasing.

Doc rumbles on. "Jesus Christ Superstar, I was Herod in that. Quite a few David Edgecombe plays."

"Wow." I have only seen one of the Montserrat-born playwright's plays, the one about Hubert Harrison, a Crucian considered by many as 'the foremost Afro-American intellect of his time' which was staged at the old Good Hope School, as part of UVI's first Literary Festival and Book Fair in 2015. I remember it as a powerful evening.

The man in the yellow shirt is quiet a moment.

"After Hurricane Hugo I got involved in the business side of things at Island Center. It was falling apart. We got a grant to stage an opera. And I was Monty Thompson's musical director for a while. We travelled all over."

I interrupt. "Monty, as in Monty from Caribbean Dance?"

He nods and sips from the bottle of water.

"Can we go back to your radio talk show? How did that come about?"

"Serendipity. Like most things. I was a guest on a show before the Constitution Convention."

"Which one? There've been a few."

"The fifth. In 2009. I was elected a delegate to the convention. Anyway the interview went well and Jonathan Cohen, the owner, suggested I have my own show, Constitution Corner. We had plans but I was kind of cocky. Ad libbed all the time. Former Governor Mapp was co-host. Then I had a music show - Nostalgia. Calypso, and I played some of my own music."

"Do you write your own lyrics and music, Doc?"

"A little. I wish I'd started earlier because I enjoy it. Island tunes. I wrote an opera based on the Bible. A friend of Monty's, Felix, wanted to reenact the whole Bible. We collaborated on the Genesis part, then I added my atheistic slant. My sister was into religion, but she liked it. Religious music with calypso."

"I thought you wrote about the songs you sang at the Synagogue, about 'the fireburn'. *Clear the Road.*" Amazingly I dredge the name from somewhere.

"No, that was a Mighty Sparrow song. I'd like to write one about Hubert Harrison and D Hamilton Jackson, though."

"They're certainly worthy." I think again of the Edgecombe play. And D Hamilton Jackson holds an esteemed place in Crucian history for starting a labour union before Transfer in 1917, and petitioning King Christian X, the Danish king, for permission to start the first black newspaper on the island.

"I did write a song, *Dancing with Stacey.*" He pauses, but before I can enquire about Stacey, he is off on another tack. "Joe Dell Anduze, he's a better musician than me, wanted to do some recordings before his voice went. Mine's going too."

"Sounds pretty good to me." I don't want to think about the loss to St Croix when these wonderful musicians stop performing.

"I'm planning an anthology - maybe a double CD - get it all recorded."

"That's a great idea. Get to it!" I harry him with a smile.

I glance down at my notes and take a deep breath. I am not sure how this question will go.

"Doc," my voice is hesitant, "having lived in a number of countries prior to, during, and immediately after independence, I'd like to ask your thoughts on independence. In an interview you gave a number of years ago you said, 'no country is ever truly ready'."

There is silence. I'm not sure whether to fill it or rush on with a softie.

He starts, his deep voice quiet. "Independence doesn't have to be acrimonious." He gathers his thoughts. "People love that FEMA check. We have to get off the nipple. But we refuse to address it. Even in the status commission. We want to vote for president and vice president, we want a full seat in the House of Representatives. How can we get that?"

I realize it is a rhetorical question and stay silent.

"It's impossible. Congress would never allow it. Or any of the territories. What would that do to elections? On the whole the territories tend to be Democratic. We can't be part of Caricom - who we are more aligned to than the US - unless we leave the US."

"A kind of free-association, like the British Virgin Islands," I suggest, thinking of the tax haven forty miles north of St Croix.

Doc nods. "That wouldn't happen either." He pauses, again. "Congress could tell us to come up with a plan to be executed over X number of years. They would agree to give us X number of dollars a year, for X number of years to help us prepare."

It seems like a lot of X's to me.

"You know, at the Centennial, the University of Copenhagen and UVI agreed to a student exchange program. Sophomore students would go to Denmark for a semester. We held a fundraiser at UVI to help pay for their housing, clothing and transportation."

I remember the event. It was a night of song and poetry.

"The Danish Government gave a gift of $750,000 in education grants. It all got murky. It took Lief Pedersen and me five years to get it sorted. Why? Because everything has to go through the Department of the Interior." Doc is silent. "I used to think we weren't ready for independence. Not now. But any decision must be made by those who live in the Virgin Islands."

I have a final question for this exuberant but, I think, tired man so generous with his time.

"There are a lot of buildings on St Croix which are a blight. Buildings that tell the history, good and bad. Should they be revitalized?"

I'm not sure Doc expects questions of this ilk, but he is gracious enough to discuss them.

"Of course, they should. We should be looking at cultural tourism. History, music, food. Not just beaches and diving and swimming. The problem is…"

I know I am about to get another considered answer.

"… the problem is that a lot of parents are able to accumulate enough wealth to educate their children but not enough to pass it along to keep the next generation wealthy."

I want to ask why it is the responsibility of parents to provide for their children from the grave but I have no time.

Doc continues, "So a little house in Christiansted ends up in probate. Kids move out. No one wants to do anything. It becomes derelict. The government is half-hearted about it. They should look at those properties delinquent in taxes. Go to the owners, then form a probate panel of three judges, who mediate an agreement. Help them form a trust, get funding. Encourage restoration to be done to the specs laid out, then when the plan is completed the trust can either sell it or keep it."

It sounds a viable solution but I have doubts as to its implementation. Too many people with different opinions in each and every family.

"That's what my dad did. There were seven of us. We formed a trust. Now everything is sorted for the next generation, the grandkids, and beyond."

"Do you have grandkids, Doc?"

"Not that I know of." His laugh bounces off the walls. "I never married."

"A busy life," I say.

"I like falling in love. I made three attempts. But I kept choosing girls from off island and when it came to a decision they couldn't see the rest of their lives here. And I couldn't see mine anywhere but St Croix."

The statement is the perfect full stop to the morning.

MOTHS, MAGGOTS AND MOLD

H ere we are in St Croix! The sea is an ever-changing panoply of brilliant blues and glorious greens and is a ready distraction as I glance from my study window. I've just watched the ferry depart - its rather odd four-hulled shape making smooth headway across the channel to St Thomas. It is a constant on an island that has few constants at the moment, after first Hurricane Irma skipped to the north, followed a week later by Hurricane Maria who skimmed the southern shores creating merry hell.

Power being the least constant of them all. Most of St Croix is still powerless though the hordes of beefy-looking linemen from the mainland, and our own crews, are steadily making their way across the island installing new poles and lines. March, or at the latest April, is the month being touted by Governor Mapp - I think that's called "hedging one's bets"!

Arriving on Wednesday after relatively stress-free flights considering we travelled with Bonnie, the cat, and her partner-in-crime, Clyde, the dog, astonishment greeted our arrival when we found we are part of that small percentage who do have light and therefore water. Along with the delight was a momentary pang of guilt - assuaged by offering 'power and shower' to people we know who are in need of a top up.

Hurricane Maria stripped the island of vegetation. Stately mahoganies tumbled. Elegant palms may be upright but their waving fronds have fallen or dangle impotently, providing little or no shelter. The genip tree across from our sturdy West Indian home is showing signs of life but until a few days ago was naked - its branches skeletal against the ocean backdrop.

But life is to be found. In our house it is in the crevices of old brick walls, or sending tendrils across walls and furniture, or in the fridge.

Moths emerge on a minute-by-minute basis. They had taken up residence in the pantry, managing to invade tightly sealed packaging to leave mounds of sawdust on the shelves. Bleaching and repainting have helped but still they flutter out to be met by a barrage of Raid.

Mold is an unsightly web of varicose veins across walls covered with anti-fungal paint, and wood furniture polished with wax. Diluted vinegar has been sluiced over every surface, left to dry, rinsed and then sprayed with eucalyptus anti-mold magic. We'll see.

And maggots inhabit every nook and cranny of the fridge and freezer. The saving grace… power came on the day before our arrival and so instead of a seething mass of blancmange-like grubs there is a bucketful of dried oat-like particles coating every surface and deep within the fridge's innards. I will never look at muesli the same way again.

Drawers, rails, the ice-maker, and various screws, bolts and important parts line the gallery catching every skerrick of sunshine as vinegar and lemon do their part in eliminating odors. I have a minor concern that there will be one vital part missing when the fridge is reassembled, and I believe it is an unacknowledged concern of the man who will be putting it back together. It has been a back-breaking endeavor and why, I have been told, my husband never went into the plumbing business. A confined space is not a pleasant work environment for a tall man. We have spritzed, we have poured, we have scrubbed, we have dug into every possible fissure with toothpicks in order to rid our cooling device of its unwelcome, though thankfully dead, visitors. Baking soda and a constantly rotating fan are now doing their job and one day, soon, we will have a functioning fridge.*

There are many small jobs which need attention. Shingles have been rudely cast aside by Maria's wrath, exposing the inner structure of our home. A few shutters now swing forlornly on broken hinges in the intermittent trade winds but the windows held true as did the roof, hurricane clipped at every conceivable point. An enterprise I, at one time, considered excessive but for which I am now grateful.

But we have it easy. Blue tarpaulins dot the landscape in FEMA's effort to keep the daily squalls out. Many have lost much. Piles of debris litter roadsides - mostly organic but sofas, mattresses and televisions are seen in some areas. There is a recycling centre but it is overwhelmed - its dumpsters out and about around the island trying to corral the odiferous detritus left in Maria's wake.

Frederiksted, on the western end of St Croix, took the brunt of the hurricane as she spumed her way to Puerto Rico where she inflicted even greater damage and hardship. This end of the Caribbean chain has been hard hit this year so we are receiving cruise ships who normally shun us. St Thomas, Tortola and many other regular cruising destinations are unable to host great numbers of tourists and so St Croix is grateful to be able to receive them - albeit offering limited delights but each day is better than the last, and the spirit of resilience is ever present.

These islands need tourism, and to those who have made plans to visit, or are considering a Caribbean adventure, please come. All are welcome. But please be patient if your credit card does not immediately work, or cell phone reception is patchy, or if the power fluctuates - this is what islanders have been managing for many weeks, and in some instances will be coping with for months to come.

Moths, maggots and mold are easily dealt with and do not dampen the warmth and friendliness of the Caribbean. Remember, it is always about the people.

*The refrigerator was replaced!

IT WAS A HONEY OF A DAY!

I had plans. Planting two cuttings people have so generously given me - what I hope will one day become a glorious shooting star (Clerodendrum) bush and a Danish flag vine (I don't know its grown-up name), except instead of red and white my clippings are red and pink. Don't know why. Then I was going to write, write, write.

Instead what did I do? I sat. First at a chair positioned just so at our dining room window, then on the barstool in the kitchen, then upstairs at the hall window. All overlooking our neighbor's garden. I had become a voyeur.

It was the men that did it. Two husky men with dreads and beards thrusting their legs into white coveralls at the bottom of our drive. A young woman covered from head to foot in all manner of garb, including a tee-shirt draped artfully around her head, completed the trio. Her job, seemingly, was to shove greenery into a kettle-like contraption which was then lit by one of the men. She then pumped and primed it until smoke blew off in satisfying curlicues to dissipate on the omnipresent north-easterly winds battering St Croix this month.

Now you must remember I was not in close proximity and so I could be forgiven for thinking, when the masks came out, that the trio were heading to a fencing tournament. And then I twigged.

Bees!

I am rather fond of bees and we are planting a garden to attract them along with hummingbirds and bananaquits, the rather charming and cheeky little yellow-breasted birds - smaller than a British robin - who twitter around any flowers. I have though in the last few months been stung twice by bees - not something that has ever happened before. I can report that they hurt like hell, then itch, then swell into an unattractive lump before disappearing. I am obviously not prone to anaphylactic shock.

But I digress. We had searched our property but could find no evidence of bees, neither had we noticed a great deal of buzzing next door. And so I was intrigued. Hence, the various watch locations in which I stationed myself.

A lot of toing and froing took place. Boxes. Empty frames. Ladders. The kettle. And, I was pleased to see, long gloves. One of the men clambered up the ladder in his ungainly gear and, with a puff of smoke, the first surge of bees was evicted from the underside of the eaves. Another flurry of activity showed the bees' displeasure when plywood fascia board fell to the ground.

It was at this stage the attendant woman beat a hasty retreat and spent the rest of the morning lying in the sunshine. I can't say I blame her.

I was though a little disconcerted to see, as the first wadge of bee-blackened honeycomb was torn from its sticky home, the second bee man remove his gloves and poke his finger along the dripping piece before dropping it into a box and hastily pushing the lid back over.

"No, no," I muttered from behind my glass seraglio. "Put your gloves back on." He didn't hear me.

Smoke, swarming bees, intense studying of each piece of saturated honeycomb was the order of the morning. More plywood tumbled down, security lights were rudely displaced to hang like giant testicles, and a thousand bees tried to attack the men who dared take their home.

One section of honeycomb must have been eighteen inches long. Then the larger of the two men scrabbled down, settled onto a step, took up one of the empty frames and began, after first shaking off more bees, to push honeycomb into the frame. Snapping off any bits outside the frame, he tossed them into a bucket and repeated the process five times. Each filled frame was carefully slotted into the box by the shorter of the men.

(I admit my description of the apiarists is not full, but you try describing men in white jumpsuits tucked into socks and boots, wearing full head masks and long gloves - well one of them anyway. I can tell you the gloveless man had black hands.)

And all the while bees dive bombed them. Outrage thrumming with every wing beat.

The clumps of comb became smaller, chiseled away from the roof, and bees began to settle on the outside of the eaves. A crawling black mass to be swept into a Tupperware container and unceremoniously tipped into their new hive.

The entertainment was over and, deciding prudence would be the order of the day, I sat down to write - why risk planting when stray, and discombobulated, bees might still be at large? But I was restless and decided to go and run errands.

Sitting by the roadside were two men with beards and dreads and a woman in all manner of garb but without a tee-shirt wrapped around her head.

"Good morning," I said through the car window, because no conversation on this island is started without a pleasantry. "Thank you. I've had a wonderful time watching you work. And you," I accused the shorter chap, "you weren't even wearing gloves!"

He smiled - his eyes were topaz, by the way.

"Good mahnin'. Hey mon, we got deh queen!"

"Great," I said, "does that mean those bees still buzzing around will go away?"

"Yeah. It called 'driftin' - the workers will look for another hive," said the main man, who I have since learned is Roniel Allembert, aka the VI Honey Man. And now, his mesh face covering removed, I can report his beard was greying, and plaited. His eyes were a muddy brown and his smile was as wide as Niagara.

"You want the best honey on the island?"

"Sure," I replied. "Thank you."

Languidly he rose, delved in the flatbed of his battered truck and returned to my car. Leaning through the window he gave me a piece of dripping honeycomb.

It was good. And I had a honey of a day!

WHY HERE?

Restoring a West Indian home up a steep hill in Christiansted has been a labour of love and which, as most love affairs, has had moments of great joy and moments of deep despair.

A web of wires criss-crossing the walls, with appliances daisy-chained into the front of the fuse box. A gas pipe suspended below a low ceiling. Fans that would decapitate anyone over 5'6". Termite eggs sounding like sand trickling into a pail whenever furniture was moved. Shutters which creaked in un-oiled anger with each gust of the trade winds that make this island such a cool place to live. A dishwasher which had been home to small furry critters with long tails. An oven that belched gas at the threat of a flame. And baths upon which no bottom should ever sit. The list was long.

But the views! Ribbons of blue as the Caribbean filters through azure, to aquamarine to emerald, and back to kingfisher navy glisten in iridescent invitation. Yachts dot the bays in bobbing abandon. And the one thing that makes any place a pleasure to be. The people.

No conversation, no matter how short, starts without 'good mahnin' or a pleasantry about whatever the time of day. If the acquaintance is more than a passing hello, then an inquiry after the health of the family, or a comment about the day, or maybe an upcoming event is the norm before diving into the purpose of the meeting. It is the most delightful way in which to conduct one's life and a reminder that courtesy is still alive in certain parts of this great land, despite the lack of civility in the political sphere.

Why here?

St Croix might be an American territory but she most definitely has a Caribbean vibe and is, to my biased view, the best of the US Virgin Islands. The hustle of the mainland is missing. "When will you be here?" is answered by "Soon come." People are warm and welcoming, and like to laugh. The market is full of fresh produce and stall holders eager to impart their knowledge of how to cook that strange looking leaf.

Don't get me wrong. This is not Utopia. There are social issues, as there are anywhere. Gun violence has taken a nasty upturn - fueled by drugs and unemployment. Domestic abuse, probably for the same reasons, runs like a fetid stream through society. Hurricanes rudely destroy homes, schools, hospitals, businesses and lives.

For someone like me, who has lived and worked in many places -12 countries, as diverse as Papua New Guinea and the Netherlands - there is a charm to St Croix that appealed from the outset. I couldn't care less about the possible health hazards of sparrows flying around inside the supermarket. And whilst religion is taken seriously, no matter what the faith, there is still space for humor - the sign, since blown away, affixed to the gates of the Lutheran Church on King Street in Christiansted admonished, "Thou Shalt Not Park Here".

Or another propped up in a window opposite Singhs, the Trini doubles* fast-food joint, which offers three directions - the lab, the morgue or the X-ray - take your pick.

Where I sit and write, often on our gallery looking out at the aforementioned view, I am privy to many amusing conversations taking place in the street below, though I am not part of them. I was though part of a conversation last night. Let me set the scene.

The Plough was glistening in an ebony sky. The channel lights were blinking red and green to guide cruisers into safe harbor should they be so foolish as to attempt a night-time arrival through the narrow channel. The breeze rustled coconut fronds and clack-clacked tan-tan pods as cicadas harmonized in accompaniment. The roosters were blessedly silent - no doubt preparing for their pre-dawn chorus of 'funky blackbird'! Jazz in the Park and a glass of Bourbon had left me mellow.

The idyll was broken by the violent gunning of an engine followed by a desperate screech of brakes, the rattling of pebbles on our galvanized roof, and a flurry of curses. I rushed out to see what was going on.

"Good night," I said, showing remarkable sang-froid in the face of a long-base ute very close to tipping down onto our roof. "Everything okay?" Which in the face of it was rather a silly question, but very British.

"Good night." A man, with large glasses and trousers slipping below his butt, responded politely then shouted further instructions to the driver before turning back to me. "W'appen de road? De road it go where?"

This was a fair question. There is no warning that the road behind our house leads not downhill in tar macadamed smoothness but into a series of steep and very rutted steps. If urban legend is to be believed, a number of vehicles have taken the plunge over the years. A little disconcerting to know, as such an event would surely disturb my slumber.

"It's been like this for many years. Certainly since before you were born," I replied.

"How old you think I be?"

"Younger than these steps." I told him. "Have the brakes failed?"

The driver, his lips pursed firmly around a cigarette, bade me good night and replied in the younger man's stead. The brakes were fine. It was the steepness of the gravel road causing the problem. That and no power in the engine. It took another five or six attempts before, with sparks and stones flying, the pick-up made its wailing way up the hill. Brake lights flashed on - amazingly both worked - and a cheer went up from the flatbed filled with three young, and perhaps a little inebriated, men before they went on their way - the driver waving goodbye.

That's 'why here' - it's fun!

*Doubles are small sandwiches made of flatbreads filled with channa (curried chickpea).

RUM RUNNERS

Brown eyes surveyed the white beach that stretched beyond the shallows glittering opaline and turquoise in a tangerine dawn light. A peaked cap hid Frank's greying blonde hair, his chest was a curly mass, his skin tanned from hours at sea. Around his waist was a tattered sarong, his favored garb whilst on board his ketch, *Palila*. For all his rakish appearance, Frank was clean-shaven.

"At last!" His words dissolved on the easterly winds as the man in an approaching tender raised his arm in welcome. Frank leant over the rail to take the line and tie it to a cleat then watched the man in tattered shorts clamber aboard.

"You're late," said Frank as the men slapped each other on the back.

"Hey, man, dis de Caribbean. Slow, slow." The words came with a wide smile. "How are you doing, Frank?" The patois disappeared. "Still naked as a native, I see. Don't they have shirts in England?"

"That, my friend," Frank said, with a laugh, "is why I'm an island man."

"Last time I looked Britain was an island." The broadly built man grinned and, walking along the deck, his hand trailing along the newly finished teak, he took in the neatly stowed mainsail. "Looking good!"

"I'll clarify, a tropical island man." Frank disappeared into the saloon and came back with a jug of coffee. Black and sweet.

"Here," he called pouring a tin mugful, "just how you like it. And yes, she should look good. She had her first complete refit in Madeira. Engines hum like a lady in love."

"How was the crossing?"

"Not too bad. Amazing how uncomplicated life was without a big black chap like you on board." Frank raised his mug to the one man he trusted above all others and continued, "Did what the ancients suggested - headed south until the butter melted then turned right."

"To?" Jem asked

"Turks and Caicos. Put in at Cockburn Harbour. That's where I added them." Frank nodded at two rods angled over the stern.

"Nice touch."

Frank laughed. "I'm told Americans love to fish. And drink."

Jem grinned, although there was an edge to his voice. "Cuba is crawling with thirsty Yanks."

"You're one."

"Yeah, but not a white one! Makes all the difference. Don't forget, the Danes only sold their stake in the West Indies - St Thomas, St John and St Croix - three years ago. 1917 they moved out and the United States moved in. Though we didn't get a say in the deal." Jem frowned. "You know it was only earlier this year that it was specified we had American nationality but, just to be clear, we do not have the political status of American citizenship."

"This is too deep for a mug of coffee. That's a discussion for whisky."

"Rum will have to do and it just so happens…" Jem bent to produce a bottle from the canvas bag at his feet. "Bacardi, man, best rum in Cuba and beloved by our soon-to-be customers in Florida."

They sat in the cockpit and watched the sky deepen as day bloomed. A bevy of egrets in a panoply of white feathers flew up from a rookery on the shore and headed to wherever they spent their days.

"Which one gives the signal, I wonder?" Jem asked watching them disappear over the headland.

"Dunno," Frank said, his eyes closed as he savored the rum-laced coffee. "You ready for this, Jem? No doubts? You might not get back to St Croix for a while."

"No, man." Laughter burst from Jem's wide mouth. "My mother wasn't happy until I promised I'd bring you to meet her one day. She's curious about the crazy Englishman I know." He paused, then said, "It'll be different to the Med."

"Yup, it will." The men sat in the gentle glow of early sunshine sharing memories of other mornings in other parts of the world. "We did well to get out of Europe," Frank said, draining his mug. "I'm fine moving goods, but no more people."

Jem nodded. "Different times, man. We had no choice. King and country."

"You're a complicated bugger, Jem," said Frank. "Neither your king nor your country. Nor your war."

"My mum's from Barbados. Made it close enough."

"Not to get shot." Frank glanced at the ragged dent in Jem's thigh. "How is it? Still giving you gyp?"

"Nah, I'm fine." Jem rubbed his leg. "Nothing a little excitement won't fix! And I was lucky." He drained his coffee, looked at Frank and, noting new lines like statements around his mouth, asked, "And you?"

"Fine." Frank looked across at the Hicocas Peninsula stretching out to Vadero, the town at the end of a spit on Cuba's northern coastline. He closed his eyes. The image of Sofia did not haunt him as much now but in unguarded moments her face floated in, not as he had last seen her, thank God, but as he had met her. Determined, fearless, vibrant, and sometimes deadly. He had loved her as a daughter he'd never had. And yet he'd sent her on partisan missions across the Aegean. Like he'd sent others. But it was her torture and murder at the hands of Turkish militants in the Dardanelles that had decided Frank to quietly disappear. There was no one to miss him. No one to know his new name. Except Jem, and his brother, Edward who, whilst being tied to a wheelchair, had a mind that ticked like a metronome. The man who managed the funds. Frank shook his head and said, "Enough reminiscing."

Jem wandered along the deck to stand on the saloon roof, running his hands along the boom, and asked, "How many aboard?"

"With you, four. One less than when I crossed the Atlantic. I gave them shore leave last night. One has been with me since the Canaries, an American looking to get home. Morose chap but knows boats. Off loaded three in the Turks and Caicos and picked up another one there, a Cuban with contacts, or so he says."

"What color?"

"Sorry?"

"What color is the American?"

"White. But's he okay."

"Okay enough to take orders from a black man."

"Yes. But if a problem arises he'll be put ashore," Frank assured him.

"Alright." Jem didn't look convinced. "What do they know?"

"I'm an eccentric Englishman. Damaged goods. Searching for something. I like my liquor but don't break my own rule of only a tot a night when aboard. I've let slip there is a steady supply of funds. Don't want anyone jumping ship at an inopportune time. I'm sure they suspect we'll be in the rum business, but no one's said anything."

"How do you know about sailing?" Jem asked with a grin, knowing the question would irk Frank. "Especially a boat this size?"

"Because I'm a bloody Englishman. We are surrounded by sodding water."

Jem stopped Frank's irate flow, his smile wide and knowing. "Oh, and you grew up rich with a yacht on the Isle of Wight. Though that shall remain strictly between you and me. So tell me, Mr Wilson, what brings you to America."

"What are you? The Coast Guard?"

"Nah. Just getting the story straight."

Frank grinned. "I go where the wind takes me. Hoping to start a fishing charter."

"You have a mixed crew, sir," Jem said.

"Sailors come in all colors, Lieutenant."

Jem smiled, "As a matter of interest, how are you going to explain me?"

"Brothers in arms. Fought together in Palestine."

"I suppose I could hint that you were my commanding officer. Though it would pain me to go that far!" Jem's laugh was a rumble.

"Not to mention it would be a lie. More like brothers in bars.

Frank showed Jem the modifications made to *Palila* since he'd last been aboard. The crew's quarters were shared and cramped. Jem nodded his appreciation when he saw the master cabin had been divided and his berth was now the same size as Frank's.

"Thanks," he said.

"Well, you are the first mate," Frank said.

"What's the stowage like?"

"Not bad. We now have a false floor. Bottles only." Frank hurried on when he saw concern cross Jem's face. "I was worried about that too, but I bumped into a chap who knew a chap - you know the story - who has come up with a clever idea. Burlap packaging!"

"What?"

"Yup, that's what I thought, but hear me out. Six bottles jacketed in straw. Three on the top, then two, then one - the whole thing sewed into burlap. Then store one package up, one down and they don't clink."

"Who's doing the sewing?" Jem asked with a grin.

"We will, the first run. When we have a regular supplier we'll get them to do it."

"Hmph. Their price will go up. Everyone's in it for the money."

Frank patted Jem's shoulder. "Let's see, huh? Have you made any contacts yet?"

"Yeah, man. The Fat Cuban. Don't know why, he's not fat. Chews a cigar. Light skinned. A younger son gone bad, perhaps."

"Wonder if he's even Cuban. What does he know?"

"That we're an English-registered vessel. You're a disillusioned Englishman. We met in the War, in Turkey."

Frank nodded. "Does he know I speak Spanish?"

"You think I'm a fool, man? Of course he doesn't!"

The men laughed, then, hearing the putter of an outboard approach returned to the deck. Jem stood back as a man clambered aboard.

"Where's Tom?" Frank asked.

"He in town. Not come." Elian's grin was gap-toothed.

"Ever?"

"No, Boss Frank, for now. He say come pronto."

Frank frowned then introduced the Cuban, who as well as a deck hand doubled as the cook. "Elian, this is Jem. If he says 'jump', you jump. ¿Comprendo?"

"Si, capitán."

Frank turned to Jem. "Tom, you will have gathered, is our American. UA, unauthorized absence, at the moment. How he thinks he's getting back without a dinghy is a mystery."

The meeting with The Fat Cuban took place in a seamy bar along the waterfront at Vadero. Frank toyed with a rum in a finger-smudged glass and remained quiet, playing the amiable Englishman looking for adventure. It was a pose that did not sit well and the fingers of his left hand beat a silent tattoo on his knee under the counter as negotiations rambled back and forth.

"Oily little shit," Frank said as they pushed through the swing doors, the brilliance of the day stinging their eyes after the dim room. "You sure about him?"

Jem nodded as they sauntered back to the tender. "If we want Arechabala as well as Bacardi, it's his name that keeps coming up."

"You reckon we need both?" Frank asked. "Can the average American tell the difference?"

"Yeah, man, I've been listening in all the bars. Buyers want a choice."

"Alright, but I don't trust him. And I'd rather drink whisky."

"I heard there's a warehouse full of it in Havana."

"Is that whisky with or without an 'e'? Irish or Scotch?"

"Glenlivet," Jem said with a grin.

"Hah, now we're talking!" Frank stopped and looked at a man staggering toward the water's edge. "That's Tom."

They threw the cursing drunk into the tender where he fell into a puddle and returned to *Palila*, where Elian helped manhandle him down to his berth to sleep off the effects of a rum-fueled night.

Tom, surly and bleary-eyed, and Elian sat on deck and listened as Frank outlined their plan to head ninety nautical miles to Havana after they took possession of a load of Bacardi arranged by The Fat Cuban, then cross the western tip of the Florida Straits and north to the maze that constituted the Ten Thousand Islands on the edge of the Everglades. Neither Tom nor Elian were surprised but Frank noticed a frown creasing the Cuban's already wrinkled brow.

"You have done this before?" Frank asked in Spanish.

"Si, capitán. *Solo una vez*," replied the Cuban.

"It was a bad voyage?"

"Si, capitán, *muy malo*. Water crazy." Elian mimed slapping himself as he also described the ferociousness of the mosquitoes along the mangrove-fringed waters off the coastline.

"And you?" Jem asked Tom, his eyes still bloodshot.

"Yeah," Tom replied, "but to Miami."

"Why didn't you say something?" Jem asked, anger close to the surface.

"You didn't ask, didya? And none of us knowed what we was gittin' into when we signed on," Tom said, his voice sounding truculent.

"Alright, alright." Frank broke through the building rancor. "Anything else we should know?"

The crew shook their heads, then Elian chimed in, "Hey, Boss Frank?"

"Yep?"

"What *Palila* means?"

Jem snorted but waited for Frank to speak.

"It's a bird. From the Pacific."

"And not just the feathered variety," Jem said, a chuckle deep in his throat.

Laughter eased the tension and Elian returned to the galley to chop onions for their evening meal. Jem told Tom to pull out the bales of burlap and twine stored in the fore cabin in readiness for a night of sewing. Jem returned to the saloon to study the chart for their sail to Havana, and Frank disappeared into his cabin to empty the safe of American dollars.

Demijohns of whisky and bottles of Bacardi filled the saloon. Frank, large scissors in his hand, cut the coarse burlap into squares, while Jem, an able sailmaker, stitched them into tight packages of six bottles each. Elian and Tom pulled straw from a bale and stuffed it around the bottles. As packages grew, they began moving them into the false hold, one pyramid down, one up.

At $4 a case of rum they would make a tidy sum even if they didn't get the $100 a case expected from deliveries to the east coast. Night wore on and as the last bottles were stored, Elian swept the saloon free of strands of burlap and sticks of straw while Jem and Tom replaced the floor of the fore cabin.

"Last warning." Frank told Tom, "Next time you'll be put ashore. I don't care where we are. Got it?"

The American glared but kept his eyes lowered as he nodded. He was the only one who railed at the limit of one rum a day, the source of contention that brewed over into his fists flaying when Jem found him slugging from a bottle he took from a locker under a bench. Tom's face showed where Jem's return punch landed.

"And while we're on the subject of behavior," Frank continued, "if Jem here says 'jump' you will jump. Got that too?" Frank waited for a nod. "Right, we'll set sail around noon.

You're on watch with me once we enter open water, then Jem and Elian. Two-hour watches through the night. Sailing time about twenty hours. All hands on deck as we near Havana. Anything else, Jem?"

The tall man looked skyward and said, "Should be a smooth passage, waves shifting from north to east as we near Havana. Probably higher seas at the beginning."

"Yes, all eyes sharp until open seas," Frank added.

"*Delfín*," Elian said, his face alive with hope as he translated, "er... how you say, dolphin, guide us."

"Damn, Jem," Frank said as they cleared the channel and saw the miles of sandy beaches on the other side of the Hicocas Peninsula, if this isn't the perfect place to build a hotel I don't where is."

"You haven't seen St Croix yet. But can we finish one thing before we move to another?" Jem asked. "Right now we're in the rumrunning business." The friends laughed and set sail across new waters for both of them.

Palila made good time and they lowered the sails as Havana came into view mid morning. Tom, somewhat chastened and nursing a black eye, kept to himself but was civil and proved to Jem he did know what he was doing aboard the ketch. After sails were stowed, Frank told the men that after shore leave overnight, they would load, stitch and store the following night then leave the next morning for the Everglades.

"Tides are minimal, so at least we don't have to wait for them," Frank said to Jem as the clang of the anchor chain ended in a thud and *Palila* swung gently until she settled. "There should be news from Edward. I told him to write Post Restante, Havana. The men can go ashore when we're shipshape, and tomorrow I'll do a bank run and check the post office. You going ashore tonight?" Frank asked.

"Nah, I'll go tomorrow too. And I happen to know where there's a good bottle of Cruzan rum," Jem said, "but first I'm diving in." He looked at Frank's sarong and bare chest. "You might want to add some clothing before you saunter the streets tomorrow?"

Frank and Jem watched the crew row ashore then dived, naked, into the clear water before they stretched on the foredeck to dry, each clad in a sarong. A bottle of rum between them, they watched the town lights shimmer as they talked of other islands, other bays.

"Buenas días." Frank, dressed in cream linen trousers and a blue long-sleeved shirt, raised his Panama hat to the clerk behind the counter at the post office, his second stop of the day. "My name is Frank Wilson. Do you happen to be holding any mail for me, please?" The woman smiled, showing deep dimples above the crisp white of her collar. He watched her go to the bank of pigeonholes at the back of the room, her shapely legs disappearing under a floral hem.

"Aquí estás, here you are, Mr Wilson, two letters," her voice a gentle lilt as she smiled at the tall Englishman.

Frank thanked her, bowed and glanced at his watch then set off for a bar he'd spotted as he'd sauntered along the shore, enjoying the feel of land beneath his feet. A gin and tonic would be the perfect accompaniment whilst he read his brother's letter, and the one from someone whose writing he did not recognize.

He sank onto a planter's chair and ordered his drink before opening Edward's letter.

March, 1920

My dear Frank (I do still struggle imagining you as a Frank), nonetheless you are dear,

   Thank you much for your last missive. The Turks and Caicos sound rather pleasant but I am in no hurry to visit America. From reports various, it sounds a hellish place, certainly at the moment, with no liquor to ease the way.

   Delighted the refit was successful. Palila - a name that conjures up grace and beauty, which from your account is exactly what the namesake had. Such a long time since I sailed. What fun we used to have racing at Cowes. Do be careful, old boy. There has been enough misfortune in this family.

   I do hope you and that delightful-sounding fellow, Jem, are managing to stay out of trouble or, at the very least, having the time of your lives. I shall always regret not getting the chance to meet him.

   I imagine you are reading this sipping a G&T overlooking Havana Bay. How that thought warms my heart on a rather dreary English day, although hope can be found in the hint of green erupting from the brown sod of flowerbeds. The raised beds - God love you for thinking of that - give me pleasure eight months of the year. Another few weeks and the daffodils will dance and life will take on an altogether sunnier view. Bob has kept the garden in good shape throughout winter and he, and Margaret, spend the rest of the time keeping me in order. How very fortunate I am to have such sterling people to help.

Frank smiled. The daffodils would be in full bloom by now.

   The house is as it has always been. Far too big for a bachelor but no point moving out or on now and, who knows, perhaps one day you will return to these shores. We have essentially closed off the top floors and when I have company we dine informally in the morning room.

Frank sipped his drink and gazed over the bay. He felt a pang for his brother with the altogether colder view from the family home. A place to which he would never return for any length of time.

To business, as Father would've said. I have spent these last winter months sorting out affairs, and going through trunks. What a lot of papers the parents kept – most have been assigned to the fire that Bob ably keeps going. There has though been a, I suppose, shocking surprise.

The deed, in Father's name, to another property in London – doors along from the old Albemarle Street house. The worthy Mr Lymington, and a private investigator he has occasion to use, have been doing some digging. It seems Father had a paramour housed there for years. I wonder if Mother knew. The woman was apparently respectable and an artist – do those words go together? There were no issue from the liaison so we can rest assured of no surprise siblings, and of our parentage, or can we? All very strange. Needless to say the woman, whose name was Ellen Elizabeth Jennings, is naturally deceased. Or deceased naturally. Or both! We have managed to track down some of her work – it almost pains me say, but she was good. Father always did have a good eye! Signed herself EEJennings, no doubt to lessen the chance of censure from the misogyny of the day. Still around today, I'm ashamed to say, even after all the efforts of the womenfolk during that ghastly War. Please, God, there is never another.

Frank kicked out the leg rests of the planter's chair and leant back, stunned, the pages clutched in his hand.

But back to Miss Jennings. She died about five years after Father so I can only assume she was of a similar age. I suppose Mother was the flibbertigibbert in his life, being fifteen years his junior. How little we know of our parents until it is too late to seek clarification. The house has had a caretaker couple all these years – not the same ones of course – whose salaries have been paid from a separate account drawn from Coutts & Co but about which I knew nothing. The determined Lymington, or perhaps his cohort, has found the solicitor dealing with the property and we have begun negotiations to regain ownership. I won't go into all the details but there have, from time to time, been others living at the property who have paid rent which is, I suppose, how it has gone so long undetected.

If you are confused by all of this, Frank, imagine my amazement. Apart from Lymington and his people, no one knows, which is how I think it should continue. What point raking old coals? So, if you are in agreement, I would like to arrange for the sale of the property. Proceeds of which I shall place directly into your account. I have plenty for my needs. As do you, dear boy, but adventure and an element of risk has always been your calling.

Without sounding maudlin, I wonder sometimes, what mine would have been. I was no doubt destined to fall badly from a horse at some stage in my life. It just happened rather sooner than anticipated. Ah well. A good life has been had. My books, my plants, my friends and the occasional delightful visit from my brother.

Now, what other news?

Churchill has announced that conscripts will be replaced by a volunteer army – 220,000 strong. A very good move. We have had enough of war, rations, and rules. Lloyd George is fighting against trade union militancy despite his initiatives for reform to housing and education, and the economy is becoming severely depressed. The Ulster Unionists have accepted a plan for a Parliament of Northern Ireland – I very much fear Ireland is a keg waiting to blow. Maybe not in our lifetime but religion is fueling the anger on both sides.

And on that happy note I think that is about all I have to relate, I look forward to your next writing. Should I consider Havana your base for the time being?

I'm not entirely sure what you are up to, probably best though I have an inkling, but do be careful, my dear Frank,
I remain,
Yours ever,
Edward

The waiter, assiduously buffing glasses, hovered nearby and Frank raised his hand and ordered another drink.

"Good God," he muttered, then let out a roar of laughter. "The old goat. All those years."

His words floated out to sea but not before a couple at a table further along the gallery looked askance.

He nodded his thanks as the gin and tonic appeared, a slice of lime lipping the rim. He picked up the other letter, and slipping his finger under the flap, slit it open. The address at the top of the page read, *Lymington, Lymington & Son, Solicitors, Mayfair, London.*

Dear Mr Wilson,

By instruction from Edward James Cooper, as laid down a number of years ago, this letter will remain vague in some instances, due to the nature of your business.

We deeply regret to inform you that Mr Cooper succumbed, due in part to his compromised health situation, to the virulent influenza that has swept the world these last two years.

The pages fluttered down as Frank's legs thudded to the floor. He stood. He sat. He swallowed a mewl that came from deep in his chest. He stood again, oblivious to the curious glances from others on the verandah. He drained his drink in one gulp and motioned for another. Sitting once again, he rotated his neck, retrieved the letter and continued to read.

By the time you receive this notice Mr Cooper will have been interred, as per his wishes, in the plot next to his parents.

Frank wondered fleetingly if EEJennings was also buried nearby.

Disbursements are in the process of being made, see Addenda A. Mr and Mrs Robert Taylor, your brother's long-term caregivers, have been released from their position with the very generous bequest left them. They offered to remain at the Isle of Wight house, which has not been named here deliberately, until the sale went through but, in the circumstances, it was decided it would be more discreet if they relocated immediately the contents were sold or distributed.

There are a number of trunks, and several pieces of furniture, listed on Addenda B, that are being stored at a nearby location until we receive instruction from you or an emissary.

The house, despite part of which has been closed for a number of years, is a desirable residence and has received a most generous offer which, again upon previous written instruction from Mr Cooper, I have accepted.

After solicitor's fees have been totaled and subtracted there will be a significant sum which will be deposited in the European account specified by Mr Cooper.

If there should be anything further Lymington, Lymington & Son can assist you with please do not hesitate to contact us. Our discretion is guaranteed.
With deep condolences,
Yours,
William A Lymington

Frank held the last page closer to read the handwritten postscript.

PS. Do please accept my personal condolences. I was honoured to know Edward for over thirty years, and his deepest regard for you was evident in the many conversations we had when I visited him on the Isle of Wight.
WAL

Frank stared out to sea, seeing nothing, not even *Palila's* mast glinting in the sun, the blue ensign fluttering from a stern stay - the only indication he was affiliated to any British yacht club. The only vanity he refused to discard. Edward would not have approved. Never do things by half, dear boy, he would have said. Either you disappear or you don't. Well, he'd done a pretty good job of not being found. But when would it cease to matter? Did anyone really care that a burnt-out spymaster disappeared? Sofia's face drifted in. She had not been the first he had sent to possible death, but she had been the youngest. After that he'd walked, or sailed. Paid his way on a broken-down boat and got back to *Palila*, where she was stored on the hard and in, he had hoped, the safe keeping of a boatman in Paphos on the south coast of Cyprus.

Frank raised his hand for another drink.

"¿*Tal vez algunos bocados pequeños, senor?*" The waiter suggested some canapés as he looked at Frank's pale face when he proffered the glass.

"Indeed, yes, thank you." Frank drained his glass, his hand steady. "And bring another of these, please." The food sat, mostly uneaten by his side, but the gin and tonics kept coming.

Visions of he and Edward growing up. A childhood free of worry, few rules but an inherent understanding of where they fit into the world. A privileged life. Never in his, or Edward's, wildest imaginations would they have considered their father unfaithful to their mercurial mother. She was the sunshine, if not always the calm, in their lives. The laughter and the song. Father's periodic visits to London were all to do with his writing. Or so they had thought.

"Hmph," Frank muttered. The knowledge of a hidden lover could not lessen his fondness for his father. He remembered Edward's accident. How his mother would not allow a pall to descend over the old house. Her strength brought his brother through the loss of the use of his legs. Her determination that her younger son would not be manacled to the family home had set Frank free to roam, to seek adventure, always in the knowledge 'home' would be waiting for him. And when his parents died, it was Edward who was the keeper of that home. Even after Frank had become Frank and no longer Giles Michael Cooper.

Lights began to flicker from boats in the bay and still Frank sat, drinking. His thoughts roving over a peripatetic, and not always legal life until a figure blocked the view.

Jem took in the two envelopes by Frank's side. He indicated the waiter should tally the tab, then pulled out his wallet and paid for a bottle of gin and canapés, now a soggy mess bleeding into wilted lettuce on the plate.

"Alright, Frank, time to go." Jem hoisted his friend to his feet, then walked him the length of the gallery to disapproving tuts, either at the drunk man's state or a black man's arm around him. Neither man cared.

Frank slumped to a bench overlooking the bay, Jem silent at his side. A pelican preened on a bollard further along the seafront before skimming the surface waiting for fish.

"Edward's dead." The words were bald.

Jem nodded. "I guessed. Man, I'm sorry." He laid a restraining hand on Frank's arm as he tried to rise. "Sit awhile."

"I need a piss."

Jem snorted. "On your own there, man!"

Frank staggered back and fell onto the bench where they sat in silence until Jem nudged him up and along the jetty. Getting the swaying man into the tender took all Jem's strength and balance where Frank slumped to the bottom.

"One word, Tom, an' I knock you overboard fas' fas', eh." Jem dared the sneering man leaning down to tie off their tender. "Elian, here," he said as the concerned cook stepped forward and hauled Frank to the deck where he sprawled, muttering.

The Cuban disappeared down to the galley and could be heard boiling water for coffee.

"He brother die." Jem said. "Go to shore. Back in de mahnin'."

"I stay," Elian said handing a mug to Frank. "I cook for Boss Frank."

Jem looked at the Cuban, his eyes dark with concern. He nodded. "Gracias, amigo." Surprise flitted across his face as Tom also elected to remain aboard.

"Hey, Frank," Jem said to the man collapsed in the cockpit clutching the letters. "Coffee and whatever our Cuban friend can rustle up, then sleep."

Frank appeared none the worse for his sorrow-soaked gin session, though shrugged off any of Jem's attempts to speak about his brother and was determined to stick to their plan. Until their contact failed to appear and a message arrived from The Fat Cuban that they should motor back to Alamar, where the rum would be waiting. Delays in delivery kept them anchored in the bay at Alamar. A week in which the crew avoided Frank as much as possible. He declined any suggestion from Jem that he go ashore and instead busied himself plotting their course, taking into account the precautions of wind against stream as they crossed the Florida Straits. Like the rest of the crew, he limited his rum intake to one tot a night.

Elian went ashore to restock the galley but Tom stayed on board, seemingly determined to win the trust of both Frank and Jem. He also assured them they would be well able to resupply, should they need to, from the flat-bottom launches and small powerboats taking liquor ashore from ships and boats moored beyond the three-mile American maritime limit.

Frank did not say they would be within the limit, hiding in the deeper channels between some of the islands. The row of ships rafted together and known as Rum Row, prevalent along the eastern Florida coast and offshore Galveston Island in Texas, not being of concern. Frank had reliable information there were not enough Coast Guard vessels, intent on keeping liquor out of the United States, to protect the islands off the Everglades.

The plotting, planning and impending adventure did little to lighten Frank's spirit, and still he had not spoken about his brother and Jem wondered if he ever would.

The passage across to Florida, despite forecasts of fair weather, took their energy and concentration as a squall swelled the seas in confusion. Frank was glad their load was protected by straw and burlap and wedged tight in the hold.

New to the rumrunning game, they kept their distance from larger ships and slipped into a small bay tucked on one of the outer islands. A lack of concern for the authorities became apparent as mast and ship lights flickered on in the short dusk, throwing eerie shadows as shapes moved around the decks.

The Fat Cuban had assured Frank and Jem that it would not take long for a buyer to appear once they hove to. And he proved right. From the cover of night and against a backdrop of mangroves, a speedboat darted toward them to bump alongside *Palila*. Again The Fat Cuban's guidance proved useful. and Frank held his nerve and turned the skipper's offer down.

"That was more than I expected," Jem muttered.

"First offer, Jem," Frank said, looking to the jagged shorelines of Ten Thousand Islands. "There'll be another soon enough. We've got quality product that's not been cut." He took a sip of rum, a bottle left out of a sack to prove the quality to any would-be buyer. Frank was inclined to agree to assurances made by The Fat Cuban that it was the purest rum ever made. Maybe pure enough to make him switch from whisky to rum from the Arechabalas family estate.

"Yeah, man, I know but we don't want to sit here too long."

"Patience, Jem." Frank scoured the island-dotted waters between for either danger or a purchaser. "There," he pointed.

Frank accepted the third offer, made by a burly man in a larger launch, whose southern accent could be heard even around the cigar glued to his lips.

Sacks of bottles passed up through the hatches, hand to hand to from *Palila's* crew to the motley group waiting to receive them on the launch. A commotion further out to sea stopped operations as dim lights were doused on both the large and small boats until a message was received that the fracas was not due to the authorities but to a deal turned sour.

"Won't make it back tonight," the buyer growled, his voice low. "If there's trouble, sail out to the three-mile mark. Then same time tomorrow night."

"Don't forget the water," Jem reminded him.

"Boy, I'll bring your water when I'm ready!"

Frank put his hand on Jem's arm, a warning in the pressure. "Mr Farrow is my first mate. You'll treat him with respect, if you please," Frank said, his smile pleasant, his tone frigid.

"Why him?" Jem asked, watching the launch disappear into the darkness, a trail of white wake the only indication it had been tied alongside moments before.

"He's rough, but despite his manners, I think he's trustworthy." Frank laughed, the first laugh in over a week. "If any of us can be considered trustworthy. And I like the idea of dealing with a one-man band. Like us. We're not treading on the big boys' toes." He nodded to the large vessels further out. "Time for a tot, gentlemen," he called to Elian and Tom, sweating from their efforts.

"Jesus, can we move away from land? With no breeze the Goddam bugs are going to carry us off," Tom complained.

They moved out to sea and spent the day offshore before returning to the island as the sun lipped the horizon in a tawny glow, rather like the rum they'd transshipped. As soon as the final payment was received and the packages offloaded, *Palila* set sails and headed back toward Cuba. Frank, surprised Tom had not abandoned ship with the tough buyer, watched as he coiled ropes then went down into the galley. The men had been paid, with a bonus for the speed with which they offloaded the cargo. Frank smiled, he wanted them sweet for the next trip. And the next.

"You feelin' better, man," Jem said to the man on the helm.

Frank nodded. "Nothing like a little adrenaline to put things in perspective. And cash."

"That man, the Florida man, he a *parass!*" Jem invariably lapsed into patois when angry or worried.

"A what?"

"Parass. Fool. Ignorant."

"All of the above. But," Frank patted his pocket, "he bought and paid."

The return journey to Havana, against the current but with the wind across their port bow took a couple of hours less and they arrived back at Alamar. Frank anticipated a quick turnaround, hoping to make five or six more trips before summer storms, or God forbid a hurricane, threatened to lash them across the unforgiving straits and closed the window on rumrunning for the year. For them.

"Six more?" Jem asked, shaking his head. "No, man, you crazy."

"Hurricane season doesn't typically get bad until the end of August and into September. Five or six, then we'll stop. Alright?" Frank patted his friend's shoulder. "A trip a week. That's six weeks, Jem. Tops."

"And *Palila?*"

"She'll be fine. She's strong. She'll get us to St Croix. Then we'll spoil her!"

"You crazy!" Jem repeated.

Tom jumped ship and disappeared with the rough-talking Floridian and his crew on the fifth trip. Despite his sailing ability and his attempted sobriety, no one aboard *Palila* missed him though it left them short-handed. Studying the charts, Frank and Jem decided to cut their losses and head back to Vadero before starting the voyage to St Croix. They would be carrying more fuel than rum for the journey east, heading into wind rather than having the easterlies with them.

"It would be rude to arrive in American waters without any rum, eh?" Frank asked, his laugh deep, his eyes crinkled, when he mentioned they would take on a small supply of liquor whilst in Cuba.

"We make rum!" Jem said.

"Not much on St Thomas. And who doesn't like a little Bacardi?" Frank asked with a grin.

Rum was not all they picked up.

"No, Frank, no, man. Not a good idea."

"Jem, it'll be fine. She'll be fine. You like her. Just to St Thomas."

"Sure I do, but not on *Palila*. No ladies on board. Your rule."

"My boat, my rules!"

"Shit, man. That's low." Jem stomped along the deck, his eyes fixed on the lights glowing along Vadero's shoreline.

Frank followed. He touched Jem's shoulder in apology. "Yeah, it was, and I'm sorry."

"Why this one?" Jem asked. "We bed them, we leave them." He looked at Frank. "Shit," he said again, "you not share breath! Damn." He paused, thinking. "Man, you tell me w'appenin' here."

Frank looked down. "She's young, Jem. She's in trouble. She reminds me of Sophia."

"Oh, man," Jem said. "Where she bunk?"

"In my cabin. I'll take the saloon."

"Man, you in deep."

"No. But I'm not leaving another woman in danger. She mixed with the wrong types in Havana and it got ugly."

"An' we not de wrong type?"

Frank grinned, knowing he'd won the battle. "Yeah, but only to the authorities. We're decent types too." He slapped

Jem's back. "St Thomas. Get her back to American soil. That's it."

"How many times I tell you. We not true America."

"Truer than Cuba."

Jem shook his head. "You better wear more clothes, man, you showing all God gave you." He heard Josie's quiet laugh drift up through the hatch where she was talking to Elian in Spanish. It seemed she had charmed not just Frank. He shook his head again. That wasn't fair. Frank wasn't trying to bed her.

Frank laughed, then added, "She's a sailor, she'll pull her weight."

"Not much of it," Jem muttered.

Frank looked at his watch, shadows lengthening as the sun eased. He checked the sky, and the ensign fluttering at the stern. "We'll leave at sunset. I don't want to be surprised by anyone looking for her."

"Wha' she do?"

"If she wants to tell you, she will. You can both take watch tonight. Get to know one another."

"Oh, man," Jem said again, "you devious."

Usually meals were eaten in the cockpit but they all ate Elian's early supper in the saloon. As if none of them wanted to draw attention to an extra person aboard, even though they didn't know why. Frank explained that Josie would be the extra hand to replace Tom. Elian nodded, unconcerned. Jem could not contain his snort, although he had been impressed to see Josie travelled light. A canvas sack all that she'd tossed on Frank's bunk after she'd lost the argument that she was perfectly happy to sleep in the saloon. Jem grinned. It didn't look as if she was used to losing. Apart from one with the wrong types in Havana.

"I know you're not happy about me being on *Palila*," Josie said from the helm, Jem keeping a close eye on her keeping a close eye on the mainsail. He was sure Frank would not be asleep and would be straining to hear from his berth below.

"Hey, man, not because of you. But women aboard ship are trouble."

"I won't be," Josie said, her voice firm. "And," she added, a smile taking the bite from her words, "I am a good sailor. You don't have to hover."

"Where'd you learn?"

"I grew up in Maine. On the east coast."

"I know where Maine is."

"Sorry, lots of Americans have trouble locating it, so why should you know?"

"I'm American. So I'm told."

"Jeez, sorry again. Look," she tucked a loose strand back into a ponytail, the scent of mint accompanying the movement. A frown flitted across her face as she planted her feet firmly behind the wheel. "Let's start again. Okay?"

Jem nodded.

"Hello, I'm Josie. Short for Josephine."

He looked at her then took her small hand and shook it gently. "Good day, I'm Jem. Short for Jeremiah."

She laughed. "No wonder they call you Jem!"

"Don't let my mother hear you say that." He joined in her laughter. The mainsail luffed and he watched as Josie turned the helm to fill the sail again. "This is going to be a long sail."

"Please God we just have to tack a lot, and use the engines. I'm never happy sailing with the threat of hurricanes," Josie said.

"We'll be good. It's early." Jem pushed the thought of his conversation with Frank to the back of his mind. "You sailed a hurricane?"

"No, but I've been in one. That was enough."

Jem's prediction was true. It was a sail of long tacks, fighting not currents but winds that ran counter to the direction they wanted to go, and *Palila's* engines ran more than any of them would like.

"Thanks be to St Elmo," Frank said as they sailed down the Virgin Passage, the deep channel between Puerto Rico and the Virgin Islands and saw the lighthouse on Savana Island flash. "Damn, I thought we'd never get here."

"I have a whole new empathy for anyone who gets seasick," said Josie. "I thought I was immune."

"Not there yet," Jem said, his tone glum.

"Cheer up, Jeremiah, mangoes any hour now." Josie ducked as Jem tried to flick her ear.

"My mother is the only one who calls me that!"

"So you've said," she grinned, "but it's so worth the look on your face! And I won't be around to torment you much longer so I've gotta get my kicks whenever I can." She turned serious. "How long will you stay on St Thomas, Frank?"

"A couple of days. Jeremiah here is in a hurry to see his mama."

Laughter drifted up from the galley as well as around the decks as Jem shook his head, though a smile tweaked his lips.

"Okay, I'll get organized," Josie said. "You all know how grateful I am for letting me come aboard. You especially, Jem," she poked the tall man in his taut belly. "I know it was a hard sell."

"No, man. You proved yourself. All good." Jem looked at Frank on the helm and nodded.

"So, Josie," Frank began, paused and pretended to check the sails, "what would you say to staying on? Coming to St Croix?"

Josie gave the men a quizzical look. "Is there a catch? An angle?"

"No, man," Jem said, laughter creasing his face. "You can meet my mother."

"I'd be scared to." She leant over the bow, watching the slight wake, then turned and grinned at both men, her eyes sparkling. "Yeah, I'd like that. But you must have your cabin back, Frank."

"Deal. But only after St Thomas. Elian wants to head back to Cuba. Seems like all my crew want to see their mamas!"

"Not me," Josie said as she gazed at the nearing land mass.

"You know the waters, you take us in to Mosquito Bay," Frank said to Jem, referring to the bay west of Charlotte Amalie. "Then you'll find your BWIR mate, yes? So we can offload the liquor."

"*Palila* won't know how to sail without a hull full of booze," Josie said.

"She needs a rest." Jem looked at the bleached teak decks. "She's worked hard these last few months."

"Not the first decks I'll have sanded," Josie said. "How long are you staying put on St Croix?"

Frank looked at Jem then toward land. "A while."

"You're done with running rum?" Her voice was surprised. "I've never known anyone stop of their own volition."

"Yeah, well, we did it for fun. And we made some money. This last run was a bit too close for my liking. Seems the Coast Guard are getting better organized. Stop whilst we're ahead," Frank said.

"So what will you do?" Josie was curious. She looked at the men who had become her friends. "I can't imagine you with your feet up, Frank. And what about you, Jem? Will your brother want you interfering with his business?"

"Oh, we have a plan." Frank's grin was broad, the broadest Jem had seen since Edward's death.

"Legal?"

"What do you take us for, Josie?" Frank asked.

"Rumrunners, perhaps!"

"And there's the thanks we get after we took her aboard," Frank smiled at Jem. "That's gratitude!"

Jem's laugh startled a gull spiraling down toward *Palila*. They watched it soar away.

"So what? What are you going to do?" Josie asked.

"We are going to open a hotel."

"We have to build it first," said Jem.

"There you go again, always looking for problems," Frank said, his face alive with anticipation.

"Excuse me, gentlemen," Josie interrupted their banter. "Details, please?"

"Our friend here," Frank nodded at Jem, "knows someone who knows someone who... well you get the picture? There is a small islet off Christiansted called Protestant Cay. By all accounts the ideal location for a hotel. The first proper one on the island. And, so our friend tells me, the town has potential. Rather attractive architecture, even if it is Danish."

"And built by slaves," Jem added.

"Yes, there is that. Not a noble time in anyone's history. But what better way to honor them than by bringing people to the islands?"

"Not to lose the history lesson and this is probably a silly question, Frank, but do either of you have any experience building a hotel?" Josie asked, "Even running one?"

"No. But we hadn't run rum before either."

"Maybe not rum, but you'd run other things." Her tone was tart. She looked south to where St Croix was a shimmer on the horizon. "Umm, I may not have mentioned this but I grew up in a hotel."

"You what?" Frank looked stunned. Jem smiled, delighted to see animation return to his friend's demeanor.

"Er, yeah, my parents ran the St Clement's Hotel in Rockland."

"Rockland?" Frank tipped his cap back and scratched his head. "Ship building, right?"

"Yeah, that's right. Among other things. Foundries, factories, fishing."

"Any other 'fs'?" Frank's chuckle started deep in his belly.

"A big hotel?" Jem asked.

"Big enough. What are you going to call it?"

"We," Frank said with a smile and a nod to Josie and Jem, "we are going to call it The Sofia."

Footnote:

Answering the call for volunteers, many men from the West Indies joined the British Army at the outbreak of World War I. Initially the British West Indies Regiment (BWIR) served mainly in support roles, guarding prisoners or building sandbag walls for example, however, as it became clear more men were needed in fighting battalions, the volunteers served in Europe, North Africa and Palestine. The 2nd Battalion BWIR, in September 1918, was ordered to clear enemy posts close to the British line in Palestine, which involved advancing across three miles of open land under heavy fire. "The objective was achieved with nine men killed and 43 wounded. Two men, Lance Corporal Sampson and Private Spence, were awarded the Military Medal for bravery during the action. On 20 September, after the campaign, the commanding officer of the BWIR, Major General Sir Edward Chaytor, wrote, "Outside my own division there are no troops I would sooner have with me than the BWIs who have won the highest opinions of all who have been with them during our operations here."

It was during this campaign that fictional Jem was injured.

At the start of Prohibition in 1917 the maritime limit was three miles offshore. To mitigate the ease of unloading their cargo onto smaller "contact boats" that could move liquor to shore faster, and hide with greater ease in shallow bays from the authorities, US officials expanded their jurisdiction to twelve miles offshore, creating a legal precedent still in effect today.

Lisa Lindquist Dorr in her book *A Thousand Thirsty Beaches* posits routes used during Prohibition by rumrunners aided not only the movement of people but later drugs, which possibly added to the "complicated processes of illicit and licit trade connecting the United States with the Caribbean."

Fancy a Rum Runner? Try this recipe!

Ingredients:

1 oz Light Rum   1 oz Orange Juice
1 oz Dark Rum   1 oz Pineapple Juice
1 oz Banana Liqueur   Splash of Grenadine
1 oz Blackberry Liqueur   Fruit to garnish

Directions:

Combine all ingredients in a blender with two cups ice. Blend until smooth then serve in a hurricane glass with fruit garnish and a straw.

CHERRY PICKING

*P*runus avium are those delicious sweet cherries that show up in our grocery stores in about July. There are many varieties, of which the leader is Bing, so named over a 100 years ago by an Oregon grower for one of his Chinese workmen. *Prunus cerasus* is the name given to the tart or sour cherry, the most widely known being the Montmorency.

Now this might surprise you, but cherries do not grow in the US Virgin Islands. Whatever the type, they prefer the northern climes of continental USA, Turkey, Chile and the southern states of Australia.

But we do have on our lovely island a cadre of tart and sour individuals who seem to think that human rights can be divided into different categories and that one is able to cherry pick which to support and which to denigrate.

June is Gay Pride month. Sadly, homophobia is alive and kicking in many parts of the Caribbean though hope is on the horizon when places like Cuba, closed so long to modernity, is proud to have held for the last four years a Day Against Homophobia, spearheaded by Mariela Castro, the daughter of former President Raúl Castro. Puerto Rico and Curaçao are also proud to hold parades supporting Gay Pride.

Yesterday it was St Croix's turn to be rainbow proud. A first for this island which, on the whole, tends to delight in its diversity. But the Pride Parade could easily have been soured by the vitriol emitted, anonymously of course, across social media.

I am not going to give print space to the crass comments, though a couple were almost humorous in their stupidity. But there was one circulating on the ubiquitous Facebook calling for violence against any and all taking part or supporting the Parade.

It was serious enough to involve the FBI, with St Croix Police Chief, Winsbut McFarlande being heard on various radio shows in the days leading up to the Pride Parade, assuring listeners that the organizers had the requisite permits and that, "The police department will do all within its resources to monitor and attempt to minimize the threat."

And they did. There was a strong, polite and friendly police presence. There had been an attempt to block the parade route with debris, probably left over from the hurricanes which did their best to destroy the island last year, but all was cleared by the time the marchers made their colorful way along the seafront at Frederiksted to Dorsch Beach. Rainbow flags were vivid against the cerulean waters, and all that was needed to complete the postcard was a rainbow in the sky.

There was a mingling of signs. *Repent of your Sins and you will be Forgiven* waved next to *Love is Love!* One has to wonder what is sinful about loving someone, anyone. There was though an upbeat and friendly mood with little actual engagement from those picketing. I wondered whether indeed they were becoming bemused at the mingling of gay and straight. Perhaps the tee-shirt proclaiming *I Can't Even Think Straight* added to their Crucian confusion.

I am not gay but count amongst my friends from around the world, some who are. By the same token I have never had to face the dreadful dilemma about whether to proceed with an abortion. I have friends who have. I have never been racially profiled despite having spent much of my life in Africa and Asia, unless you count comments called from market vendors along the lines of *"Hola, Blanca...."* or a shakedown from a policeman who hasn't been paid for months. I consider myself fortunate to have friends of all colors and creeds - not because they are all colors and creeds but because they are good company and have proven their friendship over years and continents, as I hope I have to them.

There should be no cherry picking because human rights should be across the board. If they are not, the early work of suffragettes has been in vain. If they are not, then the dismantling of apartheid in South Africa and desegregation in the United States has been in vain. Or the death of Harvey Milk and the Stonewall riots. If they are not, then the work of people like Maryan Abdulle Hassan, a 26-old-Somalian woman fighting female genital mutilation is irrelevant.

Or people like Audre Lorde - who championed the rights of gay, black women and who spent her last years on St Croix and helped found, along with Gloria I Joseph, The St Croix Women's Coalition.

So when I read a post written by someone, without even the courage to use his or her own name, urging others to wield AK-47s and shoot those holding rainbow flags and marching peacefully, and joyfully, it infuriates me. It makes me go out in the hot sun and proudly join the parade.

LGBTQ rights, women's right, every variation of color rights - they all matter because they are human rights. 100 years ago that Oregon farmer named a sweet cherry after his Chinese cherry picker. Let's lessen the *prunus cerasus* variety on St Croix and remember human rights are not for cherry picking.

JULY 3RD, 2018

THE CONCH CALLS

hadows cavort across the yellow walls of Fort
Christiansvaern as people mill about waiting for the
conch shell to call them to order. Dawn is a faint glimmer
across the hills to the east but all is not quiet. Music, blaring
from speakers on a pick-up truck, call for liberation, freedom
- Bob Marley is always a popular choice. Blue lights flash like
beacons from waiting police vehicles. Then silence.

Senator Positive Nelson, who has organized this Freedom
March for 18 years, is a tall rangy figure in white shorts and a
loose African shirt. His dreadlocks swing as his head tips back.
He raises the conch to his lips, and blows. The drum beats with
a building intensity. It is hard not to be moved.

After a twelve-year gradual freeing of the slaves was
announced in 1847, and the order that all babies born from
July 28th of that year were to be born free, anger percolated
amongst those enslaved. Why not immediate emancipation?
170 years ago on the night of Sunday, July 2nd, in what was
then the Danish West Indies and is now the US Virgin Islands,
Moses Gottlieb, known to many as General Buddhoe, sounded
the conch and led many of those enslaved on a march to
Frederiksted, demanding their freedom.

Gottlieb, a literate and skilled sugar boiler thought
possibly to have come to St Croix from Barbados, worked
at Estate La Grange but was often loaned for work on other
sugar plantations. It was this freedom of movement, combined

230

with an innate leadership skill, that allowed Gottlieb to secretly organize the march. By morning the crowd had swelled to about 5,000. Later that afternoon, Governor Peter von Scholten, fearing violence and burning, momentously proclaimed, "All unfree in the Danish West Indies are from today Free".

Back in the days before cell phones, it took a while for the news of freedom to travel and so an offshoot of the protesters, known as 'the fleet' and led by a young man called King, continued to riot, burn and plunder. It was thanks to Gottlieb, who accompanied the Danish fire chief, Major Jacob Gyllich, around the island that the mayhem did not continue, although a hundred black lives were lost. Order was restored but rumors swirled that the Governor, who had a mulatto mistress, was sympathetic to the cause and knew there was a possibility of an uprising. The sugar plantocracy was enraged with the proclamation, which immediately decimated their workforce, and von Scholten was ordered back to Denmark.

Despite being protected initially from the planters' wrath by Major Gyllich, Gottlieb was arrested, questioned and shipped off the island aboard the SS Ørnen. He set sail from St Croix as a gentleman but, once out of port, was stripped of his clothes and put to work until, in January 1849, he landed on Trinidad. Told he would be executed if he ever returned to the Danish West Indies, Moses Gottlieb, aka General Buddhoe is believed to have ended his days in the United States.

Today - July 3rd - is Emancipation Day! Celebrated each year with the Freedom March. As I watched the marchers, including my husband, answer the call of the conch, rattle the chains on Fort Christiansvaern and walk along Company Street at the start of their 15-mile march to Frederiksted, dawn trickled over Gallows Bay, pink and orange bands among grey clouds promising much needed rain.

Freedom came to the enslaved of the Danish West Indies 170 years ago and it is easy to think that freedom is global. But it isn't. Slavery still exists in all its ugly connotations. So whilst we celebrate the bravery of leaders like Gottlieb and the many who marched with him, as well as those who supported their claims for freedom, like von Scholten and Gyllich then 30 years later in 1878, the Four Queens who roused the crowd during Fireburn demanding better labour laws, we should remember those still under the mantel of oppression.

Would that the conch call for freedom be heard globally!

BED POSTS

Funny how things pop into one's head. Okay, okay, my head. Today the topic of discussion, mine anyway, is bedposts and uses thereof. Why, you might ask? Well, this morning whilst sitting on the gallery overlooking a somewhat bruised Caribbean sea - striations of purple, blue and mercury - with the sky delineated by a streak of smudgy white which, the higher the eye travelled, turned to a soft swaddling blue, I saw the two bedposts. In the garden.

That well-known ditty popped into my head. First sung in Britain by Lonnie Donegan - it reached number 3 in the late 1950s and was apparently his greatest US success. Donegan's version was adapted to the UK audience because the original version mentioned 'spearmint' which, being a trademark, was a no-no as far as the BBC was concerned. Then he changed a few more words. And actually I prefer his rendition to the one written by Billy Rose, Ernest Breuer and Marty Bloom, and released by The Happiness Boys in 1924. Donegan's is funnier.

Oh sorry, I forgot to mention the song. *Does Your Chewing Gum Lose Its Flavor on the Bedpost Overnight?* Now you get my drift. And having bedposts in the garden, with a strong possibility of squalls throughout the night, could arguably diminish the gooeyness of any lurking gum.

Oh me, oh my, oh you
Whatever shall I do?

The reason the bedposts are in the garden is simple. We need a privacy wall. So they are in the process of becoming a frame for a passionfruit vine - rather apt really. Now these are not just any old bedposts, they are mahogany. Which, as anyone who has lived in a country where termites also reside knows, is a wood somewhat resistant to their voracious attentions.

And before anyone cries foul. Sacrilege. These particular bedposts are not in pristine condition and minus chewing gum, will by the end of the week be an elegant backdrop giving privacy both to us and our neighbors.

In areas not prone to hurricanes, the season of which we are in at the moment, sticking a couple of bedposts in the ground would not be cause for the engineering operation currently being undertaken. Ratios have been discussed. Akin to how deep a telegraph pole should be to lessen the impact of hugely high winds tearing across our island. And so our bedposts have been stabilized in breeze blocks - those ones with holes - then cemented into the ground up to where the bedrail would normally be attached.

The ditty continues to swirl around my head.

If your mother says don't chew it
Do you swallow it in spite?

And those lines bring to mind Singapore. In 1992 that small island nation instituted a total ban on the sticky substance. And I'm with them.

Does it go all hard upon the floor
And look a nasty sight
Can you bend it like a fish hook?

It was an answer sought by the Minister of National Development when the Father of the Republic of Singapore, Lee Kuan Yew, was still prime minister. Whilst agreeing the depositing of said gum on mailboxes, in keyholes, on lift buttons, on pavements, under the seats of the brand new and expensive railway system, the MRT and, indeed, on bedposts was a prohibitive drain on government coffers under the heading of public cleaning, Mr Lee believed it was a drastic solution. It was not until the second-ever prime minister, Goh Tok Chong, took office that the ban was implemented.

Imports were immediately stopped. A selling off period was allowed. Discourse chittered around satay stalls and discontent caused some open defiance, which was soon quashed with the naming and shaming of chewers and spitters. A rumor, actually fake news, made the international press that the penalty for chewing gum was a right republican caning. In fact the punishment was merely a fine, oh, and possibly imprisonment.

A BBC reporter had the temerity to question the edict, suggesting the outright ban of gum chewing might "stifle creativity".

The question is peculiar
I'd give a lot of dough
If only I could know
The answer to my question
Is it yes or is it no?

It was a question Mr Lee was happy to answer. "If you can't think because you can't chew, try a banana." Brilliant!

Then in 1999 when talks began for a bilateral free-trade agreement between the US and Singapore, big business in the name of Wrigley put their sticky fingers on the goal posts. Imagine that. Two overriding issues were the stumbling blocks - the War in Iraq and chewing gum. Singapore, recognizing compromise is not a dirty word, agreed.

Does your chewing gum have
More uses than it says upon
the pack?

The sale and masticating of medicinal gum would be allowed but only when purchased in a pharmacy or dental office with all purchasers' names being recorded. Said Mr C Perille, the director of corporate communications for Wrigley, "There's many examples in our history of things that may have not made short-term financial sense but it was the right thing to do in a philosophical or long-term sense."

And there we have it. Back to Lonnie Donegan philosophizing on whether chewing gum would lose its flavor on our bedposts in the garden.

TUPPENCE A BAG

I drive through the old plantation gates and along the rutted road towards a 1960's bungalow peeking behind frangipanis whose limbs are also home to a plethora of orchids, scent and beauty mingled. I slow the truck to a crawl as the chance of an arrival committee made up of bantam hens, a Muscovy duck and perhaps a pelican is very real. Not to mention four-legged creatures.

"Hello, Zulu." The lolloping ridgeback's slathering kiss skims my face as I bend to pet the dog. "Come on, girl," I call to Sienna, an elderly Crucian mix ambling over to greet me, her tail wagging. "Good morning," my voice carries through the menagerie to Toni Lance as I avoid land crabs on the path to her front door.

About to sit, I am hustled back outside.

"Come on, we're going to feed the pelicans."

The pelicans in question are Marley and Rainbow. The former has a mending broken wing, and Rainbow, named for the beach where she was found, has a cracked beak and broken wing.

We walk across the yard, Toni hauling a hose as well as carrying a shallow container sloshing with water and sprat. I unlatch the large cage and watch as fish are tossed first into the water dish for Rainbow then, with some trepidation on my part, into Marley's beak. I imagine its crisp snap could remove a careless finger with ease. The birds toss their heads back as fish travel down their necks.

"How much do they eat a day?" I ask, as Toni passes me the container, a few fish remaining. Her hands show evidence of near misses although no fingers are missing.

"About two pounds each in captivity, four in the wild." Her answer is laconic. She turns the nozzle on and sprays the birds, to promote preening. Rainbow half jumps, half flies to a perch, an ungainly movement that turns to shimmying delight as water cascades over him. He flaps over to Marley on another perch and they do a shuffle dance on the pole, still luxuriating in the water raining down. "Did you hear that?"

I nod. A guttural hiss is coming from deep within each pelican. "Is that a happy sound?"

"Yes. Wouldn't you be happy having food delivered then a cool shower?"

I agree. "How much longer will you keep them?"

"Well," Toni pauses to watch Rainbow's wing as she tries to extend it, "Marley could go soon, but Rainbow's not ready. They get along well and were found in a similar area so they might be part of the same group. I think I'm going to release them together. They could look out for each other. Come on, they're done now."

I follow the slight, energetic woman back to her house. She transfers the remaining fish into another container to be used for supper. The pelicans', not hers.

I prepare to sit and Toni points to the iPhone waiting to record her words and asks, "Do you want to turn that thing on?"

"Not yet." As I shake my head she gestures for me to follow her into the hall leading to the bedrooms. She runs her hands along a shelf and pulls out a book I recognize. It is Paul Gallico's *The Snow Goose*, this one illustrated by well-known artist, Peter Scott. A book I grew up with and which I read to my children, crying with each reading.

Toni nods to a wooden duck sitting on the shelf as she finds another book, an 1841 *Birds of America* published by the Audubon Society. "Dad collected duck decoys. He had about three hundred." Next, a letter sent to her father from The Wildfowl Trust in Slimbridge, England - a place I have visited many times. "He was fascinated with ducks and geese - particularly Canada geese."

Back in the sitting room Toni tucks her legs up on a chair and settles, rather like a stork. I sit on the sofa draped with a counterpane - there to protect the cushions from dogs, a cat, and any stray bird that might be flying around.... indoors. The probability being great. "Where's Athena?" I ask. The peregrine falcon, often found on the gallery, tethered by her jesses to a perch, sadly can't be released due to a gun-shot injury sustained a couple of years ago.

"Outside, enjoying the sunshine." Toni launches into her childhood. "As a family we spent a lot of time outdoors, in the wild. My father had been in the Navy, then publishing, then was the West Coast rep for fishing and yachting magazines. Every summer we'd all bundle into the car and my parents would take us riding and hiking."

"Toni," I glance down at my questions, none of which I have yet asked. "You certainly come from an active family, was it also artistic?"

Her face lights up. "We all drew and sketched. Pam, one of my sisters, is very talented, in oils. And Cynthia, the eldest

- she's a neuro-embryologist - she's always drawn her own research illustrations."

An album is pulled out. In most of the fading, almost sepia-tinted photos, Toni is holding her cat, or a squirrel, or a chipmunk. Sometimes a guitar - the images are carefree.

"Mother was an amateur photographer. She was always posing us. We hated it. And I had a great aunt who was a well-known artist - Marion Churchill Raulston. She went to Pratt, and Skarbina in Germany. She was a portraitist and after World War I taught patients in a sanatorium to paint."

"She sounds a remarkable woman." I take the conversation back to Toni's teen years and say, "As someone who has relocated many times, I was interested to read that you moved from Pasadena to Laguna Beach. How old were you and what do you remember of that time?"

Toni's eyes well up and she says, "Laguna Beach changed everything."

I am stunned and wait in silence.

"I was sixteen. I moved from a conservative private school to a liberal public school where kids were into surfing, drugs and drinking. The So-Cal scene that was not my scene. It was hard. Really hard. I was an introvert."

"What prompted the move?"

"Dad retired. He was in the early stages of Parkinson's."

"That must have made everything even tougher," I say.

She nods. "Rather than trying to fit in I became a loner. Introspective. I spent all my free time in the hills behind Laguna Beach. That was where I became fascinated with hawks. I'd draw, think, and read a little. Have you read Henry Thoreau?"

"Years ago," I reply. "Some of *Life in the Woods*."

"His quote 'I find it wholesome to be alone the greater part of time' was pivotal. It made me realize it was okay to be the way I was."

Her quiet words provoke an independent, though maybe sometimes lonely, teenager despite a lively family.

She shakes her head then continues, "It was about the same time a falconer came to my high school. The wetlands at Newport Beach attract lots of migrating ducks, hawks, osprey. I've never fussed about the little birds, always big birds."

An image of Sesame Street's yellow Big Bird pops into my head.

"But you did take part in sports, you were an athlete?"

"Yeah, I was good. Competitive. Track, basketball, field hockey. I played competitive tennis from the age of seven to forty-five." Toni leans forward to check on Athena as a light drizzle begins. "I was asked to parties, you know, and went a few times, but I mostly said no."

Toni is not looking for pity, more an understanding of what has made her the woman she is.

"Laguna Beach was / is an artist's colony. Did that help?"

"Sure. In a way. I had a dark room at home. At seventeen or eighteen I was earning money from doing kids' portraits. I'd mount them in hexagonal boxes - it was quirky. I liked using natural settings."

My mind flies to my latest author photo. Toni was the photographer and posed me leaning against the textured wall of a crumbling sugar mill.

"And," Toni continues, "I got a photographic scholarship - $500 a trimester - to college. *Mutual of Omaha's Wild Kingdom* was all our favorite TV show. I wanted to be a wildlife photographer for National Geographic."

Not growing up in America I have never seen the program but assume it was similar to David Attenborough's shows. I glance at my notes. "You did two years at Humboldt State University in a Wildlife Management and Photography program and two years at Long Beach State. Why the change?"

"I never liked school. I mean, I liked the nature side of it and the drawing - which was technical art, but the science side - chemistry and physics - was tough."

I nod my head in full understanding.

"I took a year off and went to Aspen and rented a room in a cabin from friends of my parents. I hated it. The others in the cabin were playing around with mescaline and acid." Toni smooths blonde wisps escaping from her ponytail. "Again not my scene. I just drew, painted, worked in a beer joint, a cheese store."

Her sense of self, developed through time alone, is palpable. I am about to move back to her second attempt at college but Toni's voice breaks in.

"I met a guy in a bar who wanted to start a wild west show and wanted me to do the posters." Toni flips pages in another album. "Here." She points to four photos of her work. Animals in cages. "I was paid $25 a poster. I shouldn't have done it. It went against my every rule. Nothing should be kept in cages if they can be released."

It is obvious the commission still rankles. "What did you study at Long Beach?" I ask.

"Biomedical illustration. Rendering, drafting, life drawing, anatomy." Before I can comment, she continues. "Long Beach was a commuter college. Students lived all over the place so I didn't have many pals there either. Anyway, it was a five-year program. We had to take two speech classes. I was very reserved and public speaking paralyzed me."

I'm surprised, as the few times I have heard Toni speak in public she has been animated and articulate. We go off on a seeming tangent but I am beginning to recognize most stories come back to birds.

"My sister and I went to Disneyland one Sunday and driving home we passed some roadkill. Not groundmeat or a rattlesnake but a perfect barn owl. Not a single abrasion. I gutted it, cleaned out the brain and stuck it in the freezer at home. Then I found a 1945 book on taxidermy, so I stuffed, mounted and painted it. It was a huge turning point for me, to know I could do it."

"What happened to the owl?"

"I gave it to my biology teacher. I always got top marks in art class."

Toni goes to her store cupboard and comes back with a portfolio case. Drawing after drawing comes out. Her rendering of a barn owl is masterful. Another series is of a human face, stripped to the muscles and drawn in bas relief. One piece is particularly poignant. It is a self-portrait. Animals surround a boot, cage bars on the ankle encase a wolf - the analogy is not difficult to see. Surely her teachers recognized her prodigious talent.

She is pensive. "But I only ever wanted to paint birds, not humans, and after the barn owl I knew I could paint. And the science was a drag so I left."

I smile. "What did your parents say?"

"They weren't surprised. But my sister Cynthia was cross and told me I'd never make it as an artist."

It is the perfect lead-in for the next question, one I have mulled over for a number of days. "Toni, what fundamental characteristic makes you the accomplished artist and 'the bird lady of St Croix?'"

Her eyes glitter in surprise and she is still. This is a woman who has known herself for a long time, ever since walking the hills behind Laguna Beach as a teenager. I wonder if I have overstepped the mark but she answers.

"Genetics. I'm driven and focused. I've never not finished a painting. And I take care of every injured bird to the best of my ability. I'm super-disciplined and somewhat of a control freak."

"Somewhat?"

She takes my teasing in her stride. "I might not have had the best comprehension with the sciences but art and birds are tangibles. And I'm responsible, we were all raised like that. But I suppose I was a free spirit. Maybe because I was the youngest but even back then I wouldn't be put in a box. I'm comfortable following my gut. And," she adds, "I always got on better with older people."

"Not always." I contradict her, thinking of various youngsters who help with birds when their schedules allow.

She laughs, and fusses with her hair again, "Yeah, not now but when I was young."

"You are a woman who cares deeply yet handles roadkill without blinking, scurrying to collect it in order to feed birds you are rehabilitating. To me sentimental and sad are completely different feelings. What do you think has contributed to your ability to separate these two emotions?"

I am distressed to see her eyes tear again, and say, "We can move on, Toni."

"No, that's fine." There is silence as she gathers her thoughts. Her eyes are still damp. "I have a huge heart and am deeply emotional but I am also pragmatic, a realist. Things have to be cut and dried and I do what needs to be done. Blood and guts don't gross me out, probably because of all the anatomy classes. Seeing a bird gasping for breath is terrible. The suffering is traumatic." She pauses again and I am quiet. "The first kestrel I raised and released was awful. It didn't come back and I spent days trying to find the bird. Traipsing around a field, along a beach. It tormented me. That's happened other times, but I've had to learn to let go."

"I suppose that comes with maturity," I say. "Let's go back to California. You abandoned school. What next?"

Her laughter skips around the dim room.

"I lived in some sketchy neighborhoods. I didn't have much money and supplemented my cash flow working for a high-end catering company. But I always paid my own way. My parents never gave me a cent."

"Would you have taken it?" I ask the question, rather like a lawyer certain of the answer.

"No. But they never worried either. I had good sense and I checked in with them."

"What were you doing when you weren't waitressing?" Her answer highlights her lack of squeamishness.

"I'd check out study skins from the Los Angeles Natural History Museum and draw them, using my Dad's books as reference. Duck hunters would sometimes bring me birds."

(Since our conversation I have looked into study skins, not being entirely sure what they are, supposing they are the gutted and flattened skins of birds, rather like a sheepskin rug. They are not. They are the entire body, rigid in death and which lie in drawer after drawer waiting for the artist or researcher to examine the morphology of each specimen. In the case of birds, a study of the feathers, the color and length of the beak, measurements and so on.)

A chuckle comes from the chair opposite me.

"When I was still living at home, Mother would find roadkill - duck, quail, rattlesnakes - in the freezer that I used to practice my rendering and stippling. I always labeled them!"

"She must have been a patient woman," I suggest.

My comment is met with a wry smile. "Not always. She was the more volatile of my parents but she got used to it and always encouraged my independence."

"Were you selling your art?"

"A lot of sales were initially through friends of my parents, and The Festival of Arts Laguna Beach were always supportive. My bird paintings were already stylized but with a whimsical twist which people liked. Then I painted ostrich eggs with pen and ink. I used to sell them in a shop in Texas as well California. Hours of work but they sold well - $1000 each!"

"Wow! The Lance version of a Fabergé egg."

Laugh lines radiate across her face. "I lived in a small apartment with a surfboard and bike, painting, working a variety of jobs. I once au-paired five kids with an age range of six to fourteen."

"Not much fun, I would imagine." I am taken back to a weekend many years ago in London, when I was paid to look after three children whilst their parents went to Paris. When I reflect on it, I'm amazed I ever had children of my own.

I return to the present and think how fortunate I am to have seen many of Toni's paintings. Some have a strong environmental message, birds tangled in fishing line for example, and I ask her about it. She is immersed in a memory. I am not sure she is going to answer. I wait.

"In 1980, my brother-in-law, who is a property developer, purchased the old Beet Factory at Newport Beach. The factory, which was to be demolished, was home to burrowing owls but he didn't care. That was when I painted my first environmental statement - an owl in a condemned tire factory in the background."

"1980 is also the year you first arrived on St Croix. What brought you here?"

"Another sister. Wendy. She and her husband had been on a cruise and fell in love with the island, so came back to live here. She taught at Country Day School. I came to visit. And stayed."

"And had a romance of your own, to a considerably older man." Toni's glance is sharp. "Ceddie Nelthropp* is a part of your story. Was he supportive of the birds?"

She nods. "I'd been here about six months and was on the beach at Duggan's Reef when a couple of boys came along with a red-tail hawk in a box. I pretended to work for Fish & Wildlife and said I'd take it."

"And that was the start of the St Croix Avian Sanctuary?" I ask.

Toni nods again. "Sort of. Ceddie and his brother converted a dog run into a cage. I got hold of a pair of welder's gloves and fed the hawk lizards for about three weeks, then released him out there." She points to the field behind her. "He came back two weeks later, starving. So I fed him up and tried again. The animal shelter heard what I was doing and started sending me raptors. Then others brought me egrets. Then a fuzzy little pelican who probably fell out of a nest at Green Cay and should have been left there. I didn't know what I was doing so contacted the Pelican Man's Bird Sanctuary in Florida and he told me what to do."

"Which was?" I think back to the pelicans Toni fed earlier. She is fond of them, and they tolerate her.

"Not to make friends, feed him and leave the cage open. He had worms and the medicine made him sick, so I gave him antibiotics and vitamins, and he became too tame. The vet, Paul Hess, helped. Then in about 2000 someone found a peregrine falcon, who was blind in one eye. They were on the endangered list so technically it was illegal for me to be doing anything as I wasn't licenced."

"What did you do?" St Croix is a small island, and I find it hard to believe the authorities didn't know what Toni was doing.

"I called Mike Evans of Fish and Wildlife. He admitted to knowing about the birds, and suggested it was time I became licensed by DPNR. Doc Petersen helped me too, but I realized I needed to know more so started taking courses up in the States, and going to bird rehab meetings. Then Emy Thomas helped me get registered as a non-profit."

"And that's when you started taking birds to the schools? Explaining the importance of St Croix as a migratory staging post?"

Toni nods. "I enjoyed that. And maybe it helped kids know it isn't cool to shoot them. Teachers used to bring groups here too. Yeah, I might have touched a handful of people."

"More than a handful, I'm sure. This place," I motion to the land reaching down to the South Shore, "would seem to be the ideal location for a bird sanctuary." It's my turn to hesitate. "All this takes an enormous amount of energy, and time. Have you considered the future of the sanctuary?"

"Of course I have." She is abrupt. "I've tried to help others set up but it always falls through. Health will probably stop me one day. Then there'll be nothing, no one, for a couple of years. People only learn when there is a need and some pressure."

It is a cynical assessment. Toni stands and stretches her back. "I'm pessimistic for wildlife. I can see a time when there will be no pelicans. But all humans can do is try to live as positive and worthwhile a life as possible, try to do something good for future generations."

I look beyond the palm trees on the cliff edge to the sea shimmering in weak sunlight. "Have you lived here all the time?"

"Ceddie and I separated for about six years, but we remained close friends and I always had the birds here."

"What took you to Nevis in 1986?"

"I went with friends, an older couple, the Skeochs, as their friend and bag carrier!"

"And that's where you met a man at a bar?" I prompt Toni, still a lithe, attractive woman, I imagine she was a stunner in her younger years.

"Yeah," she laughs, "it turned out he was head of the Caribbean-British Philatelic Bureau." She points to albums stacking up on the coffee table. "I have always photographed my paintings and I used to carry around a stack of 3"x 5" photos. I showed them to him and he commissioned me to paint two series of postage stamps for the British Government."

"That's a big deal," I say.

"Yeah, it was. I had precise guidelines. Each painting had to be 9" x 6" in gouache, the lettering had to set exactly right, then, and I don't know if it really happened, they had to be okayed by the Queen."

I imagine Her Majesty studying the work of a young artist based in St Croix. "What were the series?"

"The history of rum making in the British Virgin Islands, and birds of prey in St Vincent and the Grenadines." She watches Jenny, the cat, saunter through the room. "Funny how things come full circle. I entered a duck postage stamp contest when I was a teenager but didn't win."

"Do you enjoy commissions?"

"No. I don't like being told what to do."

It is my turn to laugh. I remind Toni of the tiger I had to beg her to paint on a cigar box for my son. "Your cigar box show this year was a sold-out event. Did you enjoy showing in your own home?"

"It was great. Much more personal. Because of COVID it was just a few visitors at a time, and we really had a chance to talk, to visit. And people liked seeing my house."

I am not surprised. From the exterior Toni's home is a bungalow with few outstanding architectural features. The interior, however, is a sensory, spatial and visual delight. She is a collector, but the uncluttered feel is testament to her need for order.

"Tell me about your furniture?" I say as I take in West Indian antiques that fill the room.

"I grew up with antiques. Both my parents were collectors. Dad the decoy ducks, and stamps. My mother collected Italian plates, bronzes. It was an eclectic mix. Ceddie had a few pieces and, over the years since his death, I have added to them. Some I traded for art. I used to go to every estate and yard sale."

I look around the burnt red walls of the room filled with art. It is a tranquil room. Toni is not short of pronouncements.

"I think artists see color more vividly. The sky, the sea. Colors delight us."

I want to demur but I am not an artist so have no comparison.

She continues. "I know I can be a pain in the arse. I find it hard sometimes to step out and be with people. I am never happier than when I'm playing classical music and painting. It's calm, quiet, almost like a meditation."

Her comment is the perfect precursor to another question I have worried over asking.

"Toni, are you a spiritual woman?"

She looks at me and sighs. I am about to crater and move on but she starts to speak.

"Laguna Beach. I was younger than most when I found my sense of self, not ego, but being okay with who I am. In a way that's like finding God. I wasn't raised with a structured religion, but living in the US and learning the way to behave stems, I suppose, from Christian ideals."

"Isn't that morality?" I ask.

She nods and with an ironic smile says, "I had a privileged upbringing but very conservative. And there were undertones. Mother was spoiled. She came from a rich family and was in some aspects superficial. There were expectations that we dress and behave a certain way, have handsome boyfriends, fit the mold. But for all that we all grew up adored."

"What did they think of Ceddie?"

"They liked him, but not the relationship although they came to understand the attraction."

It is morning and our conversation feels it should be taking place in the small hours over a glass of rum.

"Let's get back to art and birds," I suggest. "In 2018 a young film maker, Elizabeth Herzfeldt-Kamprath, wrote and produced *Under Her Wing* - a documentary about you, a woman who guards her privacy, some might say fiercely. How did that feel?"

"It was okay, because it was authentic. I was involved in putting music to the film footage, which was fun. Jacqueline Schwab, the pianist, chose inspiring pieces to play."

I think of all that's necessary to keep this sanctuary running. "It takes more than tuppence a bag to feed the birds. You eschew social media, which could be a fundraising platform. Did the film help with donations?"

"A little but I get what I need. You know, when I was younger, it was 'wow, look at me!' I liked the attention, then I got more than I liked. Now I prefer to spend more time doing it than showing it."

"On your website you mention you dreamed of living in the tropics and painting like Gaugin. You achieved one of those goals. But your painting has been described as photorealistic. Have you ever been tempted to paint in a less meticulous, more loose-brushed style like Gaugin's synthesist style?"

Toni flips open another album and points. "I've painted like him."

"Similar subject matter maybe but not style," I say, looking at photos of West Indian scenes.

She concedes the point.

"It's my controlling streak. I only ever paint at my drafting table. I compose most of my paintings from a photo I've taken, the light and dark. And for a while I tried to make a statement with my paintings. Pelicans with fish hooks, but that made me cry. Made me sad. So for my own sanity I am trying to lighten up. To not look so deeply. Maybe that's why I enjoyed painting the cigar boxes."

I wonder whether the postage stamps from around the world, included on many of the cigar boxes, vibrant with parrots, octopi, fish and which have been so well received, is a subliminal nod to her father, and Ceddie, both stamp collectors, but time is running out and I decide not to delve in that direction.

"Your travels are chronicled by photographs. Why did you stop painting scenes from your trips, or life on a Caribbean island?"

"A little boat on a beach doesn't touch my heart. Birds do. And I don't take criticism well. I didn't like being questioned as to who was I to paint West Indian scenes."

I have strong opinions on cultural appropriation but this is neither the time nor place to voice them.

Toni continues, "Watching a peregrine falcon preen, or a pelican shiver with delight in the water being sprayed, to see the birds comfortable and safe with me is an honor bestowed. You know, I've always had a kind of heartache. A loneliness. Birds became friends to care for."

It is my turn to feel tearful.

Toni continues, "But I know I've pushed people away. I've always thought that if I got too close to another person, or if I had kids, it would take away from my art, my creativity."

I turn off the recorder, close my file and hug this fascinating, complex woman.

"I don't think that is something you ever had to worry about," I say, as I see a pelican land on the grass outside. It is Ivan waiting for an easy lunch from the hands of the bird lady of St Croix.

*The Nelthropp family arrived on St Croix from Denmark in the late 18th century and become involved in the sugar industry, eventually becoming partners in the St Croix Sugar Industries distillery. Ceddie, as well as being a farmer, began working at the distillery in the late 1940's becoming, in 1953, president of what was then Cruzan Rum, where he remained until his retirement in 1982.

Donations of money, mice and mongoose are always welcomed by the St Croix Avian Sanctuary.
http://tonilance.com/tonis-stuff/the-st-croix-avian-sanctuary/

MELANCHOLY CONFUSION

It is January 5th, Twelfth Night, the eve of epiphany, but here on St Croix, it is known as 'Three Kings' Day' and is marked by the adult carnival parade - a not particularly chaste celebration of the Magi's first sight of the infant Jesus.

But as with most things Crucian it does have its roots in history when the enslaved were given time off to celebrate Christmas. In the 1700s the streets of Christiansted and Frederiksted would be filled with costumed singing and dancing merrymakers, who would also visit other plantations to spread the holiday cheer. The modern manifestation has been in existence since the early 1950s when Three Kings' Day marks the end of the month-long celebration with ten days of fun at the Crucian Christmas Carnival. Calypsonians compete for the title of king or queen, and this year was won, for the fourth time, by Caribbean Queen aka Temisha Libert for her calypsos, *Promise* and *Karma*. The first advising the incoming governor, Albert Bryan, to stay true to his election campaign promises, and the second perhaps warning of what would happen if he doesn't! With moko jumbies keeping bad spirits at bay, cultural activities and fairs showcasing arts and crafts, food and drinks keep the revelers happy, fed and lubricated. The final day, 'Three Kings' Day', sees shimmering scantily-clad men and women chasséing down the streets of Frederiksted to the steady beat of music belting out from trucks. It a noisy, fun-filled spectacle that sets the crowds up for the coming year.

Twelfth Night, or the beginning of Epiphany, was always a subject of debate in my childhood home. Do the decorations come down on the night of the 5th or 6th of January? According to the Church of England it should be the 5th and so, over the years, I have come to adhere to their ruling. I can only assume the confusion came about due to one parent counting the 12 days from the day after Christmas Day, and the other from Christmas Day. Perhaps having the international date line between their two countries had something to do with it.

Whatever the reason, I find the day a little melancholy. The tinsel is down, the fairy lights are stored away despite knowing a fuse needs changing, the baubles that have survived the cat's delighted playing are packed away and my favorite tree decorations are wrapped in tissue and bubble wrap and wedged into stout boxes ready for any eventuality. The whole enterprise reminiscent of an international move, which was my initial reason for such careful storage practices. For many years we did indeed move every twelve months and I'd be damned if my Christmas decorations didn't travel with me.

Perhaps the melancholy comes from knowing my global relocations have spluttered to an end. That is not to say I am unhappy in life or in my current location. How could I be? I am healthy and happy, as are my family. I have the Caribbean glinting in the sunlight and trade winds rustling the coconuts palms outside my study. A new book being released in March adds an element of satisfaction, and the thrill of starting another engages my mind in pages of what ifs and maybes. But the excitement of wondering what country we might call home the following year was intoxicating, and I miss it.

Or perhaps my melancholy comes from saying goodbye to a houseful of friends who have stayed with us and shared our twelve days of Christmas - a noisy, busy, laughter-filled time of tempting smells from the kitchen and far too much rum and wine on the gallery.

Or perhaps it was because this year we did not share Christmas with our children and grandchildren, who are scattered around the world. That, perhaps, a direct reflection of their upbringing in different parts of the globe. We all lead our own lives and only rarely do they truly entwine for a few precious days of shared memories, and when new ones are made to be stored away, like the decorations, and brought out occasionally for delightful reminisces. That is the price we all pay for a nomadic existence. And whilst I might think ruefully, and with a smidgeon of envy, of families who each year gather around the same Christmas tree in the same house in the same town, I know that is not our family.

We are global nomads. Each married to or with a partner from another country. We live in three different countries and as different cultural mores are navigated, with some becoming amalgamated into our own family culture, I reflect on the differences. But more importantly I reflect on the shared values.

Because as Three Kings' Day draws to an end, my melancholy vanishes and I have my own epiphany. It doesn't matter where we live, or who we live with, or what language we speak. What matters is that when we do share time together, whether in reality or the virtual world of FaceTime, we are a family despite the miles between us.

DIRECTIONALLY CHALLENGED

P ride is a sin, or so I'm told. But like most things, it's moderation that really counts. And I'm not talking about pride in other people's accomplishments - our children, our spouse and so on. No, I mean pride in 'weself'. Although a little pride is what gets us out of our pajamas each morning. And as a writer, if I didn't have an element of pride in my work, I'd never pluck up the courage to send it out and risk the inevitability of rejection.

I do confess to also being proud of my sense of direction and, on the whole, my ability to take directions. I'm a good map reader, which is why I despise Google Maps. Something to which I will not resort unless in dire circumstances - like I'm running very, very late… because I got lost!

But that particular sense of pride, now I spend more time on St Croix, has gone. I am now regularly, totally and utterly directionally challenged. And that is on an island roughly 84 square miles in area, with the highest point being Mount Eagle at 1,165 feet. Road numbers do not always tally with actual roads. Island maps show roads that once may have been passable but are no longer - you know those little dash-dash-dash lines that promise entry and egress but in reality peter out.

Like Houston, St Croix is afflicted with potholes. Neither the powers-that-be in Houston nor on St Croix have actually figured out the sense of 'do it properly, one time'. But we have a sense of humor about it. My favorite bumper sticker here is also most comforting. It reads, "Not drunk, dodging potholes!" I almost drove off the road laughing.

I wasn't laughing though a couple of weeks ago. We had visitors from Australia. Long-standing friends who are used to the vagaries of life - be it unplanned adventures, inclement weather or crazy hosts. Rorie is the epitome of a laconic Aussie farmer. Mary's sense of humor has been, I'm sure, tested greatly throughout their long marriage, as has his. Be that as it may, they are great chums both to each other and to us. We had decided on a driving day, and so our aptly named truck, Otto (Over The Top Off-roader), was geared up and taken for a spin.

I thought we were heading along Scenic Route East - a misnomer really, apart from the east bit. The tan-tan is as tall as an elephant's eye and the glistening Caribbean Sea is merely a pencil mark through the scrub scrabbling up the hillside covered with creepers. Mainly Bride's Tears, spaghetti vine and some kind of pea, all attempting to turn the bush into a palette of pink, yellow and purple. Pretty but invasive plants intent on strangling local flora. In any event, after the nails-on-a-chalkboard scratching of thorns along Otto, Mount Eagle seemed to be where we were heading. I wasn't quite sure how we got there, but there was no turning back until we reached the summit.

I think I told you Rorie is a cool-cat, unfazed by the peculiarities of life in the left lane - oh, let me explain. The Virgin Islands, for some inexplicable reason, maneuver left-hand steering-wheeled vehicles on the left side of the road. It can at times produce, for those sitting in line of oncoming traffic, a dashboard-clutching drive. Anyway, Rorie was doing very well.

Until he wasn't.

Mary was trying to catch glimpses of the ocean, or anything rather than more tan-tan - and was rewarded with a flash of grey mongoose on the dusty red trail ahead. There was no left lane here. But she could afford some element of sang-froid. She and my husband, our driver, were on the hill side of the rapidly narrowing track and her gaze skimmed over bushes and through trees, not down the hill where remnants of rusted vehicles peeked from under vines, proof that an ill-advised spin of the wheel could be disastrous.

"Steer left a bit, mate." Rorie's words were calm. I had lost the power of speech as I leaned out the window and saw an inch of rubbly road then nothing but a tangle of scrub waiting to claim us in the ravine below. Okay, maybe not a ravine exactly, but a steep gully that would not make any of us feel good should we flip into it.

"I'm in 4 wheel-drive," John said, his voice soothing.

"Not much use if there's only air under the wheels on this side!" Rorie commented.

The view from the top was worth the drive and, taking the right fork, the road more travelled, on the way down the hill, we eventually found our way to where I had thought we were going..... It turns out my pride has been misplaced all these years. I am directionally challenged.

But then guidance on St Croix is a little vague. Landmarks long gone are still used as reference points. I have since learnt if we had only turned right, where the tall palm blew down in the hurricanes eighteen months ago, and not at the signpost that categorically stated Scenic Drive East, we would have been fine.

That's another idiosyncrasy of Crucian driving!

PRIDE, IT'S A TRICKY THING

America has just celebrated Thanksgiving, an important day in my adopted land. It is a day wherein the country is a moving mass as people try to get home, often battling inclement weather, to celebrate the pilgrim's first harvest.

I have enjoyed every national or festival day in whichever country I have happened to be living. All twelve of them. From Loi Krathong in Thailand to Chinese New Year in Singapore to the Ganzenhoedster Festival in the small Dutch town of Coevorden, where geese are paraded. Or maybe Deepavali in Malaysia. And don't let's forget Hogmany in Scotland. I admire the national pride that keeps these traditions alive.

I name these countries, these festivals as a precursor to this piece. Not only have I lived in many countries, I have also been employed by multinational corporations to help employees and their families understand the idiosyncrasies prevalent in countries in which they might conduct business, or indeed live.

In every place I have been fortunate enough to call home, whether for a year or a number of years, I have made an effort to learn a little of the language, to understand and recognize, if not always embrace, the culture. And to engage in local activities, whether as a foot soldier or a board member.

My peripatetic life began at a month old which, in essence, means I have spent my life 'not quite fitting in'. It is not something that has ever concerned me, as I consider it a privilege to be a guest in another country and do my best to be respectful of that culture.

And so the past few days, having been accused of cultural insensitivity, have been spent wondering "what could I have done better?". The details are irrelevant. It doesn't matter how carefully I worded the email that started the firestorm. It doesn't matter that the recipient found issue with subjects not addressed in that letter. It doesn't matter that I apparently provoke "*a bad taste in my* (his) *tongue*". What matters is that somehow, and I have searched my words, conscience and intent, I have caused great offense. Enough to make the man write, "*I will not allow someone from else where come to my homeland and talk to me however they would like, I am proud Crucian and I stand with pride for what I do in my community.*"

That is the sentence that rankles. No, actually it hurts. Because I do not know how this chap got to that place of intense dislike from my actions or, indeed, my words.

Then I started thinking about words like identity, ego, pride - all of which, if used with a dose of reality, are important words for defining who we are. It's when the dosage gets out of kilter that things go pear-shaped. It can happen with tyrants of tin-pot regimes, wannabe dictators of western countries, and lesser mortals. The common denominator being that all have lost the ability to recognize the world works best when we are able to feel humility, to admit to mistakes, to accept guidance. It is the people who manufacture threats from without their immediate sphere of influence. Their hubris becomes a crutch behind which they cover inadequacy, incompetency and sometimes a lack of intellect. And every culture is littered with those whose ego is easily dented.

As I consider the past few days, and give thanks for the island on which I spend most of my time, I reflect on Rudyard

Kipling's poem, *If*. He too was an expatriate, having grown up in India before returning to England then emigrating to America. He wrote:

> *If you can keep your head when all about you*
> *Are losing theirs and blaming it on you,*
> *If you can trust yourself when all men doubt you,*
> *But make allowance for their doubting too;*
> *If you can wait and not be tired by waiting,*
> *Or being lied about, don't deal in lies,*
> *Or being hated, don't give way to hating,*
> *And yet don't look too good, nor talk too wise:*
>
> *If you can dream—and not make dreams your master;*
> *If you can think—and not make thoughts your aim;*
> *If you can meet with Triumph and Disaster*
> *And treat those two impostors just the same;*
> *If you can bear to hear the truth you've spoken*
> *Twisted by knaves to make a trap for fools,*
> *Or watch the things you gave your life to, broken,*
> *And stoop and build 'em up with worn-out tools:*
>
> *If you can make one heap of all your winnings*
> *And risk it on one turn of pitch-and-toss,*
> *And lose, and start again at your beginnings*
> *And never breathe a word about your loss;*
> *If you can force your heart and nerve and sinew*
> *To serve your turn long after they are gone,*
> *And so hold on when there is nothing in you*
> *Except the Will which says to them: 'Hold on!'*

If you can talk with crowds and keep your virtue,
Or walk with Kings—nor lose the common touch,
If neither foes nor loving friends can hurt you,
If all men count with you, but none too much;
If you can fill the unforgiving minute
With sixty seconds' worth of distance run,
Yours is the Earth and everything that's in it,
And—which is more—you'll be a Man, my son!

The words might appear dated but they resonate as I try to master my anger and disappointment. If I can do that, I shall be on my way to being a stronger woman.

I shall also contemplate Kipling's other masterpiece, *The Jungle Book*. Because juggling different cultures and sensitivities can make it feel it is a jungle out there. But maybe, if I work hard enough, next Thanksgiving I can truly focus on what makes me thankful for being on this beautiful island.

GETTING SHOT!

A wonderful bird is the Pelican.
His beak can hold more than his belly can.
He can hold in his beak
Enough food for a week!
But I'll be darned if I know how the hellican?

The *Pelican* was penned in 1910 by Dixon Lanier Merritt, an American poet and humorist, although the poem is more often credited to Ogden Nash who included it in his 1940 anthology, *The Face is Familiar*. Plagiarism is a dirty word.

So too is cruelty.

Such is the risk for pelicans, and other birds on St Croix. Arid on the east end and verdant on the west - only 28 miles apart - natural beauty is surrounded by soothing Caribbean waters. There are, though, beasts who hide along the bays and inlets ready to shoot down birds skimming with magisterial solemnity above these waters.

What possible sport can that be?

There are eight species of pelicans, but here on our island we have the Brown Pelican - a dull name for an august bird whose white head above a chestnut nape and brownish-silver feathers remind me of a be-gowned and wigged judge. They are ungainly as they take flight, flapping their wings and slapping the water with big webbed feet, but as they find thermal currents they can soar as high as 10,000 feet. No wonder the Wright Brothers studied avian aerodynamics. Technical aspects of a pelican are remarkable. The air pockets in their bones are connected to respiratory airways lying under the throat, breast and wings and aid buoyancy, allowing the birds to keep their wings horizontal and steady.

"Almost like bubblewrap," says Toni Lance, artist, photographer, certified falconer, licensed bird rehabilitator and founder of the St Croix Avian Sanctuary.

Meet Gabriel, an adult of uncertain sex but of breeding age, shot down a week ago. Due to the location of the pellet, surgery was not an option. There was no sign of a break and so Ms Lance is attempting to rehabilitate the bird at the Sanctuary on St Croix's south shore. She moves the wing but it remains unwieldy, unable to be lifted. She sprays Gabriel with water to encourage preening which in turn helps get oil back into his feathers. The pelican dutifully preens. His appetite is good. If not for the shot wing, Gabriel would be flying free as a bird, preparing to mate and sustain his species.

The Brown Pelican - clever birds that they are - stuns its fish by plunging headfirst into the ocean. The air sacs in its wings lessen the impact and bobs the bird back to the surface to float, rather like a cork. If the waters are shallow or churned, pelicans have a back-up system for fishing. Unlike other birds, pelicans have four toes rather than the standard three, which allows effective paddling whilst using that huge-pouched beak as a scoop, which they then drain by tipping their head back. It is this maneuver that makes them most vulnerable to the thieving habits of others, mainly seagulls, who are wont to steal fish right out of their mouths.

Gabriel, irrespective of sex, is a breeding adult. Unlike other areas, St Croix tends not to have large squadrons of pelicans but rather three or four flying in formation. If Gabriel cannot be rehabilitated in the next few weeks, and this is by no means certain, he / she will be euthanized. That means the loss of probably two healthy young a year for the next twenty years.

You do the maths.

Avian rehabilitation is not all a flying success. Ms Lance has, over the years, seen many birds soar to freedom but there have also been those unable to be released. Some, such as a peregrine falcon, she has used as aids in an effort to educate children about the importance of treasuring our resources, and honoring the freedom of flight; others with no chance of survival in the wild - often the ones shot by ignorant and brutish people - are euthanized.

Where is the outrage? The chance of the perpetrator of this crime being caught is remote and, sadly, it is only a matter of time before the St Croix Avian Sanctuary is again called upon to rescue a shot bird.

I am assured by Ms Lance that Gabriel is, like most pelicans, a good-natured bird. They have been around for many years - the oldest fossil found is dated thirty-million years ago - and they have remained remarkably similar, if somewhat smaller. They were, in medieval Europe, considered a symbol of sacrifice due to the belief a pelican would, if no other food was available, wound her own breast to feed blood to her young.

The wound in Gabriel's wing cannot be mended by an infusion of blood. It may not mend at all. The chance of seeing this magnificent bird fly again is slim. Grounded and unable to swim in seawater, Gabriel's paddled feet, even on a padded perch, will break down with pressure sores. An inhumanity that cannot be countenanced.

"I'd need to be set up like Seaworld to keep pelicans in captivity," Ms Lance explained.

Disgust should be filtered through towns, school halls and social media at the wanton cruelty and 'sport' of shooting an innocent bird, animal or human. There is too much of it.

"A wonderful bird is the pelican...."

But this is not a humorous story. Gabriel's life is likely to be short. A sanctuary can only do so much. Birds have to deal with the elements. That's enough. That's natural. Getting shot is not.

RAISING CANE

If I was a tad intimidated at the thought of the upcoming conversation, I should never, ever have watched his interview on Greek SKAI TV as part of my research. The man being questioned gave a masterful lesson in unsettling the inquisitioner, deftly avoiding questions on the debt burden of the country and the state of its finances in general. Pericles and Euclid were tossed back at the man holding the clipboard as examples of how Grecian culture has spread around the world - not least of which is democracy.

I first came across Bob Apfel two years ago when I could have been excused for thinking he was a field hand. He wore raggedy jeans, a long-sleeved dress shirt that had seen better days, and his face was hidden under a tatty straw hat. The notion was soon dispelled as he explained his venture to a group of people, including a number of Danes visiting on the biennial St Croix Friends of Denmark / Danish West Indian Society exchange trip.

I arrive at Raising Cane, the old Estate Prosperity on the west end of St Croix, and wend my way past restored stone cottages, gardens overflowing with pepper, papaya and all manner of local produce. I'm a little early so I wander around a ruin which, I am later told, was the farm hospital and manager's house.

There is no one around so I phone Bob. As I wait for him to appear I wander over to a field of undulating sugarcane. The only sound is a whisper magnified as tall canes sway in a syncopated rhythm of their own making. It is serene, beautiful, hopeful. The quiet is disturbed by an approaching Jeep.

"Hi, I was with the men." Bob clambers out and hooks on a mask. He is wearing rolled-up denim shorts and a pink-checked, long sleeve shirt, opened or maybe torn-off buttons exposing a brown chest. He wears flip flops.

"Good afternoon, no problem. Thanks for agreeing to chat," I say from behind my mask.

"Shall we drive around the farm?"

"Sure," I reply, fast realizing my questions are not going to be of much use as an aide-memoire.

"Your vehicle or mine?"

"Yours." I figure I might at least be able to glance at my notes if he's driving.

We get into the Jeep, and I reach for the seatbelt. Instinct.

"Do you want to drive the tractor?"

"Sure," I say again, relieved I tossed sensible shoes into my bag as a just in case. And who visits a farm in a skirt?

It is a very big, red tractor.

Bob climbs up first and sits in the driving seat. The cab is surprisingly roomy and very much more comfortable than I expected. On the roof strut to the right of the steering wheel is a digitalized screen, and within easy reach is a touch-screen console. Beeps sound.

"This is the clutch. These are the brakes."

I ask why two but his answer is lost in the rumble.

"What's that third pedal?" I want to know just in case I do actually get to drive this behemoth.

"It raises the steering wheel." He demonstrates then flicks the lever behind said wheel and we are in drive mode. Easing the clutch, we judder to a start and inch forward.

I tell him the last time I was in a tractor was forty-five years ago in New South Wales, Australia. It was the only way my friends and I could reach the blacktop through floods. We were not escaping rising waters but trying to get to a wool-shed dance.

Bob nods, stops and says, "Okay. You drive."

We juggle to swap seats in the confines of the cab.

"Ease that stick to go faster, or you can press one of those buttons."

I glance down. There are two icons, a hare and a tortoise.

"Which is the speed up one?"

"Aesop," I say. He smiles.

"Okay, clutch in, gear on, ease off the clutch and off we go."

Easing the clutch takes a bit of getting used to. I'm glad I'm not wearing flip flops.

Bob talks, all the time. His enthusiasm is infectious and, as I drive along the bumpy lane beside a field of cane, I struggle to hear, let alone remember everything. A recorder is useless. We near a deep trench and the lane narrows. I am grateful when he says he will drive around it. The thought of tipping a quarter of a million-dollar tractor is not appealing to either of us. We change seats again and he negotiates the turn. "Let's walk."

The best way down from a high tractor is as if climbing down a companionway on a boat. We jump the trench, about three feet wide. I am relieved I do not miss my footing. He is off and I scurry over bumpy ground to catch up.

"I have a consultant here from Lubbock, Texas." Bob removes his mask and points to PVC pipes, a streak of white in the dirt. "He designed this sub-surface irrigation system, but it's made in Israel."

It's an impressive eleven miles of pipe laid eleven inches down, seven inches below the cane. "Where does the water come from?" I ask.

"There are wells at the edge of the property. They used to supply Frederiksted."

"What about Creque Dam?" I mention the reservoir leaking water on the eponymous road   heading east from Highway 63.

"Maybe one day," he replies with a lopsided smile.

We leap back across the trench and keep walking. I am distracted by the beauty sloping away. Sugarcane wafting almost to the water, just a narrow strip of road away. There are yachts moored in the roadstead and to complete the tropical idyll, a couple of palm trees are silhouetted like sentinels to the ocean. Bob's voice brings me back.

"This clearing will be where the factory and distillery are built. And a visitor's center. And a shop."

Before I can ask when, he continues.

"It's here. In eleven containers. We're just waiting for it to clear customs."

I imagine a Meccano set and men holding pieces trying to figure out where things go. Then I look at Bob and know it will be planned and organized down to the last bolt.

"It'll take about three months to build. We've got to lay the foundation before we can start processing."

"And you will only use sugarcane juice?"

"Yes. It's the purest kind of rum. *Rhum agriocle*, the French call it. Crucians and islanders call it cane rum. Cruzan Rum and Captain Morgan use molasses brought in from South America. They produce *rhum industriel.*"

"If it's not as pure, as good, why make it?"

"Subsidies. The government pays for the molasses. Suntory/Cruzan Rum and Diageo/Captain Morgan make the rum. Under the Revised Organic Act of 1954, the governments, here and in Puerto Rico, get a rebate on the federal excise taxes - the 'rum cover over'." He gestures. "Look at it. A hundred and seventy acres, perfect for cane production. So many acres on St Croix allowed to go to bush." He gazes across his property. "One day I'd like to see all the abandoned, flat land developed and under cane."

"A sort of cooperative?" I question him.

He agrees.

"But how would local farmers be able to afford hi-tech machinery?"

"There's always a way." His response is cryptic.

"Captain Morgan hasn't been on St Croix long," I comment, kicking a pebble from my shoe.

"They were promised the world. Puerto Rico's loss."

"You've got a farm there too," I confirm. He nods, puts his mask on and climbs back into the tractor grumbling quietly in wait. "You drive." I have a chance to gather my thoughts as he pushes buttons on the console. "Have you support from local government?" I ask.

"Not support, but neither censure." Bob engages the clutch. "You know I went to the University of the Virgin Islands (UVI) when we first started up here? Suggested a program in hi-tech agriculture, but the new head of department was too busy. I invited him to visit the farm when he was less busy. He never came."

"What about PR?" I ask.

272

"Different story. The university there set up a program. I sent funds and we had twenty-two students last year. Some of them intern on the farm there, and here."

"It seems such a lost opportunity for students."

"UVI is more interested in quoting Shakespeare."

"I imagine you could quote him back to them," I suggest, remembering the Greek interview.

Bob drives past the old plantation house, the shiny new roof at odds with scaffolding that appears to be holding up the walls. Boards are hammered across the windows as if the eyes of the building are permanently closed.

"I seem to remember the great house was going to be used as a research center?"

"Eventually," Bob confirms. "Not much point having a research lab without any cane. We need the product first." He stops and we drop down again to terra firma. "Why do you think there aren't any women farmers?"

"There are," I reply, thinking of friends who toil alongside their partners on sheep, cattle and agricultural properties. "In Australia. All over the world."

"But actually farming by themselves."

It is a discussion for another time and so I ignore the comment, but not graciously.

"Push that button." He rubs his hand across his face.

I do as I'm told. The plough lowers into the ground. I raise it by pushing another button.

"Get in, you can plough a row."

Bob is used to getting his own way it seems, but I clamber up again because I rather like the idea of ploughing my own furrow. I'm instructed to push prompts on the screen so the huge red tractor will steer itself. A computer much better at keeping a straight line than a mortal. I'm warned not to touch the steering wheel. I'm getting better at easing off the clutch and we glide off although I have to be reminded not to touch the wheel. It is an instinctive reflex.

"Turn that dial," he tells me, "then look behind."

I have metal rods in my back and don't twist well, but not having to hold the wheel meant I could shift around.

"See, you're ploughing. Turn it more. See, deeper furrow."

We came to the end of the line. I lift the plough with the greatest of ease. Anyone can turn a dial. "Does the tractor turn on its own?" I ask and am disappointed to learn it doesn't. But power steering is a wonderful thing. I reset the plough, the automatic steering and back we go.

"The GPS is on the roof," Bob says. He is delighted with the beast I am driving. I forget to ask him its name. Or maybe I think he'll laugh at me. "My men love it."

On the slow drive back to the farm buildings I ask about land maintenance. I am asked a question in return. Classic Greek interview technique.

"If you had a lawn at your home, I know you don't but if you did, would you replant it every year?"

I admit I wouldn't.

"Sugarcane is like grass. It doesn't deplete the earth."

"Huh!" A sound of meagre intelligence and I lift the plough as we near the end of the row. I am instructed where to park. I hand over the key and follow Bob into the huge domed workshop, open on each end.

"Everything has to be automated," he says. "I don't want any connotations of slavery."

Next I'm shown a digging machine. Different blades for different tasks. One churns rough ground and the other continues to break down clods of earth. I don't consider myself a machine buff but, bloody hell, the next one was fantastic. I decline to follow Bob up on five wobbly pieces of timber in

order to reach the hub and peer inside the planting machine.
He jumps down and I have a lesson on the planter. It's brilliant.

"Sugarcane is a vegetatively planted crop."

I am sure I look nonplussed.

"That means billets, cane stalk sections, are planted not
seeds."

I nod and the tour continues.

"See that?" He points to a closed trough. "The billets are
bathed in fungicide, then fertilized before planting. Billets fall
at a steady rate from the hopper into the opened furrow dug by
the same machine, precisely four inches deep. The earth is then
pushed back by these blades here, then tamped down to get rid
of air pockets," he points to two small wheels below the belly
of the hopper. "All done by one machine."

Next on the tour is a wide attachment for the tractor, with
three separate arms about six feet apart, each with fine spokes,
which reach over the germinating and newly-growing cane
stools to keep weeds at bay.

We walk into the open to fields at different stages of
growth that sway green in the softening day.

"Have you had any pushback from local farmers?" I ask.

"Not really. Some people objected when we burnt off the
rubble after we'd cleared. Sent men out from the Department
of Agriculture to tell us we needed a permit. We didn't." He
pauses and a frown appears above the mask. "An official came
the other day and tried to close us down because we didn't have
a permit for pesticides."

"Do you need one?"

"No. He tried to intimidate my workers. He didn't even
leave a card." It obviously rankles. "We use only non-restricted
fertilizers or pesticides. We don't use anything you couldn't get
from Home Depot."

I had visions of spray cans of pesticide being loaded onto flatbeds to be delivered to Raising Cane. The reality is that for the quantities needed, vats are shipped in.

"What happened to the Department of Ag man?"

"He was sent away and told to read the rules. They did apologize when I phoned."

As we move across to the office, the old plantation stables gussied up, I ask, "Why, Bob? Forgive me, but you're a rich man. Most men would be looking to slow down, to sail around the Caribbean, play with their grandchildren. You were a financier not a farmer. Why?"

"You've got to keep learning and growing. The alternative is not appealing." Again he turns the question. "You keep writing books. What's the difference?" His eyes are very blue in the deepening day.

He has me there, so I resort to another question. "But what made you decide to raise cane?"

"This is the ninth company I've started. The first was a newspaper, Securities Industries Daily. It grew from me and one part-timer to fifteen reporters. Then I sold it and moved on." He rubs his face again. I know the feeling. Masks can get itchy. "Got to keep learning," he repeats.

"You bought Fortuna Mill Estate on St Thomas, and had plans to refurbish a building at the Sub Base in Charlotte Amalie and turn it into a micro-rum distillery and naval museum. What happened?"

"It's going ahead. Just not there. It'll be in the Grand Hotel."

I wait as he covers computers and printers and bolts the stable door.

"Farmers are generous with their knowledge." He jumps back to what fascinates him. Farming. "I went to an agricultural show, in Florida, the largest in the US. Full of farmers. We were all staying in the same hotel, saw each other at meals, I got to know some. They pointed me in the right direction when I was looking for machinery. Do you know what farmers ask each other first?"

I shake my head.

"Red or green? What do you think that is?"

My mind swirls to ecology but that is not the right answer.

"Farm equipment!"

I am still confused.

"What color is John Deere machinery?"

The penny drops. "Ahh, green," I say, looking at his farm equipment. It's red.

"Who is red?" I ask in return.

"Case IH."

I tell him my father imported and sold the first Massey Ferguson tractor in Malaysia back in the sixties. "It was yellow." We laugh.

"One last question," I say to this innovative farmer. "In the Greek interview you talk about the first loan there in 1832 wherein 50,000 small farms were sold to 50,000 farmers - in essence spreading the economy. You also mentioned working with the Thatcher government in Britain and talked of her belief that expanding ownership encourages commitment. Is what you are doing here at Raising Cane, the Apfel way of encouraging people on island to have a stake in the future of St Croix?"

He looks down at the soil. "I suppose it is. Old-timers tell me they like to see all this, reminds them of their childhood," he waves across to the sugarcane growing tall and green, hopeful.

"Thank you, Bob," I say from behind my mask as we move towards our vehicles. "I've really enjoyed this, and learnt a lot." It is awkward in these COVID days, not being able to see smiles, to shake hands.

A red Bobcat trundles past. "Wasn't sure if I really needed one of those," Bob says, "but it's used every single day. Arguably the busiest piece of equipment we've got."

He laughs, waves and climbs into his Jeep. "Follow me, I'll see you out."

I wave to employees returning to the workshop in all manner of red vehicles. I remember Bob saying most are long-time St Croix residents, but from down island or Vieques. We drive past provision gardens surrounding the restored stone cottages, which are lived in by some of the farmworkers, and the man Raising Cane. The chain is across the entrance. As Bob opens the carabiner and waves me out, I glance in the rear-view mirror and see him locking the chain before he drives off in his Jeep. Red, of course.

INTERREGNUM

A recent Sunday morning was spent speaking to a small congregation of Unitarian Universalists, whose seven principles would seem to be a pretty good guide for decent living. I promised that *Same View, Different Lens* would discuss cultural awareness in a world wherein countries, and some peoples, are reverting to an insular and intolerant outlook.

But this isn't a piece about the brilliance of my talk! Rather it is the coincidental nature of it as the precursor to the hell happening around the world as COVID-19 shuts down our borders. An action wholly understandable but which threatens to make us more inward looking and parochial, quick to lay blame beyond our boundaries.

Pico Iyer, a philosopher and travel writer I much admire, says in his book *The Global Soul,* "The airport was a rare interregnum - a place between two rival forms of authority - and the airplane itself was a kind of enchanted limbo.... And so, half-inadvertently, not knowing whether I was facing east or west, not knowing whether it was night or day, I slipped into that peculiar state of mind - or no-mind - that belongs to the no-time, no-place of the airport, that out-of-body state in which one's not quite there, but certainly not elsewhere."

It is this feeling, this interregnum, in which I find myself now. Not, however, the anticipatory kind of limbo that airports induce but rather in a discombobulated state of nowhereness. I should be used to that feeling. I grew up a 'Nowherian' as

Derek Walcott, the St Lucian poet, called us. An in-betweener, accustomed to often being on the outside looking in, not always quite fitting into a prescribed mold.

My family is global. My daughter is married to a Trinidadian and lives in Port of Spain, my son is soon to marry a Polish woman. They live in London. I have no doubt we will continue to live in different parts of the world, that their children will grow up with an inherent cultural awareness -and I remind myself that cultural awareness and common sense go hand-in-hand. In these days of COVID-19 I have to get a better handle on the latter because I have a constant refrain in my head.

What if they need me?

I know that is highly unlikely. I believe and trust in their ability to deal with anything thrown at them. That was how they were brought up, around the same world they now have the temerity to call their playground. This morning, as I walked Clyde along the empty Boardwalk in Christiansted, I realized what is causing my somewhat irrational mood. It is grief.

Grief for a world that has changed beyond anything I could have imagined. No one knows how long borders or skies will be closed. Sorrow for those whose family and friends have died from this rampant virus. But my newly understood grief is also selfish.

It is grief at the freedoms I have lost, the freedom to hop a plane to see my children. It has sent me to find words vaguely remembered from when my father died. In his desk I had found a book of quotes, snippets of Latin and Greek, Malay and Urdu, he jotted down. Words that took his fancy. The words I wanted were written by the British doctor and eugenicist - not a science I agree with but, in the current context, wise words nonetheless, "All the art of living lies in a fine mingling of letting go and holding on."

So in this interregnum, this limbo, I must accept that some things have changed, maybe forever. That is the grief. I must embrace the ease of virtual communication which, for a while, is replacing the joy of real and tactile social intercourse. With vigilance, COVID-19 will be contained and, once it has run its course, our borders will be reopened, and our minds once more excited about the infinite possibilities and cultural awareness that travel provides. But for now it is a time of letting go, and holding on, and remembering we see the same views through different lenses.

THE MASKED LADY

U S Virgin Islanders have been fortunate in the management of COVID-19. Our governor has listened to health experts, instigated common-sense practices and after a period of lock down has been opening the islands up in a measured manner. There is a strict mask policy, with shops stating in large letters, No Mask, No Service, No Exceptions. Big burly men comply. Children over the age of five comply. There appears little reason to not comply. Our islands have had some deaths but nowhere near the numbers seen on the mainland, which has allowed our hospitals to withstand the stressors of treating those seriously infected. We wear our masks!

I, along with everyone else, am learning a whole new way of reading people. Are the eyes crinkling in laughter or distaste? Is a slipped mask a sign of belligerence, or just a slipped mask?

I don't go in for public shaming but I did feel moved, after dancing around a young man wandering the aisles of my local supermarket, to suggest that wearing his mask across his chin was as much use as a condom on his big toe. His girlfriend, suitably masked, burst into laughter and dug him in the ribs.

"I told you," I heard her chortle, as her beau got caught up in gold chains in his haste to protect himself. And others.

I was encouraged to encounter them again, this time at the cashier, and see his nose and mouth were suitably covered. The girl grinned and waved.

My weekly outing revolves around the supermarket. Actually three of them. The only way I am able to gather items on my list. On Monday, as I tied my mask in timely fashion before approaching the ramp to the store, I was surprised to be hailed by a tall, masked woman I did not recognize.

"Wait!" she called. "Can I ask you something?"

Her tone was peremptory. I am, by nature, suspicious of unknown, over-friendly people, dreading a monologue on the glories of Jehovah. But what the hell? In these days of isolation and fear, a brief encounter might help ease someone's day. Mine included.

"Sure," I replied, waiting by Otto, our truck, as she ferreted around in her handbag.

"Which do you think?" She waved two strips of paint swatches in front of me. "I can't tell the difference. They're both grey. And that," she jabbed at a duck-egg blue square, "is meant to go with both."

"Um," I replied.

"My decorator said I must decide."

"Well," I said, pointing, "that grey has yellow undertones which is why it's a bit murky. And that one has blue tones which makes it sharper."

"How do you know that?"

"I was an interior designer."

"Hah! And I found you in the parking lot." Her laugh trickled around her mask.

"So it would seem," I said, hoping my eyes reflected my amusement. "What room are they for?"

"Kitchen and lounge. Together."

"Have you lots of windows? Lots of light?"

"No."

"Then I'd go with the blue grey."

Her brow wrinkled above her mask - a clue I took to mean she wasn't relieved at my profound judgement.

"Um…" I said again, dithering in the blistering heat as to whether I really wanted to continue the conversation. "Do you like the colors?"

"I'm not sure."

"That usually means you don't. If I were you, I'd get some more samples. Good luck."

We parted ways, she to her car, me to my trolley. My mask hid my smile.

Scanning the shelf for ginger cookies, my sole reason for being at the store, I was surprised to feel a tap on my shoulder.

"Oh, hello," I said to the woman, again noting the intricate braids and marveling at the patience required to attain them.

"Are you still a decorator?" She asked.

"No," I replied, hoping my tone was firm. "I haven't practiced in twenty years."

"I don't know what to choose. Or which paint. Sherwin Williams. Behr. Benjamin Moore. Who?"

"Why don't you get your decorator to put together another storyboard with different colors, a different theme," I said.

"Storyboard?"

"Oh," I said, and explained. "Look, the color should reflect you, not your decorator or what she deems is in vogue. Do you have favorite plates, dishes, or a sofa or cushion you can take a color from? Something that ties the walls to your things."

"Huh," she said, looking again at the two strips of paint samples.

"Then buy a small sample tin of a couple of colors you like, brush a bit onto each wall. Each wall will show the color differently depending on the time of day and night. But ma'am," I said, "it must be something you like, not something someone else thinks you should like."

"I'll tell my friends I found a decorator in the parking lot!" She laughed and patted my arm. "Thank you."

"My pleasure," I assured her.

The masked lady went down the ramp and I wandered along the aisle in search of ginger cookies. My heart laughing and my smile broad behind my mask.

No mask, no service, no exceptions taken to new dimensions.

LÁSZLÓ

The steel structures of the power and water company rose in ugly defiance against a pearlescent pink sky, across which cirrus clouds streamed streaks of white as the sun lowered with a slow sigh in the evening breeze.

Music from bars drifted in step with women - tourists with little regard for their host island, as they sauntered in neon-colored mesh which showed skimpy beachwear barely covering dimpled buttocks. Men, some bare-chested, followed their womenfolk, hands clutching bottles of beer. Tattoos either rippled or quivered to the beat of the island.

The man known on St Croix as Jim, pulled the starter cord on his little outboard and puttered out to the wreck swinging at anchor in Christiansted harbor. He was of indeterminate age. Some thought him in his late forties, others, who might have seen him showered and shaved, put him ten years younger. His hair straggled around his neck like a shaggy Komondor. He sounded American to most, but he could just as easily have been Hungarian, like the mop dog he resembled. Jim was clad in a grimy tee-shirt, a tear under the armpit showing reddish hair, and shorts that had also seen better days. He wore heavy work boots.

A canvas satchel rested across his thighs and, tucked under the thwart in the middle of the tender, was a metal toolbox. It was locked.

Jim noticed a couple from a newly arrived catamaran watching as he neared his boat.

Their voices carried on the wind. European, but speaking English. From the corner of his eye he caught their arms raised in greeting, solidarity of the seas, no matter the state of the boat. He pretended he had not seen them and, as he reached for the pushpit, angled the tender with his legs so his back was turned. He heaved the metal box aboard and slid it across the deck.

A crooked smile showed a cracked tooth as odd words reached him across the mercury-colored bay - solar panels ... strange ... wreck ... unfriendly. "Yup," his voice could have been a sigh as he hoisted himself aboard, ducked under the solar panels attached to the top of the unused davit and tied off the dinghy. He kept his back to the curious couple as he eased open the unlocked companionway hatch and bent to pick up the box.

His shoulders relaxed as he climbed down the steps to the galley. The daily façade shaken off as he surveyed the pristine interior at stark odds to above deck. Teak gleamed, and a hint of vinegar mixed with sea air gave a clue to his relentless battle against mold. He placed the metal box under the saloon table and turned to the galley where a pan of black beans soaked in the sink and, slipping the satchel from his shoulder, pulled out a bunch of cilantro and a bottle of rum.

"Not much longer," he said as he raised a toast to himself and thought of the previous eight months.

The man leant against the bar of a pizzeria and gazed at boats riding at anchor or moored in the bay in front of him. His neighbor at the bar, a garrulous old-timer on the island, had needed a steady supply of rum but little prompting to give him a rundown on who owned which boat.

"What about that one?" Jim had pointed to a mastless boat whose paintwork was dull and, as she rose with each swell, showed algae along her hull. "She is unluffed."

His companion laughed. "Unluffed. Where'd you say you were from?"

"I didn't," Jim said, an edge to his voice. "I was born in Hungary. But left many years ago." He slapped the man on the back, "So, who owns her?" He paused, then said with care, "she is unloved."

"Been there for years. Lost her mast in a hurricane. Can't remember which one. The guy, a statesider, flew down, took one look at her and left. Never seen him again." He dribbled black sludge down the neck of his beer bottle as he spat juice from the wad of tobacco that gave his lower lip a warped bulge, as if he'd been slugged.

Jim tried not to shudder. "And she just sits there?"

"Yeah. She'll sink, like the rest," he pointed to a mast just visible in the still water.

"Huh! You t'ink I could buy her?"

"Why bother?" The man looked at him strangely. "Just take her. What'd they say? Possession is nine tenths of the law. You'll need a dinghy. I know someone wanting to sell one." He laughed. "It would be me! I'm Mick, by the way. Pleased to meetcha!" There was a question in his voice.

"Jim," he'd replied shaking the man's hand. "Why you wish to sell it?"

"Been here long enough. Twenty-seven years." Mick looked down at his swollen ankles. "Time to go while I can still walk. Get me some help. My daughter in Texas has been begging me to go live with her. Not sure I want to, but what's the alternative, eh?"

The younger man nodded. "It has an engine? Your dinghy?"

"Yeah, four stroke, rigid bottom but no oars. Lost 'em."

"How much?"

"One fifty."

Jim looked out at the wreck, then nodded. "Show me."

"You wan' a trailer too?"

Jim shook his head. "*Nem*, no."

Jim unlaced his boots and wriggled his toes free, then poured another rum and set the glass down by the sink. He drained the beans, chopped the cilantro, added some oil, cayenne and salt and put the pan on the gimbaled hob to simmer.

Taking his glass he sat at the chart table and applied pressure to the top right side of the panel facing him. It swung open to reveal a tin-lined cupboard built behind black-out blinds. Inside was a cell phone and an envelope.

A waft of body odor assailed him as he lifted his arm to push his hair back.

"Jesus, I stink," he muttered. He glanced at his watch, the face scratched, the band sweat-stained. He had time to shower. "Not much longer," he said again as he tore off his filthy clothes and stepped into the shower cubicle in the head. He hoped never to have to work on a construction site again but it had been a good cover. A bum from New York looking for warm-weather work. A job that helped explain to those curious along the Boardwalk how he got funds to pursue his dream of being a professional photographer. A cover for the hikes he took around the island armed only with an expensive camera. He had brushed off any jibes about the boat's chance of sinking and rebuffed any attempt from those at the bar to go aboard. It was his space. His moments of solace. No one needed to see how he had made the space livable. Jim touched the photograph tucked into the mirror frame, his eyes damp. He shook his head.

Showered, he hauled on clean clothes, picked up his rum and returned to the chart table. He looked at the amber liquid as he sat. Cruzan rum would be the only thing he missed. He checked his watch again and waited for the phone to ring.

"*Dobryy vecher*," Jim said, his tone quiet, as the crackle on the line cleared.

"English!" The voice whipped back.

Jim rubbed his eyes, took a sip, and started again. "Good evening."

"Hi, how are you?" There was no hint of an accent, although he suspected she was Russian. "How is the Caribbean? Still sunny?"

"Yes." Jim sipped his rum then choose his words with care. "Since we last spoke I found the track to the waterfall you mentioned." He waited for the response, to see if his code was picked up. It was.

"Lovely, and was there water?"

"Yes, there has been rain."

Jim heard a chuckle, then the voice said, "There has been a lot here too, but sadly no sunshine between the showers. Unlike where you are. Many would be envious of such a life."

"I am sure."

"And it is still cold here." The woman's voice gentle over the airwaves. More chilling than if the hidden threat had been voiced. Jim knew the steel behind the façade. "How much longer do you intend to stay, enjoying the weather?"

The roar of a cigar boat racing across the bay swung yachts on their anchor chains as it passed. The boat lurched and Jim clutched his glass. "Not long. The project is almost complete. And hurricane season is soon to start."

"Of course. Not a good time to be on a boat. What of your photography? Are you still intending to have an exhibition at the gallery in New York you spoke of - I'm sorry, Jim, I can't remember the name of it."

"Yes, I hope so. The gallery, it's called Views, seem interested." Jim faltered before continuing. "Perhaps you could come to the opening?"

"I would like that, thank you. Let me know the dates?"

The line began to crackle. Not, Jim knew, from outside interference but from the woman's end, the precursor to the call ending.

"Sorry, Jim, the line's breaking up, I can't hear you. If you can hear me, let's chat again when you get back to New York. Take care, now."

Jim, not bothering to respond, turned the phone off and grunted. "Bitch," he murmured as he put it back in the locker then returned to the beans on the stove top.

He lay awake a long time listening to the soft slap of the water against the hull. Sounds from the Boardwalk died as bars closed. He lifted his head to look out the porthole. Lights from the catamaran still glowed but there was no movement. He wondered where they were from. He envied their freedom. In the gloom he could just make out the photograph in the mirror. Not that he needed to see it to know every contour of her face. The memory of their meeting and time together etched in his mind.

New York, January, 2015. A blizzard that shut down the city. A hardy few daring out once the worst was over. He needed booze. She needed milk. "I cannot drink coffee without milk," she had said with a laugh as she tugged open the cooler door in the only store open in the neighborhood. "I cannot drink it without rum," he'd replied, stamping snow from his boots. They found they lived a couple of doors apart. She an appraiser at an auction house. He a loner, a would-be photographer. They saw each other every day. And some nights.

Until she disappeared. His calls went unanswered. At her office, they told him she had taken a leave of absence, and no forwarding address. Her friends said the same. Social media provided no clues. Nothing.

Until the call came. A distorted voice telling him to check his mailbox downstairs. The race down four flights to the dingy hall where mailboxes, some with doors hanging open, lined one wall. He wrenched the key into the metal door and pulled it open, then drew out the brown envelope. Photographs. Ellen. Stripped and bleeding. Her face crumpled in fear and pain.

His phone was ringing as he ran back to his apartment.

"Hello," he shouted as he punched the cellphone. "What the fuck?"

The line was dead.

He paced the room. He looked at the photos again. He shoved the computer aside on his desk and studied them under his angle light. They were genuine. He was sure. He should know. The master manipulator of photographs. But that was behind him. Or so he had thought. Free in the West. Lost in New York. One immigrant among many. Now he just photographed beauty. And not even women. Just nature. Until Ellen. He touched the photo of her on his desk. She was laughing. Her blonde hair a long plait draped over her shoulder. Her eyes sparkling as she blew him a kiss. Then her face transposed to the puffy, bloodstained image in his hands.

Jim twisted in his bunk, the last image too painful to bear. Soon. A month maybe. Photographs of the main building plans, the scrubby areas behind the razor-wire topped wall, the beach to the west of the property, approaches from the sea taken from an evening sail on a tourist yacht, all were saved on a thumb drive tucked into a hollowed-out hammer handle stored in the locked metal case. Or when he was hiking, in his camera bag. He'd built trust with Ken, the site foreman. He knew he'd be chosen. Just he and Ken to finish off the extra build-out. The project for which they both had to sign non-disclosure papers. More a bunker than a building. Sound-proofed with fiberglass insulation attached with metal strips to the studs, before they fastened new drywall to the resilient channel. Studs into which he had inserted minute listening devices. The project for which he had been sent to St Croix. He did not bother to wonder the point of the photographs when the Russians would now have listening capability. He didn't care. Just about the final photos needed to free Ellen.

He sighed. Not long now. Ellen's laughing face accompanied him as his eyes closed.

New York jangled his nerves. The traffic. The subway. All that had once energized him now did the opposite. The anonymity it provided gone. St Croix, despite the job, had charmed him. But he could never go back. The shakes of heads along the Boardwalk as he watched the boat blow up in a gas explosion. One he had set. Ken's kindness. Jim hoped suspicion for whatever was about to happen at the facility he had helped build would never fall on the foreman.

Jim checked into the hostel he had been ordered to stay in. He waited. Three days. Only going out for food. He watched television. He checked his cellphone. He paced. They would leave New York. Find another island. He'd fix up another boat. Maybe sail it this time.

Then the call came. He grabbed the phone.

"Welcome back, László," the bitch's voice was harsh. "Is it strange to no longer be Jim, or even Michael? No matter. You may be who you like soon. Deliver the thumb drive, in a padded envelop to the address of the gallery you so hoped to exhibit in. I regret it is no longer a gallery."

"Where's Ellen?" His heart thudded as the line went dead.

Four days later, three days after he made the delivery, his phone rang again.

"Hello!"

"I'm sorry, Michael."

"Ellen?"

"I'm sorry," she repeated.

POWER TO THE PEOPLE

Not long ago, but which in what COVID times seems a far-off galaxy, I lived in a small despotic West African country. It is a country run under harsh measures, with even harsher punishments for those who dare to question the ultimate authority - the president. He, it should be noted, came to rule through murderous machinations that removed his uncle from power.

And power is one way in which he exerted control. Switch electricity off or limit access to light as the blanket of night falls and it is harder for the 'common' people to meet, to plot, to demand greater freedoms. It is a ploy used by many over the years - owners of plantations worked by the enslaved also used the tactic to lessen any chance of rebellion.

But even if the power was on in Equatorial Guinea, many did not have the luxury of being able to afford it.

In Malabo, we had moved into an as-yet unfinished apartment. We had doors and windows, a floor and a roof, plumbing and power.... sometimes. I had been promised a generator but that was months away and had to be shipped from the mainland. Days after moving in, I watched the sun drift behind the hills beside us to leave the jungle a jumble of dark greens and greys as the frogs began their nightly chorale.

A movement caught my eye and I saw a flicker from a flashlight and what looked like a very tall man dressed in very little. In the half light of a brief equatorial dusk, it took me a moment to realize his height was unnaturally elongated by the fact he had clambered onto the roof of a dilapidated car that graced the entrance to our mud-baked and overgrown road. He looked to be hanging.

"Stephen!" I called down to our guard, a delightful Ghanaian who had about as much chance of saving us from anything as my dead grandfather. "Stephen, there's a man on a car by the electricity pole."

"Oh, madam, he is stealing your power."

It took a moment to digest this information. And another moment to shrug. This was WAWA at work. West Africa Wins Again. The chap had no chance of getting electricity to his shack, so why not nick it from the house down the road? Good luck to him, I thought, as our power winked off, on, then off again. It could have been deliberate, it could have been a malfunction.

In 2013, long before these COVID times, we were fortunate enough to find another 'in-need-of-work' place on St Croix, the largest of the US Virgin Islands. We fell to renovating with a vengeance. The immeasurable assistance of Barry Allaire and his duo of merry men, Mingo and Easy made a somewhat daunting task very much easier.

The plumbing wasn't too bad but, oh my, the electrics were not good. I spent a lot of time on island by myself and as darkness drifted across the bay silhouetting yacht masts in a melange of pinks and mauves, I would turn on a light only when absolutely necessary, and never more than one at a time. Oftentimes a fizz would accompany the action. We rewired - thank you, Leroy - and my confidence grew.

However, my new found belief in power was short lived. I came to understand another acronym, although not nearly as catchy as WAWA. WAPA is our Water and Power Authority. After nearly eight years of intermittent power or brown-outs -

those rolling, blinking outages that cause permanent damage to electronics and appliances despite having surge protection - the phrase "We've been WAPAed" has entered the family lexicon.

I fully understand the fragility of power services during hurricanes that are hurled our way at, sadly, more frequent intervals. What I do not understand is why a power company in America is allowed to function badly, with seeming impunity, through continuing performance failures, compromises to payment and billing systems including the, almost, unbelievable loss of $2.7 million when invoices were paid to a purportedly legitimate vendor. A scam referred to by WAPA as a 'Business Email Compromise'. I wonder if that scam will be found by the FBI to have been initiated in West Africa. In which case WAPA and WAWA are not so far apart.

Why are heads not rolling at the continued farrago of an "autonomous agency of the Virgin Island Government" that does not deliver power? To the idle bystander it could be construed that local accountability has gone the way of federal accountability.

Not too long ago and in these COVID times, in frustration, I posted a comment on social media. It read, "I have lived in 12 countries, a number of them considered 3rd world developing countries. Never, ever, have I had such a poor power service as I get here in the US Virgin Islands."

Comments flooded in. From those known and unknown. Comments like, "Have you lived in Nigeria?" Yes, I have. "Knowing that you've lived here in Thailand that is really saying something." Yup! Closer to home people said, "And at such a high cost" and "The worst". There were many more such helpful insights.

What they all failed to mention is that I do not now live in a developing country. This is the United States of America.

Please, WAPA, power to the people!

HOW DOES MY GARDEN GROW?

My mother's gardens around the world bloomed in abundance. The five-acre garden in the centre of Kuala Lumper, where the Twin Towers now loom over the city, is the one I remember best. Huge rain trees under one of which a King Cobra could often be found, much to human and canine consternation. A mangosteen grove, home to all manner of frightening things that I knew must lurk behind trunks and amongst decaying leaves and fruit on the ground, led to the perimeter fence where I rarely ventured. But oh, the fruit, juice dripping from the plump, white flesh hidden deep beneath a thick purple skin, was heavenly and worth the risk of who knows what. And row upon row of my mother's pride - orchids - purple vandas, striped yellow tigers, whites and pinks. Red hibiscus - *bunga raya* - the national flower of Malaysia, and canna, boisterous in their yellow and orange and red finery but also home to snakes who relished the damp ground. And frangipanis.

Mum had two and a half gardeners to help her. One permanently pushed a mower, one helped with the garden itself and the half came in each afternoon to help tend the hundreds of pot plants. I showed no interest in the mechanics of gardening but loved the beauty.

My foray into horticulture did not take place until, as an adult, I was again in the tropics. We lived in Bangkok, on Soi Attawimon. The garden was an expanse of grass which bordered one edge of a fishpond. An ornate *wat*, high on a pedestal placed in the corner was, morning and night, adorned with joss sticks and offerings to the temple gods by Es, our house girl. Cannas and crotons rimmed the house.

Frangipani trees have always been a favorite, perhaps because their many-forked branches invited climbing, despite my irate mother shouting at me to get down. I don't think Mum was concerned about a broken arm or leg, rather more the imminent snapping of her tree. Whatever the reason, I like both the delicacy of the flowers, whether white, pink, or yellow, and their fragrance.

And so I decided to plant a frangipani. Bangkok used to be known as the Venice of the East. *Klongs*, canals, threaded their way through the city before many were filled in and tarred over. The knock-on effect, apart from dreadful traffic jams, was a severe flooding problem caused, in part, by the dense red clay just below the topsoil. Each tropical deluge merged our pond with the garden, snakes and koi swimming freely. That clay translated into heavy digging.

The Chatuchak weekend market provided the tree, about three foot tall. I can't remember why I didn't wait for the man who mowed the lawn to dig the hole. Most likely my normal impatience. Whatever the reason, I regretted it.

"Madam?" Es, her voice hesitant, looked at me from the shade of the veranda, concern etched across her smooth face. "Madam, not good."

I glanced up. "What?"

"Not good."

Es had a green thumb for herbs, and I expected a horticultural lesson.

"Cannot plant."

I looked at the hole, painstakingly dug. "Why not?"

"Tree for *wat*, not house." Her tone was adamant.

"Why?" I asked, sweat dripped from my face to my drenched tee shirt.

"Call *lân tom*. Sad flower. By wat," she repeated.

I looked at her gentle face and all arguments fled. Who was I to ignore a cultural taboo?

I waited until the mower man came and he dug the next hole. By Es' wat.

Thereafter, in various countries around the world, I have asked before digging. Each time we have moved on, I have been sad to leave my garden and I wonder how my gardens grow.

Thirty-five years later, on an island in the Caribbean, I have a garden I'm not leaving.

From a tan-tan and coralita jungle over which two coconut palms presided, emerged a quarry of rotten rock, glass and Chaney, the shards of crockery from bygone eras. From that has come, with a lot of sweat, some blood but no tears, a garden that offers respite, calm and abundant pleasure.

Loathe to remove the palms, sanctuary to wasps, bananaquits and iguanas, I agreed to their removal after my husband's magic words, "falling coconuts on grandchildren's heads". I missed the sound of the fronds in the trade winds. I did not miss the downward thump of nuts landing.

We had a plan. The garden we have is nothing like the plan. Rather it has evolved. Our only hard and fast proviso demanded a garden for birds, butterflies and bees. We have all three, and even on occasion play host to a gluttonous night heron who, with great patience and stealth, steals fish from the pond. Iguanas are regular guests too, the vivid green of the newly hatched reptiles merging with the passionfruit vine. And we have learnt that the chickens ranging free in Christiansted love pomegranates.

Our planting to a true horticulturalist might seem haphazard, but it works. Portlandia rubs shoulders with lemon grass and duranta. Natal plum nestles next to gardenia. Lantana (a weed to my Australian friends) plays nicely with ixora. Plumbago and jasmine share purple and white space. Cuban palms reach skywards, their trunks adorned with orchids. Hamelia and snow-on-the-mountain nudge the fence line with Ginger Thomas, the national flower of the Virgin Islands. A few we've bought - one, a bottle brush, in a nod to my Australian heritage. Some plants were in the garden - a China rose hibiscus, milk and honey lilies, mother-in-law tongues although, it must be said, my MIL's words were never sharp.

Plant sharing is a way of life on St Croix and so, as I wander from the patio to the pergola to the perch on the peak, I am reminded each step of the way of friendships made. Parakeet flowers, poor man's orchid, hibiscus and gingers from Emy, cacti from Pat, orchids from Susan, all manner of unnamed seedlings from Rosalie, jatropha from Don, and from Toni and Isabel respectively a yellow and crimson frangipani.

How does my garden grow, the one I won't be leaving? Very well, thank you!

PERFUME AND POLITICS

A quartet of women, all the wrong side of sixty, stand around a beaten-up SUV in a glow of their own making as well as light spilling from the glittering interior behind them. Their shadows cavort. They are gleeful, like teenagers discussing the cute new boy in math class, or eight-year-olds released from school. The air is perfumed by an array of scents emanating from their bare arms. From musky to sweet, floral to citric, their noses crinkle in delight or dislike. The same scent smells different on each of them. Chemistry, an active ingredient that comes both from the ornate bottles spritzed onto their wrists and their friendship.

Laughter surrounds them as they display their purchases, boxes of perfume that could last them their lifetimes, on the sea-and-sun-ragged vehicle. A mascara rolls down the slope of the hood, caught before it reaches the tarmac of the parking lot.

Lyrics from the songstress perched on a barstool, playing her guitar, mingle with the trade winds that cool them, even in the quadrangle of a low-slung strip mall. A melange of orange blossom, jasmine and cedar waft a myriad of aromas. The hood is also a table for loot from swag bags. Mont Blanc and Coach, Boss and Cellcosmet jostle for space as exclamations swirl amidst the mirth. Swaps are negotiated, generosity fills the night.

The quartet's conversation quietens and turns to the master class in marketing just witnessed. Their instructor,

Raymond Kattoura, Director of Purchasing for Duty Free Retail whose base is in Miami, is also the host for the opening of Rouge - St Croix's latest high-end perfumery and luxury goods emporium, situated at Orange Grove Shopping Center. A seemingly lacklustre choice lacking in the charm and beauty that makes up so much of St Croix.

"The store is located," he told them, "not in Christiansted along the Boardwalk or on King or Company Streets, because the company's target market is people who live on island rather than tourists passing through." The staff at Rouge, their black clothing a foil to the shimmering array of bottles, added to the ambience with not only their quiet guidance but a willingness to join in the laughter as wrists and arms were held out for another scent.

"The senses must be stimulated and comfort is a major factor. The body and brain feeling in harmony. Freedom to choose in a relaxed environment. Pleasant staff. Good lighting. And ease of parking contributes to the equation." His goal achieved, Mr Kattoura's last statement has added import as the friends loiter around the car.

"Even if I'm dressed like a tramp," says one of the women putting her new perfume back in the bag, "I want to smell good!"

Fueled by Prosecco and fed by Teddy, an event planner with flair, the opening night of Rouge and their evening ends, and fond farewells are made.

"A luxury brand is about more than just products, it is about lifestyle and experiences too." Kattoura's words reverberate as one of the women, me, prepares for bed. Fun and friendship, even behind masks, help the four of us, all vaccinated, enjoy an evening out - the first in a long year.

As my eyes close, I am glad I made a pact with myself during the turbulent year just past, when the airwaves and ether were filled with reports unconducive to sleep. I no longer listen to, watch or read any news before bedtime, and so words from a song of my long-gone youth drift in and I smile, *Oh what a night!*

Daylight filters through the loose-weave curtains and I come to a consciousness of dawn and Bonnie, the cat, yowling. As I wait for the kettle to boil, she curls around my ankles but rejects the offer of a cuddle. I take my mug of tea to the gallery and rejoice in the glorious place I call home. An island that embraces any newcomer willing to be polite and open to idiosyncrasies unique to every individual place.

I am relaxed, happy.

I press my phone for CNN. It was my first mistake of the day.

I read of the travesty of voter suppression just signed into law in Georgia - the state, not the country. I see images of Governor Brian Kemp surrounded by white, predominantly middle-aged, balding men looking over their masks in front of a painting by Olessia Maximenko of Callaway Plantation. Now an open-air museum that tells of its inglorious former existence as a slave plantation where runaways were hunted by dogs, in a state wherein the tyrannical Jim Crow laws demanding segregation of public buildings and blocking the right to vote for Blacks were embraced with complete disregard for human dignity - or, in easy language, White Supremacy.

Gone, in the swoop of the Governor's signature, are the results of the Civil Rights era.

Gone, also, in handcuffs was a State Representative, Park Cannon who happens to be a Black woman, a Democrat knocking on the door of the staged signing asking to witness the travesty. She was arrested by white, uniformed male Troopers in Georgia - the state, not the country.

Heather Cox Richardson in her *Letter from an American* this morning writes of South Carolina Senator James Henry Hammond who, in March 1858 rejected "as ridiculously absurd" the idea that "all men are born equal." He continued by warning that the ballot box was stronger than 'an army with banners' and that appears to be the belief of those currently in the Georgia administration.

The Military Reconstruction Act in 1867 began, Cox Richardson reminds us, to establish impartial suffrage which Maine politician, James G Blaine, wrote in 1893 "changed the political history of the United States."

Yesterday in Georgia - the state, not the country, Governor Kemp and his minions began an attempt to change the face of the United States in 2021 back to the bad old days.

All Americans, whatever color, whatever political persuasion, should be incensed.

The glee, the frivolity and joy in the company of Black and white gone in a puff of perfume, and the stroke of a pen.

Oh what a night!

FUTURE PROMISES

I arrive early in order to snag a table at the Bistro in Gallows Bay. As I wait, I watch a clutch of chicks squabble and chase the one with the worm as the hen pecks her own path. I have met my next interviewee once, briefly, a couple of years ago at Havana Nights, a fundraiser for Project Promise. I remember her being glamorous and, despite the flurry of the event, a woman with a wide smile.

Resa O'Reilly, wearing a fuchsia pink top with ruffles at the shoulders, approaches the table holding a cup of strawberry lemonade and a breakfast sandwich. "Apple?" she asks.

"That's me. Please, have a seat and thank you for agreeing to this." I am delighted to see the smile is still intact. I leave her to guard our table and go into the Bistro to order coffee. I'm not sure why, as I rarely drink anything during these interviews, but it will give her a chance to eat her breakfast in peace. Resa is a woman juggling many things, eating included.

I return with my coffee and sit down. "We are of course going to talk about Project Promise but what I'd like to know is how you got to where you are. So firstly," I say, "I'm always curious about names. O'Reilly is a well-known name here with distinctly Irish overtones. Are you interested in, or have you researched your family lineage?"

Her eyes glow. "We've started. I'd love to go to Ireland and trace our heritage. It's on the 'to do' list, but not yet though. The pandemic has put everything on hold."

I nod and think of lives on pause around the world. "Do you know which part of Ireland?"

"No, we don't yet. But here on island we've traced our ancestors back to Estate Clifton Hill, just east of Central High School."

"This is so off topic," I excuse myself, "but I was involved with Friends of Denmark and it was fascinating to meet Danes coming to St Croix, some of whom were able to trace their lineage back to an enslaved woman. In all probability not a consensual relationship but nevertheless important to know."

"Finding our roots," Resa says, "is important to knowing ourselves. I love all those ancestry research shows on TV, and I can't wait to get a complete picture of mine."

I agree. "It's important from an historical view too. If we don't know where we came from we don't always know how to get where we are going."

Resa, a master of inserting Project Promise into her conversation, jumps on my comment, "That's one of our perspectives with the Caterpillar Project, the importance of cultural awareness. Who we are, what's our story, so we can move ahead."

I want to know a bit more about her before we discuss her non-profit. "You were born and bred on the island?"

"No, I was born in Puerto Rico."

I want to slap my forehead. "Oh no," I say with a laugh, "It's hard to find people born here."

"I'm the youngest of four and none of us were born on island. One of my brothers was born in New York but the rest of us in Puerto Rico."

"How old were you when you came to St Croix?"

"Three days!"

"Thank goodness." I already know this conversation is going to be filled with laughter. "That almost counts as 'bahn' here."

"Not born here but raised and rooted on St Croix," Resa says.

"Indeed, all the way back to Clifton Hill. What schools did you go to?"

The list is long. "I started kindergarten at the Moravian School in Christiansted, then St Mary's until 7th Grade, then Country Day School for junior high before I resumed my Catholic school education at St Joseph's, from where I graduated in 1995."

"Bleah, we don't do dates! Far too aging."

"I'm okay with my age. I think we are as old as we feel, so I'm about thirty."

"Well then, I'm about thirty-five then add almost thirty years and you're there!" People at the adjacent table look across as our laughter drowns out the chickens.

"It sounds as if your parents were involved and supportive."

"Absolutely," she says, "we were given every opportunity to succeed."

"After St Joesph's you went to college on the mainland?"

"Yes, I did one semester at Temple University in Pennsylvania."

"What happened?"

"It was too cold for this island girl. I enjoyed seeing snow which was pretty but too cold for me."

We agree it's great for a day.

"Snow, check." Resa's hand ticks the air. "Then I transferred to UT, University of Texas at Austin."

I nod and explain that I spent many years in Houston.

"But you know what happened?"

I shake my head.

"Austin had a totally unexpected snowstorm. I couldn't believe it."

We laugh again then I ask, "Resa, I'm curious, what prompted you to a degree in psychology?"

"I've always enjoyed people. And psychology can be a broad field which I felt could lead to something interesting. But I totally missed home even though two siblings were in Austin."

"Did you come back for holidays?"

"All of them, except one summer. This is home, and I could not wait to come back. I did not even wait for graduation."

"When you were at UT," I pause before I ask a question that is not on the pages in front me, "um, Texas does not always have a good reputation as far as race relations go, did you have any issues whilst you were there?"

"No, not really. It was just different and I missed home. I wasn't in many social circles. By nature, I'm quiet and it just wasn't home. Where I'm rooted."

There's that word again. "In some ways I envy that," I say. "My whole life has been on the move, and I've loved it. The flip side is I don't have an embedded sense of belonging anywhere although I feel at home wherever I happen to be." Resa smiles at my words but I can sense a kind of sorrow too.

We talk briefly about my travels, particularly in Equatorial Guinea, in West Africa, where the government was cruel and despotic but the man on the street was great and certainly an experience I wouldn't have missed.

Resa nods. "We are where we are supposed to be in every moment." We drop back to Texas when she tells me, "My brother and sister lived in Austin too so when I wasn't studying I spent time with them."

"Was that Rudy?" I ask of the one brother I met at an Orchid Society Show where he was displaying bonsai trees.

"No, it was Randy."

"Are you all 'R'?"

Laughter flits around us. "Yes, Rudy, Randy, Rema and Resa. And we all have the same middle initial."

"Good grief, that must have been confusing in the days of snail mail!" I love her laughter.

Resa bubbles with joy. "When I got home, my first job was with Marshall and Sterling as a receptionist. Sometimes you gotta take what you can until you get what you want. My first job in my field was at the Department of Human Services, as a vocational counselor for children with disabilities."

I ask if she thinks government services have improved for special needs children since then.

"Probably not." Resa's answer is disappointing.

"Why not?"

"You know, there is a lot of programming out there that is wonderful, great concepts but the implementation was not always good."

"From there you moved to Frederiksted Health Care where you were involved in a school-based pilot program at St Croix Educational Complex."

"Yes, I was the first mental health counsellor. I loved getting to know the children, all children, not only those with problems. Some would drop in just to say hello. Being there was when I realized that was what I wanted to do with my life, help children in need."

Resa's hands are moving in time to her words but there is no laughter now. "It was a window into their world, so many had issues I had never had to face. No food on the table and violence in the home were just some of them. I got to learn about their families, and their dreams, their wants and needs.

These students just wanted to be seen, they wanted to be heard. That window into their world revealed their lack of support." She pauses, lost in reflection. "It was there I developed the idea of a holistic approach program. We have to focus on all aspects of their lives."

"So it's in balance," I suggest. "And giving positive role models, as you had?"

"Exactly, as I had."

"I admire you. There are many who grow up with opportunities and privilege, as I certainly had, but most of us don't give back to the extent you do. Huge kudos."

This woman does not take compliments easily and her laugh trills, almost with embarrassment. Before we delve deeper into her passion I want to know a little more about what sent her on her current trajectory. "You also worked as a teen project coordinator for the Family Planning Program. As a woman who has spent her life involved with at-risk children, some of whom may not have been planned or wanted, I imagine you have seen a number of unwanted pregnancies. I'm interested in your take on the push in some areas of the country to teach abstinence only."

Resa's hands are still, for a moment. "What's important is education. That's where it starts. I believe it is our duty to educate our youth so they can make informed choices. That's what I loved about working as a teen project coordinator, being in the classroom and that sense of responsibility gained from teaching. During this period, I had the awesome opportunity of presenting to students from all the schools on island, and even UVI."

It is my turn to nod. I take a deep breath and ask, "I think it fair to say that there would be few who would choose abortion as a prophylactic, yet Roe v Wade is under attack. What are your thoughts on this?"

"I think that everyone has a right to make their own choices. It goes back to education and making informed choices. So yes, I'm pro-choice."

Then I ask, "What prompted you to get your masters degree in criminal justice?"

We are distracted by a chicken chasing a child, and merriment ripples along the tables.

"I wanted to not only focus on education, but to focus on prevention as well. I wanted to help prevent children from making bad choices that would introduce them to the juvenile justice system."

"Is that why you worked with the VI Department of Justice (DOJ)?"

"At the DOJ I was the sex-offender registry manager, I didn't work with youth and wasn't there very long. I missed my time in the classroom. I was laid off in 2012, I had just had my son and…."

I interrupt, "That's Nyan?"

"Yes, that's right. He's making ten in September. I can't believe I'll have a ten-year old, that's so wild. He's a cutie." Her voice is soft.

"And how old is your daughter?"

"Nnenaya is thirteen and heading to the 9th grade."

"What a pretty name!"

"Yes, it's Nigerian."

"Huh, do you have roots there as well?"

"Her dad has Nigerian ties."

"And Nyan, is that the same?"

"No."

We jump back to the DOJ.

"I got laid off the day before I was due back to work after maternity leave, my pink slip was hand-delivered to me in my driveway. My son was three months old and my daughter three, she had just started pre-school."

"Not good timing."

"No. It was like, oh my gosh, what now?"

"Was your partner supportive?"

"Yes, but it was my parents who were there for me. I could not have got through it without them." Her eyes are glassy with unshed tears. "You know it was, at the end of the day, a truly definitive time for me. I could have given in to the moment, or I could look at that moment as an opportunity for me to do what it is I'm supposed to do with my life. I literally had that conversation with myself. That lay off forced me to look into myself."

"Then serendipity?" I ask.

"Yes. A few months into my layoff, an opportunity to purchase a building presented itself, actually owned by a cousin…"

I interrupt Resa again. "Another O'Reilly?"

Her eyes now sparkle with glee, "No, Hendricks. Vaughn Hendricks."

"Oh come on, I wanted you to truly keep it in the family. So tell me about the building."

"It was a wreck, it had been abandoned for about twenty years, and had been passed down to my cousin from his father. It eventually went up for auction because the property taxes hadn't been paid. Once I became aware of the building, I decided I wanted it. I approached Vaughn, I had my whole spiel ready and offered to pay the tax debt. A win-win situation. Keep it in the family. Right?"

I shake my head. "Because with a newborn and a three-year-old you had nothing else to do?"

Resa's hands are in full flow. "Well, it didn't matter because my cousin rejected the idea, so really and truly I forgot about it.

I thought if it was supposed to be mine it would be, so I went on with my life."

I am amazed Resa was able to shrug off the loss.

"But," she continues, "the government gives the owner a year to get their finances in order before the property goes to the auction's highest bidder. I tried to figure out which building it was," she picks up the story, "then about a week before the year was up my cousin contacted me and asked if I still wanted the building. So I told him, 'of course.'"

"That was quite some commitment," I say, imagining a young mom trying to finance such a project. A building which variously had been a tavern, a cobbler's, owned by a ship captain, a mason and finally a wig shop.

"We worked out an agreement and I purchased the building sight unseen."

"What," I asked this determined woman, "did you think when you finally got in? Was it an aha moment or more of an oh my God moment?"

"Excited. Life is fantabulous. The first time I went into the building it was knee high in trash, mattresses everywhere but I couldn't wait to get my hands on it. I saw the purchase as an opportunity not an obstacle, right." Resa pauses, lost in reflection. "Anyway we eventually closed on the building and one day I was driving by, and I looked up under the rear-view mirror and I knew, it came to me. I said to myself, 'I'm going to start a non-profit organization, it's going to be housed in this building and I'm going to work with at-risk youth' and, at that moment, I knew what my life's purpose would be."

"That's wonderful. You've come a long way in such a short time with your holistic, long-term approach to helping at-risk children, rather than with a brief, sharp intervention-style program. Do you think your model should be incorporated into government funded programs?"

"Yes, I do. A holistic approach is the best way to make the biggest impact."

"Which leads us to the Caterpillar Project, really your signature program. I love the imagery invoked by the metamorphoses of young people, girls and boys, into responsible achievers in the community. It's an eight-year program that starts in fifth grade. Was that a hard sell to the government?"

Resa chooses her words. "I wouldn't say it was a hard sell. I pitched it to the deputy superintendent, Miss Faith George, who liked the possibilities and my enthusiasm. She was the one who approached all the elementary schools. It was Lew Muckle Elementary and its principals, Daphne Williams and Cecilia Espinosa, who agreed to host the pilot program. I will be forever grateful to them for their willingness to take a chance on a new program."

"Was there a concern that the project would breed a sort of elite cadre of students?"

"That was definitely a question in the beginning. Some skepticism. You're going to be doing what, who, where, when. But they welcomed us."

"It must have made a bit of difference, and this sounds a little crass, but they had nothing to lose. You weren't asking for funding. Again it was a win win."

Resa nods. "We only asked for space and help in identifying the children."

I read from my notes. "The criteria stated for acceptance to the program was for twenty-four students with C or D averages, minimal to no behavioral issues and with an involved parent. Is that correct?"

"Yes. We had a slight challenge at the beginning in that we were given names of 'A' students. A push to make the program academic and not holistic. Of course academics are important, but so is cultural awareness, life coaching, community service. But we got through it."

"I read a clinician was brought down from Chicago to administer social and personality tests in order for you to whittle the first group down to twelve children. Why were you set on that number?"

"The program works on quality over quantity, and I felt a smaller group would be more impactful."

My heart plummets to think of an eager child being rejected because a recalcitrant parent might not make a commitment and ask, "Was an involved parent a make or break?"

"It had to be." Resa looks down, her hands still. "We must have them on board because we have to be able to give the parents the tools they need to reinforce the message we are giving their children."

I'm about to ask a question when Resa tells me a story that ties in with her belief that things happen for a purpose.

"It was my responsibility to find my purpose and I did. You know something amazing happened. After we closed on the deal and about four months later Project Promise was incorporated after lots of work behind the scenes. We did a lot of different programming in the following two years, then the day," Resa emphasizes the coincidence, "the day before the Caterpillar Project started I found out that Lew Muckle, the man, had worked in the building as a young man. Everything stopped, my world, my heart, everything stopped, and I knew I was on my way to fulfilling my life's purpose."

"Oh, I've got goose bumps."

"Yes, that happened to me as well!" Resa says. "I knew then I was on the ride of a lifetime. So every morning I wake up with gratitude in my heart for the impact I am able to make in children's lives."

I ask, "Was there any fallout from those twelve children not chosen?"

Resa considers her words. "No. But, just to clarify, even though, we were given twenty-four names, not all twenty-four of those students and parents were interested in participating. So, we screened the parents and students who wanted a chance to participate in the program and, going in, they knew that there was a possibility that they wouldn't be chosen to participate."

I can only imagine the difficulty in making those decisions. "So the children all came from one school so probably knew each other. How has that worked? Was it an advantage?"

"I've never really thought about that," Resa answers. "It was advantageous to us, everyone was in one place, and we advocated them to be in the same class going into 6th grade so they are all getting the same homework, the same classroom experience."

"Are they a tight-knit group now?"

"There is camaraderie, again born of shared experiences. A kind of this is who you're riding with."

Again I think of those not chosen and ask, "Has there been a knock-on effect from the Caterpillars as far as their non-caterpillar peers?"

"I think so. But nothing blatant. The Caterpillars are definitely looked upon as different but are not necessarily celebrated. I think it has been hard for them to sometimes recognize the benefits of being a Caterpillar, but I believe that will come with maturity."

I consider the enormous benefits the Caterpillars have and ask if all twelve are still involved in the project.

"Sadly not. Some have dropped out, which was to be expected. We have two boys and three girls. You know," Resa says before I can follow up, "very early on it became clear that some parents did not want the responsibility, the challenge if you like, of ensuring their kids attended programming. Nor did they want to be held accountable for their actions. That doesn't exist in some families."

"And from the kids themselves?" I ask.

"One girl didn't want to join as she preferred to play baseball. She was ten years old. That's too young to make that kind of decision. There is no way one of my kids is going to make life decisions at that age. The other students we lost mostly because of their parents. For example, one mom thought yoga was a religion and she didn't want her daughter participating in that."

"And is there a religious aspect to the Project?"

"No, no religion."

I flip through my notes as we are rather hopscotching around. "You mentioned in another interview that you hoped to have a second group of children who would be mentored by the first. Has that happened?"

Resa's smile is broad. "It's about to. I love every single aspect of what I do, and we learn from everything. This time the children will be drawn from different schools, creating different dynamics."

Logistical difficulties swim in front of my eyes. "How will you handle that?"

Resa starts with her customary enthusiasm. "It's going to be a different experience for us and them." Her laughter competes with a noisy chick. "You know, we've waited longer than I wanted to start a second group but the time wasn't right. Now is the time to start because now we have the building and we will build on the lessons that we've learned from the first group and apply them as needed for the second group."

"The pandemic changed so much, with everything being virtual. But we're excited about introducing a new group of Caterpillars and seeing how it all unfolds."

I am struck at Resa's insistence that this is a long term project and that everything is as it should be at this time but I wonder if she isn't a little disappointed at the lack of closeness between the Caterpillars.

"Not really. They are close in the sense that every day after school we get together, this is who we are, this is what we do. They are tight enough, it works."

"Perhaps sometimes it is better not to be too close, too joined at the hip."

"Yes," Resa says, "and we have always to remember they are still children. Also that this is the first time anything like this has been done. We knew what we hoped for but we didn't know how it would play out. We still don't know. I've embraced the uncertainty and I can't wait to see where it leads."

"Well," I say, "it is a pilot program and, as such, some areas could be tweaked."

Resa agrees.

It's time to move tack. "You have formed a number of partnerships with local entities, such as the National Park Service (NPS). Have they all been successful, and are they ongoing? Pandemic restrictions notwithstanding."

"Yes, we have three other programs. Our Buck Island Program partners with Big Beard's Adventure Tours and the National Park Service (NPS), and the Salt River Bay Program with the NPS. The Buck Island Program has been sidelined this past school year; however, we were able to implement virtually our Salt River Bay Program. I can't wait for us to be able to run these programs in person again, and for the visitor's center to be reopened."

"Does Benito Vegas lead the hike?" I ask, thinking of the energetic NPS education officer.

"Yes, he does. We also have an Excellence and Leadership Program in which one student from each high school is acknowledged for their overall accomplishments."

I remark, as someone with an international background, how impressed I am that Project Promise and the Caterpillar Project have a global component."

"It's important these kids grow up as global citizens, with a perspective beyond our shores. It's equally important to take care of our local communities and to assist international communities."

"Like Toys for Tanzania, and Walk for Refugees Awareness?"

"Exactly! And don't forget our Educate South Africa Initiative, we raised funds for school children in South Africa." Resa bubbles with delight as she tells me of the success of their Summer of Service, a 4,000 mile coast-to-coast trip on the mainland with four of her Caterpillars. "It was wonderful! It gave them a different perspective on life, with experiences they will never forget. We tried to see something iconic from each city we visited - like the Liberty Bell in Philadelphia - experience the different foods, Philly Cheesesteaks in Philly! And of course, our experience didn't stop there, we gave back to some of the communities we passed through."

Before I can speak the dynamo across the table rushes on.

"It's important for the Caterpillars to know, despite their challenges, they can still make a difference in the lives of others, which is why the service component of the program is so important."

It is an outlook from which many of us, children and adult alike, could learn.

"What do you think was the Caterpillars' biggest take away from the trip?"

"A wider perspective on life, something they probably don't recognize yet. But they will."

There again is the long-term view, and Resa's unshakeable belief that things happen for a reason. I consider how the Caterpillars have become involved during the pandemic with the Heart to Heart International COVID program and how, after training, they have become COVID-19 Youth Ambassadors helping to launch a 'stop the spread' educational campaign.

"You are," I say, "a master fundraiser."

"Not really," she responds, "I think our success is a testament to the powerfulness of this journey! The things that we need, seem to show up just as we need them. For example after Hurricane Maria, Island Therapy Solutions stepped in and gave the Caterpillars space to meet."

"Can we talk about the dilapidated building in Christiansted that prompted the whole Project Promise concept and how you have, literally, raised the roof?"

Her optimism and outlook on life are so infectious I can see how people appear to fall over to help her.

"COVID has given me the time and space needed to focus on the building renovation. Back in March I was approached by Humanitarian Experience for Youth (HEFY), a summer travel camp looking for a service project - a construction project - a living lab for their volunteers. It just so happened I had one!" Her laugh is deep and all encompassing. "We just needed to replace the roof and raise the money to do so."

"$50,000 in five weeks is daunting for most," I comment with a wry smile.

"If the intention and will is there I firmly believe anything and everything is possible. You just have to figure out a way. Our community has been incredibly generous. We received a grant from Home Depot, and HEFY donated $25,000 which paid for the professionals to teach the building skills needed for the renovation. Amazing!"

"I think I read in one of your Project Promise updates that St Croix Trading did the rafters. Is that right?"

"Yes, and a contractor did the demo for free. Through a combination of donations and crowd funding we were able to raise the monies needed. I made a direct ask to 50 businesses for $1,000. Some gave that amount, some responded with much more, Haugland VI, for example, who also gave $25,000."

Our time is running out, even the chickens have moved on, but I have one final question.

"What next?"

"Oh my goodness, it never stops!"

I have no doubt about that.

"Summer camp is virtual this year, as will be the first semester of the school year. Last year we focused on job readiness - resumé writing, leadership and so on - in preparation for actual job experiences this summer. And I've hired the Caterpillars as junior camp counsellors so they can start to implement the skills they learned last summer."

"And the building?" I ask.

"Once it's completed we'll be able to implement more programs, with weekend programming too, which will be for different age groups, not just the Caterpillars. And Havana Nights, I hope in person next year. But only for those who are vaccinated."

"Resa," I look at my phone, "would you have time to show me around the building?"

"Oh, I'd love to show it to you. Follow me."

We drive into Christiansted and pull into an empty lot beside the building that started this whole venture. The volunteers, all young, grin and say hi as they trickle in after their lunch break, plonking hard hats on their heads as they ready for an afternoon of labor.

"Look," Resa says as we step gingerly over uneven floors and planks leading from level to level, "that will be the kitchen, over there is the reception area. Here will be the computer lab, there will be the laundry room and a bathroom, that's a classroom. Upstairs will be multipurpose room, offices and two more bathrooms."

I look around the construction site, interior walls framed out earlier in the morning. There is still a massive amount to do but I have no doubt this woman, wrapped up in a vibrant bundle of energy, will get exactly what she wants.

"What are you going to call the community center?"

"Still to be decided. It used to be called Hansen Hus. But we'll see."

Whatever this new space in Christiansted is called, the Project Promise concept and the Caterpillar Project, the renovation, the programing is a direct result of a deeply embedded belief that anything can be done, particularly when you are following your purpose in life, as Resa O'Reilly is.

"You really are a remarkable woman, Resa, thank you for all you do."

https://www.projectpromisevi.com/donate

HOPE

The last eighteen months have been a strange and convoluted time. For some a year and a half of hell as friends and family have succumbed to the scourge of COVID-19. For those in abusive relationships, lock-down restrictions must have added terrifying tension to an already untenable situation. For those with families, trying to juggle work and online classes for children, the pressures have also been immense. For others, loneliness.

I recognize how fortunate I have been. My family and those dear to me are all safe and the biggest frustration has been not being able to see them, dotted as we are across the world, although with the recent lifting of Trinidad and Tobago's embargo on entry, we have been able to see our daughter and her family. Now I look forward to our son and his fiancée having their long-delayed marriage on St Croix. It is a wedding contingent on the US lifting its embargo on Brits and Europeans entering the country.

For many the beginning of 2021 saw a level of anxiety lifted and, as the year has progressed and my loved ones became vaccinated against this rampant virus and its mutations, I have felt an element of hope. That feeling is of course tempered by the uncertainty of the vaccination's longevity, and the dismay at so many people, for whatever reasons, who choose to risk their lives, and those near and dear to them by choosing not to vaccinate.

I struggle to understand those in developed countries who seem unable to grasp the proven reality that vaccines work. Polio, diphtheria, measles to name just a few illnesses that have, to all intents and purposes, been eradicated except in pockets where people refuse to take the shot. Mostly these people are in the developed world. Those refusing vaccination in third-world countries do so because of a lack of education, lack of means, or because sometimes of their conviction that good ju-ju will always win.

But what is the excuse for those in the west? Are we so focused on our personal rights that we have lost sight of the bigger picture? Do we really have more faith in politicians desperate for re-election, or shock-jocks eager to pander to their fan base? Have we no faith in science?

It would be easy to lose hope in humanity's humanity.

The restrictions in the US Virgin Islands have eased. Tourists from mainland America may once again enjoy the beaches, the art, the food, the culture of these beautiful islands. And, despite our governor being a strong advocate for doing the right thing - no mask, no service - is our new mantra, and offering numerous venues to receive a free COVID shot, our numbers are rising. There are gaps left around the dining table, in the classroom, at work. Families are being left bereft.

I recently spent an afternoon in a shop that was closing down. I was the only one in a stifling, airless room and so had pulled my mask aside for a moment. A masked man walked in. I apologized, immediately re-covered my nose and mouth and told him I was double vaccinated.

He said, "No problem."

"Are you vaccinated?" I asked.

His eyes crinkled and he laughed. "Me? No! I drink jumbie tea every morning!"

Every instinct told me to argue with him but I didn't. He was placid. Sure of his health and wellbeing. I wonder if he is alive. I hope so but, if he's not, there is no one to blame but his false beliefs, an arrogance perhaps.

It would be easy to lose hope in humanity's humanity.

After my conversation with Resa O'Reilly, I had to stop in at Seaside Market for some asparagus. I ran in, made my purchase, and as I walked back to the truck, clutching unwrapped asparagus spears, a stream of damp children toting swim towels engulfed me. Judging by the weary-looking adults accompanying them, I imagine they had all been to Altona Lagoon as part of a summer camp.

One bright-eyed child of about seven said, around a huge grin, "Hello, I love asparagus. It's my favorite."

"Mine too," I replied. "Have you had fun?"

He nodded then said as he walked by, "I think asparagus tastes like Heaven!"

His words made me smile and have been with me since that day and, if he is the youth of St Croix, then we adults have nothing to worry about, and Heaven, well, it sounds okay too.

There is hope!

GLOSSARY

Caricom: Caribbean Community is made up of twenty developing countries in the Caribbean - fifteen Member States and five Associate Members who meet twice yearly to discuss issues affecting the Community.

Christmas   Labels placed on mail during the Christmas
Seals: season to raise funds and awareness for charitable programs.

DPNR: Department of Planning and Natural Resources

Down   A phrase used to describe people coming from
island: other islands down the Caribbean chain.

Jumbie: A spirit.

NEGS: New England Girls School - my boarding school in Armidale, New South Wales, Australia.

St Croix   A monthly magazine highlighting what's
This Week: happening on St Croix.

Tan-Tan: An invasive species of tree, *Leucaena leucocephala*, known in the Virgin Islands as tan-tan or guinea tamarind. It is an erect woody plant that grows as a shrub or tree which can reach 10 to 15 feet. Also the name of a tour-guide company on St Croix.

The Beast: A hellaciously steep road on St Croix. Beauty and the Beast is the name of the annual triathlon.

TCK: Third Culture Kid, of which I am an example, is a child who was raised in a culture other than their parents' or the culture of their country of nationality, and who also live in a different environment during a significant part of their child development years.

Twin City: A coffee shop in Christiansted, so named for the 'twin cities' of Christiansted and Frederiksted.

WAPA: Water and Power Authority.

Wat: Temple in Thai.

ACKNOWLEDGEMENTS

There are eight people integral to *Crucian Fusion* - those eight men and women willing to chat to me, on record. Without Hans Lawaetz, Stanley Jacobs, Lucien Downes, Nina York, Doc Petersen, Toni Lance, Bob Apfel and Resa O'Reilly there would be no conversations. It truly was an honor, not to mention fun, to speak with them and hear of their lives, their accomplishments and their hopes for St Croix. Thank you!

The essays, which were originally published as blogs, can only be blamed on me, so too the short stories. Pure self-indulgence.

A huge thank you to Emy Thomas who read and commented on each stage of this book, and whose patience and encouragement is endless. My thanks to Janet Newman, whose prowess with the red pen I first experienced last year when she proof read the manuscript for The St Croix Writers' Circle latest anthology, *Mondays at Ten*. And once again my dear friend of over thirty-five years, Kay Chapman, who has cheered me on ever since I started this writing gig, thank you.

Crucian Fusion is dedicated to five people, Isabel, Emy, Barry, Mingo and Easy. All of whom made the first few months on St Croix so very much easier with friendship, knowledge, professionalism and plain good humor.

My love and thanks as always to my husband John, who is the recipient of my thoughts, fears, and occasional rants. It is he who keeps me sane and who pours me a bourbon at the end of the day when we sit on the patio in the garden he created, and gaze across the bay and raise a toast to St Croix.

ABOUT THE AUTHOR

A nomadic life has seen Anglo-Australian Apple Gidley live in twelve countries as diverse as Papua New Guinea and Scotland, which is chronicled in her memoir, *Expat Life Slice by Slice* (Summertime Publishing, 2012). She lives on St Croix with her husband and deaf cat, Bonnie.

Gidley's roles have been varied - editor, intercultural trainer for multi-national corporations, British Honorary Consul to Equatorial Guinea, amongst others. She has two historical novels, *Fireburn* and *Transfer,* released by OC Publishing in 2017 and 2019, which are set on St Croix, in what was the Danish West Indies and is now the US Virgin Islands. Her next novel, *Have You Eaten Rice Today?* takes place in 1950s Malaya and modern-day England and Australia and will be published by Vine Leaves Press in September 2022.

She is currently working on a contemporary novel, and researching her next historical book.

Gidley writes a regular blog, *A Broad View*, and leads The Writers' Circle of St Croix.

www.applegidley.com